FILTHIEST OF THEM ALL

DIRTY TEMPTATION SERIES
BOOK 3

SAMANTHA BARRETT

*For all the girls who never feared the monster under their bed
but instead embraced the dark and depraved things that
monster wanted to do to their body. This one's for you, now
turn that page...*

Good Girl...
The Butcher is waiting for you....

CHAPTER ONE

Tatum

Silence.

For some it can be daunting and drive you mad but for others, there is solace to be found, you can revel in it.

Fear.

It can have you looking over your shoulder and making you see things in the shadows that aren't there.

Caged.

That's the feeling that consumes you, makes you feel trapped with no escape and has your fight or flight instincts kicking in.

For the past six months I have been living in silence, keeping everyone at arm's length and never allowing them close enough to see through the mask I wear. Every corner I turn fear grips me, thinking he's waiting in the shadows to finally make his move. I'm living like a caged animal. I've tried to regain control of my life and live normally but I fail daily. I change my plans at the last minute, never sticking to the same schedule, wanting to keep them on their toes if they are tracking me.

I still work for Vivian Tempest or should I say Ezy A. I expected to be fired after she learned my true age and my brother rescued me, leaving her behind to face the wrath of the previous Lord of the Saints—better known as my sperm donor—Thomas Valerian. A month after I escaped, her husband reached out and offered me my old job back. Given I was living on ramen and sleeping in a car with my brother, I didn't have any choice. I haven't seen my brother in person since I accepted the offer. I limit my calls and texts with him and always change phones. I never call him on my personal cell, only on the burners I have stocked in my suitcase.

I don't even have a home, I live out of hotels, always traveling to oversee the builds of the new hotels and running Lividica when I return to Hollow Hills. That place still gives me the creeps, I hate going back there. My skin crawls and I always feel like I'm being watched. It's the waiting that is killing me. I know I'm not free of the Denver Kings and that they will come for me. It's the fact I have no idea what they look like or who they are that worries me the most.

Alexander 'The Butcher' Denver. His name alone has people pissing themselves in fear and hiding out of worry he will suddenly appear like the fucking boogeyman.

I grew up in foster homes where men thought they could take from me. I have looked the devil in the eyes and survived. Alexander doesn't scare me but the unknown does. The phone ringing pulls me out of my thoughts. I sit forward in my chair and push the stack of papers scattered around my desk to try and locate my cell. When I find it I see it's an unknown number. A pit forms in my gut and I know it's irrational to worry over a strange number but every day I always think 'is today the day he makes his move'?

I answer the call and place it on speaker as I finish typing out my email. "Hello?"

"Miss Lawson." The husky voice reverberates through my office. I still have my hands hovering above my keyboard.

I can feel it, this is him.

"Who is this?" I keep my tone calm and my breathing even, not giving away how terrified I am.

"Introductions aren't necessary. You know who this is." I suck in a sharp inhale, my eyes dart around the room as if waiting for him to jump out of a dark corner and finally kill me.

"What do you want?" The tremble in my voice pisses me off, I'm trying to appear unaffected but failing.

"I've given you space and kept my distance, not using you as bait to lure out that piece of shit. I expect the same courtesy in return." His voice is raspy and sends a shiver down my spine, how a voice can do that is beyond my knowledge but just the sound alone, I could listen to it for days on end and never tire of hearing it.

"I haven't done anything and I don't know what you're talking about," I fire back, grateful that my outrage is beginning to spur me to life. I focus on that instead of the reaction I'm having to his voice.

"Don't play stupid, it's not a good look on you, Tatum." Hearing him say my name has my flight instinct kicking in. I slam the lid of my laptop and begin gathering everything I need and shoving it in my bag.

"You don't know what looks good on me, Butcher," I grit out through clenched teeth.

"The mismatched teal bra and black lace thong wouldn't have been something I chose for you." I freeze, my jaw unhinges as I stare down at the phone while terror roars to life inside me. "How's that for not knowing what looks good on you?" I swallow a couple of times trying to regain my composure. He's here. How do I know? Because I'm wearing the teal bra and black thong right fucking now.

"You stay the fuck away from me. I'm not like the girls you're used to dealing with. Unlike those hussies, I fight back and my bark matches my bite, asshole."

"Stop looking into me and the Denver Kings and we won't have an issue. Keep digging and next time we'll be having this conversation face to face." He ends the call but his warning hangs heavy in the air. My breathing is rapid and my heart is working double time to try and keep up with the panic flaring inside me. I debate my options—which aren't many. All I can do is get out of here, grab my shit from the hotel and get on the next plane to head to Miami.

No!

If he is watching then I need to switch it up. I'll head to Chicago. It may raise questions with Vivian since the construction on that one is taking longer than my grandmother to orgasm. It's bullshit the amount of permits you need there just to open a hotel with a sex club. Lividica is in high demand and I have numerous people reaching out to me to get them in contact with Vivian so they can buy the clubs. She of course shoots down every offer, she'll never sell Lividica, that place is her baby.

I tear out of there without so much as a goodbye to

anyone. My driver is out front waiting. When he sees me running toward him, he drops his cigarette and then climbs inside the vehicle, clearly surprised to see me so early—normally I am the last one here.

"Where to, Miss?"

"My hotel, wait for me out front. I'm grabbing my things then we're heading straight for the airport," I say breathlessly. He doesn't comment which I'm grateful for. I make it a rule now to never befriend any of my drivers because for all I know they could be a plant from The Butcher. I can't stop looking out the back window and all around to make sure we aren't being followed.

The second we pull up in front of the hotel I'm jumping out of the car before it comes to a complete stop. I dash through the lobby like my ass is on fire, then push the button for the elevator so many times. Rationally I know pushing it repeatedly won't get it here faster, but I'm not in my right frame of mind and I can't be held accountable for that considering my phone call with the fucking Butcher!

The second the doors open, I don't even wait for the people to exit, I barge through them and stand in the back, ignoring their sneers and outbursts at my rudeness. When the doors close, I punch the button to the eighth floor and pray it doesn't stop.

When I get off, I run all the way to room 824. I don't fuck around trying to fold my clothes or pack them nicely. I shove everything I own into the bags, clear out the bathroom and shove my files into my suitcase, then I hightail it the fuck out of there. The driver loads my bags while I climb in the back and pull my laptop out to book a red eye flight. The cost of the airfare is almost double my normal fee but I don't bat an eye as I input my credit card details and pay for the fucking thing. Eight months ago I barely had two pennies to rub together, but thanks to a fake ID and Vivian trusting me to run her club, I now have financial freedom. She pays me more than I could have dreamed of or even hoped for, so I bust my ass every day to make sure these builds, the clubs, the girls and guys as well as the contractors are all doing their jobs and not taking advantage of her.

Even after learning the truth about my age, she didn't fire me. I expected to be thrown out on the street and told to never step foot back on the premises, but I wasn't. We were thrown into a fucked up situation and fought for our lives. I still feel guilty for leaving her behind when my brother showed up and saved me..

"Ma'am." I jerk my head up from my laptop and meet my driver's gaze in the rear-view mirror.

"Yeah?"

"Are you okay?" The sincerity in which he asks me makes me suddenly feel bad that I have been so cold toward him.

"Yes, thank you, I'm fine. I just really need to get on that flight." He nods but doesn't reply. I open my browser and begin looking up Alexander Denver. His case was public and so was his trial but there isn't a single fucking photo of him—how is that even possible? Given the fact my boss was the head of a secret society, and knowing that she had people in high places doing things for her, has me believing Alexander may have someone of his own taking down any images of him. Why would he do that though?

What is he hiding from?

Or, is it a who not a what?

Everyone knows he is the leader of the Denver Kings. Everyone has speculated what they are but no one knows for sure. Some say they are an MC club, mafia, street gang and so much other shit, but no one actually knows for sure what the Denver Kings are. It must be a full time job keeping all the information about a gang and serial killer off the web.

That's it!

I need to find who is scrubbing the evidence from the public. Maybe if I find that person then I can... what the fuck am I going to do?

Kill him?

Threaten him?

Maybe the answer is a lot simpler than that. I just don't want to go down that road, because if I do, I probably won't like the answers. This nagging voice in the back of my head is telling me that I need to woman up and stop avoiding it. Given the phone call from the man himself, I know I can't bury my head in the sand any longer. I need to know the truth, so I type her name in the search bar.

Elenor Denver.

I stumble my way through security and barely register the voices of the people around me as I walk toward my gate. My mind is a jumbled mess, I avoided looking up Elenor for months, wanting to believe my brother and not trust what Vivian said about him. The evidence online is damning to say the least. Nexus was never named or anything and it has been labeled as a cold case. The killer was never found. There was one image, an image that had my blood running ice cold. It was a picture of a man with his back to the camera on his knees clutching the lifeless body of Elenor. Her face was blurred but you could see from the way he held her that she was his everything and I have no doubt in my mind that the man in the image was Alexander.

The report said she was drugged, raped and then strangled to death. She was only sixteen, the girl had her whole life ahead of her. She would have been the same age as Nexus now, twenty. I'm only two years older than her when she was killed. I may not have much or anything to show for my life, but I still don't want to die and I can only imagine that she was feeling the same thing as her last breath was robbed from her.

I shiver, still feeling the chill in my bones as I hand the lady my ticket, then make my way onto the plane. I sigh in relief when I notice it isn't a full flight. I wish it was a direct flight but we have to stop over in Colorado before flying into Chicago. I'll be sad to leave Texas but I'll be back soon enough, I always am. Most of the hotels are near to opening except for Chicago. Vivian is trying to set up another one in Colorado but she is still trying to find the right location there. It would make my life easier if she would just finish building the fucking ones she has now before planning more.

I look for my seat toward the back of the plane, which is empty. When I find it I want to pout at the sight of a guy with a baseball cap and sweater on with the hood pulled up covering his face, sitting by the window. I decide to suck it up and wait till we take off then ask one of the hostesses if I can move to an empty row. I stow my bag in the overhead compartment, then step in to take the end seat until a man clears his throat. I twist and look back.

My mouth parts on a silent gasp, I know him!

I wrack my brain for a moment wondering where I have seen him before. He shoots me an impatient look so I grit my teeth and claim the middle seat. When he squeezes his large frame into the chair beside me, squashing me between him and the stranger beside me, I have no choice but to suck it up and wait for takeoff. I hate getting the middle seat! I decide to remain silent and close my eyes and just wait, it won't be long before we are in the air and I can switch seats.

"I warned you what would happen if you kept looking into the Denver Kings, Miss Lawson." My eyes snap open and I turn my head to the side to face the asshole. It hits me all at once why he looks so familiar. He was the guy that came to Lividica and spoke to Vivian–the Aztec god.

"Alexander," I breathe out as fear begins to spread its tendrils throughout my body. When I see three other people wearing baseball caps and hoods I start to panic. One claims a seat in front of us, one sits behind us and the last one sits in the row opposite Alexander. I peer to my other side to see the guy has pushed his hood back and is looking directly at me.

This was a set up.

CHAPTER TWO

Alexander

Her bright blue eyes are as wide as saucers as she slowly swings her gaze back to me, her full pouty lips pinched as she eyes me warily. She's trying to put on a brave face but I see through it. The way her breaths are coming in short rapid pants gives her away, so does the way she keeps clenching and unclenching her fists in her lap. She knows she's trapped. When she tries to stand, Vatican places a hand on her shoulder keeping her seated. A soft whimper escapes her but she bites down on her plump lip to keep quiet.

"I warned you," I growl. Her brows raise a fraction. I watch as her chest rises and falls, drawing my attention to her tits that are practically begging to be set free from that tight, black, cotton shirt she wears. I drag my gaze back to hers to find she is still staring at me with a mixture of fear and something else. I cock my head to the side and study her for a second, and that's when I see her mask slowly fall. The fear in her eyes vanishes as the hostesses begin to run through their safety procedures before takeoff.

"Normal people give you three chances before the final strike," she bites out, then smacks Vatican's hand off her shoulder and scowls at him. "You ever touch me again and I'll snap your fucking wrist." Her tone is firm and low, she knows she doesn't need to raise her voice to capture our attention, she has it without any effort. Vat raises his hands as if surrendering but I don't miss the hint of a smirk on his face. When she faces me again her blue eyes resemble a storm. "I'll stop looking into you and your little freakshow when you stop hunting my brother and stalking me."

I raise a brow in surprise, it's been a long time since anyone has spoken to me this way and it's oddly... refreshing. Even when I was in prison, my name alone had men turning and running in the opposite direction.

"Give me the rapist and all this will end."

She grinds her teeth, not liking my insult but I don't care about her or her pathetic feelings. She shares blood with the motherfucker who took the only person I have ever loved from me. If she had a cock I would have ripped her apart months ago and forced her to talk.

"No." Her answer still comes as a surprise, even though I expected it. I thought the show of force and the fact she is trapped on this flight with the five of us would have scared her into changing her mind.

"Put your seatbelt on," I grit out and sit back in my chair to do the same. I feel her gaze boring into the side of my head. I can feel her temper rising the longer I ignore her. When the plane finally takes off she lets out a soft mewl. I suppose she thought it was a growl but she's too soft and the sound has no effect on me. When the plane finally evens out, she unclasps her seat belt and stands but I don't move.

"Let me pass," she grits out through clenched teeth.

I lull my head to the side and slowly let my gaze travel up her body until I meet her eyes. I can tell my perusal of her makes her uncomfortable. Good. "Sit down, Miss Lawson. We aren't finished here." She huffs and stomps her foot causing my brows to raise to my hairline. "Did you just stomp your foot like a spoiled brat?" My tone holds no amusement.

"I was picturing your balls on the floor," she snaps back. I can see Vatican behind her hiding his smile, he clearly likes her spitfire attitude.

"Sit down," I snap. The little shit just stands there glaring down at me, so I meet her anger with my own. I stand and have to hunch so I don't smack my head on the overhead lockers. I didn't realize how tiny she was until now. She stands as tall as my chest, my body covering hers with ease. When I lean in, brushing my chest against her, she starts to tremble, she has nowhere to run and is forced to endure whatever I do. "I'm not like your little masked friends. I don't play with my... toys, I break them." A soft gasp escapes her. "Don't play games with me, Miss Lawson, because you won't like what happens when you lose," I say low enough for only her to hear. Her eyes swim with a range of emotions but I don't try to decipher them.

"What if you lose?" Her retort has me jerking back and staring down at her skeptically.

"I never lose," I snap back.

Her features harden as she tilts her head back to meet my hardened glare. "Everyone loses, maybe this will be a first for you." Before I can say anything she continues on, "Now are you going to let me pass so I can use the bathroom or are you going to make me cock my leg and mark my territory?"

"Only males mark their territory," I bite out, not liking her vulgar mouth.

To my surprise she presses in closer until she is flush against me, cranes her neck back and smiles sweetly. "Out of the five of us here, *Alex*, I'm the one with the biggest set of balls." My guys can't contain their laughter. I glare at the little shit and remain where I am. She huffs out her annoyance and climbs onto the seats, then jumps into the aisle, heading to the back of the plane toward the bathrooms while I stare after her wondering what the fuck just happened?

"I don't think I have ever seen you so rattled." I shoot Pope a dark look. He raises his hands and smiles, then moves to join Omen in the middle row. Halo is next to follow him and claims the vacant row in front of them.

When Vatican stands, I glower at him but he just smirks and shoves me back so he can get past. "The girl does have a set on her and I don't want to be in the firing range when she snaps." I shove Vatican in answer, which just makes him laugh. I remain standing, ignoring the idiots behind me as I wait for the blonde blow up doll. When five minutes pass and she still hasn't returned, I growl and storm down the aisle ignoring my guys telling me to just leave her. When I reach the bathrooms, I find all four lavatories unlocked. I shove all the doors open and growl out my anger.

The little bitch is trying to run away but she won't get far on a plane. I cross through to the next aisle and stalk toward the very back. I shove the curtain open that blocks off the hostess area from the rest of the plane. The sight before me has me wanting to murder a woman for the first time in my life. The area is empty except for the blonde, sitting on the small counter with a hot cup of coffee in one hand and a fucking cookie in the other. She meets my furious gaze and smiles sweetly while batting those long fucking lashes.

"Coffee's hot, help yourself," she says in a sickly sweet tone that has my hackles rising. I push forward and force my way between her legs, wiping that smug look right off her face. Her mouth pops open in shock, displaying her half eaten cookie.

"Close your damn mouth and swallow," I snarl. She does as I demand and gulps down her food. Even in this position I'm still looking down at her. I reach between us and grab the cup from her hand and place it to the side. Before I can snatch the fucking cookie, she stuffs it in her mouth and chews loudly, then swallows and smiles.

"Never touch my food, Alex, you won't like what happens when you do." I strike out and wrap my hand around her throat, her eyes widening in surprise. My grip is firm but not restricting, never in my life have I ever wanted to strangle the life from a woman except for this infuriating one. Her chest rises and falls in quick succession as I lean in close so my lips brush the shell of her ear.

"Breaking you is going to be fun," I whisper.

In a move so fucking bold my own eyes snap wide, she wraps her arms around my neck, her movements sluggish which just makes me smile. "Many have tried before and failed, you'll... just be..." Her mouth clamps shut so I pull back and smile down at her, her eyes are glazed and she starts to sway. "What you do ta me?" Her words are slurred and come out sounding like a toddler.

"You haven't been paying attention, Miss Lawson. I've been watching you for months. I know your weaknesses and your strengths. I knew you would flee and find comfort in coffee." Her gaze flicks to the coffee pot before slowly coming back to me.

"Drugged me..."

I smirk. "Yes. Now let's hope this makes you more compliant."

"Muder... fooker," she rasps out before she slumps forward. On instinct, I wrap my arms around her and trap her against my body. The smell of her strawberry shampoo assaults me. I don't like fruit but the smell wafting off her is strangely... pleasant. She jolts in my embrace and I find myself pulling her closer until she is nothing but dead weight in my arms, so I switch to holding her bridal style. I peer down at her face and marvel at it for a moment.

Her black lashes are so long and her plump lips look delectable and beckon me to taste them, but I ignore that urge and make my way back to our seats. When the guys hear me approaching, they all turn to stare at me with varying expressions. I know they won't support my choice to drug her but Tatum isn't like most people, when she's scared or worried she doesn't retreat inside herself and hide away, she goes on the offensive and uses her quick wit to her advantage and fights.

I gently place her in her seat and secure the seat belt around her waist. Her hair falls onto her face and I find myself brushing the strands back and tucking them behind her ear. She looks so young and the thoughts I was just having about this eighteen-year-old *child* are disgusting!

"She's gonna be pissed when she wakes up." I pull away

from her and drop into my seat beside the mouthy blonde and scowl at Halo who stares directly at me without an ounce of shame.

"That's my concern, not yours," I bite out.

"It seems everything is always your call these days," Pope snarks, earning a dark look from me.

"You got a problem with how I'm running things?" My tone is cool and filled with a challenge. We aren't like most... I don't even know what the fuck we are now since we broke off and are doing our own thing. I guess we're a crew? Nah, we don't need labels we're just a family of fucked up misfits that run things in Denver.

"I got a problem with you bringing her to our home. She is his fucking blood and I don't want anything to do with that cunt—"

Before Pope can finish, I'm on my feet. He matches my move with a hard look on his face. I don't rule my guys with fear. I may be the so-called leader of the Denver Kings but these guys are my equals which is why none of them fear me. They may fear my rage when I snap but they know I would never intentionally hurt them.

"She is the key to finding that fucking worm. I want him on my table so I can saw him limb from fucking limb like the rest of you." Pope's eyes darken with bloodlust, I may be The Butcher, but these four are just as hungry for blood as I am. "We need to play this fucking smart. We can do whatever the fuck we want in Denver, as per our deal, but he isn't in Denver, is he?" I clip out. Pope's eyes flicker but he's too proud to back down. "We need her to bring him to us or we risk being caught and this time, I won't be able to buy our fucking way out. I would rather be the one being butchered than work for them again."

"I'll never go back," Omen grits out as he stands and places a hand on Pope's shoulder, forcing him to reclaim his seat.

"We end this fucking thing soon," Vatican says.

I nod. "As soon as we get home, Halo will start tracking and narrowing down where the fucker could have gone." Halo grunts his agreement.

"He's smarter than we thought," Omen announces as he claims his seat. I mimic his move and nod stiffly, hating to admit that the little cocksucker has eluded us for this long. We thought after Thomas was taken by the CIA and the Haven Saints were brought down by Vivian Tempest, that Nexus would be forced out of hiding thanks to all his friends getting arrested. It's no secret that Vivian and the Filthy Few want him dead, so I know for a fact that they aren't the ones aiding him.

Speaking of Vivian, she won't be pleased that her general manager will be away from work for the foreseeable future, but she knows she fucking owes me and unless she wants me hunting her boyfriends, she will honor our deal and keep her fucking nose out of my business. I may have a soft spot for the girl because she reminds me of my sister, but that won't save her from my wrath if she gets in my way.

CHAPTER THREE

Tatum

My head feels like someone is jack hammering it from the inside of my brain. My throat is drier than a nun's pussy and I don't have enough spit to swallow and moisten the fucking thing. I gather my willpower and slowly blink my eyes open, only to slam them closed again when a sharp pain starts making itself known in the back of my skull. I take another minute to breathe through the pain and slowly blink my eyes open again. The pain is still present but it's more of a dull ache now. I look around and frown. Where the fuck am I?

I sit up and swallow my gasp, I'm lying on a fucking bed!

I leap off the thing and instantly regret it when my head begins to spin and the ache starts pounding again. I clasp my head between my hands and grit my teeth through the wave of pain. When it finally subsides enough I search through my memory of what the hell happened.

Alexander!

"Son of a bitch!" I snarl.

"Don't call my mother a bitch." I whirl around and fight the haze of dizziness that washes over me from the sudden movement. I sway on my feet and have to reach out to steady myself on the edge of the bed. When I gather myself, I turn my head and glare at the infuriating Aztec god standing in the doorway. His hair is loose and sits around his shoulders, the top pushed back, no doubt from him combing his fingers through it. He's changed. He's wearing a pair of black sweats and a gray cotton shirt that is pulled taut over his chest. "Here," he says as he walks toward me with a glass of water. My mouth waters at the sight of it. I want to smack the glass out of his hand but I bite back my pride and snatch it from him.

"Asshole," I bite out as I bring the glass to my lips.

"Wait, take these." He extends his other hand to show me two white pills sitting in the palm of his hand.

"No."

"They'll help with the side effects," he grits out through clenched teeth.

Rather than answering him I keep my eyes locked on his as I greedily drain the glass. When I'm done, I make a show of sighing just to be a brat. "Only one glass?" I taunt.

His eyes narrow into slits. "You'll be the one in pain now," he snaps.

"Pain is a reminder of what you have survived." He cocks his head to the side, studying me for a moment. His gaze is unnerving but it's more than that. I don't know what it is but when Alexander looks at you, it's like he's trying to peel back the layers of your armor. Almost like he is trying to see through the bullshit to analyze the real person beneath the persona we all put on for the world to judge us by.

It's fucking creepy, to say the least!

"Who hurt you?" His question floors me and has my knees so weak to the point I have no choice but to plop my ass on the edge of the bed. He doesn't move or try to fill the charged silence, he just stands staring down at me expectantly like I owe him an answer.

"Where am I?" I counter.

He pinches his lips to the side and hardens his gaze but allows the change of topic. "You're in my house."

Swallowing razor blades would have gone smoother than his answer. "Why?" I dart my gaze around the room and take in the minimal furniture and decorations. The walls are bare of any pictures, the paint a dull gray color. The sheets I sit on now are an emerald green, and aside from the bed and two dressers there isn't much in here, not even a rug.

"You know why you're here." His tone is hard and unyielding.

"Why drug me and not just force me to tell you on the plane?" I snarl as my anger begins to simmer inside me.

"Because you aren't the type to respond to pain. Unlike most people, you seem like you can take a fuck load of hurt and still keep your mouth shut." His assessment of me is astounding.

"Did you learn that from stalking me?" I sass.

"If you're looking for me to feel some type of guilt for the events that led us to this moment, then don't hold your fucking breath." I bristle at the bastard.

"You're a real prick, aren't you?"

"You know, I've killed people for a lot less so if I was you, I would watch that vulgar fucking mouth of yours."

"You going to kill me, Alex?" I press. His nostrils flare and it's clear he's battling within himself to control his anger. I do nothing to try and help ease his torment because fuck him, he kidnapped me. "How the fuck did you get me off the plane unconscious with no one noticing?" I blurt out.

He ignores my first question. "When you have the right amount of money, anyone can be bought." I gape up at him, utterly speechless.

"You can't just drug women and fucking kidnap them!" I shout and instantly regret it when my head begins to pound again. I grind my teeth and breathe through the wave of pressure.

"Take the pills, it will help." He almost sounds sincere.

"Fuck off, Alex," I exclaim as I continue to ride the wave of pain.

"Suit yourself. Shower is through there, clothes are on the counter. Welcome to your new home, Miss Lawson." The smug bastard strides out of the room without another word or even a backward glance. When he closes the door behind himself, I wait to hear the sound of a lock engaging. I keep waiting but the sound never comes. All I hear is the sound of his retreating footsteps. I know without a doubt this is a trap of some kind. Given the state I'm in, I decide to take him up on the offer of a shower and pray that the water helps wash away some of the after effects of whatever drugs he used on me.

I'll kill him for drugging me!

Have you ever tried standing under the shower head and keeping your eyes open? I don't fucking recommend it, that shit is harder than I would like to admit. But there was no fucking way I was going to close my eyes for even a second while I'm standing here naked. I did a quick sweep of the bathroom and tried to spot any cameras. I know that these days they can be the size of a pin but a part of me is hoping Alexander isn't some creep and watching me shower while stroking one out.

The clothes he left out for me are huge!

I'm not exaggerating! You know how girls wear their boyfriends clothes and they look cute in the oversized shirt? Not me. I look like one of Snow White's dwarfs in Shrek's clothes. This is so not fucking hot. I've rolled the sweats' waistband so many times that I have a fucking camel toe and they still drag along the ground. The shirt, oh God, don't even get me started on that. Then there is the hoodie he left that swallows my entire body the way I wish I could swallow a dick whole.

I growl in frustration, then storm out of there with a billow of steam following me out. I don't have a brush so the best my hair is getting is a finger comb. Do I feel better after a shower? Yes, I do, but that isn't the point. I had bags with me, could he not have stolen those as well like he fucking stole me? Like if you want to hold me hostage he could have at least had the decency to make me comfortable.

"That fucker is so going to regret this," I bite out as I grip the door handle and turn it. To my surprise it is actually unlocked. I slowly pull it open and stick my head out. I look both ways and frown, there are no guards standing outside. I quietly slip out of the room and plaster my back against the wall. I feel like a knock off of Rambo right now as I slide against the wall, trying to find the fucking exit.

Including the bedroom I just escaped from, there are four rooms. The doors are open so I take a quick look inside. All of them are clearly lived in if the mess is anything to go by. The room I was just in was clean and bare, unlike the others. I approach the end of the hallway and freeze at the sound of voices.

"We had a tail, Alex," a guy says.

"I know. Thomas sending those fucking heads to Vivian brought heat on us." Alexander sounds troubled and that brings a smile to my face.

"They think it was you, don't they?" another guy asks.

"Yeah. It didn't help that I was released around the same time. She won't believe us, she'll want to see the remains to prove her point but it's a bit fucking hard when Vivian had them all cremated." They're talking about the severed heads that were sent to Vivian by my sperm donor, but who the hell is the woman they are referring to?

"What's our next move?" This guy's voice is deep and holds a dark edge to it.

"Well, that depends on our guest, why don't you ask her?" I still, my breaths turning shallow. "Why don't you come join us instead of hiding, Miss Lawson?" My brows leap to my hairline. I dart my gaze back toward the way I came and debate if I should make a run for it or face these assholes head on. The decision is made for me when that snarky bastard speaks again. "We don't have all night." I grit my teeth, square my shoulders and hold my head high as I round the corner. I spot Alexander immediately, leaning against the wall and staring directly at me, the intense look in those green eyes has my skin breaking out in gooseflesh.

I tear my gaze from his, not wanting to try and decipher

what that look is about and scan the living room. Two of the guys I recall from the plane sit on a leather sofa, one is looking directly at me while the other sits there with a laptop on his knees and his eyes glued to the screen. Another guy from the plane is leaning against the far wall with his arms crossed over his chest. I nearly shriek when someone brushes up against me. I jump away from him gasping in shock. He smiles softly and there is something about his soft brown eyes that has my anxiety easing.

"I'm Vatican." His voice is deep and husky, his crooked smile makes him seem youthful and easy going.

"Tate," I rasp out. He nods, then holds out a bottle of water. I stare at it but don't make a move to grab it even though my mind is screaming at me to take the cold liquid that will soothe my throat.

"It's sealed," he offers. I purse my lips and tentatively take it from him. He doesn't wait for a *thank you* as he moves to join the others and plops down onto the vacant loveseat. I uncap the water and ignore them as I guzzle it down greedily. I nearly drain the entire bottle in one go, then sigh in contentment as I recap it and face Alexander again.

"What is it gonna take for you to let me go?" I ask. If he's surprised by my question he doesn't show it.

"The truth," he answers.

"About?" I throw back at him.

"The whereabouts of your brother," he says without missing a beat.

I keep my composure as I fire back. "If you let me strap a dildo on and fuck your ass, I'll tell you where he is." It takes a whopping three seconds before all five sets of eyes are on me, then laughter breaks free from the four guys, bringing a winning smirk to my face. Alexander on the other hand looks like he is plotting ways to disembowel me.

"You think this is a fucking joke?" he roars. The room falls silent and suddenly for the first time since meeting him on the plane I feel it, *terror*. I gulp and try to appear unaffected by his outburst but the instant he pushes off the wall and stalks toward me, I lose the fight. My fight or flight instincts kick in and this time, I choose flight. I turn and run through the house not knowing where the fuck I'm going but the sound of his thundering footsteps chasing me spurs me on to find the nearest exit.

When I spot the entryway up ahead, I almost weep at the sight of it. I hear him getting closer but I don't dare look over my shoulder, knowing that will cost me precious seconds of time I don't have. I extend my free hand that isn't carrying the stupid bottle of water ready to rip the door open, but then a scream of shock and pain tears from me when he grabs my hair and yanks me back. My feet slide out from under me, I'm about to land on my ass until an arm bands around my waist, securing me to his front. I barely have time to process what happened before he pushes me forward. I manage to turn my head to the side at the last second before I headbutt the front door. I push back but the asshole uses his body to hold me in place, his hands landing on either side of my head, caging me in.

For a solid minute all that can be heard is the sound of our ragged breaths. I don't know what the fuck came over me. Rationally I know I would never be able to escape but the fighter within me refuses to give up and roll over and show this wannabe alpha my belly.

"I've *never* wanted to slaughter a woman so badly

before," he pants out. The sick twisted bitch inside me preens like what he just said is a compliment. I have no idea why I have the urge to push this man until I find his breaking point. I know who he is and what he has done, yet... I'm not afraid.

"Well, I guess I should be proud that I get to pop your cherry then, huh?" His answer is to growl and I can't keep the satisfied smirk from my face.

"This isn't a game."

"Then what is it?" I fire back.

He grabs my arms, then spins me around and slams me back against the door. I grunt and glare up at the fucker. I hate the significant height difference between us. I may be little in stature but not in fight. I have faced hellhounds that wanted to rip me apart and survived. Alexander Denver is a fucking puppy compared to those monsters. When he bends down so we are eye level my breath hitches. Our breaths intermingle and the scent of mint and smoke hits me, I should be repulsed but... I'm not.

"This is your life on the line." His voice is hard and firm but it's the look in those green eyes that has me tensing.

"Why do you sound so concerned about what happens to me?" I find myself asking. His eyes harden as his hands grip my waist in a bruising hold. He pulls me forward until I'm plastered against his front. I drop the water bottle and place my hands flat against his chest.

CHAPTER FOUR

Alexander

Her blonde hair hangs around her face like a shield. I itch to brush the strands back but I keep my hands on her waist, resisting the urge. Her big blue eyes stare up at me with curiosity and hatred, but it's the sight of lust mingling in the depths of them that has me wanting to say fuck it to my rules and claim her.

To claim her would be to kill her.

Her innocence shines in her eyes—her mouth suggests she is older than her eighteen years but her eyes are what give her away. They show you everything without meaning to. She is impressionable and hardened from something that hurt her in the past and I find myself needing to figure out what that was and destroy the cunt. I shutdown that line of thought, she is a means to an end and it has to stay that way.

"You are the only one who seems to know where the rapist is." She flinches as if my words physically hurt her.

Her eyes darken and her features harden. Her grip on the front of my shirt tightens as she presses in closer, ghosting her lips over mine which has me tensing in surprise. It takes a lot more self-control than I want to admit to keep my impassiveness.

"Do what you must, I'll never give up my brother." My upper lip pulls back in a snarl. I shove away from her and the darkness that lurks beneath the surface of my skin bristles at me for not inflicting pain. She grunts out her annoyance as I turn my back and stalk away. I make it four fucking steps before I grunt when something smacks me in the back of the head. I whirl around to see the bottle of water she had resting on the floor in front of me. I dart my gaze from it, then back to her. I was fully prepared to ignore her temper tantrum until she cocked her hip and placed her hand on it smirking.

I rush her, her eyes widening in terror at the sight of me coming at her. She doesn't have time to react. I grab her waist and toss her into the air like she weighs nothing and she shrieks in fear. I don't use my hands to break her fall. I push forward and trap her against the door with my body, her legs and arms banding around me by instinct. Her breathing is erratic and her eyes are as round as saucers.

"What the fuck—"

I cut off her tirade before she can continue. "You ever fucking throw something at me again and I'll show you who really has the biggest set of fucking balls out of the pair of us. Do you understand me?" I yell, her nostrils flaring, clearly not liking my tone or the way I just manhandled her. Truth is, I don't give a fuck what she wants or what pisses her off. She is here for a reason and once she gives me the intel I need, she'll be sent packing and never thought of again.

"Fuck. You," she screams in my face.

"Not even in your wildest fucking dreams would I let your vulgar ass touch me." Her mouth slackens as her eyes fill with indignation. Victory has never felt so fucking sweet. My train of thought is corrupted when her legs tighten around my waist and her fingers tangle in the back of my hair. She tugs on the strands, tilting my head back far enough so she is looking down at me, clearly loving the height difference between us now. Her blue eyes are filled with a cunning look. She slowly bends down and runs her nose along my jaw, a small moan escaping her and without permission my hands grip her ass to keep her steady. She darts her tongue out and licks the shell of my ear. I hiss in both intrigue and surprise. I loathe to fucking admit it but my cock is hard.

Her lips ghost over the shell of my ear just as she grinds down and feels what she is doing to me. All my threats from a minute ago are proven redundant now.

"Hmmmm," she purrs in my ear, my hold on her ass turning bruising as I war within myself to either keep her steady or help her grind on my dick. "See, this is a game you will lose." I grind my teeth so hard they begin to ache. "Want to know why, Alex?" She doesn't give me a chance to reply. "You like to think you are the one calling shots but you're not. I am. You showed me your hand when you didn't rape me while I was passed out. You gave me clothes and water. You let me out of the room and allowed me free roam of your house. You just let the wolf into your straw house and I'll blow this motherfucker down before I ever give up my brother."

I release my hold on her and step back. She clearly anticipated the move because she lands on her feet with a smug smile. When she opens her mouth, to fire another insult I'm sure, I go with a different tactic of shutting her up. I wrap my hand around her throat, force her head back, then smash my mouth to hers. She turns to stone for a split second until I lick across her lips. She gasps, granting me the access I need. I swipe my tongue across hers and have to force my groan of pleasure down at the taste of her. Her hands fist the front of my shirt, I'm unsure if she wants to pull me closer or shove me away, but I don't let that deter me as I step forward, forcing her back against the door.

She grunts into my mouth but I swallow the sound. I start to forget the reason why I started kissing her when she kisses me back with a hunger only matched by my own. The kiss turns from exploration to a fight of dominance, our teeth clashing as we fight against each other. The moment I wrap an arm around her waist and pull her against me so she can feel my raging hard on, she relents and allows me the control I fucking crave. Her submission strokes the darkness inside me.

"Alex." At the sound of my name, I jerk back and take a step away from her. I try to appear unaffected when I face Omen but I can see from the look in his dark eyes that I failed. I hear Tatum panting beside me, gasping for air. I feel exactly like she does. I'm just better at hiding it than she is. That kiss was supposed to be a test to see how far I could push her, I was never meant to enjoy it or crave another taste of her. "We got a situation," he says, then darts his gaze between me and Tate. I see her from the corner of my eye ducking her head in shame.

"Give me a minute," I say. He nods then stalks off. I

know without a doubt he's pissed at what he just witnessed. I turn to her. She keeps her gaze on her feet and nibbles on her bottom lip, avoiding my gaze. I reach out and grip her chin, forcing her gaze back to mine. The sight of unshed tears in her eyes has my breath lodging in my throat and anger brewing in the pit of my gut. She flicks her eyes away which just has me hardening my hold on her chin. She winces, then skirts her gaze back to me. I'd much rather see the fire burning in them than that look from a second ago. "Me not chaining your ass up wasn't me showing you my hand. That was me treating you like a human being."

"Do you treat all the people you are going to kill like that?"

This fucking girl makes it hard not to want to strangle her!

"No, just the ones I'm trying not to fuck."

"I thought you wouldn't touch my *vulgar ass?*" she throws back at me.

"Did you miss the part where I just kissed you?"

She shrugs. "I may have been a participant in that."

"Clearly I was talking out of my ass," I grit out.

"Nice, so you are a killer and a liar—noted."

I release her and step back, then run a hand through my hair in frustration. "Look, I'm sorry. I shouldn't have kissed you." Her features pull taut, I can see she is uncomfortable. "It won't happen again."

"And if it does?"

"It won't," I bite out.

"You just admitted to being a liar so how can I trust you?"

"Jesus fucking Christ!" I snap then throw my hands in

the air. "I swear to God I have never met someone so annoying and infuriating!" I growl.

She beams and bats her lashes. "Well, thank you. You should get used to that because I'm not planning on telling you shit, Alex, so you may as well chain my ass up."

All traces of emotion vanish from me when I step forward, she can see the darkness rising to the surface inside me. Her body stiffens and her mouth remains shut as I glare at her.

"Stop pushing me, Tatum. I'm not like the other guys you know. I have a breaking point. I swore I would never harm any woman or child, but if you continue to taunt me and remain tight lipped, I will tie your ass up and I promise you I won't stop until I break down your carefully crafted walls and force you to face the demons of your past. I'll make you beg for death but I'll never grant you that freedom until I'm done playing with you. I hope he loves you enough to trade his life for yours, because if you don't give him up soon, I'll break my own vow and start sending him pieces of you—starting with your tongue."

She pales and stumbles back a step. I leave her standing there looking like a fish out of water. I no longer care if she escapes through the front door, she will learn soon enough there is nowhere for her to run out here. We are surrounded by thousands of acres, there is nothing out there but open land. It seems like a sick joke that my last name is Denver and I live on the outskirts of the place itself. This ranch has been in my family for generations. I never wanted anything to do with this place but my sister loved it here so much.

I find Omen and the other's gathered around Halo, who is sitting at the counter in the kitchen with his laptop in front of him. As I approach they all look up at me, none of them have to say a word. I know Omen has already told them what he witnessed between me and Tate a moment ago. I ignore the question in their gazes and ask.

"What'd you find?" Pope shoots me a look that only a teenage girl could pull off which has me scowling at the fucker. "Mind ya fucking business," I grit out. The cunt laughs which just irritates me more.

"Dez is the one tracking us." Halo's tone is filled with rage and I can't blame him, we've flown under the radar for years. My release from prison and the murders happening at the same time has fucked us.

"I need a meet. The only way to prove we didn't do this is to have a sit down." All four of them stare at me with wide fucking eyes and varying looks of outrage. Before they can all start firing off their dislike of this decision I push on. "We can't afford for them to get in the way. Going after that little cunt is already going to put us on the chopping block."

"I don't give a fuck. I'll take whatever those dicks throw at us as long as that cunt is dead," Vatican declares.

"Agreed. Smooth shit over with them now so we can move freely, then we strike. They'll come for us with every-thing they have when they realize we did it," Halo says.

"Let them come. I'm ready to meet my maker with the blood of that motherfucker on my hands," Omen agrees.

"The decision is yours, boss. Just know we all have your back and will do whatever you say," Pope adds.

I run my gaze over each of them and nod. Five years ago I bought our freedom and that is a decision I will never come to regret. The only thing I regret in life is not being there to protect my sister. I should have been by her side, but instead

I was too busy trying to build the Denver Kings. We aren't a crew, gang or an MC club. We are a family.

"Set up the meet with Dez. If they aren't covering their tracks, then they want this meet as well," I announce.

"How many men do you want watching your back?" Omen asks. The Denver Kings is country wide, we don't have a banner or a fucking patch to state who we are. We run our business undercover so if any one of our locations was busted no one would be able to trace it back to us. That is the only way we have been able to operate as per our deal.

"The five of you and that's it. They can't know about the rest of our operations," I mutter, pissed off that I still have to worry about those fuckers figuring out that I reneged on our deal. At the start I had planned to adhere to their rules, but then I realized I would never be a blue collar type of guy, and I had four guys relying on me to keep them fed and sheltered, so I went back to doing what I know. My own parents disowned me. They lost this place a couple of years ago to the bank. I had the guys swoop in and buy it while I was locked up, there is no way I would ever let my sister's dream be sold to developers. My parents hate who I am and blame me for what happened to their daughter. I can't say I blame them, the things I have done would make any parent disown their own child.

"What about her?" Vatican says, flicking his chin behind me. I peer over my shoulder to see Tatum standing there, looking uncertain. I can't say the look suits her but the sight of my clothes on her body does. Fuck! I push that thought away and narrow my eyes.

"She remains here." Her jaw locks and the twin balls of flames in her eyes rise as she glares at me.

"*She* is standing right here." I raise a brow at her outburst.

"You are irrelevant, Miss Lawson. Your wants and needs are not something that will be taken into consideration. You will remain in my *straw house* until I say otherwise. No one here will help or aid you in any attempt to escape. Welcome to your gilded cage."

"You're a real fucking prick, you know that?" she snaps back at me.

"So I've been told, but as you can see, I don't give a flying fuck what you think." She reels back as if I hit her. I refuse to allow her reaction to have any sway on me, so I turn back to my guys. "Send me the details when Carnage responds. I'm heading to bed. We leave in the morning to head to the warehouse." Halo opens his mouth but before he can utter a word I add, "Yes, she will be coming with us. Now, how about you fuckers stop worrying about the girl and do your fucking jobs." I ignore their snickers as I spin around and stalk past Tatum, heading out the back door.

CHAPTER FIVE

Tatum

I stand here watching him retreat outside. There are no lights to mark his path.

"If I was you, I would be running after him before you get lost." I spin around to face the guys and frown. The guy with unruly brown hair rolls his eyes. "You aren't staying in here with us." I jerk back and cock my head.

"Who are you?" I blurt.

"Pope. Now, chase after him before I throw your fucking ass out of our house." I scrunch my face and stay where I am until the guy with black eyes—Omen I think his name is—takes a step toward me and I dart out the back door Alex just disappeared through and squeal as the moist ground touches my feet. I run blindly into the darkness. The moon offers no fucking light tonight. Fear begins to wind its tendrils around me as I don't see Alex ahead. I hear leaves crunching to my right and I veer that way but my breath hitches and I slam to a halt. I spin around in a circle and instantly my eyes widen. I'm surrounded by... nothing. The lights from the house behind me are nothing but a faint glow. I hadn't realized I had run this far.

I inhale and all I smell is nature. This place is nothing like Hollow Hills or any of the places I have lived before. It's quiet and... peaceful. Suddenly I don't care. I'm alone in this strange place with a serial killer and his four sidekicks. I feel the hairs on the back of my neck stand up a second before I feel his heat at my back. He doesn't touch me but he stands close enough to shroud me in his shadow.

"Do you see now?" he asks me quietly.

"See what?" I whisper.

"There is nowhere for you to run, Tatum. Even if I let you go you would never find your way to town. This place can be a prison without having any need for bars on the windows."

I shake my head as I look out at the night sky. "I don't see a prison," I admit.

"What do you see?" The curiosity in his tone is clear and I choose to answer rather than fight him and ruin this moment.

"Freedom," I say barely above a whisper.

"That's what she said." Hurt laces his tone. I turn and face him ready to ask what he means but he silences me when he grabs my hand and drags me after him. A whimper escapes me when I step on something. He stops, then turns to peer down at me. "What happened?"

"I stepped on something," I mutter. He curses beneath his breath, then suddenly I'm being swung into his arms bridal style. My arms band around his neck on instinct. His scent overwhelms me and I know for sure that whatever this attraction is between us, it isn't fucking healthy. I'll admit the first night I saw him in Lividica I was stunned, he's not like any man I have ever seen before. He is fucking stunning yet he doesn't walk around with big dick energy. He has no idea how fucking beautiful he is.

"I'll have Vat bring your bags to my place," he mumbles. I'm about to ask what that means but then he rounds a bend and suddenly my train of thought derails at the sight of a small cottage nestled in a gully next to a creek. The moon shines enough light on this side for me to make things out. Alex kicks the door open, clearly he doesn't need to lock it living out here. He places me on my feet then steps away, a moment later I'm bathed in light. It takes a minute for my eyes to adjust, I turn in a circle and marvel at the beauty of this place. It's all open—the kitchen, the living room and even his bed is all in here. I see a door off to the side and I'm guessing that's the bathroom, at least you can pee in private then I guess. "What? No smart-ass remark?"

I turn back to face him with a frown. "Huh?" I ask genuinely confused.

He shoots me a deadpan look. "You aren't going to say you'll blow my *stick house* down?" I cringe and shoot him a sheepish smile.

"I'd much rather blow the straw house down and keep this one, thank you very much." If my reply shocks him he doesn't show it. I leave him there as I make my way around the tiny space and gaze at the photos that decorate the walls. I can feel his gaze boring into the back of my head but he doesn't stop me when I reach out and trace my fingers over a picture of him with a beautiful girl. I don't need him to say it,

I know without a doubt that the girl in the photo with him is his sister.

Elenor Denver.

God, she was stunning. She has his eyes. Her long strawberry blonde hair reminds me of Blake Lively's. He has his arm wrapped around her while she stares up at him with the biggest smile on her face. You can see the love she has for him in her eyes. Suddenly it becomes too painful to look at the picture, I close my eyes and turn away from the image.

Alex moves behind me and I tense in anticipation but when I spot him moving toward the closed door, I frown. He's really just going to take a shower and leave me out here to dig through his personal items? When the door clicks shut behind him I have my answer. I make my way to the kitchen and check the fridge, nearly crying at the sight. I grab everything I need to make a sandwich.

I decide to be gracious and make the Aztec god one as well. I carry our plates over to the bed and sit down, tucking my legs beneath me and resting my plate in my lap. My stomach growls. I collect the sandwich and my mouth waters as the scent of turkey hits me. I open my mouth to take a bite but freeze when the door opens and Alex steps out wearing nothing but a white towel wrapped around his waist.

My mouth is watering for an entirely different reason now.

Steam billows around him, his hair wet and slicked back. All his tattoos are on display and I greedily run my gaze over him but freeze at the sight of the tattoo in the middle of his chest.

Ellie.

It doesn't take a rocket scientist to know that *Ellie* is

Elenor. The next tattoo that captures my attention is the one in an upside down U shape around his abs.

De Santis Cosa Nostra.

My eyes bug out of my fucking head, I'm not dumb I know what Cosa Nostra stands for. Mafia. Is that what he is, a made man? Alex's gaze meets mine and I can see the warning in them, if I ask the question that is burning in the back of my mind he'll shut me down. But, if I keep my mouth shut and wait it out, I could do some research on whoever the fuck Da Santis family is while they go to that meet.

"Whatever you are plotting, don't," he scolds as he stalks toward me. I drop my sandwich on my plate and stare at him, partly praying that he stays the fuck away from me but also wishing he would drop that towel and rid me of this sexual tension I can feel pulsing between us. When he veers off at the last second toward the dresser, I hate that I'm annoyed he didn't attempt to touch me.

"I wasn't plotting anything," I mutter as I finally pick my sandwich up, which doesn't taste as good as I hoped. It was the sight of *him* that ruined this beautiful snack for me. I was fine and happy until he walked out here looking like a fucking God and making me want to take a bite out of him and not my actual meal.

"This for me?" I swallow and peer over at him to see him standing there in a pair of gray sweats. I want to fucking whimper at the sight of him. Jesus this is so fucking unfair. Why did he have to be a raging asshole who wants to ruin my life?

"Yes," I snap. When he continues to eye it warily I growl, then snatch half the sandwich, meet his stare and take a bite. "Happy?" I say around a mouthful of food. His eyes narrow in disgust so I swallow and smile sweetly. "No rat poison was used, scouts honor," I say, holding up two fingers. His face slackens.

"I'd bet my fucking life that you were never a scout," he mutters as he snatches his plate off the bed and stands there eating the sandwich I made for him. I hate that his sandwich now looks more enticing than mine! We both eat in silence but it's charged. Not in the awkward kind of way but in the way that you can feel so many unasked questions hanging between you both. I get so lost in my own thoughts, I don't realize he has taken the plate from my lap and turned out the lights until I feel the mattress dip from his weight.

I gasp and scoot around on my ass to face him. He sits there on the edge of the bed with his phone in his hand, reading something like nothing is wrong.

"What are you doing?" I ask when he locks his phone and places it on the bedside table. I may not be able to see him but I can feel his eyes on me which just heightens my awareness of him in the dark. Goose flesh begins to break out over my skin and a small shiver works its way down my spine.

"Tatum, I'm a twenty-seven year old man who is quite fucking capable of sleeping next to a woman without sinking my cock inside her." I feel a blush coating my cheeks but what's worse, I can feel myself growing wet at the picture he's painting and without consent, images of him pop into my head of him naked and on top of me as he thrusts— "I'm tired. Now lay the fuck down and go to sleep." I swallow and suck in a ragged breath, trying to calm my thoughts. I have never, and yes I mean fucking never, met a guy and wanted to fuck them. I normally steer clear of the opposite sex and don't find any of them attractive, but it seems like that isn't the case where Alexander is concerned.

Yippee!

"Why did they say I couldn't stay in that house with them?" I blurt, trying to buy myself some time to think of some plan so I don't have to sleep next to the fucking Butcher.

He sighs and I can tell he is at the end of his patience with me. "Fine. If I tell you, will you shut the fuck up and go to sleep?"

"Pinky promise."

"They won't let a female near them. They have their reasons why and you being around for the foreseeable future until we... get what we want is going to cause problems. Now, go to fucking sleep."

"Asshole," I mutter as I toss the sweater I'm wearing onto the floor, then stand so I can rid myself of the sweats. Just as I kicked them to the side and peel the covers back his words stop me.

"What are you doing?"

"Uh, going to sleep?" It comes out as a question.

"Why are you undressing?" The tightness in his tone has my brows raising.

"I thought you said you could control yourself? Or were you lying again and you do actually find my vulgar ass attractive?"

I roll my lips over my teeth to keep from laughing when he growls out loud. "I may just decide finding that cunt isn't worth it after all," he mutters to himself. I preen and climb in beside him. I lay on the edge of the bed, not wanting to touch him. Silence stretches between us, I have no idea if he's asleep or awake but I can't shut my mind off long enough to even try to sleep. It doesn't help that I suffer with insomnia and have no melatonin to help put my ass to sleep.

I start to delve into everything I have learned. Alex is clearly part of some mafia. His sister is dead, he blames my brother. He wants me to give up the only family I have left because he thinks Nexus is the one who murdered his sister. I know Vivian and her friends think he did it as well, but the brother I know, he would never hurt anyone. He saved me from our father. He's never asked me for a thing, I was the one who promised to help him hide.

"He didn't do it," I whisper.

I feel him shift beside me and lay on his side facing me. I keep staring up at the wooden beams not wanting to look at him. It seems whenever he is around I can't keep a level head and that is a huge problem considering what he wants from me.

"How well do you really know Nexus Valerian, Tatum?" His tone is soft and that surprises me more than his question.

"He would never hurt anyone."

"How do you know that?"

"Because I've looked evil in the eyes and know exactly what the devil looks like. Nexus isn't bad." I don't know why I'm getting so emotional speaking about this but I find myself fighting back tears.

"Who hurt you?"

I clench my jaw and inhale through my nose. "No one."

"Halo will return your laptop to you tomorrow. All your emails and searches will be monitored. You can work from here but you will be watched."

"So, I'm a prisoner?"

"Only if you want to be."

"What the hell does that mean, Alex?" I cringe, since when did we become familiar enough to shorten each other's names?

"It means your freedom is your own. You can have it whenever you want but you know what the cost of that freedom is."

"Yeah." I scoff. "I just have to sell my soul to Satan."

"If that's how you want to see it."

"Let me ask you this, *Butcher,* if the roles were reversed and I was forcing you to give up your sister—" The remainder of my question dies on my tongue when he yanks me toward him, then rolls so he is nestled between my legs and hovering above me. My breaths turn ragged. Twenty minutes ago this exact image was burned into my mind but now, it doesn't have the same feelings attached to it like my daydream.

"This is your one and only fucking warning, Tatum. Don't *ever* mention my sister again. I told you I had a breaking point earlier, she's that point." His raw honesty is astounding and refreshing.

"Who hurt you?" I ask.

"I wasn't hurt, I was annihilated."

"Who annihilated you, Alex?" I whisper.

"Your brother. Then your father framed me for murder." I gasp.

"What?" He tries to roll off me but I wrap my legs around him, holding him in place, surprising us both.

"Tatum," he says my name like a warning.

"Did you drug me again?" I blurt. That is the only explanation why I am acting like a hussy around him.

He jerks. "What?"

"Did you or not?"

"Why the fuck would you think that?" I decide not to answer and release him. He rolls over and I scoot back to my side. This time I close my eyes and force my mind to go blank, willing sleep to claim me. Everything will look different in the morning... I hope.

CHAPTER SIX

Alexander

I wake to the sound of someone moaning. I snap my eyes open and freeze. I tilt my head down to see Tatum practically laying on top of me, her hair a wild mess across my chest and her leg is resting dangerously close to my morning wood.

"Hmmmm," she purrs again as she rubs her cheek against my bare chest. She looks peaceful and undisturbed in sleep. The fact she is quiet and her vulgar tongue isn't being put to use may be another reason why I find the sight of her sprawled across me so endearing. My train of thought is wrong and I know it, but after watching her for months, I half expected her to be a scumbag like her brother. I've never seen her go on a date, hang out with friends or even go shopping for herself. She just lives out of hotels on fast food and works. She's a creature of habit and something about that surprises me. She's so young and should be thinking about college and partying, yet all she does is work her ass off for Vivian.

My phone vibrates beside me and I slowly untangle myself from her and slip out of the bed. I check the message and realize I have about twenty minutes to get ready. I fire off a reply to Halo, telling him to bring her stuff to my house.

I could have given her back her things yesterday but I chose to test her, I wanted to see how much she would fight me. Low and behold, she didn't do what was expected and wore my clothing without a fuss. I head for the bathroom to grab a quick shower. When I'm finished I give my beard a quick trim and debate on shaving the fucking thing off or not, but there isn't time. When I walk back out to change, Tatum is sitting up in bed and staring at me. I don't have time to argue with the vexing little shit so I ignore her and make my way to my dresser, I hear her gasp and curse myself. I yank a shirt out of the drawer and pull it over my head.

The only way I know how to get her mind off the scars on my back is to drop my towel. I can feel her eyes boring into me but she says nothing as I finish dressing. I pull my hair into a bun just as a knock sounds out.

"It's open," I call out. Halo lets himself in and places her bags and laptop down. Tatum stares at them with an open mouth but it's the look on Halo's face that stumps me. He looks from me to her, then to the floor beside the bed and that's when it hits me. He can see her discarded hoodie and pants on the floor. "It's not what it looks like," I defend.

Halo scoffs. "Yeah, I've never heard that line before." I grit my teeth and snag my phone off the bedside table just as Tatum says.

"Oh, it is totally what it looks like." I snap my head

toward her and gape at the fucking minx. She smiles sweetly at Halo and bats her lashes. "Don't worry, he didn't tire me out too much. All that time in prison caught up with one minute man over there," she says, nodding toward me. Halo the little fuck doesn't even try to mask his laughter. I shoot Tatum a scathing look as I storm toward my boy and shove the fucker out the door. "Where are you going?" she rushes to ask as I attempt to close the door.

"Out. You run, I'll catch you and show you just how well prison didn't diminish my stamina." I close the door with the picture of her sitting there, eyes wide and mouth hanging open, to keep me company as I head to the main house to meet the others so we can get to this fucking meeting and the De Santis Cosa Nostra off our asses.

"Do you think they believe that you had nothing to do with the murders?" Halo asks from beside me. I pause around the bend from the house and look at him. He may be the second oldest out of the four of them but he is the one with the baby face. His blue eyes try to hide the worry he feels but I know him as well as I know myself and seeing the De Santis family again has him on edge. He stabs a hand through his short black hair and sighs. "I won't go back, Alex," he says quietly.

A whoosh of air rushes from me. I place a hand on his shoulder and bend a little to meet his gaze so he can see the resolution in mine. "I'll burn the four of those sons of bitches to the fucking ground before I ever let them take you and the others. I swear on my sister's fucking grave, Halo. I will never let any of you go back there." My words seem to ease some of his worry but not all of it. The only way to squash it completely is to get this meeting over with. Before we can take another step, my phone begins to vibrate in my pocket. I pull it out and shake my head. Halo nudges me so I turn the screen toward him and he just snorts and continues onto the house leaving me here to answer the call. "Vivian, what a surprise," I say as I connect the call.

"Alex, I thought you and I had a deal." She's trying to disguise her anger but is failing miserably.

"What deal would that be?"

"The one where you don't fucking touch Tate—" Her raised tone and the fact she thinks she can tell me what I can and can't do grates on my fucking nerves. It took Tatum less than three minutes of getting her shit back to call her boss. Her laptop and phone are bugged, we can see and listen into everything she does on them.

"You don't call the shots. I held up my end of the deal, I kept your brother and those other fuckers alive and saved you. You got Thomas and I get his cunt of a kid. That was the deal," I snap, my tone filled with venom and ice cold. It takes her a minute to gather herself before she speaks again.

"Alex, please don't hurt her." The pleading edge to her tone does nothing to make me soften. She may remind me of Ellie but she isn't her. At the start when she first came to visit me in prison, I was floored. She looks nothing like my sister but the way she spoke and how she carried herself... her ambition is what had me seeing similarities between the two. I allowed that to cloud my judgment for a moment and offered my services to keep her and her *friends* safe. Not only that, I also got Nexus out of the deal. Halo is the best fucking tracker in the country and the fact he isn't able to find Nexus Valerian is worrisome to say the fucking least.

"She'll conduct her work for you from here. She will do

her job and you will stay out of this, Vivian. You try to sniff around my business or get your boyfriends and brother to put on their bat suits and I'll place an anonymous tip through to the CIA myself. We had a mutual agreement but we aren't friends. Don't ever try to tell me what to do again." I end the call and force myself not to throw my phone in a fit of anger, Vatican wouldn't let me live it down if I broke another phone.

Killing used to be my release for all my pent up anger. I earned the name *Butcher* because of the precise cuts, no medical examiner could ever pinpoint the exact cause of death because I was that fucking good. I don't believe in numbing the pain of my victims or even giving them a shot of adrenaline to keep them up. I loved what I did but the toll it took on my soul wasn't worth it in the end. I got out of that life and chose to run straight for a while but the urge is always there. It never goes away and is always present, begging me to let the monster inside takeover and give us both the outlet we need.

"We're moving out," Omen shouts. I nod and head inside their place. I slam to a stop on the threshold when I see them all. They are all strapped with firearms and wearing bullet proof vests. Vatican tosses me a vest. I catch the fucking thing and just stare at it.

"Put the fucking thing on and don't argue. We aren't taking chances with these fuckers, Alex," Pope says. There's an edge to his tone but I can also hear the worry and that is the only reason I don't argue with him. I pull my shirt off and unlike Tatum, these four don't balk at the sight of my scars. They hate seeing them and they serve as a reminder of what happened but I never want Omen, Vatican, Pope or Halo to feel any type of guilt over this. I made my choice and I wouldn't change it.

I secure the vest then pull my shirt back on. All four of the guys are staring at me when I turn around. Vatican and Pope's brown eyes are dark and swirling with guilt. Omen and Halo's blue eyes have a storm brewing in them.

"Stop. It's been fucking years and you all need to get over it. We survived, we got out and we're here now," I grit out. They all drop their gazes and return to their earlier tasks, not saying a word. I sigh and scrub a hand down my face. "I need you guys to stop feeling guilty over this shit."

"How the fuck are we supposed to do that?" Omen snaps, twin fires burn in his eyes, his black hair flopped forward onto his forehead.

"By not fucking thinking about it every time you see my back!" I roar. Halo and Pope both look away but Vat and Omen stare directly at me. "I made the fucking choice—"

"We would never have let you go through with that shit if we knew what those cunts had planned!" Vat defends.

I shake my head. For years we have been having this same argument and I'm over it, they need to deal with it and let this shit go. "It wasn't your call to make." My tone is ice cold and filled with dominance. "Get strapped, we're leaving," I clip out, ending the conversation and heading out the front to the car, only to stop dead in my tracks at the sight before me. Two of my guys that patrol the grounds are standing there with their assault rifles aimed at the blonde leaning against the back of my car with her arms crossed. She looks... sexy as fuck. The aviators she wears cover her blue eyes, a white crop exposes her toned stomach, her belly button piercing catches the sunlight and the leather jacket she wears adds to the bad girl look. But what sets it off is the black leather pants with the black knee-high boots that have me picturing her wearing those as I thrust inside her.

"Don't worry, the panties and bra match today," she calls out just as the four guys come up behind me. I push my lips to the side to keep from smirking, this girl is crazy with a capital C but the sex appeal on her is fucking real.

"Now all I'll be wondering all day is what color they are," Halo mutters.

The devilish smirk on her face is pure sin and I know she is about to tell him what color they are so I cut in before she gets the chance. "What the fuck are you doing, Miss Lawson?" I growl.

She waves her hand as if she is talking to a friend. "Stop with the *Miss Lawson*, I think we can use first names now, Alex, since we slept together." The four guys behind me all begin sputtering and barking questions. Adrian and Phillip even start lowering their guns and shooting me questioning looks. I grind my teeth and stalk toward the little hellcat who is beaming at me. I wave the guards away as I grip her arm and drag her around the front of the car. "Nice to meet you!" she calls out to Phillip and Adrian, both of them chuckle in answer. I shove her against the front of the car. She grunts and tries to push forward but I pin her in place with my body. I reach out and push her sunglasses to the top of her head, revealing her eyes burning with anger but there is no masking the lust I see in them.

"You think this is a game?" I snap.

"You're the one who said you always win, Alex. I'm just evening the playing field and proving to you that you're not invincible."

I lean down and grip the back of her head, tangling my fingers in her locks as I brush my lips against her ear. A shiver works its way through her and I relish in the knowledge that she isn't immune to my nearness. "Get your ass back to my house. I don't have time for your shit today."

The fucking hellcat throws her arms around my neck and pulls me in closer so she can mimic my move. I detest admitting that her lips on my skin have me heating the fuck up and my cock leaping to attention. It's been a long time since I have had this type of reaction to a woman and it's unnerving to say the fucking least, especially considering who she is related to.

"I'm not the type of girl you just leave behind," she purrs. I tighten my hold on her hair and relish in the hiss that escapes her. I've learned that she likes the feeling of my beard against her skin and I'm not above using that to my advantage, so I brush up against her face. A small mewl escapes her before she clamps her mouth shut.

"And I'm not the type of guy you can push around and play games with. The news articles you found about me were all true." A gasp escapes her and she stiffens against me. "They called me The Butcher because of how much I loved carving through the flesh of my victims and got off on sawing through their bones with their screams of agony to keep me company as I worked. Want to find out how they felt in their last moments?" I hear her gulp. She begins to tremble in my hold and I know she is starting to realize that her life really is in danger now.

"I scoured the internet, I read everything there is to know about you. I bribed the cops for your case files." Her admission shocks me, not once did Halo tell me she had some cops in her pocket. "You never hurt a woman."

"Want to be the first?" I ask as I pull back just enough to look her in the eyes—we're so close our breaths are mingling. Her blue eyes search my own, trying to decipher if I'm bluffing or not. She won't find what she's looking for because I haven't even decided if she will be my first or not.

"Why do you want to hurt me?" she blurts out quietly. The way her eyes widen tells me she never meant to voice that question aloud but she can't take it back now.

"Because the pain of my victims tames the monster inside me and gets me off," I answer.

"If the only way for you to get hard was to kill someone then why are you hard for *me* right now?" Before I can answer, Omen appears beside us. I can see the disgruntled look on his face from the corner of my eye. He can think what he likes, his worries aren't my problem.

"Prison was lonely, don't flatter yourself." Her jaw unhinges as I push back from her and turn to Omen. I climb in the car with the four of them following my lead. When Vat starts the car Tatum still doesn't move, she spins around and places her hands flat on the hood of the car and glares at me through the windshield.

"You leave me here and I'm running!" she yells. I lull my head to the side and nod at Vat. He slams the car in reverse and plants his foot. Tatum stumbles forward and manages to right herself before falling face first into the ground as we speed away, leaving her standing there in our dust, screaming.

CHAPTER SEVEN

I hate that we have to rely on Halo hacking into the cameras around the building we are meant to meet the De Santis family in. I could only manage to get four of our guys to perform some drive-bys. I couldn't risk Carnage or the other's spotting them and figuring out we are running our own game now.

"It looks clear, boss," Halo says from the back of the car. I nod and take a second to get my head right. I haven't seen these fucks since we walked out of there five years ago, seeing them after twenty years would still be too soon if you asked me.

I grip the door handle but pause as I say, "They don't own you anymore. You are free men and don't have to be here for this meeting. I will never make you do anything you don't want to do." When a hand lands on my shoulder, I peer back to see it's Omen. His eyes are hard as he stares at me.

"You're our family. We'll always have your back no matter what," he vows. Their loyalty is something that can never be bought. These four are the only family I have and I will do anything in my fucking power to protect them. Unable to say anything else I just nod and step out of the car. It takes me three seconds to spot five of their men trying to blend in with the crowd of people on the street. Halo nudges me and flicks his head across the road where four blacked out Range Rovers sit. At least they aren't trying to be discreet about the fact they came with a mini army.

"The Don's here," Pope says. He's right, the only reason there would be this many men is because the boss has left the safety of their home. I grunt in response. I was expecting to meet the gruesome threesome, not the four of them today. I head inside the restaurant, which is empty except for the table in the back.

Of course they shut down the restaurant for this impromptu meeting. At the sight of the five of us walking toward them, three of their guards try to intervene to search us but I grip the first one by the throat. The other two stop in their tracks and reach for their weapons, but Halo and Omen already have theirs drawn and aimed at their heads.

"You touch me or my guys and I'll rip your fucking head off." My tone is filled with bloodlust. All of these cock-suckers know exactly who the fuck I am and if they don't, they should ask about me because it would save all of them this type of embarrassment in front of their boss.

"Let him go, Lex." Hearing her call me *Lex* grates on my fucking nerves. I release the cunt with a shove. He falls into the other fucker who helps straighten him. We stalk past the three of them and come to a halt in front of the De Santis family. The four of them sit there, looking smug as fuck. They all hold an air of superiority. They are the type of rich people who would spit on a janitor and laugh.

Carnage, the fucker, sits there looking like the fucking Grim Reaper. His pale blue eyes are filled with malice. He's cut his black hair, it's now short on the sides and longer on top. When he cuts his gaze to Halo and winks, I nearly leap across the fucking table and rip his throat out.

Wrath and Rage sit on either side of the other two, keeping them secure in the middle. They are fucking trouble. These are the two you need to watch, they have no rhyme nor reason for doing anything. They will shoot first and not even care to ask questions later, they're fucking idiots. They look like charming frat boys with their blond hair and honey brown eyes but it's their dark personalities that make them despicable. Having one of them roaming the earth is bad enough but the fact they are twins is worse than anyone could have conjured in their worst nightmare.

"You look good, Lex," she says in that sickly sweet tone. I tear my gaze from the terror twins and finally look at the devil herself.

Desire De Santis.

Raven hair, bright baby blue eyes that lull you into thinking she is innocent and a woman who you could fall in love with and build a home with. She is nothing but a facade. Everything about her is designed to lure you in and suck the essence right out of you without you even noticing until it's too fucking late.

"Desire, always a displeasure to see you," I say, making sure she can hear the venom in my voice. Her left eye twitches. Years ago she could have inflicted punishment for my tone but not anymore, she has no control over me and she hates it. She may be able to control some things in my life but not me as a person. I'll never allow the cunt that kind of power ever again.

"Have a seat, Lex." Her tone is laced with a command but I don't heed it, nor do my guys.

"Cut the fucking shit, Desire. Why the hell are your men following me?" Carnage is the one to react first. He pushes back from the table and stands. Halo pushes in front of me with his gun drawn, it's no surprise to me when more men flood the restaurant exposing her hand. Pope nudges my shoulder subtly letting me know he has signaled our own men to move in closer —now that all of her minions are inside with us there is no chance of our guys getting spotted. Carnage and Halo don't flinch or even bat an eye at the men surrounding them with their weapons raised. Omen, Vat and Pope remain by me, knowing Carnage would never allow his men to take Halo out.

"Still playing on the wrong side, brother," Carnage taunts Halo.

"Still eating our sister's pussy I see, *brother*," he spits out. Carnage just smiles, it's dark and would have any man shitting themselves but not us, we know that Carnage is deadly but the true monster of their dysfunctional family is the one wearing the thong up her ass.

"You should try it, brother, she tastes good. Just ask Alex." Carnage flicks his gaze to me for a second, trying to taunt me to do something but I remain where I am. I force my hands into my pockets so I don't do something stupid, like snap his fucking neck and start a war.

"Enough, we didn't come here to kill our brothers,"

Desire announces. Carnage still remains standing until the devil herself stands and places a hand on his shoulder. Like a good little dog, he does as his master says and reclaims his seat.

"We aren't your anything," Omen snarls. Desire finally looks into the eyes of her twin and that's when I see it, hatred.

"*You* will never be anything to me, Toscano," she bites back.

"I'd rather be a Toscano than a sellout De Santis, like you, *cagna.* (bitch)" Omen is hanging onto his rage by a thread. I turn to him and shift so I'm blocking his view of Desire. His eyes are mirrors of hers but unlike the she-devil, his holds pain in them.

"Take a walk, brother. We got this" He shakes his head once and stares at me. I give him a slight nod, telling him it's okay. He blanks his face of all emotion before turning on his heel and storming out of the building, regret churns inside me. I knew bringing them with me to see these cunts was a bad idea but there was no way they would have stayed home and let me come on my own.

"Put the gun down, Halo," Desire snaps. I whirl around knowing Halo won't listen to a word she says. I reach out and push his arm down. Desire looks to me as she speaks. "Unless you can control them—"

"You don't fucking address them, you want to speak then you speak to me. Am I crystal fucking clear?" Her eyes widen and blaze with outrage at the way I just spoke to her. I see her men creeping in closer and I shoot her a dark grin that holds promise. "They make one more move, just *one,* and I'll tear your entire fucking army down, Des. You want to bury your soldiers or talk like real men?"

Her jaw locks and I know I've pushed her just enough now. She fucking hates when people refer to her position as a man's. "I'm the fucking Don of the De Santis Cosa Nostra, Alexander. Never fucking forget that."

"And I'm the motherfucking Butcher. Never forget that," I roar. I hear a gun cock causing Pope, Vat and Halo all to draw their own guns.

"You're what I made you to be!" she yells.

"You didn't make shit, Desire! I made you. I gave you the throne your frigid ass currently sits on." My outburst has her eyes blazing and her true colors showing.

"It's a great thing your precious Ellie isn't here to see the monster you have become." I step forward until my thighs smack into the table, forcing it forward. The twins and Carnage all get to their feet and flank their sister who is staring right at me.

"Say her name again and it will be the last word you ever fucking utter. Mark my words on that," I force out through gritted teeth.

"Enough. We came to discuss business," Rage snaps. "All of you, lower your fucking weapons and stand down. Halo, Pope, Vatican, please lower your weapons as well." The three of them turn to me for confirmation. I nod which just causes Rage to narrow his eyes.

"Why are you following us?" I ask.

"Because you broke the terms of your deal with my sister," Wrath answers.

"I didn't fucking break my word," I bite back.

"We have proof, Alexander. We know The Butcher's

work and the severed heads you sent to that girl was a calling card of yours."

I roll my eyes which just pisses Rage off. "I didn't send the fucking heads. Thomas Valerian sent those heads to the girl, trying to fool her into thinking I was coming after her. She can validate my story and so can half a dozen others." I can tell these cocksuckers don't believe a word coming out of my mouth. If they decide to take action against me because they think I broke the deal, then we'll go to fucking war. I didn't go through everything I did just to lose to them. I won't fucking die until I have avenged my sister, after that they can do what they like with me.

"And you think we'll just take you at your word?" Carnage sneers.

"His word is all you're getting, asshole," Halo snaps, answering for me. The hatred between him and Carnage runs deep. They may be twins, but much like Omen and Desire, there is no love lost between the two of them.

"So, if I'm eating our sister's pussy does that mean you're sucking his cock?" The sigh has barely finished leaving my lips before Halo is launching across the table and tackling Carnage to the ground. Pope and Vatican are the next to jump the table to stop Wrath and Rage from intervening. I cross my arms over my chest and let Halo have at it. Carnage isn't weak. He'll give as good as Halo can give. They may hate each other, but even if they won't admit it to themselves, we know they would never kill each other, which is their greatest flaw.

"You idiots!" Desire screams as she tries to separate Halo and Carnage, but one of them flings their arm, knocking her on her ass. Her soldiers scramble forward but when I face them all they stop in their tracks. They know she can order their death for not protecting her but they also fear me. They all know what I have done for her and in her name.

"You touch him or the other two and I'll make you dig your own grave before I bury parts of you in it and send the rest to your families." When none of them take another step, I move around the table and shove Carnage off Halo. Before Halo goes after him again, I grab the back of his shirt and pull him across the room. I shove the little shit against the wall and get in his bloodied face. "Enough," I growl right in his face.

He's panting and sweating from exertion, his eyes are wild and filled with the need to maim and inflict pain.

"Look at me." It takes him a second to do as I ask. "Go outside and wait with Omen."

"I'm not—"

I cut him off before he can finish. "Yes, you are. Go wait with your brother. Vat and Pope will remain with me while we finish this. Now, go." He shoves me away from him and storms out of here with anger wafting off him in waves. Halo is always level headed and calm until Carnage is added to the equation. I scrub a hand down my face and take a steadying breath before facing Desire who is glaring balls of fire at me.

"The next time one of them steps out of line—"

"You'll do what?" I snap, cutting her off.

"Don't fucking push me, Lex," she warns.

"Make your point known so we can all get out of here and you can fuck off back to Chicago," I snarl.

"The agreement still stands. You try to build a family of

your own, you die. You kill without my blessing, I slaughter you," she reminds me.

"Look at where I fucking live, Desire," I shout and spread my arms out wide. "Does it fucking look like I'm killing for hire or building a family of my own?"

"You have four of my brothers with you," Wrath snarks. I cut my gaze to him and glare at the little fuck.

"They aren't your anything, you little shit stain. They are *my* brothers and *my* family. They may share your DNA but you'll never have their loyalty." Wrath's nostril's flare in anger. He tries to step toward me but Pope shoves him back a step.

"Make a move against him and the blood we share won't save you," Vatican promises.

"We'll make inquiries into the situation. If I smell a rat or something seems off, I'm coming for your fucking head, Butcher," Carnage warns.

I smirk at the cocky fucker. "You can try and hunt me all you like but I'll always be the predator and you will always be the prey, little De Santis. Never forget that." I turn to leave, fucking done with this bullshit meeting but her words hold me in place.

"The deal extends to Nexus Valerian. Kill him and it won't be my brothers hunting you down, Lex. It will be me." My breathing turns choppy as I try to reign in my temper. I know if I face her now, I'll blow the deal out of the fucking water and rip that vile bitch apart.

CHAPTER EIGHT

Tatum

Night has fallen and still there is no sign of headlights coming down the long ass driveway. How do I know it's long you ask? Because I gave up walking the fucking thing after a few miles. When he said we are in the middle of nowhere he meant it! The guards he left behind didn't even try to stop me when I took off after them. By the time I made it back to the house, four of the assholes were standing there grinning at me. I wanted nothing more than to smash them across the head with a fucking rock but I'm a lady, so I flipped the fuckers the middle finger and stomped my ass back to Alex's cabin.

I refused to sit there and wait, so I stole one of the asshole's duffle bags and stuffed some clothes inside. Since I couldn't trust he hadn't tampered with my burner phones, I opened the hidden compartment in my suitcase to grab one I knew was safe. I pop the bottom out and snatch the phone out then stuff it into my pocket. Before I left, I decided to be a petty bitch and I took his comforter with me because fuck being cold. I even stole some food for my escape. I may not be able to navigate my way out of this fucking place but that doesn't mean I won't try. I hate that he was so cocky and just left me here unguarded. I found this place far enough away I can't even see the lights from the house. I'm lost and it's dark as fuck, but if I'm lost then that means he won't be able to find me, right?

I push that thought away as I pull the burner phone out and hit call on the only contact number I have saved. It rings five times before he finally answers.

"Tate?"

"Yeah, it's me," I breathe out.

"You didn't call yesterday, is everything okay?" A whoosh of air escapes me hearing the concern in his voice. It's strange, I still marvel at the fact that I can care about someone this much. I've grown up never caring for anyone and only watching out for myself, to find out I have a brother who I have grown to care about a lot.

"I have to tell you something," I mutter.

"He found you?" The anxiety in his tone is clear.

I run a hand through my hair and sigh. "Nexus, don't panic, okay—"

"Where are you?" he snaps.

"You can't help me, brother."

"The fuck I can't. I have something in place to take that fucker down—"

"I'm at his house," I blurt, the line going silent for so long I have to double check and make sure the call is still connected.

"Why are you there?" The hint of accusation in his tone has me bristling.

"Oh, because he invited me over for a tea party. Why the fuck do you think I'm here?" I snap, unable to hide my anger.

"Fuck. Okay, I can make this work." I reel back.

"What the hell do you mean you can make this work? I'm his prisoner, Nexus. I can't exactly make demands."

"You're calling me aren't you? You must have some freedom or something." His tone is starting to rub me the wrong way. I thought at the very least he would be concerned and ranting about how he's coming to get me or something but no, I haven't heard any type of concern from him.

"I'm fighting for my life here, Nexus. I'm trying to find a way out of this place and away from him in order to keep you safe." Hurt laces my tone and I'm pissed for allowing emotion to slip through my tone but I won't lie, I'm fucking hurt over his reaction.

"But, the best place might be for you to stay there." I choke on my spit.

"Say what now?" I rasp out.

"Has he hurt you?" I mull over his words and bite the inside of my cheek when I get where his line of questioning is going.

"No," I grit out.

"So, he's treating you okay-ish then?"

"Where are you going with this?" I bite out.

"You're a beautiful girl, Tate. Men seem to talk more freely when they are *relaxed*." Bile rushes up my throat. I swallow a few times and try to control my outrage.

"Are you suggesting that I... seduce The Butcher?"

Disgust laces each of my words. Not because I find Alexander repulsive but because my own brother is suggesting I whore myself out for intel.

"Call it what you want but if he—"

"Do you even know what he looks like?" I ask.

"Of course."

"How?" I know I sound shallow asking this but for all he knows he could be some fifty-year-old balding, overweight trucker.

"I've seen pictures."

"Where?" I shout. "Where the fuck have you seen him, Nexus?"

"Why are you being such a chick about this?" Tears prick the backs of my eyes.

"You're just as bad as all those foster fathers I had. I'm nothing but a way for you to pay your debts."

"Hey, hey, hey, come on now. You and I both know I never hurt that crazy fuck's sister—"

"He isn't crazy!" I snap.

"Wait, are you defending him right now?" I bite back my retort and remain silent. "How long have you been with him?"

"A couple days," I mutter.

"Wow, all it took was two days for you to turn against your own brother."

I scrub a hand down my face. "He didn't turn me against anyone. He also isn't crazy, Nexus. Someone hurt his little sister and he won't stop hunting until he finds out the truth."

"How do you know that?"

"I can see it in his eyes. His sister is his purpose and reason for doing all of this. He loved her, Nexus, you can feel it!" My voice rises as I begin to doubt everything I know. "He really loved her and this won't end until he—" I hear rustling behind me and tense when the hairs on the back of my neck stand on end. "I have to go." I end the call, power the phone off and slip it in the side of my shoe. My breathing turns ragged as I wait. When a couple of minutes pass and nothing happens I find myself praying that it's Alex out here with me and no hungry mountain lion.

Oh my God.

Wouldn't that be a way to go, escape my captor only to be eaten by a lion! A shiver works its way down my spine when the rustling begins again. I wait with bated breath and clench my eyes closed, not wanting to see the animal as it takes my life. I feel it approaching and when I feel a presence beside me I deflate.

"How'd you find me?" I mutter as he takes a seat beside me on *his* comforter. He stretches his legs out in front of him and rests back on his elbows, getting comfortable.

"Being able to sit out here and look up at the stars is one of the reasons why I keep coming back to this place." He doesn't sound angry, he just sounds... tired. I mimic his position and look up, my eyes widen. The stars are everywhere, there's no buildings to obscure your view of them, they're so bright and beautiful. We sit here for a long while just looking up at the beauty of the universe. "To answer your earlier question, there isn't a place you can run to where I won't find you, Tatum." On most guys, that answer would sound cocky but when he says it, I just hear the truth.

"How come you can find me but not my brother?" I push.

He sighs and I can't help turning to look at him only to

freeze when I find his gaze already on me. "I thought about that a lot today. The only conclusion I have is that someone with enough knowledge about me and my guys is hiding him."

I frown, then study him for a second trying to sense if this is a trap. "Why would you think that?"

His green eyes burn with an intense look and I find myself trying not to fidget. "Want to know something I can't figure out?"

I purse my lips and decide to throw caution to the wind, he hasn't killed me yet so may as well push my luck. "Sure, why the hell not," I mumble which has the corner of his mouth lifting into a smirk. It's amazing, there is no light out here yet I can see him perfectly thanks to the moon and stars shining so bright.

"How someone like you could share blood with a piece of shit like him." I recoil.

"Don't call my brother that." I tear my gaze from him and huff as I stare up at the sky, but I can't find the beauty in it any longer because he ruined it for me. Alex reaches out and grips my chin, then forces me to face him. I scowl at the fucker.

"What would you have me call him?" His question stumps me. He searches my eyes for a second, trying to see something. I have no idea what it is but his features change and anger enters his eyes causing my breath to hitch. "Who hurt you?" I jerk free of his hold.

"No one hurt me, you couldn't hurt me if you tried. So if you've come out here to drag me back by my hair, kicking and screaming, then go for it," I snap and pluck a handful of grass and toss it at him. His eyes blaze and I match his glare with one of my own.

"What did I tell you about throwing shit at me?" he grits out.

I roll my eyes and pluck another handful of grass. He eyes it and cocks a brow in warning. "You're not going to kill me, you aren't even going to beat me. You have no leverage here, Denver," I taunt, then throw the grass at him with a smile. My smile vanishes in an instant when he strikes out with his body, pinning my own flat against the comforter while he looms above me. I try to lift my arm to hit him but he's quicker. He captures both my wrists and pins my arms above my head. I open my mouth to yell at him but he beats me to it.

"If you try to spit on me, I'll say fuck it to my no torturing women rule and flay you the fuck open." I gape up at him.

"Eww. I'm not a spitter." The second the words leave my mouth and his eyes widen, I realize what I've just said and how he took it. An uncomfortable second of silence passes between us, then I feel it. My eyes widen at the feeling of him growing hard. Unlike me who starts fucking blushing, he just remains stoic, nestled between my legs with his hard cock pressing against my pussy.

Our eyes remain locked and suddenly the air around us thickens and feels charged. My skin grows hot and my nipples start to harden. My breaths turn shallow when suddenly a wave of need pulses between my thighs. My mouth parts on a silent gasp as realization crashes into me.

I'm turned on and I can't deny it. I'm attracted to The Butcher.

I should feel repulsed and hate him on sight and the principle that he wants to murder my brother but... I don't.

What's wrong with me?

Alex slowly bends down while keeping his eyes locked on mine. Suddenly unable to control myself, I lean upward and meet him halfway, pressing my lips to his. We still at the contact. When he doesn't move or even breathe, I pull back and stare up at him in shame but his hand grips the back of my head holding me in place.

"This goes any further, I won't stop. You want this to end, then run now and run fast because I'll hunt you down, Tatum, and take what I want from you." I suck in a sharp inhale.

"What if I want you to catch me?" I find myself saying. A devilish glint enters his eyes and I start to panic that I've pushed too far.

"Then run, Bambi, and pray I don't catch you." Excitement fills me at the prospect of me being hunted by him for a different reason. I've never behaved this brazenly before with any man. I don't know what makes him different but I think it's the fact that at any given time since I met him on the plane he could have taken what he wanted from me but didn't. He's always held back and now I want to see what he's like when his restraint snaps.

He's a killer.

He'll fucking slaughter me.

My brother's words play on repeat in my head but as I stare up into his eyes, I don't see the killer, I just see... him.

Fuck it.

I push him off me and relish in the sound of his dark

chuckle as I make a run for it. I have no idea which way to go that will lead me back to his cabin so I just wing it.

"You have three minutes!" he shouts. I shiver but this time it's from excitement and need that is building low in my belly. The thrill of being chased by him is erotic. I've never experienced this kind of thing before but I would be a liar if I said being chased by a serial killer didn't have me soaking my panties. I break through a line of trees and slam to a stop as I scan the area trying to remember if any of this looks familiar.

"Fuck!" I growl and take off, sprinting through the woods. I dart between trees, trying to gather my bearings but fail as the trees begin to blur and become one and suddenly I realize, I'm utterly fucked and lost. I know my time has run out and he'll be closing in on me so I quieten my steps and try to navigate my way out of the woods. Hopefully I can find a hill or something so I can get a view of the land and hope that I can spot the house from this distance. Just as I round a tree I nearly weep in joy when I see an opening up ahead. I take another step only to be halted when an arm wraps around my waist. A scream escapes me a second before I'm shoved against a tree and then he's right in my face, panting.

Fear grips me but there's also arousal at the fact I know what's about to happen. I shouldn't want this but fuck, I do. That sick twisted bitch inside me is feigning for this moment and the prospect of being fucked against a tree by a stranger. I open my mouth to ask him what happens next but before the words can escape me, he smashes his mouth to mine, robbing me of air and rational thought. My arms wrap around his neck as I press up on my tiptoes and deepen the kiss. I pull the elastic from his hair and tangle my fingers in the strands. He breaks away and scrapes his beard along my neck sending a shiver of need through me as he places open mouthed kisses on my shoulder.

"Shit," I hiss when he sucks my flesh into his mouth. I tilt my head back, offering better access. His hands grip my waist in a bruising hold. He pulls back and I nearly pout thinking he's putting a stop to this until he grips the front of my crop top in his hands and tears it down the middle. I gasp in surprise but it melts away the moment he grabs the cups of my bra and pulls them down, exposing my tits to the cool night air.

"Fuck, I've been dying to taste these." His words shock me to my core. I had no idea he's been thinking about me like that! When his hot wet mouth latches onto my nipple, I arch forward and cry out as he swipes his tongue over my hardened peak.

"Oh shit, Alex," I whimper and tug on his hair, holding him in place. I'm panting like a fucking dog but I can't find it within myself to care. I've shut off all rational thought and allow myself to live in this moment and the feelings he's drawing out of me without much effort at all. He switches sides and I moan loudly. I need him to dull the ache he's caused between my legs. I lift my right leg and lock it around his waist, pulling him forward. He bites down on my nipple, drawing a pain-filled cry from me. He soothes the ache by licking away the sting but his message is received.

He calls the shots.

He releases me with a wet pop. I expect him to kiss me, but instead he surprises the hell out of me when he crouches down and begins undoing my pants. I stand here with my legs parted, shocked at the sight of Alexander Denver kneeling before me. Jesus that sounds like a line from a cheesy Rom Com but it's true. He rids me of my shoes and I step out of my pants which he tosses to the side. I start to nibble on my bottom lip, suddenly nervous thanks to the way he's staring at my lace covered pussy.

He flicks his eyes up to me and smirks. "Looks like they do match after all."

I scoff. "You're cracking jokes right *now?*" I hiss. His answer is a dark chuckle and I fight the urge not to smack him over the head. All thoughts of violence flee me when he grabs my leg, throws it over his shoulder and presses his nose against my pussy. I suck in a sharp intake of air.

"Fuck, you smell so good, Bambi," he purrs. His praise sends a bolt of heat through me. I never thought hearing a man tell me that my pussy smells good would be so erotic but God damn it is. He darts his tongue out and licks me through my thong. I throw my head back and cry out. I'm shaking with need and he doesn't seem like he's in any rush. He continues to lick me through my thong and it feels fucking amazing but I need more!

"Alex... please," I beg. I'm not proud of it but honestly, I don't give a fuck now. I need him to make me come more than I want to live right now.

"You want to feel my tongue inside this wet little cunt, Bambi?" God, his fucking mouth is an aphrodisiac on its own. My pride is telling me to deny him but my mind is screaming at me to give in and hand myself over willingly and let someone else take control for once in my life.

My mind wins.

"Yes, please, please, please—" My plea is cut off when he

pushes my panties to the side and a whimper escapes me when he blows his breath along my moist slit.

"Fuck, you're so wet." My answer is a small moan. I'm ashamed to admit I even buck my hips, trying to gain some type of friction. I fucking need it. I've never been this heightened or aroused in my life and it's both addicting and aggravating. I want him to hurry up and eat me out but the darker side of me wants him to drag this out and make me beg him for my release. "Beg me."

"What?" I ask and drop my gaze to his.

"Beg me to eat this pussy and I'll consider it. If not you can get on your knees and choke on my dick." I loathe to admit I actually contemplated his request, choking on his dick doesn't seem like such a bad idea, but the need coursing through me makes my mind up.

"Please eat me out and make me come on your tongue, then I swear to fucking God himself I'll do whatever you want, just let me come," I beg.

"Jesus, calm down, Bambi. I had planned to make you come, I just didn't realize how much you wanted it." I balk at the fucker when he smirks and I itch to smack the look off his face, but then his sinful tongue glides through my slick folds and all rational thought flees me once again.

Holy shit.

He has the skill of a porn star. He grips the globes of my ass and pulls me flush against his mouth. He flattens his tongue against my clit and I cry out, bucking my hips shamelessly as I grind against his face. When he pushes his tongue inside me and groans at the taste I'm fucked. I cry out so loud I have no doubt I scared every fucking animal out of this forest.

"Alex!" I pant. He sucks my clit into his mouth as he pushes a single finger inside me, it stings but the feeling of him assaulting my clit overrides the pain. He pumps his finger in and out of me, stretching me out to prepare me for taking him. I've felt how big he is and I know no matter what, taking him is going to sting like a bitch but I'm so ready for it. "Oh shit, please don't fucking stop," I plead as I continue to grind against him. He adds a second finger and I fucking erupt, smacking my head against the tree as I throw it back and scream. My orgasm rips me in half—it's the most intense orgasm I have ever experienced and it's ruined me for any other man. Waves of pleasure flow through me, causing my body to tremble uncontrollably.

Alex withdraws his fingers and pushes to his feet, grips the back of my head and pulls me forward so he can kiss me. He forces his tongue inside my mouth and I gasp at the taste of myself on his tongue. Jesus, tasting my own release from his tongue is fucking pornographic. I reach out blindly, fumbling with the button on his jeans. He doesn't try to help me or even growl in impatience. He keeps kissing me, allowing me to take my time. I push his jeans and briefs down his legs but make no move to touch his cock.

I can't.

CHAPTER TEN

Alexander

I can feel her apprehension the second my dick springs free. I know there is more to her that she isn't telling me. I don't need the words to know I'm right, I can see it in her eyes and feel it in the shift of her body. I don't let her get caught up in her mind. I grip the backs of her thighs and hoist her up against the tree. She comes back to herself and gets lost in the kiss, then pulls away and stares down at me as I line myself up with her entrance. Her eyes widen as I press against her opening. My brows furrow when I push forward and she winces, horror fills me as realization crashes into me.

"Bambi?" Her eyes meet mine and I see it. "You're a virgin," I whisper. Her mouth opens but no words come out. Fuck! I attempt to pull back but she tightens her legs around my waist and slams down onto my cock. She screams in pain and I grit my teeth, trying not to bust a fucking nut from how tight she is.

Fuck, she feels amazing.

"Oh, fuck, fuck, fuck, shit!" she screams out. I see her eyes glistening with tears and anger fuels me.

"Why the fuck did you do that?" I roar.

Her nostrils flare and she blinks back her tears as she meets my angry glare. "Because, I wanted to. No one hurt me, Alexander, and now you know for sure I'm not a liar." She throws her words at me with a heavy dose of venom.

I lock one arm under her ass, the slight movement has her wincing. I grip the back of her neck with my other hand in a punishing hold. "Someone hurt you and you will tell me who but tonight," her eyes widen, I can see when she opens her mouth she's about to lie so I push on, "Tonight, you're going to let me erase that pain and hopefully make this a better experience for you." Her eyes fill with emotion that I don't try to decipher as I maneuver and lay her down gently on the forest floor while keeping my cock inside her. She stares up at me with a look of uncertainty. I had planned to fuck her hard and work out my frustrations on her perfect little cunt but it appears tonight will be a first for both of us.

I lean down and seal my lips to hers, forcing her to relax and melt into the ground. Only when she is fully relaxed do I begin to move inside her. I draw almost all the way out before sliding back inside her slowly. She gasps into my mouth but I don't break the kiss, knowing she needs me to keep her distracted until the pain bleeds into pleasure. I keep my thrusts slow and measured even though it's killing me. I want nothing more than to slam inside her and chase my orgasm.

But, I can't, not with her.

When her moans begin to grow, I break the kiss and

keep the same tempo as I peer down at her. "You like it?" I grit out. She arches off the ground when I stroke that sweet spot inside her. She pushes her hands under my shirt and runs her fingers over the scars on my back. She's too lost in the feelings I'm pulling from her to notice them again.

"Yes, Alex, it feels so good," she moans.

"Lift your leg and wrap it around my waist." She does as she's told, her blind trust in me to know that I can give her the pleasure she seeks is... crazy, but the fucking monster inside me loves it. Relishes in it even. This time when I push inside her I hit a different angle, her eyes widen and a sharp cry pulls free.

"Oh my God, keep doing that." She pants. I bite down on my lip when she digs her nails into my back as I thrust inside her again with more force. "Hmmmm," she purrs, she likes it hard! I repeat the move twice more, getting her used to the feeling before I allow myself to slam inside her harder. We both cry out and I lose the battle against my control. I draw back and place her legs over my shoulders, then bend forward and fuck her like a savage. Her cries will be heard for miles and the sick satisfaction that gives me has me fucking her harder and deeper. "Alex, I think I'm going to come," she screams. I pinch her clit and love the way she shudders beneath me.

"Come for me, Bambi," I growl and she does. The sight of her coming on my cock is a sight that will be ingrained in my memory for years to come. Unable to hold off my own release any longer, I slam inside her once more before emptying everything I have inside her without remorse.

Shudders tear through the both of us, the only sound

that can be heard is our panting. I'm slick with sweat and feeling fucking lighter than I've felt in years.

"Not a one minute man after all, huh?" I taunt, her mouth popping open in surprise. Before she can say anything, I brush her legs off my shoulders and bend down to capture her lips in a kiss. This kiss isn't like any of the others. This one is more of a... let's call it a truce type of kiss. I break it and slowly ease out of her. I feel like a prick when I see her wince. I yank my shirt off and reach between us but she darts her arm out gripping my wrist stopping me.

"What are you doing?" She sounds horrified.

"Bambi, that was your first time and there is going to be a mess of my cum and your blood. Let me clean you up and then I'll take you home for a shower." She stares at me with a dumbfounded look but doesn't try to stop me again. When I clean her as best as I can, she winces and cringes but doesn't make a sound. I help her to her feet and we both get dressed. I cringe when I face her again and see the mess I made of her shirt. I reach back and rub the back of my neck, she narrows her eyes.

"You couldn't just take it off or something?" I smirk and shrug.

"Ripping it seemed like the better option since I get to stare at your tits the whole way home." Her jaw unhinges.

"Asshole," she mutters when I grip her arm and begin to lead her out of the woods. It takes a minute for the awkwardness to surface between us now that we have rid ourselves of the sexual tension, there is only tension left and it's fucking suffocating! I release my hold on her and lead her back to where she ran from. She keeps her head down and every couple of steps I see her wince or cringe slightly and I feel like a prick. I assumed from the job she has and how she carries herself that she was... fucked if I know what I was thinking, but I never thought she was a fucking virgin. Believe me, I'm not the type of guy you want to remember for the rest of your life as your first sexual encounter. As we round the bend I frown at the sight of the two guys waiting on the hillside. Tatum lifts her head and when she spots them she slams to a halt.

"Are you fucking serious?" she seethes. I whirl around and face the little devil with a frown.

"What?"

"Your little fucking ass lickers have been here the whole time?"

I snap my arm out and grip the back of her neck in a firm hold, not caring that I'm hurting her. "I may have just fucked you like a nice guy but don't get shit twisted in your head. I'm still in charge here, Tatum. I call the fucking shots." Her eyes widen and hurt filters through her eyes. I release her and stride toward the guys. I toss Pope the phone. He hands it to Omen who turns and stalks away, no doubt to take it to Halo.

"You son of a bitch!" she screams, then shoves me from behind. I stumble forward a step then face her. Tears glisten in her eyes. I know what this looks like, but I don't have time to worry about how I hurt her feelings. "You stole my phone..." Her eyes widen as she looks between me and Pope. "You set me up, you heard my phone call and knew it was Nexus." I can see the wheels spinning in her head as she pieces it together. "You made them hang back. You knew if you asked about the phone I'd destroy it, so the only way to get it back intact was for you to..." She clamps her mouth closed and shakes her head, then snatches the duffle bag off the ground. When she meets my gaze again I see nothing but hatred. "I hate you," she spits out then shoulders past me. I know she'll follow Omen back so at least I won't have to hunt her ass down if she gets lost.

"That was fucking low, even for you," Pope mumbles.

"How about you keep your fucking nose out of my business, huh?" I snap as I snatch my blanket off the ground and storm back toward the house. Pope catches up to me in a couple of strides, then cuts in front of me. The look on his face can only be described as concern, which irritates me further than I already am.

"You don't just screw anyone."

"What the fuck's your point?" I snap.

"My point is that you just used that girl. She may be the fucker's sister but she isn't him."

I scoff. "Since when did you fucker's start caring about Tatum Lawson?" I snarl as I press into him.

He pushes his forehead against mine, not backing down. "Since we have all been spying on her for six months. You aren't the only fucking person here who is confused where she is concerned."

"She knows exactly who the fuck I am and if I have to resort to old measures then so be it." His eyes widen at my declaration.

"You would subject her to your demons?" The disbelief is clear in his tone as he takes a step back and looks at me like I'm a stranger.

"I told all of you, I would do whatever the fuck I had to in order to get justice for my sister. If that phone is a dead end, then she is the key to getting me what I want." I brush past him without waiting for a reply. I've never tortured a woman or hurt a child but I will do it if it means getting vengeance for Ellie. My little sister deserves that much and Pope of all people should fucking understand that.

I'm a mile or so out from the house when my phone begins to ring. I fish it out of my pocket and hit answer when I see it's Damon.

"Yeah?"

"Boss, we have a situation that needs your attention." Damon is my head of the Colorado area and he keeps my men armed through his connections in Russia. He swore he would never work for anyone but himself, but that all changed while I was inside. His wife's rapist was sent to the same prison, so I offered him a deal. I kill the fucker and he arms my men—he took the deal.

"What is it?"

"We caught two guys tailing you, they're from the De Santis Cosa Nostra."

I grind my teeth. "I'll be there soon. Have them ready for me." I end the call, quicken my pace as I scroll my contacts, then hit call when I find his number. The phone rings seven times before the fucker finally answers.

"Well, hearing from you is never a good thing," the fucker says.

"You keep following me and I'll be forced to take drastic measures to prove a point, Carnage," I say in an even tone.

"You're going fucking crazy, Denver. I never put a tail on your ass."

"Bullshit, come say it to the two fuckers I have strung up." He's silent for a second and that unsettles me more. When Carnage is silent for too long it never ends well.

"Send me the location."

I snort. "You want to join your men?" I taunt.

"Fuck you, Alex. If what you say is true, then the order didn't come from me." I can hear the waver in his tone, something is going on in the De Santis family and it's clear Carnage is trying to smooth things over. But, why?

"They aren't leaving my shop... intact."

"No repercussions will come from my family if what you say is true. You have my consent, *Butcher*." Hearing him give the green light to embrace my monster and allow him out to play sends a thrill through me.

"I'll text you the address," I say, then end the call as I stride into the main house. Vatican, Halo and Omen all turn to me with weird looks on their faces. "What?"

"She's in Omen's room," Halo says. I shrug, then head toward the internal garage with Omen and Vatican following after me. I toss my blanket on the back of the sofa as I pass by.

"What are you doing?" Vat asks when I start punching in the code to one of the floor-to-ceiling safes we have. I have all my tools locked away in here, it's been years since I have touched these instruments and just the sight of them is getting my dick hard again. My mouth is watering at the sight of my favorite hunting blade—the weight is evenly distributed and makes it perfect for flaying the skin from my victims.

"I got the green light, we have two strung up and waiting," I answer as I start placing my tools in a bag.

"Who gave you the green light?" Omen bites out.

I stop stuffing my bag and turn to face them both. "Carnage." At the mention of their brother's name both of them begin cursing.

"Why the fuck would he give you the green light?" Vat pushes.

"Because Damon picked up two fuckers who were tailing us. Carnage swears it wasn't him who had us followed." Omen frowns and drops his gaze mulling over my words.

"If Carnage didn't order the tail, then who did? Wrath and Rage don't have that kind of pull in the family to go behind his back." I raise my brows and shoot him a deadpan look that has his eyes narrowing to slits.

"Desire is making moves of her own without the family knowing," Omen supplies. I nod.

"Suit up, we leave in ten minutes," I bark.

"Who's gonna stay with the girl?" Vat asks.

"Pope and Halo—"

Omen cuts me off before I can finish. "Halo won't hang back if he knows Carnage is going. I'll stay with Pope and keep an eye on her."

My features harden as I stare at him. I fight against the need to rip his head off as a spark of something foreign flares to life inside me. "You don't touch her," I grit out, then stalk past them both.

Halo, Vat and I pull up in front of the warehouse we have on the outskirts of town. Unlike the De Santis family we don't peddle drugs, we only distribute guns and Kevlar piercing ammo. I don't fuck with narcotics, I won't be the reason someone else loses a loved one because of that shit. I may peddle guns but that's a different beast entirely. The three of us climb out and make our way toward the blacked out Lincoln that's idling out the front.

At the sight of us approaching, Carnage kills the engine and steps out. Both him and Halo are sporting bruises from their earlier fight but Halo knows he needs to keep his shit in check tonight or he will be dealing with me.

"You better be right about this, Denver," Carnage growls as he falls into step with us.

"You better hope he's wrong or you'll need to find a new pussy to pound," Halo snarks as we enter the warehouse. Carnage doesn't feed into his bullshit. I lead them through the vacant space toward the back where we take the stairs down to the basement level.

"How'd you find them?" Carnage asks.

"I have my ways," I answer. I called Damon on our way here and had him and our guys move out for the evening. Carnage can't know about the Denver Kings and seeing a production line of guns being readied to ship out is one way to fuck us over and get us killed. I had Damon move the fuckers to our empty warehouse where we conduct our... business.

Vat pulls his keys from his pocket, unlocks the door, then waves us in. I smile at the sight of the two bastards chained to a beam with their arms above their heads. They wear only their pants. Damon has already worked them over pretty well—one of them has a flap of skin hanging from his cheek.

Thanks to the lights being hung above their heads, we can see them but they can't see us in the shadows. Both of them tug on their chains, trying to get free, then their movements still, they can sense the apex predator has arrived. The notion of them sensing their impending death has excitement thrumming through me. I move toward the back of the room, keeping to the shadows and place my bag on the metal table. Carnage follows and stands beside me.

"You say nothing about me while you extract your information," he says low enough for only me to hear.

"Same rules apply as before. This is my show and you have no say here. I conduct my operation as I see fit," I snap, then begin setting up my instruments. Once I'm satisfied with how they are laid out, I grip the edge of the table and drag it in the light. Both of the guys jerk and fight harder at the sight of me and the tools I have on display.

"Butcher," the one on the right breathes out in a tone riddled with fear.

I smirk at the fucker. "Answer my questions and I'll have no need to use any of my methods to extract the information I need." My tone is relaxed and almost friendly. I love lulling them into thinking that if they are good, they get to go home and live to fight another day but that's a lie. No one has ever been strung up in front of me and lived to tell the story.

"They'll kill us!" the one with the flap of skin shouts.

I reach for my scalpel and hold it up. Both of them start jerking and kicking their legs. It's useless, they'll never break those chains. I twirl the blade in my hand, I know from the reaction they're giving me already, they won't last long and I won't be able to play with them for as long as I would like. It's the quiet ones that always last the longest, I love forcing them to break.

"Hmmm, see, if you don't tell me what I want to know I'll kill you slowly but, I'm not unreasonable. I'll let you pick who gets my undivided attention first." I look between them both as I rub my beard and flick my brows. When I hear a dripping sound I know what it is without even having to look, one of these fuckers just pissed themselves.

"Me!" the one with the flap of skin yells, causing surprise to course through me. The other one turns pale as he looks at his friend.

"No, take me first." I roll my eyes, that fuckers bravery is bullshit, he just said that so he didn't look like a pussy.

"I'll tell you whatever you want to know, Butcher, just let my brother go."

Fuck!

"I hate killing siblings!" I groan. Both of their faces morph into a look of hope, fucking fools. "In that case, let's begin." Both of them fight harder than they did before to get loose. I go for the guy on the right who pissed himself. The fact the other one offered himself means he would take longer to break. The easiest option is to force him to watch his brother die because that shit will break him worse than me cutting him open.

I place my blade in the center of his chest and glide it down slowly, making sure he can feel every ounce of pain. I never rush my masterpieces, they all get my undivided attention and time. The other fucker starts yelling and spewing threats but I ignore him until I reach the waist line of his brother's pants. The cut is deep enough to fit my separators inside so I can peel the flesh open while I start removing parts of him while he's still alive.

"Fucking stop," his brother screams as I retrieve my separators. I frown at the sight of the fucker passed out. I hate when they don't stay awake for the show. It's poor manners. I slip one end under the skin and the guy jerks awake with a horrid scream tearing from him. I force the other end under the other side, relishing in the pained yell he lets loose. I never use the separators to break bones, I love doing that individually. I just love using them to hear the sound of flesh tearing and inflicting as much pain as possible. If he thinks it hurts now, just wait till I start cranking them open, there is nothing like hearing the sound of flesh being torn. Just the thought of hearing it in a second has my cock growing hard.

"I'll tell you whatever you want to know!" I roll my eyes and keep my gaze locked on the other fucker as I turn the crank. The bastard starts flailing and screaming as I keep ripping his flesh open. "Fucking stop, you crazy cunt!"

I pause and shoot the motherfucker a dark look.

"Butcher, you have information to extract. Stay on track," Vatican says as he comes to stand by my side. My nostrils flare as I try to calm myself. I loathe being called crazy, what I do is a fucking talent and a craft that I have honed over years of practice. This is fucking art. Vatican nudges me and shoots me a look, bringing me back to the present and out of my bloodlust.

"Tell me who sent you after me and my guys," I snarl.

The fucker swallows, I keep my eyes on his so I can see if he lies. "The De Santis family sent us."

"Which one?" I push. When he takes too long to answer, I return my attention to his brother and smile, the sight of his rib cage and insides on display is a sight I could stroke one out to. It's beautiful. I retrieve my reciprocating saw from the table and hate that my toy is passed out with his chin resting on his chest. The other cunt starts yelling and screaming but I drown out his noise when I start the saw. I grab the first rib and start working only for the fucker to wake up and start jerking, messing up my cut. Blood splutters from his mouth and lands on my cheek but I don't stop until I have his rib resting in the palm of my hand.

I glide toward the other bastard who is still issuing threats and push his brother's rib into his pocket. He starts sobbing and goes lax in his restraints and that's when I know we have him, he'll tell us everything we want to know. He was easier to break than I had hoped, which is annoying but it is what it is.

"Tell me what I want to know and I'll end this." His head slowly lifts and when his brown eyes meet mine, the look of resignation is there, he's given up.

"Desire De Santis sent us to tail you," he admits.

"Why?"

"She said you were making moves and wanted proof." Carnage steps out of the shadows and comes to stand beside me. The guy's eyes widen but there isn't an ounce of fight left in him. He thinks I've set him up and is ready to die.

"What else did my sister tell you?" Carnage sneers. The guy's face contorts in confusion, clearly not understanding what the fuck is happening right now.

"Nothing." When I swivel toward his brother and raise my saw he starts talking again. "I swear, I only overheard her on the phone!" I turn back to the fucker and narrow my eyes.

"What did you hear?" I yell. He recoils on instinct.

"Just that she would have proof soon. She said that the deal you and her made wouldn't save you this time. She said you would have no choice but to come back to her and she would make sure you never knew what really happened."

"That makes zero fucking sense," Carnage roars. The guy takes a shuddering breath.

"I swear, that's all I know. I'm just supposed to follow them and report back to her when I find their home base." Rage overcomes me. I dart forward and grip the cocksucker by the throat, his eyes bulge as I cut off his airway.

"From now on you work for me. You report back to that bitch what I tell you to, am I clear?" He nods as best he can. I release him with a shove as he gasps and coughs. I turn to Vatican, he can see the look on my face and knows I'm about to resort to my old ways. "Get that fucker medical attention and bring that bitch to the house. I want to find out exactly what that cunt is up to."

"I'm not letting you go after my sister," Carnage snaps.

I pin the bastard with a look that urges him to try me on this one, because I'll kill him where he stands. "We're at war now. Your sister broke the agreement when she came for me. Choose a side, Carnage." I press into him until we are chest to chest and eye to eye. "This time, when I turn my back on your family, none of you will be standing. She's making moves without you."

"She's doing what she has too!" he defends.

I drop my tone to a whisper. "Why don't you ask your darling sister what really happened to your father and how she became the Don."

CHAPTER TEN

Tatum

After taking a shower in the room I first woke up in, I pull some clothes from the duffle bag, then climb onto the bed, still wearing the towel wrapped around my body and clutching the clothes in my hands, unable to find the will to change. Tears prick the backs of my eyes and I take a deep breath, trying to ward them off. I'm not the type of girl to cry. The fact Alexander is the one who is causing the urge to shed tears angers me further. My phone rings and I sigh, I may be kidnapped but unfortunately that doesn't mean I can stop working. I find my daily cell inside the duffle and pull it out to see it's my boss.

With a sigh I answer the call. "Hey," I say.

"What's wrong?" Vivian asks.

"Nothing, just living my best life in the Bahamas," I snark.

Vivian sighs. "I'm sorry Tate—"

"For what? You didn't kidnap me, that was all that asshole." Bitterness laces my words.

"Can you talk?" I straighten and dart my gaze around the empty room.

"Yeah?"

"I'm working on a way to find you but unlike Alex I don't have a hacker as good as Halo, so it may take us some time to find you."

I reel back in surprise. "Why are you helping me?" I ask in disbelief.

"Because you're my friend, Tate." The honesty I hear in her words surprises me and honestly, floors me a bit.

"T-thank you but I wouldn't waste your time. You can't reach me where I am." I explain how I'm surrounded by nothing but open land and woods and that the driveway is so long I gave up trying to escape. "He's a fucking asshole. I want to slap him so fucking hard his teeth come loose," I growl.

"Tate, are you attracted to Alex?"

I scoff and shake my head even though she can't see me. "Fuck no, never. He's hideous and I hate him."

"Yes, you've said that but for someone who has been kidnapped you don't seem desperate to leave him."

I growl low. "Vivian, this isn't some fucking love story where I fall in love with my captor. This is real life where the cunt uses me and then kills me because he wants to hurt my brother, who you hate as well, I might add."

"Then answer me this, has your white knight of a brother tried to save you?" Her tone is loaded with accusation and I cringe when I recall my conversation with him from earlier. "I didn't think so." A knock sounds at the door.

"I have to go. I'll finish the reports and email them to you and place the order for the restock at Lividica," I say then end the call just as the door opens. Omen stands there staring at me with a mix of unease and loathing in his eyes. "I guess this is your room?"

He works his jaw side to side then nods. I sigh and stand, then stuff my clothes back into my duffle and zip it up. When I sling the bag over my shoulder and move toward him he raises his hands halting my movements.

"Why aren't you changed?" he grits out.

"I was about to but then you knocked," I answer.

He scrubs a hand down his face and sighs. "Get dressed, meet me in the living room." He doesn't wait for a reply, he just closes the door behind himself. I exhale and make quick work of changing and running my brush through my hair, then piling it into a messy bun on top of my head. I toss my bag in the corner of his room, then dump my towel in the hamper in his bathroom before heading out to the living room. I pause in the entryway and look between him and Pope. Omen has black hair, it's long enough that it can be slicked back while Pope's is short and brown in color. Pope has soft brown eyes, Omen's are blue but you can see an edge of danger in Pope's while Omen's eyes are riddled with ghosts and pain. Out of the four of them, Omen is the one that scares me.

Pope notices me and nods for me to join them. I slowly make my way toward the sofa that has Alex's blanket draped over the back. I pull it over my lap and look between them both. Pope has his gaze focused on the laptop in his lap while Omen just sits there looking off into nothing, clearly lost in his own thoughts.

"Are you hungry?" Pope asks. I shake my head. "When was the last time you ate?"

I scoff. "How about we skip the part where you act like you give a fuck about me and just ignore each other?" I snap. I don't wait for a reply as I pull my phone out of my pocket, bring up my Kindle app and search for a book to read. I nearly laugh out loud when a book pops up but it's the name of the author that has me shaking with silent laughter.

Alex Denver.

That's the fucking author's name and she even has a duet called *Bloodlust.* Either this is the universes way of mocking me or fate has a cruel sense of fucking humor. I can't decide which one it is right this second. I download the book and start reading it. Just as I hit chapter three and start really getting into it, I'm dragged out of my book by the sound of Omen's voice.

"He won't keep you." I flick my gaze to him and narrow my eyes.

"Well that's fine with me because I'm not a woman who wants to be kept," I snark at the fucker.

"You cloud his judgment and need to go before you destroy what he's worked for." I scoff and roll my eyes.

"What exactly have I done, Omen? I never came to any of you. I kept my head down and tried hard to stay off your fucking radar. *He* sought me out and hunted me down!"

Pope shakes his head, urging Omen to shut up but he ignores him and pushes on. "He watched you for months, for the four of us it was a job. We waited for you to fuck up and lead us to that cunt but he obsessed over you." My face slackens and I suddenly feel cold.

"W-what?" I sputter.

Omen's features darken as he leans forward and rests his arms on the tops of his thighs. "The night on the plane may have been the first time you spoke to him but it was your second time seeing him. Want to know how many times he's seen you in person?"

"Omen, that's enough!" Pope snaps trying to reign him in but it's too late, Omen is on a roll and he wants to prove his point that I am fucking things up for them without even trying to.

"How many hotels did you stay in thinking you were safe because you locked the door? Want to know how easy it was for him to break in and stand over you while you slept?" My chest rises and falls as terror grips my airways making it hard for me to breathe. "You are a fork in the road that needs to be removed."

"I don't want to be anything to him," I spit out.

Omen just sits there with a ghost of a smirk on his face and shakes his head. "I would have believed that if I didn't hear you fucking him a couple of hours ago. Seems like my opinion about you was correct."

Anger ignites inside me. "And what opinion is that, asshole?"

"That you're like every other bitch in the world, you spread your legs to make your point," he fires back.

"Fuck you!" I scream at the bastard. "I fucked him because I wanted to, not because I wanted anything from him. And let's get something straight, asshole. I don't fuck men, ever point blank period, bitch." Realization dawns on his face. Pope coughs and gapes at me.

"Alex was your first?" Pope mutters. I cross my arms over my chest and slouch back into the sofa. I fight the urge not to blush in shame. I hate that he brought up hearing me and Alex but I have no one to blame but myself.

"Shit," Omen mutters. I see him and Pope share a loaded look before they both turn to me.

"Get your ass up," Pope snaps then tosses his laptop to the side.

"Why?" I ask.

"Because you can't stop what's done to you, you can only survive it and you won't survive him if you stay here." I stare at Omen in confusion. "Does he know you were a virgin?" I duck my head. "Answer me!" he roars. I flinch and nod. "Get up, we need to move now before he gets back."

"Why?" I push as I climb to my feet and keep the blanket wrapped around me, suddenly chilled to the bone. Omen rushes out the back door as Pope comes toward me. I take a step back, making him halt his advance.

"Alex is a fixator. He may not have shown it tonight, but him knowing he was your first will make him hyper focus on you and he'll want to work out your breaking point. He'll destroy you if you stay, Tatum."

"Why do you suddenly care?"

He sighs. "Because I was in love with a girl who gave me the gift you gave him tonight and much like Alex, I would destroy everything in my path to get to her. We need him to keep his head clear and finish what he started so we can all move on. Until he accomplishes that, we're all stuck here living like this."

I scrunch my face. "You all hide out here because you're hunting for my brother. Why do you stay with him?"

Pope's eyes darken. "Because he's the only person in this fucking world that we trust without question. What he did for us we can never repay. Alexander Denver is our brother and we would die for him without a second thought. Having you around will complicate things. We'll take you to the airport and put you on the next flight out. We'll keep Alex from coming after you."

"Why? I don't understand what the fuck just changed."

"What changed our minds is you telling the truth, and Omen knowing that you don't use your body to get your way swayed him. Omen hates every female because our stepmother raped him." My eyes widen and I gasp as remorse thrums through me for him. "Let him save you, he needs some form of redemption and helping you will give him that."

"Redemption from what?" I whisper.

He takes a shuddering breath. "For killing my mother."

I haven't allowed myself to relax for a single second. I was waiting for Pope and Omen to declare this was all a joke or drive me to Alex so he could kill me but they didn't. True to their word they dropped me at the airport with all my bags and wished me well. The part that shocked me to the core was Omen inputting his number into my phone and telling me to call him if I ever need anything or I'm in trouble. I cleared security and kept checking over my shoulder. Even when I found my seat on the plane I started to get anxious, but my row was empty.

I finally take my first full breath as the plane evens out in the sky and I actually allow some of the tension to flee my body.

I did it!

I escaped. I actually fucking did it and I'm still alive to tell the story. I close my eyes and rest my head back against the headrest, inhaling the sweet scent of freedom. I'm heading to Chicago and it may be one of my least favorite places to visit, but right now I'm so fucking excited to be surrounded by buildings because it means I'm far away from *him*.

Jesus, why the fuck does my chest constrict when I think about him?

Nope, I close off that train of thought and focus on work. I pull my laptop out and place it on the tray in front of me and start reading over the reports the contractors have sent. I may not have gone to college or even have a degree, but I'm smart and I know how to read through this type of shit and spot when they are fucking us over. Which is why I can already see these assholes in Chicago are deep in the shit right now with all this red tape.

I make note to read through all the legislation in regard to opening a hotel and sex club in the city and find out why we are being hard-balled at every turn. I get so lost in reading over everything and catching up on the shit I missed that I don't realize we're about to land until I'm asked to pack away my computer.

I'm bone tired and still sore from Alex fucking me like a crazed man. I shiver and I hate to admit it but it isn't from disgust. The way he took what he wanted while still making sure I felt good was so unexpected but utterly addictive. I've never wanted a man as badly as I wanted Alex, and that notion frightens the fuck out of me. I follow the crowd off the plane and collect my luggage, then head out the front to meet my Uber. I didn't organize a driver thanks to my impromptu escape. The drive to the hotel passes by in a blur and by the time we arrive, my movements are sluggish and I'm practically falling asleep on my feet.

After checking in, I head to my room and nearly weep at the sight of the bed. I dump all my belongings on the desk in the corner, pull the curtains shut, then turn out the lights and climb into bed. A sigh escapes me when I get comfortable and close my eyes, ready for sleep to claim me until my fucking phone starts ringing. I want to cry and debate ignoring the call but if it's a work emergency I'm the person they call. I reach for the fucking thing blindly then hit answer without checking the caller ID.

"Yeah?" I croak out.

"Do you know what it's like to be hunted by a predator?" My eyes snap open and I bolt upright in bed. Suddenly the darkness that envelops me starts suffocating me as I panic that he is hiding in the darkness.

"Leave me alone, you got what you wanted."

"Hmm, see the thing about that, Miss Lawson, is that now that I have satisfied one craving tonight, I realized that I crave the taste of your blood on my tongue."

I shudder. "Fuck you."

His dark chuckle fills the line and I start panting. I hate my body's reaction to just the sound of his voice. "No one escapes me, Tatum, never forget that."

"Go to hell, Alex," I snap, then end the call. My heart is racing and suddenly I'm so fucking wired I don't know if I'll be able to sleep now thanks to that Aztec fucking god and the memories of how good he felt inside me.

How can you hate someone yet crave them?

CHAPTER ELEVEN

Alexander

"You two ever pull a fucking stunt like that again, I'll do more than smack you fuckers around," I snap at Pope and Omen, who both stand in front of me with their fists clenched at their sides and dark looks in their eyes. When I returned I expected to find Tatum hiding somewhere but then those fuckers told me they let her go. I lost it and laid into them. Halo and Vat tried to stop me but they couldn't, so they resorted to fucking tasering me!

"You have lost focus on what we are doing here ever since you started stalking that girl," Pope snaps.

I cock my head to the side and study him. "I've never lost focus. She was our way to finding that cocksucker, and thanks to her giving up that phone we can finally track the snake," I shout.

"You fucking used her like a cheap whore," Omen bites out. I cringe. I know this shit is hard for him to understand given his past, but he needs to see that Tate isn't Rosalina. I didn't take advantage of her, she wanted me as much as I wanted her.

"Omen, I never used her. Yes, I had planned to take the phone from her but what happened between me and her wasn't me asserting my power over her. She wanted me and you're just gonna have to take my fucking word on that." He opens his mouth to argue but I push on. "We have bigger things to worry about. Desire De Santis is making moves behind Carnage's back. We need to find out what she is up to and why she is coming after us now after all this time."

I can't figure out why she would be making a move now. For five years the De Santis Cosa Nostra has left us alone, but even before I got released from prison there was some stirring in the water. We played it off until I got out, then they became bold and made their presence known. When I went to Hollow Hills to Vivian's masquerade night at her club, I bailed on her because Omen alerted me to the fact we were being tailed.

"She mentioned Nexus Valerian," I mutter aloud.

"When?" Halo asks.

"At the meeting." I turn and face them all. Each one of them looks confused.

"How does she know about him?" Pope hedges.

I shake my head as I try to think back if I mentioned something about him. "I don't know. She told me the deal extended to him. Why?"

"What if they're linked?" Vat says.

"How? Nexus meant nothing to us until *after* we left the family," Omen clarifies.

Vatican's eyes widen as he faces me. "Desire is the one

hiding Nexus. There is no way that little fuck would be able to hide from us on his own. Desire's helping him. She knows Halo's blind spots and is playing on them." My face slackens as his words sink in. I pull my phone out and dial Carnage. This time he picks up on the third ring.

"What?" he says as he answers.

"How the fuck does your bitch of a sister know about Nexus Valerian?" I snarl.

"Who the fuck are you talking about, Butcher?" He sounds irritated and that is a sign that Carnage is telling the truth. He always gets angry when he doesn't know shit.

"I'll say this one fucking time, De Santis. If I find out you or your sister had a hand in anything to do with Elenor—"

"Whoa, whoa, whoa, you stupid fucker. I may hate you but that hate doesn't extend to your sister. You fucking know that, you fucker. I never went after your sister!" he roars. "I was the fucking one helping you protect her and getting her ass into the good schools and making sure no one fucked with her. Don't you ever fucking accuse me of ever laying a hand on her!" His anger is felt and I know now, without a shadow of a doubt, he's innocent, which means either the twins are in on it with Desire or she's acting alone.

"Carnage, pick a side quick because your sister fucked up. She showed me her hand at the meeting and now, I'm coming at her with everything I fucking have," I yell, then try and calm myself, not wanting to get in a fight with this fucker.

"You have my word, Butcher. If Desire had anything to do with what happened to Ellie... I'll deal with her."

"No. If she did, I'll deal with her myself," I answer.

"You really gonna torture the woman you were in love with?" I grind my teeth and work my jaw side to side.

"That was a long time ago," I force out through clenched teeth. "Get the intel fast or I'll extract it from her the only way I know how. You have one week." I end the call, then face the guys. "Work with the angle that Nexus and Desire are somehow connected. Figure out how they know each other. We find that link, we find him." I turn to leave but Halo's words stop me in my tracks.

"Best way to find that link is to go to Chicago." I peer over my shoulder at him.

"Your point?" I push.

"Your pretty little blonde is in Chicago."

I growl in annoyance. "Get a flight out of here tomorrow. We work from there. Pope, call Damon and tell him to meet the Luther's for the shipment on Friday. Omen, deal with Adrian and have him and some others fly out separately to us and set up a perimeter in Chicago to watch our backs." I don't hang around for them to reply, I storm out the back door to call my little Bambi who is going to learn what it's like to be hunted by *me*.

I fucking hate the busyness of the city. I've been in Chicago mere hours and I already miss the peace of my home. I don't get how people can live in a place like this and even hear themselves think. Omen drives us through the city. I don't know what the connection is, but I can feel it in my bones that Tatum is somehow tied into this web of bullshit between Desire and Nexus.

"We're coming up to the location," Omen says, pulling my attention to him. I nod and wait for him to park across the street from the hotel Vivian has purchased to open her new club. The location is prime and will garner a lot of traffic. There is no doubt in my mind that her sex club will be profitable.

"Why was construction halted on this?" I ask Halo.

"The permits keep getting knocked back. Someone is black balling them," he answers. We all know this has Desire's name written all over it, she wouldn't allow a hotel with a sex club to be built here. It would take profits from her brothels she has around town. Unlike the ones she runs, Vivian's embrace kinks, its upper class and all her girls *and* guys are tested regularly.

"We got a situation." The urgency in Pope's tone has me going on alert. I follow his gaze to the alley next to the hotel. My breath lodges in my throat when I see Tatum standing there, she looks pissed off but it's the sight of her in those jeans that hug her like a second skin and that tight yellow long-sleeve shirt she wears that falls off one shoulder that has my mouth watering. "Why is Wrath here?" I shake my head and push away those thoughts. I cut my gaze to the guy standing beside the one she is arguing with and my anger soars. Wrath De Santis shouldn't be anywhere near her. He is fucking poison and I know for a fact he loves to take what isn't being offered. I'll be fucking damned if I let him take a single fucking thing from her.

Only I get to fuck with her.

"Well, I guess we know who is blocking the permits from going through now," Vat mutters. I grunt my agreement without taking my eyes off Tate. Wrath is grinning like a fool, he's loving the sight of her all fired up.

"This isn't a coincidence, I don't believe in that shit," Halo voices. I nod in agreement. "There is no fucking way Desire suddenly comes back to haunt us, then drops Nexus's name and now suddenly, Wrath is here with your girl." I bristle at the whole *my girl* comment but remain silent as I watch her throw her hands in the air, then stalk away from those two. She pulls her phone from her pocket, then brings it to her ear. She suddenly pauses, then turns and faces our car. She may not be able to see us through the tinted windows but she doesn't need to, she can feel me watching her.

"Go. We need to get recon done," I order. Omen obeys and drives us away from Tatum. I plan to pay her a visit later tonight. After seeing Wrath with her, I'm now more certain than ever that she is linked to the De Santis family without even knowing it. My money is on her piece of shit of a brother making a deal with them and using her as leverage.

We make it back to our home base which isn't much. We rented a house under Adrian's name that's on the outskirts of the city. Damon is handling our shipments while we are away. Omen and Vatican are my guys who handle coordinating our other runners. Unlike most networks, we are based in one spot and ship from there. Which is why Desire will never figure out how things are because we have runners. They fly in and collect one of our trucks loaded with guns and drive them across state lines to where they need to go. If anyone was really looking they would see that Halo owns a moving company. We do have a crew that is completely legal and does inner state moves to keep the books steady while we use the other trucks to run guns. We're opening another base of operation in Hollywood under Pope's name to help with the demand.

"Where do we start looking for the link?" Vat asks me from his spot at the small, round dining table where he sits with Halo. Pope and Omen are out doing a sweep of Tatum's hotel, making sure she isn't being tailed and to watch and see if Nexus comes to her.

"Go back to when we left the Cosa Nostra." Both of them jerk in surprise.

"Any reason why we are going back that far?" Halo presses.

I scrub a hand down my face and sigh. I have no idea if my hunch is right but something in the pit of my gut is telling me I'm right. "Desire is a jealous bitch, she let us go too easily—"

"Too easy?" Pope snaps. "I've seen the fucking scars, Alexander, she didn't let us off easy at all!"

"She let us live!" I roar.

"Why?" Halo yells. "Tell me why the fuck my crazy ass sister let us leave with our lives?" I open my mouth but clamp it shut as Omen and Vatican enter the house. They look between the three of us and frown.

"What the fucks going on here?" Omen barks.

"Nothing." I answer.

"Alex is about to tell the truth," Halo says at the same time. I pin the little shit with a glare which he ignores and continues to stare at me.

"Truth about what?" Vat hedges.

"Why Omen's twin let us live," Pope answers. Both Vat and Omen snap their gazes to me expectantly. For years I have kept this secret, I thought I would take it to my grave but it turns out, I was wrong.

"I did something that guaranteed she could never turn against us!" I admit.

"You have leverage on her don't you?" Pope breathes out in surprise.

I nod. "Yes. It was the only way I knew that she wouldn't come after us or send the fucked up twins and her army after us. I have a failsafe. If Desire ever took us out, a letter would be sent to Carnage."

All of them look confused but it's Halo to ask the question. "What do you have on her?"

I exhale and run my gaze over each of them, praying they understand and don't hate me. These four are the only family I have, they are my brothers. "When I made the deal with Desire, it was originally for six of us to go free."

"What?" Pope pushes.

"The deal was for not only my freedom from the Cosa Nostra but for the four of yours and Carnage's." My answer is met with fucking crickets. No one moves or utters a single word for a minute but my gaze is locked on Halo.

"You made a deal to save my twin. Why the fuck would you do that?" The anger is crystal fucking clear in Halo's tone.

"Because your brother was my best friend, Halo. Carnage wasn't always a piece of shit. He was good but the more time he spent with that vapid bitch, she corrupted him."

"He was always fucked up. He still thinks we killed our father. None of us put the hit out on him. Roberto De Santis was murdered by the Vatel family." When I say nothing,

Omen narrows his eyes and pushes on. "He wasn't taken out by a rival family, was he?"

I blow out a loud exhale and shake my head. "No, he wasn't."

The four of them lose it. They all start shouting and Halo goes as far as throwing one of the dining chairs across the room, shattering it against the wall. I say nothing. I stand here and take the hate and shade they throw at me, knowing I deserve it. They hated their father but it doesn't mean they wanted him dead. Only one of their siblings did and she is the one who gained everything while they lost their family.

"Who did it and don't fucking lie to us, Alex." Vatican's tone is firm and unyielding. The four of them stand shoulder to shoulder staring at me expectantly.

"I did. I killed your father and helped Desire take over the De Santis family."

CHAPTER TWELVE

Tatum

"Those assholes think they can keep issuing fines for bullshit reasons and I am about to go fucking ham on their asses, Vivian," I seethe as I continue to pace my hotel room. My anger hasn't lessened. I just received eight-thousand-dollars' worth of fines for bullshit reasons today.

"Okay, calm down. I can get on a flight and be out there tomorrow afternoon. Does that work for you?" I sigh and nod.

"Yeah. I'm honestly at a loss at what to do. They have stonewalled us and I don't know what the hell to do anymore," I admit, feeling like an utter let down.

"Tatum, this isn't your fault. These things happen and we just have to roll with the punches."

"Yeah. I guess so."

"The guys and I will fly out after I hand in my paper. So... will I just be seeing you or..."

I groan and hate the sound of her laughter. "Yes, Vivian. The Aztec god is gone and I'm fucking thrilled to be rid of his overbearing ass."

"Hmmm."

"What the hell does that mean?" I snap, then cringe when I remember she's my boss and I shouldn't be giving her attitude.

"It means you don't sound like someone who is happy to be free and you're the one who called him a god, not me."

"Argh, I'm going, I'll see you tomorrow." I end the call as soon as she starts laughing. I toss my phone on the bed and stare at the burner phone resting on the bedside table. I picked up a new one today with the plan to call Nexus but... I haven't. It has nothing to do with what Alexander said about his sister, it's the fact that when I did call him he implied I should use my body as a way to get Alex to spill his secrets. I've never told anyone what happened to me as a kid except for my brother. Him knowing what happened and still suggesting what he did makes me feel sick.

I nibble on my bottom lip, debating if I should just push through my reservations and call him to at least let him know I'm okay and... free. I feel weird even thinking that I may have been his prisoner but I never really felt like it. I wasn't chained up or tied to a bed and hurt. Well, I got my ego fucking torn apart in the end and lost my virginity to The Butcher.

"Argh," I growl into the empty room as I scrub a hand down my face. Guys complicate everything and this is the reason why I have always been grateful that I have never felt intense attraction toward the opposite sex or ever had the urge to throw myself at someone until, Alexander–The fucking butcher—Denver!

Jesus Christ!

The moment I saw him enter Lividica my body felt like it was on fire, and my world stopped spinning for a split second when he met my gaze. He became my focal point and no matter how hard I tried not to look at him I couldn't control myself. My eyes kept darting across the room to catch a glimpse of him. I loathe to admit I even felt envy toward my boss when she threw her arms around him and hugged him. I don't know what it is about that fucking man that has drawn me in. Rationally I know I should be terrified of him and I was until I met him. Everyone has heard the rumors about the infamous Butcher, tales of his actions spread like wildfire. Of course each time a story was told it would change and people would put their own spin on it, but none of that mattered to me when I was with him.

"Cut your bullshit, Tate," I scold myself. I need to keep my head on straight and prepare myself for Vivian and her guys to arrive tomorrow. I decide to take a quick shower, then call it a night. I need to get some sleep or I'll be up all night obsessing over the construction and paperwork I need to sort for the other locations. The closer we get to the builds being almost complete means my work load nearly triples. Vivian is going to have no choice but to hire more people to run each individual club with me overseeing them all. I can't be in every place at once and I have to admit, I need the help because this shit is a lot for one person to deal with daily.

I feel slightly less tense after my shower. I snag one of my oversized shirts from my suitcase and pull that on. The shirt is big enough to reach my knees, I love not being restricted when I sleep so I forgo panties. I climb under the covers and sigh. God, I didn't realize how tired I was until now. I yawn and close my eyes ready for this day to be over and fall asleep almost instantly.

I begin stirring, I can't shake the feeling I'm being watched. I'm woman enough to admit that I'm fully awake now but I refuse to open my eyes. I may be a bad bitch in the streets but I've seen enough horror movies to wonder if ghosts are actually real! I keep my breathing even and remain still as I strain my hearing. I hear nothing but that doesn't mean something or someone isn't in here with me. I wait another minute before I slowly open my eyes, keeping as still as possible, waiting for a sound or fucking anything really but I get nothing. I still have the feeling of eyes on me. I know now it isn't a ghost in here with me. I exhale and slowly sit up. Once I'm in a seated position, I slowly look around my room only to freeze when I see a silhouette sitting on the chair in the corner of my room. My heart bangs against my ribs trying to escape in fear. My breathing turns choppy as I wait for whoever it is to kill me.

"I never said you could leave, Miss Lawson." Call me fucking crazy but I instantly relax and release a long exhale at the sound of his voice.

"I don't recall ever asking for your permission, Butcher," I bite back.

I watch as he leans forward and looks directly at me, I hate that it's too dark to make out his features. I may not be able to see him clearly but I know without a doubt he'll have a scowl on his face. "Are we playing a game, Tatum?" The level tone of his voice sends a shiver down my spine. I expected him to be mad and frothing that I escaped but instead, he just sits there talking calmly like we're old friends.

"No. I'm not a toy for you to play with and discard when you get bored, Butcher. I don't want to be the center of your attention. I don't want to be anything to you. Stop breaking into my hotel rooms and following me—"

"Which one?"

I frown. "Huh?"

"Which. One. Told. You?" This time his tone isn't calm, it's edged in darkness.

"Why does it matter who told me that you have been breaking into my hotel rooms and watching me?" I snap, my tone laced with accusation and I refuse to cower to this bastard.

"Here's the thing, Tatum." He slowly climbs to his feet and I scoot back against the headboard, keeping as much space between us as I can. Alexander Denver is an enigma, he is someone women fantasize about because they think they can handle the bad boy, but they're foolish. He isn't someone who can be owned or molded to fit into society. He will never blend in amongst normal people. The aura that surrounds him pulses with predator energy and that is the reason he will always be set apart from everyone else without even trying. "My motives don't need to be explained to you." He takes a step toward the bed and I brace myself.

"W-why not?" I stutter.

He continues stalking toward me and I hate that my body begins to hum with awareness at his close proximity. "Because I will take whatever the fuck I want and have no regrets about it. Don't try to psychoanalyze me, you will never figure out what makes me who I am."

"Alex—" I clamp my mouth closed when he snaps his arms out and grips my ankles. I scream when he yanks me down the bed toward him. I claw at the sheets but it's no use, I just pull them from the corners. He releases me when I'm at the edge of the bed with him standing between my legs, my chest rising and falling in rapid pants.

He reaches down and trails his fingers around my throat. I inhale sharply. "I never meant to encounter you or ever meet you." I shiver as he continues to trail his fingers down my body. "I was just meant to watch from afar and never interact with you." My breath hitches when he gathers the hem of my shirt and pushes it up, exposing my bare pussy to him. The deep growl in his chest has me trembling, I may not be able to see in the darkness but he clearly can. "You were just supposed to lead us to your brother." I tense but then he skirts his fingers along my inner thigh, my body temperature skyrockets and my breathing turns ragged as he skates those fingers to my pulsing core. Fuck, I'm already wet for him and that makes proving my point a lot harder when my mouth tells him to *fuck off* but my pussy begs him to *fuck me.*

"My brother isn't here." I pant as he trails a finger through my slick folds, then groans when my arousal coats his finger. I may not be able to make out his features, but I can see him lift his arm and I stare wide eyed and breathless when I hear him suck his finger.

He just tasted me!

"Hmm, you taste fucking exquisite, Miss Lawson." A whimper escapes me without consent. He lowers his hand and this time he doesn't ease me into his touch, he circles my clit like he has a right to touch me however he wants and in this moment, I am nothing but a willing participant eager to take his form of punishment if it means he relieves me of this ache burning within me.

"Alex," I plead unsure if I am begging him to stop or give me more. He presses the pad of his thumb flat against my clit and I cry out, bucking my hips off the bed.

"This time, you don't need to question if there are any hidden motives, Bambi." His words don't register as he slips a finger inside me, causing a distraction from my wayward thoughts, he's forcing me to feel and focus on only him. I clench the sheets in my hands and arch my back from the bed as he curves his finger and strokes a spot inside me that has me gasping and begging for him to do it again. "That's it, Bambi, ride my finger and show me how much you want my cock inside you." His words cause a shudder to roll through me, the pure dominance and the command in which he speaks them has me wanting to obey like a puppet.

He continues to inflict pure pleasure as I try to gain control of my own body, but I'm fighting a losing battle. He's playing me like a fiddle and I have no choice but to endure the glorious torture he is inflicting on me. I want to say I scream for him to stop and get the fuck out, but I'm not a liar and the feelings he's invoking inside me are fucking perfection. I'm craving the release I know he can give me.

"Holy shit, I need..." I clamp my mouth closed, I have no idea what I need. I just know I need more. As if he can read my mind, Alex lowers to his knees while still keeping his fingers inside me. I gasp when I feel him blow his hot breath against my aching pussy. I whimper when he curves those skilled fingers.

"You open these legs for only me. I catch anyone else

sniffing around you and I'll tie your ass to a chair and make you watch as I tear the fucker apart and cut him into tiny pieces." My eyes widen as I push up and rest on my elbows, staring down at him. I can feel the intensity of his gaze on me and I am certain he isn't fucking around. "If you try to open these legs for anyone else, I'll take your punishment further and make you try a couple of pieces of him." My jaw unhinges. I'm about to tell him to fuck off when he swipes his tongue through my folds, then sucks my clit into his mouth, drawing a scream from me.

Jesus, I'm not a prude or anything and have made myself come before, but I never imagined it would feel this fucking amazing to have a guy eating my pussy like it's his favorite meal. I flop back against the bed and begin grinding my hips against his beard. He keeps his tongue out, allowing me to take my pleasure from him while still fingering my cunt. Reaching down I tangle my fingers in his hair and tug on the strands, loving the sound of the growl that comes from him. I feel my body begin to tense and my muscles lock up in preparation for my orgasm. I don't fight it, I latch onto it and let it slam into me.

"Alex!" I scream as I come so fucking hard my body spasms. The feeling of his fingers and tongue on me is too much, I shuffle backward only for him to leap on top of me. He grabs my wrists and pins them above my head. I have zero time to gather my thoughts before his lips are on mine, demanding access. Like a slave to its master I open for him and relish in the taste of my own pussy on his tongue. My stomach muscles clench when he grinds against me and I feel how hard he is.

He breaks the kiss and stares down at me, both of us

panting. "I'm gonna fuck you and then you and I are going to talk."

I scoff. "You can't make me fucking horny, eat me out and then dangle sex above my head, then drop a bomb like that on me," I hiss.

"Get my cock out." I want to ignore the fucker but in doing that would mean denying myself the pleasure I crave so much. I do as he says and reach between us, freeing him. I wrap my hand around him and feel emboldened when he groans and drops his forehead against mine. I pump him twice, then swirl my thumb over the head of his cock and gasp when I feel his pre cum. Without overthinking it, I bring my thumb to my mouth. He watches me as I wrap my lips around it and suck it clean, moaning at the taste of him.

I release my thumb with a pop. "You taste sweet, Butcher."

"You taste better," he purrs before claiming my lips and thrusting inside me in one swift move. I scream in pain but he swallows it. He remains still, giving me a chance to accommodate his size. I turn my head, needing to suck in lungfuls of air to breathe through the pain. He cups my face between his large hands and forces my gaze back to his. "I'll break down every wall you have and force you to let me inside." I balk up at him. "But, I will never force myself on you. I'm taking what you are willing to give because you refuse to admit it to yourself that you crave my touch as much as I crave yours."

My breathing accelerates for a whole new reason now. "Craving you doesn't mean I like you," I mutter.

He chuckles and pulls almost all the way out of me before slamming back inside. I cry out and bow off the bed.

Alex leans down and bites the soft flesh between my neck and shoulder. A heady moan tumbles from me and I feel myself growing slicker when he licks a trail to my lips. I wrap my arms around his neck and hold him in place as I kiss him. My move shocks him, so I use it to my advantage and lock my legs around his waist and pull him inside me deeper.

Alex starts rocking his hips and I whimper, his fingers felt amazing but Jesus take the fucking wheel because his cock feels like pure silk, gliding in and out of me with ease. The only sounds that can be heard are skin slapping skin and our ragged breaths. I don't know whether it's the feeling of him inside me or the sounds we're making but I feel untouchable, like nothing in the world could tear me down. I feel a sense of completeness with him inside me. It sounds fucking crazy and stupid but all my life I have felt hollow and out of place until the first time Alexander Denver plowed through my hymen and made me whole.

"Fuck, Bambi, you feel so good, baby." His praise bolsters my confidence, this may be only my second time having sex but I have no doubt he has fucked a lot more women than I care to think about.

"Keep going, I'm so close," I plead.

"Beg me," I grind my teeth and consider strangling him but then his thrusts pick up tempo and rob me of rational thought.

"Please, fuck... please make me come, Butcher." A feral sound escapes him, he grips the back of my neck in a bruising hold and presses his forehead against mine.

"Eyes on me while you come on my cock." I obey without thought. Our breaths mingle as he continues to pound inside me, chasing his own release while I latch onto mine. The eye contact only heightens my need.

"You feel so good," I whisper as I start meeting him thrust for thrust.

"Fucking you is my new favorite thing to do," he growls as he hits that sweet spot again and I'm at his mercy. The orgasm that rips through me is like a tidal wave, consuming every surfer on the beach. I'm powerless to fight against it. I'm forced to ride the wave of bliss while he continues to fuck me and drag out my climax, like it's his life mission and right now, I can't be certain it isn't with how savage his thrusts have turned. "Fuck, Bambi," he roars, then tears away from me. He rests back on his haunches, grips his cock in his hand and pumps himself three times before I feel jets of his cum covering my thighs, pussy and stomach.

I stare at him with wide eyes, knowing I should be pissed he just came on me and marked me as his but... I'm not. If anything, I find it sexy as fucking hell that he just used my body to get off, then marked me as his own.

I'm so fucked up in the head!

CHAPTER THIRTEEN

Alexander

I grip her arm and pull her to feet, leading her toward the shower without flicking a single light on. She says nothing as I strip us both off and begin washing her. Neither of us say a word when we step out and dry off. I grip her hand again after I pull on my boxers and lead her back to her bed. I wait for her to try and complain that she needs clothes or something, but she doesn't. She slips beneath the cover and lolls her head to the side to look at me.

"You staying the night or running back to the bat cave?"

"I expected you to kick me out," I answer.

She scoffs. "Did you steal my phone this time?"

"No," I grit out.

"Did you steal anything of mine?"

"I would have stolen your thong but you weren't wearing one so no, I didn't steal any fucking thing." Her quiet chuckle feels like a balm to my tattered soul. I find myself relaxing at the sound but it ends all too quickly.

"Get in the bed, Alex." I climb in beside her, wearing nothing but my boxers. This is new for me. I don't sleep next to anyone. Tatum lays beside me silently. I've watched her long enough to know she takes a while to fall asleep. The awkward silence is weird. Normally it never bothers me because I don't have a lot to say to anyone, but with her I have this need to make sure she is comfortable so I ask, "Who hurt you?"

I feel her tense beside me. "I'm not weak." Her softly spoken answer is one I didn't expect.

"Never said you were, Bambi."

"What's with the nickname?"

"You were the prey and I was the hunter the other night, the name fits."

"Whatever you say, *Butcher*." I say nothing because the truth is I hate her calling me that, it's not a name I chose for myself. She rolls onto her side and faces me. I can feel her overthinking from over here but I don't say anything, giving her time to work it out in her head. "Why are you here?"

"If I knew the answer to that question, then I wouldn't be here lying beside you." I can't hide the edge to my tone.

"Wow, you sure know how to make a girl feel special after you just fucked her." Bitterness laces each one of her words.

I loll my head to the side and look at her. "Tatum, I shouldn't be here." Conviction is clear as I speak. "Your brother is someone I want dead and groveling at my feet as I tear the son of a bitch apart slowly. I want his blood covering every inch of my skin. I want to inflict the most amount of pain on him as I can so he can pay for what he took from me. You share his blood and here I am making myself at home inside you." She recoils and tries to scoot away but I snap my arm out and wrap it around her waist, pulling her flush against my side.

"Get out," she snaps.

"No. Don't let your anger cloud your judgment. I know what he asked you to do to get intel on me."

"How?"

"I heard enough of your conversation with him. I would never have asked such a thing of my sister, she was mine to protect and that little cunt stole her from me."

"And what? You plan to steal me from him and force me to face the same fate as your sister?" When I don't answer she gasps and struggles against me to get free. I roll over and use my body to pin her beneath me. "Fuck you, get the fuck off me!" she screams. I pin her arms above her head and grind against her pussy so she can feel how hard I am.

"Does that fucking feel like I want to kill you?" I snap, she stills beneath me.

"What are you doing here with me then?"

I exhale and decide to be honest. "I have no fucking clue. You were meant to lead us to your brother and never know we existed, but then you had to start digging and bringing attention to us so we had no choice."

"Who are you worried about finding you?"

I grind my teeth. "No one. The endgame here is finding your brother, and I won't let whatever this is between us cloud my judgment. He will die and there isn't a thing you can do to stop it." She sniffs and I fight back the growl that wants to break free.

"You kill my brother and you can forget I ever existed."

"You're not someone who is easy to forget, Miss Lawson," I mutter.

"Stop stalking me and then it won't be so hard."

"You need to stop crossing my path, then I might."

"How the fuck do I cross your path?" she splutters.

"The guy you were with today—"

She cuts me off. "You were watching me?" She doesn't give me a chance to answer. "Of course you were, I knew those two fucking dicks played me." I snort.

"Omen and Pope never gave up your location, you just happen to be in the same place as the fucker we are hunting."

She squirms beneath me. "Can you let me go now?" I mull over her words for a moment.

"I kind of like this position."

She snorts out a laugh. "Of course you do, I bet you're really mad now that you decided to put your boxers back on?" Her sarcasm has me glaring at her. I release her wrists and decide to teach her a lesson, reaching between our bodies and pushing my boxers down to free my cock. "You are not sticking that thing inside me after you just admitted to wanting to kill my brother—" I thrust inside her, silencing her rant. Her back arches off the bed and a long drawn out moan escapes her.

"You never should have allowed me to touch you," I growl as I continue to thrust inside her. "Now, you're mine and I'll take whatever the fuck I want from you when I want, am I clear?"

"Alex." She pants as her nails run along my back, drawing a hiss from me.

I slam inside her harder, loving the sharp cry that tears from her sinful lips. Unable to control myself, I smash my own lips on hers and swallow her moans as I fuck her like a rabid man. When her nails dig into the flesh of my back, I grunt. She turns her head breaking the kiss. "Let me get on top." When I pause and stare at her in surprise, she uses my moment of shock against me and shoves against my chest until I'm lying flat on my back.

She shifts and swings her leg over me and straddles my lap. I fight the urge not to thrust my hips when she grips my cock and lines it up with her soaked cunt. A shiver of excitement works its way through me as she slowly glides down on my dick.

"Oh fuck," I growl as I grip her waist and help guide her until I'm fully sheathed inside her perfect pussy.

"Shit, you feel so deep!" she pants out. It sends a thrill through me knowing I'm the only one who has seen her like this. Needing to see her in the light, I reach back and fumble around for the bedside lamp. I flick it on. Instantly my cock jerks inside her when I feast on the sight of her tits. I reach up and cup them in my hands, she throws her head back and moans.

"Ride me, baby." She drops her chin to her chest, places her hands flat on my chest and begins to rotate her hips. I keep my eyes on her, loving how her pupils dilate and her gaze grows hazy as she uses me to find her own pleasure. I pinch her nipples and relish in the sounds she makes. When her movements turn sluggish and hurried, I grip her waist and begin to guide her movement, meeting her thrust for thrust. The whimpers and mewls that escape her only fuel my own need. My balls are tightening with the need to spill everything inside her.

"Oh God, I need you to make me come, then I want you to come on my face." Her demand has me stilling beneath her. Her eyes meet mine and I can tell that my reaction has her feeling slightly ashamed about her request. Rather than allow her time to rethink it, I quicken my pace and slam her down onto my aching cock, wanting nothing more than to get her off so I can fulfil her request. "Yes, fuck, just like that," she screams and digs her nails into my chest as she screams my name when her orgasm slams into her. I keep fucking her, drawing out her release. When I can't hold off any longer, I lift her off me and climb off the bed, reach out and grab her hair, then use my hold on it to guide her to her knees before me.

My other hand wraps around my shaft but she reaches out and bats my hand away, wrapping both her own around my cock and pumps me. I hiss at the feeling. I'm two seconds away from exploding! The sight of her opening her mouth to capture my release pushes me over the edge, my grip on her tightens as I roar her name and cum all over her perfect fucking face. She keeps stroking my dick, forcing me to draw back from her touch. I look down at her and a sick sinister part of me loves the sight of my cum all over her cheeks, chin and mouth. She fucking pushes me over the edge when she reaches up and swipes her finger along her cheek and brings her cum covered finger to her lips, then sucks it clean while maintaining eye contact with me.

"Hmmm, you taste delicious," she purrs.

I can't stop my smile from breaking free. I reach down

and cup her cheek. "You are certainly not what I fucking expected and I am so fucking glad to be wrong for once."

Tatum groans beside me and I furrow my brow until I hear knocking again. I sit up and rub my eyes, then look around the room and that's when I remember. I came here after I dropped the bombshell on my brothers but I didn't expect the night to go how it did. I was just meant to sit here and watch her until I calmed down, then head back to deal with that situation.

"Tate!" I jerk at the sound of a woman's voice. I gently shove Tatum and smirk when she shoves me away.

"Leave me alone," she grumbles as she rolls over.

"Bambi, your boss is here," I say, fighting back a smile. It takes two seconds for my words to register, then she is leaping from the bed like she was zapped. She stands at the edge of the bed with her wild hair pointing in every direction. My gaze drops to her nipples and I smirk at the sight of them hard and ready for me. The sight of my bite marks on her neck and shoulder has me feeling like I need to beat my fists against my chest. I've never been the type of guy to get possessive over a female or want to stake my claim, but with Tatum I can't seem to mark my territory enough, and that is the type of shit that will get me in deep fucking trouble when it comes time to enact my revenge against the motherfucker she calls brother.

"Tatum, I know you're in there!" Vivian calls out as she pounds against the door. Tate's eyes widen and I see a hint of panic in the depths of them.

"You have to hide," she shrieks then darts across the room and grabs my discarded shirt off the floor while I remain where I am on the bed. I quirk a brow when she pulls my shirt over her head, then darts into the bathroom for a second before returning with an elastic band. She piles her hair into a messy bun atop her head, then looks at me while Vivian continues to pound on the door like it somehow wronged her. "Alex, hide!" she snaps, then rushes out of the room to answer the door. I ignore her so-called demand and climb out of the bed and pull my jeans on, leaving them unbuttoned.

I hear Tatum open the door and I pause in the threshold of the bedroom, remaining out of sight. "You're early," Tate breathes out like she's just run a marathon.

"Oh shit." I hear one of Vivian's boyfriends mutter and it pisses me off that they are seeing her in just my shirt.

"Well, you look well fucked." Vivian's tone is filled with mirth and I can picture Tatum glaring at her.

"Vivi baby, now I have pictures I shouldn't have in my head," another guy whines. I grind my teeth as I round the corner. I know Tate can feel me drawing near because she tenses. I grip the door and plaster myself at her back and stare right at Vivian and the three fuckers.

"Keep your thoughts off *her*," I snarl. The brown haired fucker smirks cockily at me.

"It seems The Butcher *butchered* your girl, Vivi baby." I narrow my eyes at the son of a bitch in warning. The blond guy, Ezekiel, smacks him across the back of his head.

"Learn when to shut the fuck up, Hayze," he snaps.

Vivian smiles and moves around Tate. She grabs my arm

and pulls me away from Tate to hug me. I stand here stiffly and shoot Tatum a look to help me out here, but the little fucking minx stands there smirking and crossing her arms over her chest. I sigh and pat Vivian on the back awkwardly. She steps back and stares up at me with a loving look in her eyes, which just fucking floors me.

"I knew she liked you," Vivian exclaims, making her three boyfriends sigh and grumble. She waves her hand and ignores them. "So, I think we might have interrupted something..."

I shoot her a deadpan look, knowing that she is just fishing for information about what's happening between me and Tate so I keep my mouth closed.

"How about, I meet you in an hour and then we can discuss... things," Tatum says in a tone laced with guilt, which just pisses me off.

Vivian pouts and shoots me a pleading look that I ignore and I look to Tate. Without me needing to say it, she knows it's time for her to get rid of her boss and her toys.

"Vivian," Tate says as she grabs her arm and gently pulls her away from us. Ezekiel reaches out and grabs his wife's arm, pulling her into his side. "I'll meet you guys downstairs in an hour and I'm... sorry about this," she says, then closes the door. She keeps her back to me for a minute before slowly turning around. Her eyes are filled with fire as they meet my own, but I stand firm and cross my arms over my chest, not giving a shit that her boss knows we're fucking. "Did you really need to do that?" she hisses, then attempts to push past me but I snap my arm out and wrap it around her waist, halting her escape. With her flush against my front, I reach around with my free hand and force her head back. She opens her mouth to curse me out no doubt but I silence her with my lips.

CHAPTER FOURTEEN

My mind is still a jumbled fucking mess. After I kicked Vivian out, I had planned to get rid of Alex and be done with him and his bullshit, but then he had to go and kiss me and confuse the hell out of me. The bastard knew what he was doing. I'm now wound up with no relief because he fucking left! When he broke the kiss and peeled his shirt off me, I expected him to fuck me or at the very least finger my pussy so I would be able to concentrate on something other than his filthy promise.

Stay wet for me all day and I'll come back and destroy that perfect little cunt, Bambi.

The bastard pulled his shirt on, then waltzed out of my room, while I stood there gaping at the closed door for so long my eyes started to water. To say I am on fucking edge is an understatement. My nipples are sensitive and my pussy won't stop fluttering and clamping down on fucking air. By the time I reach the lobby to meet Vivian and the guys I'm a fucking hot mess. The four of them take one look at me and fight back smirks. Bosses or not, I glare each of them down until any hint of a smile vanishes from their faces.

"I thought we wouldn't be seeing Alex." Vivian's tone is filled with mirth and I have to bite my tongue to keep from snapping at her.

"Yeah well, same, but the bastard seems to like breaking into hotel rooms and watching me sleep." Her brows raise in surprise. Before she can comment further I push on. "We have a meeting at ten with the inspector at the site. If we leave now we can grab coffee on the way." I don't wait for a response from them as I make my way toward the exit.

"Am I that bad when you three don't give me what I want?" I hear Vivian say. I grind my teeth and quicken my pace so I don't have to hear their reply. It's bad enough they all know I spent the night with the infamous Butcher but I have to admit, seeing Vivian touching Alex had me wanting to claw her fucking eyes out and rip her hands off him. The possessiveness I feel over him is wrong. We may be fucking, but that doesn't mean I have to complicate things and bring feelings into this because at the end of the day, he is still the guy who wants to take away the only family I have.

After grabbing coffee we made our way to the hotel. Vivian and Archer are the first to voice their upset over the sight of the place.

"Nothing has been done!" Archer bites out.

"Why the hell are they holding it up? We have every-thing in order and none of the other locations are this far behind." I can hear the disappointment in Vivian's voice. I don't blame them for being pissed, they are losing money by the day with how long this one project is taking. "New York and Miami are set to open in a couple of months, Texas is mere weeks from opening."

"We'll get to the end of this before we fly home, baby, I promise," Hayze says as he wraps an arm around her and places a kiss on the top of her head. Ezekiel flicks his head, motioning for me to follow him. I leave the three of them to talk while I follow Ez far enough away that they won't be able to overhear. When we come to a stop, his gaze bores into mine and I fight the urge not to fidget.

"What the fuck is really going on?" His tone is firm and unyielding.

I sigh and run a hand through my hair. "Honestly, I don't know. Everything has been done by the book, we have followed all regulations and standards to a T, but we keep getting setbacks for bullshit reasons."

"Like?"

"The plumbing isn't up to state regulations, the windows are safety glass. The wiring in the building needs to be redone, the fire sprinklers need to be spaced out further. It's all bullshit. I have read up on everything and this inspector is just picking on us and I am so fucking close to breaking his nose—"

Ezekiel smiles and places a hand on my shoulder, silencing me. "That would just make shit worse but I won't lie, I'm starting to think someone doesn't want us opening Lividica." I frown and cock my head to the side.

"What makes you say that?" I push. He grips my shoulders and turns me so I'm facing the opposite direction where three blacked out Lincolns are parked.

"Something tells me our inspector is being paid and

whoever the fuck is here in those cars are his benefactors."
My jaw unhinges and my left eye begins to twitch as anger
courses through me.

"Give me five minutes before we go in. I need to make a
call." I don't wait for his reply as I move away and pull my
phone out and dial a number I never thought I would have to
use. It rings five times before his deep baritone voice flows
through the line.

"Since I never give my number out and all my contacts
are saved, I'm gonna take a wild guess and say what do you
want, Tatum?"

I bite the corner of my lip feeling suddenly nervous.
"Omen, I need help."

"Where are you?" His tone instantly changes from
annoyed to worried.

"No, it's not that kind of trouble," I reassure him.

"Then why the fuck are you calling me?" he snaps.

"I know Halo can hack the cameras around the city and
before you lie and say you guys aren't even here, don't." He
snickers but remains silent. "I think someone is stonewalling
my build for the next hotel and I need to know who it is...
please."

"Halo, bring up the feed around Lividica in the city." I
roll my eyes, my point has been proven, these men have no
fucking boundaries. "What am I looking for?" Omen asks.

"There are three blacked out Lincoln's parked in the
alley next to the hotel. Ez thinks they are the ones paying off
our inspector."

"Give me twenty minutes," he says, then ends the call.
Vivian motions for me to follow them inside. I sigh and do as
she asks, but just before we enter the building she comes to a

stop and faces me. Her eyes hold a hard edge and I start to worry she may fire me.

"This is your show. We may own the hotels but you are the one who knows everything about them. When we get in there, we'll follow your lead. This is your show, Tate." My jaw drops, I'm at a loss for words.

"Vox and Nova just arrived," Archer says as I turn away from Vi and sure enough, Nova and Vox are making their way toward us. Vox is wearing his usual scowl while Nova is beaming at me. When she is within reach, she wraps her arms around me and holds me tight.

"I freaking missed you, Tate!" I melt into her embrace and can't help but smile.

"Yeah, I kind of missed you too," I mutter as she pulls back and shoots me a wink.

"So, what's the plan?" Nova asks. Vivian tells her what she just told me and to my surprise both her and Vox agree without complaint. I'm so used to rich people always thinking they know everything and taking control but not this lot. They are leaving me to handle everything and I fucking respect that shit so damn much. I never thought I would ever be in the position that I am. I'm just some kid from the system who was never wanted and yet... I have people that actually care about me and come when I call, that's something that will take a long time to get used to.

"Let's do this," I say as I lead the way inside the lobby that is still under construction. My jaw locks when I see the builders we have employed sitting around doing fucking nothing while they get paid for it. I pause in the center and look around and not once do any of these greased up pigs try to act like they are actually working. They just continue on with their conversations and scrolling on their damn phones. "If you sons of bitches want your paycheck at the end of the fucking week, I suggest you do some damn work!" I shout garnering the attention of everyone.

"Who the hell is she?" one of the guys asks.

"Your boss," Vox snarls as he steps forward to stand at my side. A silent gasp escapes me. "I suggest you listen to her or you're all fired." His threat seems to do the trick, all of them scramble to get off their lazy asses and return to work. The sound of clapping draws my attention to the other side of the room where a woman stands. She wears a white suit with no shirt beneath her jacket to show off the swell of her tits. Her black hair is tied in a high ponytail with no loose strands but it's her eyes, the blue, it stands out against her tanned skin. I look at the three guys flanking her. I cock my head to the side and frown. The one covered in tattoos reminds me of Halo for some reason. The other two are twins, both of them look vicious. Their brown eyes are filled with mischief, both of them have their blond hair spiked and cut short on the sides.

"Tatum Lawson, I presume?" the woman says in a stuck up tone. I hate the way she stands there looking down her nose at me. I can tell she is wealthy just from the way she holds herself and from what she's wearing. The three guys are dressed similar to us, casual. Well, I'm wearing a loose tee that is knotted in the front and a pair of jeans I've had for years that didn't start out with rips in the knees but after years of use they now have them.

"Should I know who you are?" I ask. Her upper lip twitches in distaste, good. I have no interest in kissing this bitches ass. I know for a fact now they are the ones stonewalling us. I can smell it on them, she's here to intimidate me and push me out of town. She can try as much as she likes but I never fucking run from a fight. The woman takes a step forward but the Halo clone darts his arm out and stops her. She scowls at him but he doesn't budge, just shakes his head in warning.

"The meeting is about to begin," Halo 2 says, then turns and heads back through the doors. The bitch shoots me one last glare before following the guy with the other two. I crack my neck side to side and follow after them.

"Let the fucking fun begin," I growl. As we enter the room, I snort at the sight of a large oval table and chairs that weren't here yesterday. "Made yourself at home I see?" I snark. The four of them sit at one end of the table with the bitch at the head, so I make a power move of my own. I claim the seat at the other end, sitting across from her. Nova and Vivian are both grinning as they sit on either side of me with the guys claiming the seats by them. Just to piss the bitch off further I slouch back in my seat while maintaining eye contact and nod my head for her to begin. Halo 2 has a ghost of a smirk on his face but it isn't him I'm worried about, it's the twins. I can tell they are unhinged and I would hate to face those fuckers in a dark alley alone.

"It's *my* city. I'll make a home where I want," the cunt grits out. The red lipstick she wears just adds to her cunt vibe and has me rolling my eyes.

"Is that so..." I let my sentence trail off. Vox and the other three guys recline in their seats, happy to leave this meeting to me which means a lot, they could undermine me at any time but won't. Nova and Vivian sit there with blank looks on their faces, ready to intervene if I need them—I won't, I got this.

She sits forward and steeples her hands on the table and stares at me with hatred. I keep my own face free of emotion, knowing it will drive someone like her insane not being able to get a read on me.

"You think you can come into my city and try to open an establishment without my blessing?" I don't bother answering, knowing she isn't done and clearly loves the sound of her own voice. "I own Chicago. Everyone in this city knows all new businesses must pay a tax to my family."

Laughter bubbles out of me which just has her nostrils flaring and her eyes burning with hatred. "Let's get something straight here. I won't and never fucking will pay a tax to you and your family. You keep stonewalling me and hindering the opening of my hotel and you will learn really fast how resourceful I am."

"Do you have any idea who the fuck I am?" she grinds out.

I purse my lips and pretend to think for a second before shaking my head. "No idea and honestly, I don't give a shit."

She pushes back and stands, laying her palms flat on top of the table as she glares across at me. I don't move or even react. "You little—"

"Sit the fuck down, Desire." My breath hitches at the sound of Alex's booming voice but I don't react. I remain composed with my gaze on the bitch before me. Her eyes twitch, she wants to look at Alex but doesn't want to lose the glaring match. The man himself makes it easy for her when he comes to stand behind me. I see out of the corner of my eyes he isn't alone. I don't need to see their faces to know it's

Omen and the others. "Sit the fuck down," Alex grits out. She reluctantly obeys him, me on the other hand I feel like stirring the pot so I purse my lips and blow her a kiss.

She doesn't like that. She catapults out of her seat and tries to round the table, but Halo 2 grabs her wrist and pulls her back as he stands. "I'm gonna snap her fucking neck," she seethes.

"Touch her and our deal is off," Alex snaps, drawing her attention to him. My brow furrows when I see recognition in her eyes. I reign in my jealousy and keep my composure, not wanting to show her that she is getting to me.

"You know the rules. She came into my city and everyone knows there is a fee to be paid." Desire sounds unhinged and it makes me smile, knowing I'm getting to her.

"Why the sudden interest in her and the hotel now?" Vatican volleys back.

Desire's face blanks and I know without a shadow of a doubt she is about to spin some bullshit. "I've been busy, it's a lot of work running a city. Someone had to fill our father's shoes when the four of you ran away like little pussies." This time my jaw pops open in shock, the cunt swings her gaze to me and winks. "Oh, you didn't know?" she says in a sickly sweet tone.

"You don't speak to her. You want to play your fucking games, then you play them with me," Alex roars. The anger in his tone has me sitting up straight. Desire cuts a glance between me and Alexander, it takes her two seconds to figure it out then her features darken.

"No, the game has only begun and I plan to fucking ruin her and destroy her like the trash she is. The De Santis family bows to no one," she bites back. I push to my feet and feign disinterest. When I see Alex look at Omen, I use that moment of distraction to my advantage and leap onto the table, ready to rush the cunt and smash her face in. Alex the motherfucker grabs my waist and yanks me back like I weigh nothing, and uses his arms as a vice to keep me plastered to him.

"I'll beat the shit out of her!" I scream.

"Bambi, you need to calm the fuck down," he snarls.

"Control your bitch, Lex, or I'll do it for you," Desire snarks.

I meet the bitches scowl with one of my own but it vanishes when I see the green eyed monster lurking just beneath the surface. That brings a megawatt smile to my face.

"Oh, darling, he controls me just fine, don't you worry about that," I purr in a suggestive tone that has Halo 2 growling and holding her back when she tries to come at me. The twins stand and help him restrain her while I stand here wrapped up in Alex's arms, which she hates.

"I think this meeting is over," Nova says as she stands. Vivian and the guys follow her lead.

"You want your hotel to go ahead, get rid of the bitch and you won't have any issues," Desire suggests in a tone filled with venom.

Vivian scoffs. "No thanks. Tate isn't going anywhere and by the looks of things, you poked the wrong bear so I'll stick with my girl and Alex." I shoot Vivian a grateful look before looking back at the cunt across the room.

"Keep blocking the build, it won't stop me from fucking him every... single... night." Her face turns a bright shade of red at my admission.

I expect her to fire back. The bitch just goes lax and pulls free of the guys hold, straightens her jacket then smiles at me. The look is filled with promise. "Did you like the taste of my pussy on his cock?" I feel Alex stiffen behind me. Her answer is like a sledgehammer to my chest but I refuse to allow her to win. I lock down the hurt her words caused and force a sinister smirk to my own face.

"I prefer the taste of my own pussy on his tongue." Her jaw locks and I know I've won. "See you around, Desire. Next time how about you leave your guards behind and we settle this for real because I don't surrender, bitch. I'll never go down without a fight, just ask Alex the next time you try slamming that retched cunt on him." I tear out of The Butcher's hold and storm out of there with my friends hot on my heels. I don't look back. I'm so angry at myself for letting my jealousy overcloud my rational thought. I'm better than that.

"We're getting drunk," Vivian calls out as we hit the street. I grunt my agreement. I need something to take the edge off and help me calm down before I claw that bitches face off and punch Alex in the dick for letting me get blindsided by his ex.

CHAPTER FIFTEEN

Alexander

I'm vibrating with anger as I stare at Desire. I had just gotten back to the house when Omen told me we were rolling out because Desire was making moves on Tate. I didn't ask questions. I have no idea how he knew what was going on and I didn't ask, I just knew I had to get to her before Desire could do any real damage.

"You go near her again or you try and fuck with her, I'll come at you with everything I have and this time, I won't stop. I'll take your family from you and smile over your grave," I spit out.

"You can try, Butcher." Wrath sneers as he pulls a blade from his side. Pope draws his gun and aims it at the little shit but he doesn't bat an eye. The crazy cunt wouldn't care if we all had our guns aimed at him, he thrives on chaos.

"I'm going to enjoy breaking that little bitch," Desire

announces. I nod my head and shoot Carnage a glance before turning back to the bitch before me.

"Then this is war," I say.

"You kill again, the deal is off. We'll take you down," Carnage barks. I can see the torment in his eyes.

"You can try," I say to him, then focus back on the vapid bitch. "No holds barred this time. I'm going to destroy you and your family."

"The four fools you have at your side are *my* family," she fires back.

"No!" I roar, then slam my fist down on the table. "They aren't anything to you. They are *my* brothers and I will fucking die before I ever allow you to get your claws into them again."

"You'll die at my hands, Butcher," she vows.

I smirk. "And you'll die on my table as I tear you apart piece by wretched fucking piece, you heartless cunt." I turn my back to her and stalk out of there without a backward glance. The time for fun is over and now it's time to stop playing in the shadows. She thinks she's won already but she has no idea what we have built. I'll dismantle their empire and have her running scared before I finally strike and take her down.

The second I step outside and inhale, I feel freedom. I no longer have to hide or work in the darkness. My whole operation will be out in the open, which means more doors will be opened for us. I know without a doubt our business will take off, we'll be able to reach out to other connections without having to worry about Desire finding out. The amount of guns and ammo we'll be moving now means we'll need more men to help with the workload.

"Where to now?" Halo asks from beside me.

"Home, we need to start preparing the men and get ready to make our first move," I answer as I open the car door.

"What about the girl?" Omen hedges.

My shoulders bunch. I debate his question, now that Desire knows she means something to me, she will hunt Tatum. The safest place for her is with me. "We'll grab her on the way to the airport." Their answering laughter grates on my nerves but I don't comment. My mind is too occupied with the knowledge that I'll finally get the war I have longed for. I am now more certain than ever that Desire and Nexus are linked. She targeted Tatum, there is only one person who would have put her on that path. "We need to destroy them. We do that and then that little rat they are hiding will come out."

"You really think she is working with him?" Vat asks as he puts the cars in gear.

"Without a doubt. She went after Tate and there was no reason for that. I have a feeling Desire was meant to take Tatum today and return her to Nexus," I answer.

"Why didn't she?" Pope pushes from beside me in the back.

I sigh and scrub a hand down my face. "Because I showed her that Tatum Lawson means something to me," I answer bitterly.

"You still owe us an explanation about what the fuck happened with you and our dad," Omen clips out.

I nod. "I know. I'll explain everything when we get home, I swear." I just fucking hope they understand my reasoning for doing what I did. It's no secret that all the De

Santis hated their father Pope, Omen, Vatican and Halo changed their last name to Toscano when we left, they wanted nothing tying them to their former life. Me getting framed for those murders and sent to prison wasn't part of our plan, but now more than ever, I feel like that is somehow connected.

The drive back to the house is tense to say the least, we always knew it would come to this but I didn't expect it so soon after being released from prison. I know we have the manpower and the guns as well as the skill to go against the De Santis family, but I also know how cunning they are. Desire may be a rotten cunt but she's smart. She's the type of person who would rather chew off her own fucking arm than admit she was ever wrong. The fact she was called out today by Tate doesn't bode well for her, Desire doesn't like being made a fool of and Tate did just that by throwing me in her face.

I don't particularly like the idea of being used, especially since Tatum has made clear that she's not a fan of whatever is happening between us.

Do I enjoy losing myself inside her?

Fuck yes.

Am I happy she is related to the cunt who killed my sister?

Hell the fuck no.

Do I like her?

That is a question I can't answer because half the time I envision strangling her because her vulgar mouth irritates me. Then on the other hand, I enjoy her mind and how she thinks and views the world. I know she didn't have an easy childhood and fought her way out of the system for a better life, but she doesn't hate the world for the injustice she suffered like I do. I hate everything because some cunt stole the light of my life from me. Ellie was my everything, she is the reason I stopped being The Butcher. She hated what I did. She knew I killed for a living and still... she loved me regardless.

Pain shoots through me as the memory of holding my sister's body in my arms as I screamed for her to come back. I've never shed a tear since that night. I don't believe in God, if he was real why the fuck would he allow my angel on earth to be taken? Ellie was good. She had a heart of gold and loved everyone. She would have given you the shirt off her back.

"Head in the game, no mistakes or we won't make it out alive," Halo says, pulling me from my thoughts. I climb out of the car and stand there just staring at the four of them.

They are all I have.

My parents disowned me after Ellie died, they said it was my fault and deep down I don't blame them or hate them for their decision because I blame myself.

"You all have a choice. I'm not asking you to fight along-side me—"

Vatican cuts me off before I can finish. "Shut up, Alex. We made our choice when we left our siblings to follow you. They may share our blood but this right here," he says as he waves his arm around the five of us, "this right here is our family and we will always have your back." Unable to put into words the gratitude I feel for these fuckers, I just nod.

"Let's go to war," Omen grits out.

I'm going to put a fucking microchip in that little fucking minx!

At least then if she gets fucking lost they scan her and return to sender—*me*!

"I thought she was at *Hell Bent*?" I snap at Halo, who is sitting in the back of the car with his laptop. The fucker snaps his head up and glares at me.

"She was! The drive from the house to here takes twenty fucking minutes. I'm tracking her now," he bites back.

"Alex, he's trying," Pope says in his brother's defense.

I cut a glance to him and growl. "We need to find her before your fucking sister does." All four of them turn their heads to me. "What?"

Omen rolls his eyes. "She wouldn't be on Desire's radar if you had kept your dick in your pants." I clench my fists and fight the urge not to punch him.

"You know she has a crazy streak," Pope adds, like that small detail had slipped my mind.

"How the fuck was I supposed to know your crazy bitch of a sister knew about her?" I fire back.

"Oh, shut the fuck up," Vatican snaps. "You know Desire has been keeping tabs on you since we left. That jealous cunt will kill anyone who bats their lashes at you. You were just stupid enough to go ahead and fuck this one. Now, she is definitely going to do everything she can to rip Tate apart." Before I can tear this smart mouth motherfucker a new asshole Halo speaks.

"Found her, she's at Mint Kitty a block away." I turn in my chair and glare out the windshield.

"They're all under age and out clubbing, what does that say about us?" Pope mutters. I ignore him, too focused on getting to Tate. I had some of my guys swing past her hotel and grab her shit. I know that little spitfire is going to fight and try and throw her weight around, but I'm not budging. She'll be getting her ass on that plane even if I have to drug her again. I warned her to stop looking into us, I almost pleaded with her to stop but she ignored me.

I've spent six months watching her, getting to know her from afar. She became an obsession for me, something to fixate on aside from the need to destroy her brother. At the start, the sight of her made me sick just from knowing who she shared blood with. But as time drew on and I realized she was nothing like her father or brother, something shifted. I don't know when or how but it did. Seeing her again on the plane and the fact she didn't cower and cry like most would was intriguing.

She didn't have to flaunt herself or offer her body to hold my attention, she already had it. Tatum Lawson is an addiction for me. I loved stalking her and breaking into her hotel rooms just to watch her sleep. I even resorted to stealing panties just to see if she would notice that they were missing, but she was too focused on work to take stock of her own belongings. She isn't shallow and wants nothing from anyone. She wants to earn everything she has and won't accept handouts.

"We all going in?" Omen asks when we pull up out front of the club. I manage a grunt and climb out. The bouncer takes one look at us and steps aside. Patrons who are lined up outside shout and curse but I ignore them. The bouncer may not know who the fuck I am, but even he can sense that I'm a predator and I'll make him my fucking prey if he tries to stop me from getting to my Bambi.

The bass from the music and the sound of people shouting just to be heard over the music grates on my frail nerves. I don't come to places like this because I hate the noise. Halo and Vat motion to me that they will search the left side while Omen and Pope take the right, leaving me the center.

Great, I get the fucking dance floor.

I push my way through the crowd. The guys take one look at me and shut their fucking mouths, the girls on the other hand, they're thirsty fucking Twats I shudder in revulsion when one gets bold and cuts into my path. I glare down at her when she places a hand on my chest. I grind my teeth so hard they fucking ache, she has three seconds to get that fucking hand off me before I lose it.

"You look like you need some fun." She tries to sound sexy but the smudged mascara and glassy look in her eyes has disgust rolling through me. If this is what kids these days think is hot, then I'll fucking pass.

"Unless you want my girl to snap your arm for touching her man, I'd remove that hand if I was you." I cut a glance to my side to see Vivian standing there with Archer and Ezekiel flanking her. I've never been more happy to see her in my life. The look she is giving the girl in front of me is cold enough to freeze hell over.

The girl clearly can't take a hint. She looks at Vivian and then back to me and decides I'm not worth the trouble, but then she bats her lashes at Ezekiel, who shakes his head trying to warn the drunk idiot not to do it but she ignores him and smiles.

"I have a thing for blonds," she says. Vivian's eyes darken to almost pitch black as she steps forward. Ez wraps his hand around her arm to keep her from moving far.

"You try and hit on *my* husband again, you nasty little bitch, and I'll break your fucking nose." I bite my lip to keep from smiling at how territorial Vivian is being. The drunk girl pouts then looks at Archer who raises his hands and shakes his head. "You even think of trying anything with him and it will be your jaw I break, they are both mine, bitch." Before more can be said I push the girl aside and face Vivian who is trying to peer around me to find the drunk bitch trying to climb her men.

"Where is she?"

Vivian purses her lips as she looks up at me. "Why would I tell you that after what happened with your ex today?" she says. I respect the fact that she is sticking up for her friend but now isn't the time for her bullshit.

"Either tell me where she is or I start breaking necks in this middle of this fucking club to find her. Choose," I growl. Ezekiel and Archer press in closer to their girl while scowling at me.

"Watch it, Butcher," the blond punk says.

I meet his angry glare with one of my own. "Start talking or I start killing and your wife knows for a fact I don't make idle threats."

"Why do you want her, Alex? She was fucking certifiable today and I won't help you hurt her," Vivian pleads.

I sigh and scrub a hand down my face, utterly exhausted and just wanting to get the fuck out of here before I really do start killing cunts for fun if they keep bumping into me.

"Desire will hunt her just to get at me. She knows I care about Tate and because of that she has a target on her back.

Help me and I swear to you I will keep her safe, but I can't protect her here. She needs to come with me, Vivian."

Vivian sighs and looks at each of her guys. I clench my fists at my sides trying to reign in my anger. She finally focuses back on me and I wait with a thread of patience for her answer.

"She's near the back by the DJ, dancing with Nova and Hayze. Vox is watching over them." I nod, then turn and start shoving cunts out of my way to get to my girl.

I spot her right where Vivian said they would be and trip over my own feet. I stand here and stare at her in a trance. She's wearing a gold dress that hugs her curves perfectly. The top of it is bunched and hangs low enough to show the tops of her perfect tits. She spins and I get a look at the back. It's open, the two thin straps that wrap around her neck are the only thing holding the bottom of the dress so it doesn't expose the top of her ass. Her blonde hair is straight and loose, she looks like a fucking angel.

I see red when Hayze steps in closer to her, leaving only a couple inches of space between them. Rationally I know he is in love with Vivian and is only dancing, but he's too fucking close to my girl for my liking and I'm about to change that shit.

CHAPTER SIXTEEN

I needed this.

I thought we were just going to have a couple of drinks but then Vivian and Nova declared we needed new outfits and to have fun. Wanting nothing more than to keep my mind off Alex, I agreed. Vivian loaned me the dress. Nova did my hair and makeup. When I saw myself in the mirror, I couldn't stop staring, I have never thought of myself as beautiful until now.

The guys have been awesome. The four of them refused to even have a drop of alcohol because they wanted to be alert while me and the girls drank. I admit, I have been jealous seeing Nova and Vivian with their men, it makes me miss a certain someone who I will not name because he is *nothing* to me.

My mind agrees with me but my body burns for a hint of his touch. Just his presence alone has me burning hot with need. Today I was blindsided by that bitch. I never expected him to show up when I called Omen for help, I thought at the very least he would text me with a name or some background information on the owner of the cars. My mind has been a mess since we left. I started to unwind after a couple of drinks, but then we went to Hell Bent and everything was great. The music was good and the drinks were going down easier than Alex's cock sliding inside me but I had to go to the bathroom. The girls offered to come but I waved them off and went by myself.

Big mistake.

I just rounded the corner out of sight of them and the guys when I was yanked into a dark corner. I screamed but then a hand clamped over my mouth.

"Shh, it's just me." My eyes widened at the sound of my brother's voice. I threw my arms around him and held him tightly. He pushed me back and looked down at me with an unreadable look in his eyes that had me feeling uneasy.

"What are you doing here?"

"Why the fuck are you with them?" he snapped.

I recoiled at his harsh tone. "They're my friends, Nexus."

"They are trying to kill me and ruin my life," he argued. Guilt churned inside me. I dropped my gaze to my gold stilettos unable to meet his gaze. "You need to come with me." When he grabbed my arm I yanked it back.

"Why?" I asked.

He shot me a scathing look that had my hackles rising. "We need to get back to the De Santis compound."

"*De Santis?*" I hiss.

"Yes," he growls.

I shake my head. "I met that bitch today. I'm not going anywhere near that cunt."

"Desire is the one helping me and she will help you too if you just learn to keep your mouth and your fucking legs closed."

I gasp, my hand itching to smack him but I refrain. "What the fuck are you saying, Nexus?" My tone is filled with ice at his insinuation.

"Stop fucking that bastard and she will let you go free but if you keep—"

"Weren't you the one who told me to fuck him?" I snap.

"Yeah well, things change and Desire doesn't want you near him. I can't keep saving your ass if you keep fucking up."

I stare at him in shock as hurt threads its way through me. "All I have done since I found out you were my brother is save *your* ass. I've been bending over backwards to keep you safe—"

"How is letting that cunt inside you helping me?" This time I can't control my anger and I do slap him. We both stand here stunned at my actions. He slowly turns back to face me. My eyes are wide and my mouth is agape, unable to believe I just hit my brother.

Nexus's eyes darken and I still as he presses in closer until my back is flush against the wall. "You made the wrong choice. All you had to do was distract him while we made our move and you couldn't even do that because you went and caught feelings for the fucking Butcher."

I jolt. "What are you talking about?"

A cruel smile crosses his face. "We knew he wouldn't be able to resist you, you remind him too much of *her* for him to turn his back. We just needed him to fixate on you enough to get sloppy and he did. She knows everything now and it's only a matter of time before I'm free of him and *you*."

Tears prick the backs of my eyes. "What are you saying?" I whisper.

"I knew about him and the De Santis family. I know everything." He pulls back and smiles wickedly. "I knew exactly who his sister was. All of this has been a game and you just got caught in the middle."

Shame washes over me, everything I have been told about my brother is true, he used me. "You murdered an innocent girl, didn't you?" My voice trembles but I don't care.

"It was a condition of our working arrangement." I reach out to grip the front of his hoodie.

"He's going to kill you." Nexus reaches up and cups my cheek. I implore him with my eyes to tell me this was all a joke and that he didn't mean any of this. My heart is racing and I'm praying I wasn't a fool and blinded by my need for a family so bad that I didn't see I was getting played.

"He can try, but we'll get to him first." I drop my hold on him and shake my head. "You were supposed to choose me. I really do care about you, Tator Tot—"

"Nexus, you're my brother and I love you, please don't do this."

"It's because you love me that I know you will never let him come after me even if Desire loses. You can't sell out your own brother and that is my greatest strength and your biggest weakness." He releases me and disappears out the fire exit without a backward glance.

After Nexus left, I started doing shots, needing to

drown the pain. When some girl bumped into me I lost it and started hitting her. We were kicked out, which is why we're now at Mint Kitty. I'm buzzing and loving how the alcohol is numbing my pain and washing away the memory of what happened. I know the girls are worried about me and want to know what has put me in a mood but I ignored them and dragged Hayze to the dance floor. Nova joins us while Vox stands off to the side keeping an eye on us. Vivian and the other two have gone to get us another round.

Just as I start to let loose and spin around, the hairs on the back of my neck stand up and I know he's here. I don't bother looking for him because I know he'll find me, he's proven there is nowhere I can run or hide where he won't catch me. I continue dancing with Hayze but the second his gaze snaps above my head a small smirk crosses his lips. I know he can see him. Hayze steps back and shoots me a wink, then moves toward Nova as an arm wraps around me from behind. I close my eyes and inhale. His scent engulfs me and I hate how just his smell and presence can ease the ache in my chest. I shouldn't want him like this, even with all the alcohol in my system it still doesn't dull how my body reacts to him.

He bends down and brushes his lips against the shell of my ear, sending a shiver down my spine. I don't bother trying to mask it, he already knows the effect he has on me.

"It's time to go home, Bambi." I close my eyes and melt into him and allow myself a minute to relish in the feeling of him holding me. When I open them again, I see Nova, Vox and Hayze all staring at me with looks of concern. I smile reassuringly before turning in Alex's hold and looking up at him. He searches my eyes and whatever he sees in them has him clenching his jaw. "Who hurt you?"

I shake my head. "Why are you here?" I ask, avoiding his question.

He reaches out with his free hand and grips the back of my neck. "I'm here for you." The honesty in his tone floors me. "You can either walk out of here on your own or I'll throw you over my shoulder, but either way, Tatum, you are leaving here with me."

The fucking balls on this guy!

"Ah, no. I'm staying here with my friends," I rebuke. He sighs tiredly and nods. I smirk triumphantly until he reaches his arm out to the side as if he's Thor calling *Mjohir*. Not a second later a jacket sails through the air. I follow where it came from and see Omen standing there with a smirk. I frown but then Alex wraps the jacket around my waist. I'm about to protest but the fucker bends down and launches me over his shoulder.

"Put me the fuck down!" I scream as I begin punching his back. I look up to see my friends all standing there smiling. I spot Vivian who mouths *sorry*—boss or not I flip her off, then go back to punching Alex's back and kicking my legs.

"Unless you want to give everyone a view of my pussy stop fucking kicking!" he snaps, then lands a swift smack to my ass that has me yelping.

"It's my pussy, asshole!" I scream. When I hear laughter, I look up to see his four asshole friends following behind us.

"Wrong. It's mine and it's time you start admitting that shit to yourself."

"Like fuck, Butcher," I growl, then clamp my mouth closed when a wave of dizziness washes over me and I start feeling nauseous. I swallow the bile I feel rushing up my throat. "Alex, I don't feel good," I groan when he steps outside of the club.

"Fuck," he curses, then carefully sets me on my feet. I sway. He grabs my waist and keeps me steady. I try to focus on his face but suddenly all the drinks I inhaled have finally caught up to me. "You're going to be rethinking your life choices when you wake up tomorrow."

I pout and flop forward against him, resting my head against his chest. His arms band around me like armor.

"I'm rethinking them now," I mutter. A deep baritone laugh escapes him and I realize I love the sound of his laugh and want to hear it more.

"We need to move," I hear Halo say and shake my head. Alex sighs and lifts me but this time it's bridal style. He slides into the back of his car but doesn't release me, he keeps me on his lap as the others climb in. I find I don't mind being this close to him and snuggle in closer.

"Airport?" Vatican asks.

"Yeah, the plane's waiting," Alex answers. A yawn escapes me and when he starts running his fingers through my hair, my eyes close and a moan escapes me. I feel him tense beneath me but say nothing.

"If you two start getting handsy I'm pulling over and you can catch a fucking Uber," Pope barks. I smile tiredly feeling utterly content.

"Just fucking drive, Pope, the quicker we get to the plane the faster we get the fuck out of here," Alex snaps.

"My feet hurt," I groan. I don't open my eyes when I feel someone removing my shoes, I just sigh and melt into Alex further.

"Shit, I just got a text from Sean," Vatican growls.

"What happened?" I think it's Omen who spoke but I can't be sure because I'm slowly drifting off to sleep. I'm grateful because my head is spinning and if I open my eyes I'm going to throw up.

"Desire stopped their plane from taking off, some of the guys have been arrested." My eyes snap open at Vatican's mention of that bitch. Instantly I regret opening them when my stomach churns. I swivel on Alex's lap and roll the window down. He tries to hold me but I shove him away and pop my head out the window just in time for me to empty the contents of my stomach.

"Oh, that is fucking classy," I hear one of the guys mutter.

"Shut the fuck up!" Alex roars as I continue dry heaving. He gathers my hair in his hand and holds it back from whipping my face. The car doesn't slow, if anything our speed picks up. When I'm sure I have nothing left to throw up, I flop back inside the car. Alex instantly locks his arms around me and secures me to his front. He pulls the jacket from my waist and wipes my mouth. I admit, that move makes me swoon a tiny little bit.

I sit up straighter and look beside us to see Halo staring at me with a look of disgust. I roll my eyes. "Oh, but a girl choking on your dick is hot?" I bite out. The little shit just smirks at me.

"Ask any guy, they would agree—"

I cut him off before he could finish. "Can you track my phone?" Halo cuts a glance to Alex before focusing back on me. I almost kiss him when he hands me a breath mint. I smile my thanks and shove it in my mouth.

"Uh, Alex will just get you a new one," he says.

I roll my eyes and instantly regret it when my stomach rolls. "I don't give a shit about the phone, you idiot." I ignore him then tilt my head back to look at Alex who is staring at me with a weird look. I suck in a deep breath and woman up, blood or not, what he did was fucking wrong. "I'm assuming since you kidnapped me again, you collected my belongings?" Alex's brows furrow.

"If you plan to punch my balls I would rethink that option," he grits out.

"The thought hadn't crossed my mind but now I am thinking about your balls..." Heat enters his green eyes, I would blame the alcohol for me reaching up and stroking his beard but that was all me.

"Someone switch fucking seats with me!" Halo shouts, pulling me from thoughts of Alex's dick.

I shake my head trying to get my drunk brain to focus. "Did you get my stuff or not?" I push. His lips pinch and I narrow my eyes which has him nodding stiffly. "I need my laptop."

"Why?" Vatican asks.

I hold Alex's gaze as I answer. "I need to track my phone," I say quietly.

Alex's green eyes burn with an intense look that has me swallowing audibly. His hand grips the front of my throat tight enough to warn me to tread carefully but not enough to restrict my breathing.

"Why?" he grits out through clenched teeth.

I dart my tongue out to moisten my lips. His eyes track the movement but I force myself not to get distracted. "Nexus came to me." No sooner have the words left my mouth does the car skid to a stop. I can feel everyone's eyes on me but I ignore them as I keep my focus on Alex who is vibrating with rage. He says nothing but I can see it in his eyes that he is warring for control over his emotions.

"Butcher," Omen says in a tone that is filled with lead and dominance. "Let her go before you hurt her." I see it now.

He isn't the Alex I know right now, he's the Butcher. The man who thirsts for blood and destruction. A hint of fear works its way through me as his hold on me tightens slightly.

"Butch, you need to let her go before you do something you will regret." The urgency in Pope's tone tells me I need to do something before he really does snap my fucking neck. I suck in a steadying breath then turn in his hold so I can straddle his lap. He keeps his hold on my neck and I don't dare try to pry myself free. Instead, I cup his face and brush my thumbs along his cheeks letting my touch soothe the monster inside him.

I'm fucking praying my touch helps and doesn't push him over the edge.

When he starts blinking rapidly I hold my breath, hoping that he will be able to win the war against his rage and bloodlust. When his green eyes slowly focus on me again I push on.

"He came to me and tried to get me to leave with him." His hold drops from my throat to grip my waist in a bruising hold.

"You're mine, Bambi." His tone is filled with gravel and promise. The way in which he says that has need pulsing inside me and my thong grows damp with my arousal.

"I'm right here, Alex," I say reassuringly. I've always been the girl who would roll her eyes at parts like this in movies or books, when the guy would go all caveman and declare the woman his like she is property to be owned. Yet here the fuck I am, getting turned on by the prospect of this killer wanting me for himself.

"What did he want, Tate?" Halo asks. Alex snaps his head toward him and shoots him a look like he would peel the skin from a lesser man. Halo doesn't cower, just raises his hands, he knows his friend is on the verge of losing control to the beast inside him. This is my first real encounter with the *real* Alex and rather than running away in fear, I find myself wanting to bring back the Alex *I* know.

"He's working with Desire. She's been helping him and he told me he is at their compound. She's been helping him hide I think."

Alex's gaze bores into mine. "What else?" His tone is low and deadly.

I swallow and exhale a whoosh of air. "He said if I kept my legs closed and stopped fucking you, she would help me too." Alex's eyes darken as he slowly trails his hand down my body to grip the tops of my thighs.

"Planning on shutting me out are you, Bambi?" he asks in a seductive tone that has my core clenching when he pushes his hands higher and brushes his thumb over my lace covered pussy. I gasp and thank God it's dark in here so the guys can't see what he's doing. I squirm when he applies a small amount of pressure to my clit and bite down on my lip to keep the moan that's lodged in the back of my throat from breaking free.

I shake my head. "No," I answer.

"Hmmm, what else did he have to say?" he purrs as he leans forward and runs his nose along the column of my neck, making sure to scrape his beard against my skin. He fucking knows I love the feeling of that shit, and like a puppet I tilt my head giving him better access. "Answer me, Bambi," he says quietly, then places an open mouth kiss to my neck.

"I...um...huh?" I breathe out.

"Alex!" Omen snaps, breaking the spell I was under. My eyes widen in horror when I realize I forgot all about them being in the car with us. Horror fills me when I realize I'm grinding against him. I freeze and shove against his chest, pushing him back. The son of a bitch just smirks like a cocky bastard.

"What else did your cunt of a brother have to say?" Alex asks. I take a second to compose myself which is a lot harder now thanks to him! My pussy is fluttering and clenching on air. The self-satisfied look he shoots me tells me he knows exactly what he just did to me and doesn't give a fuck. This motherfucker and his need to stake his claim is annoying and hot, which frustrates me more because I hate it but I also love it.

Fuck! He is a mind fuck.

CHAPTER SEVENTEEN

Alexander

I look up at her, loving the lust I see swirling in the depths of her blue eyes. I may be fucking livid and thirsting for blood but the feeling of her hot cunt pressed against my hard cock is the only thing keeping me in this seat and not scouring the city for that little bitch and ripping him apart. I stroke my thumbs along the tops of her thighs, knowing exactly what I'm doing, she'll spill more than she wants to because she's so distracted by how much she wants me to relieve her of the ache I've caused between her thighs. I'll be all too happy to let her ride my face as soon as she tells me what I need to know, then I'll reward her and make her beg me for her next orgasm.

"He said I was supposed to distract you but I ruined his plan because..." She clamps her mouth closed. I press the pad of my thumb against her clit, she jolts and shoots me a glare.

"Answer me, Bambi or I make you come in front of them." Her eyes widen and her jaw unhinges, knowing what's at stake. My brothers remain silent, allowing me to do whatever it takes to get us the intel we need. To drive my point home, I push her thong to the side and circle her clit, she gasps and tries to back away, but I lock my arm around her and hold her in place.

"Alex, stop," she pleads.

"Not until you tell me, baby." I apply more pressure and she shudders—I would never allow these fuckers to see her come but she doesn't know that.

"He said I ruined their plan because I went and caught feelings for the Butcher," she shouts, her declaration has me stilling as my brows leap to my hairline. "He said they knew you wouldn't be able to resist me because I reminded you of her. He said you would fixate on me over time and you would grow sloppy and slip up. Apparently you did and now *she* knows everything."

"What the fuck does that mean?" I growl.

She sighs and looks out the window. When I see her bottom lip tremble, I grip her chin and force her gaze back to me. The sight of unshed tears I see has me dropping my hold on her and staring at her in horror as dread begins to fill me.

"He knew about you and the De Santis family," she whispers. "He said he knew who your sister was and it was all a game and I was just caught in the middle." I turn cold and grow rigid. "I asked him if he killed her and all he could say was it was a condition of them working together. I told him you would kill him. He said you can try but they'll get you first. Can I go now?" I jerk in shock.

"What?" I snap.

Her eyes fill with rage as she stares down at me. "You didn't have to do all of that to get me to tell you the truth, now let me out of this fucking car!" she screams at me and the guys all recoil. She begins fumbling around for the door handle. I try and grab her but she keeps hitting my arms away. When I finally have enough and grab her neck she blows my fucking mind when she slaps me across the face. "Don't you ever fucking touch me again!" I release her instantly. She grabs the handle and shoves the door open, falling toward the ground. I'm not quick enough to get out and stop her fall. When I reach for her she backs away and shakes her head, the way she is looking at me right now scares the shit out of me.

"Bambi—"

"Shut up, Alex!" I snap my mouth closed. The guys climb out of the car and flank me. She looks between them and scoffs before focusing back on me. "He also told me that because I love him I would never let you go after him. He said my love for him is his greatest strength and my biggest weakness. The thing is, you are all wrong about me. He may be my brother and I would never be able to kill him, but that doesn't mean I would try to stop you after knowing what he did to your sister."

"Alex, we're sitting ducks here, we need to move," Halo clips out but I ignore him.

The way she is looking at me right now fills my veins with ice. I had suspected she went through shit but I didn't realize how bad until now.

"I'm sorry—"

She cuts me off before I can continue. "Don't be. I guess I did my job without even knowing it. I distracted you for him and got the proof you needed to carry out your plans. I want nothing to do with you, Nexus, or your crazy ass fucking ex." Sadness fills her eyes and my heart pounds inside my chest. "Track my phone, Alex. I slipped it into Nexus's hoodie pocket before he left."

I step forward but she takes one back. "Tatum, I can't let you go."

She smiles sadly. "You lost me the moment you tried to use my body to get the answers you needed. Go win your war and slay your demons, Alex, then forget all about me."

"I can't do that," I snap.

She shrugs. "Goodbye, Alex," she whispers, then walks away. I try to go after her but Omen grabs my arm. I shove him back but he rushes forward and gets in my face.

"Go after him and I'll go after her. You have my word I'll keep her safe," he snarls. I look from her retreating frame back to him and growl in frustration. I grab the front of his shirt and yank him to me.

"You fucking keep her safe and alive. Do you understand?"

He nods. "I know what she is to you. You have my word, brother." I release him with a shove.

"Fuck, just go," I roar. Omen nods then takes off after my girl. "Get in the fucking car. Halo, track her fucking phone now!" I roar as I punch the side of the car.

Calm has never been one of my strong suits nor is patience. Halo tracked her phone and sure enough it's last location pinged at the De Santis mansion before it cut out. Sitting out front, knowing that the little cunt who ruined my life is behind those gates is the worst kind of torture. My mouth is watering at the thought of getting my hands on him and strapping him to my table as I drag out his last breath making sure to inflict as much pain as I can.

"We need to get our men released before we make a move," Pope announces with an edge of darkness to his tone.

"I'm working on it," Vat replies as he continues to type away frantically on his phone. My guess is he is filling our lawyers in—the same lawyers who got me freed from prison are now on our payroll.

The charges against them are fucking cooked. Desire could have come up with something better than bullshit unpaid tickets and a couple of them are said to have had warrants out for their arrest, which we all know is bullshit. Any of my guys with a record never fly with us, we leave them back in Denver to keep up with the shipments we get in so Damon can ship them out to our buyers.

"We can't sit out here all night," Halo declares, which just earns him a glare from me. Now is not the time for them to start telling me what to do, I'm hanging onto my sanity by a fucking thread after what happened with Tatum.

"Heads up," Vat hisses. I look out the window and see a car exiting the gates, it's one of the blacked out Lincolns from earlier. Pope and Vatican slouch down in their seats in the front but when the car drives straight toward us I know who it is. I jump out and ignore their orders for me to get back in. I stand in the middle of the road. The Lincoln jams on the brakes at the last second, leaving an inch of space between me and it. I slam my hands flat against the hood. The driver's door swings open and Carnage steps out.

"You have a fucking death wish?" he snarls.

I push off the car and stalk toward him, he doesn't shift as I get right in his face. "Hand the cunt over and I give you my word I'll end you quickly."

The son of a bitch scoffs and steps back. "Get in the fucking car, Alex." He doesn't wait for a response as he climbs behind the wheel and slams the door closed. I look back to my guys and motion for them to follow us. Halo leaps out of the back and stalks toward me with a glare firmly in place.

"You may trust him but I don't," he spits out as he shoulders past me. I grit my teeth and jump in next to Carnage. I've barely closed the door before he plants his foot. I check the side mirror to make sure Vat is keeping pace with us. Given the fact that most of my men are in Denver and the ones I did have here with me are currently detained, we're outnumbered.

"How'd she know I had men?" I ask as Carnage maneuvers us through the city.

"She knows a lot more than you think, like how you're the one supplying the Vatel family with guns." I fight not to smirk.

"How long has she known?"

"Since you got out of prison."

My brow furrows. "Why did she start tracking me, Carnage?" He white knuckles the steering wheel. I look at him and the tight set of his shoulders and the way he's working his jaw side to side tells me everything I need to know. "She ordered the death of my sister, didn't she?" My tone is unwavering and firm.

Carnage takes a shuddering breath and pulls over in

front of a hotel on the outskirts of town. He kills the engine then turns to face me. "I had no fucking idea until tonight when that little cocksucker walked through my fucking front door." My breathing accelerates as I fight for control of my rage.

"She won't survive this, can you handle that?" Halo speaks for the first time.

Carnage keeps his eyes on me as he answers his twin. "I gave you my word that I would deal with her if you were telling the truth and I stand by that."

"I'm going to fucking rip her and that little cunt apart," I vow. He exhales and nods.

"I know."

"Why are you here?" Halo asks.

"Believe it or not, I do have a moral compass and what Des did is unforgivable. Ellie was innocent and didn't deserve to become collateral damage in a war she had nothing to do with," he answers.

"There was no fucking war! I bought our freedom from your fucking family!" I roar.

"No!" he snaps, meeting the intensity of my tone. "You bought yourself time before my sister came after you. You're a fucking fool if you think for a second that she would ever let you go, you know her better than that."

"His back is proof enough he paid the fucking price!" Halo spits.

Carnage stabs a hand through his hair and nods. "We need a plan. We have a max of two weeks before she throws everything she has at us."

"*Us?*" Halo scoffs.

Carnage finally faces his twin and scowls at him. "Yes, *us* you little prick."

Before these idiots can continue bickering I cut in. "Why the fuck are we here?" I ask.

Carnage flicks his gaze to the hotel behind me. "Go get your girl so we can get on a fucking plane and head back to Denver." My eyes widen. Carnage just shakes his head. "You forget I know you, Butcher. I knew that would be the place where you hunker down because it was your sister's haven. Don't worry, Desire has no idea where your homestead is, she only knows you stay in Colorado."

"You're not as smart as you think," I force out.

"Yeah, whatever. Go get our girl, she's closing down the airports and I don't feel like driving all the way back to your house so get out." He reclines his chair, forcing Halo to shift or get his leg caught by the backrest. I decide to leave grilling him for answers until we get back to my place. I push the door open, ready to climb out, but before I do he speaks. "I also want an explanation about my father as well, Alex."

CHAPTER EIGHTEEN

Silence.

I can't find a moment of peace because of my thoughts and the memories of earlier tonight plaguing me.

Fear.

I feel none. All I feel is numb. I used to live in constant fear until I met the monster I was running from.

Caged.

That's how I feel right now. I'm trapped inside a hotel room with Omen and I have nowhere to run. I built the cage I am trapped in right now. I should have turned my back on Alex and went to CHU and hid out with Vivian and Nova but I ignored caution. I was too enthralled by all things Alexander Denver and now look where I am.

My life was my own. I had financial freedom, thanks to my amazing job that I am neglecting right now. I even made some friends who actually give a shit about me and expect nothing from me. I had everything until I had to go and seek out my family. Thomas used me to get to Vivian and I stupidly led him to her without knowing. My own father was going to kill me! Then my brother turned up and saved me, only to turn around and use me.

I feel so stupid. I let Nexus in and trusted him. I was so desperate for a family that I trusted a snake. His betrayal hurts so fucking badly. Which is why I'm standing in the shower right now so Omen can't see me cry, I never cry. My emotions are all over the place and I can't seem to get a hold on them. The way Alex touched me earlier and used my own body against me brought back memories I thought I had long since buried, but turns out I was fucking wrong.

Tonight I made a choice and at the time I thought it was the right one. Nexus admitting that he hurt an innocent girl showed me the true monster that he is, but Alex using me, that hurt more than I want to admit. When a sob escapes me, I cover my mouth with my hand to muffle the sounds. When I feel a gust of air hit my back I spin around, a scream lodging in my throat when my face is gripped and he smashes his mouth against mine. For a second, just one blissful second, I let myself get lost in the feeling of him and how he makes me feel stronger.

I break the kiss and push him back, He stands there fully dressed, staring down at me with guilt in his eyes. "I'm so sorry," he whispers.

I shake my head and fight back my tears. "Am I just someone you can use to get to my brother?" I hate how meek I sound but I'm so far past caring right now.

He shakes his head and sighs, then rubs his beard. I respect the fact he hasn't once dropped his gaze from mine to get a look at my naked body. I see regret which just inches that knife into my heart further. I try to push past him but he blocks my escape. I snarl at the fucker.

"Would you give me a fucking second to explain!" he shouts.

"Fuck you, get the hell out of my way, Butcher." I relish in the feeling of my anger roaring to life inside me, this is a feeling I can latch onto and embrace. It feels so much better than the pain consuming me a minute ago.

"Don't call me that."

"Why the fuck not?" I yell.

"Because she's the one who gave me that damn name!" he roars. I snap my mouth closed and stare up at him in astonishment. "I'm so sorry, Tatum. I never meant to hurt you."

"But you did."

He inhales shakily. "I know," he says quietly.

"Ask me," I grit out.

He frowns. "What?"

"Ask me your most favorite question that you have asked me more than a dozen times."

His eyes widen in understanding. "*Who hurt you?*"

"My foster father. Want to know why I've never made a move to suck your dick?" I don't give him a chance to answer. "My last foster home was the worst. I escaped all the others before they could touch me but not Ray. He was smart, he knew I wasn't like the other's so he used my four-year-old foster sister against me."

"How?" His tone is laced with venom.

"I either suck his dick whenever he wants or he rapes Emily while I watch." Alex steps back and stares down at me with a mix of unfiltered bloodlust and rage. I expected to see pity or at the very least for him to tell me he was so sorry for what I went through, but he does neither.

"Do you remember his last name and his address?"

"Yeah, why?" He grips my hand and drags me out of the shower. I stand here confused as hell as he grabs a towel and wraps it around my body, then leads me out of the bathroom without uttering a word. I spot Omen as he stands from his seat in the corner of the small room and stares at Alex with a mix of uncertainty and worry. When he cuts a glance to me I just shrug, a minute ago I was fucking broken hearted then angry and now I'm down right confused as hell.

I'm getting whiplash from my own emotions and I don't like it!

"I want a current location on Ray..." When Alex turns to face me I recoil and look around the room trying to see what he is looking expectantly at. "I need the last name and the address," he barks at me. My eyes widen.

"Why?" I sputter.

His eyes darken. "Because I'm going to kill the son of a bitch. Now give me the name, Tatum."

I bristle at his tone. "Charles," I force out.

Alex turns back to Omen. "Find everything you can for a guy named Ray Charles—" Alex snaps his mouth closed, then slowly turns back to me and narrows his eyes. I smirk and cock a brow. He opens his mouth to no doubt have a go at me but I beat him to it.

"If you thought it would be that easy, you are out of your damn mind, *Butcher*." His eyes spark with challenge, which is fine with me because I'll always rise to a challenge and never back down. "You don't get to walk your ass back in here and fuck with my head more. You hurt my feelings and I'm not forgiving you, so fuck off." Omen chokes on thin fucking air while Alex stands there staring down at me with a bored look on his face.

"Two options, that's all you're getting. You can change yourself and walk out the fucking door, or I'll change you and carry your ass out. Pick one."

I step into Alex and place my hand flat against his chest and bat my lashes, he knows I'm up to something I can see in his eyes. "*Beg me.*"

"Omen, out!" he roars.

I poked the bear too much it appears.

Before he can move, I dart away from him and into the bathroom. I slam the door and lock it, knowing he could bust it down if he wanted to. But he won't, because he knows he's still on my shit list. I won't lie, a part of me was so close to telling him what Ray's last name was but I refused because I didn't want him to think he could be my white knight after what he did!

I'm stuck between Omen and Alex as we make our way out of the hotel. Alex keeps his hand firmly placed on my lower back and the heat of his touch sears me, which only further fuels my vexation toward the asshole. I bite my tongue and say nothing, allowing him to lead me outside. I slam to a halt at the sight of one of the blacked out Lincoln's idling at the curb in front of Alex's car.

Alex gives me a gentle push. "It's not what you think, Bambi, keep walking," he urges. I stow my apprehension away and shift further into Alex's side. My unease only grows the closer we get, when Alex reaches out and opens the back door. I hold my breath expecting to see Desire sitting there but it's not, it's just Halo who smiles reassuringly at me. I look to the front and my brows raise at the man.

"Halo 2 is here?" I hiss.

Alex's brows are furrowed and Halo looks downright pissed at my comment. Omen begins snickering with laughter beside me.

"There is only one fucking Halo and I'm it!" OG Halo snaps. I purse my lips and nod.

"Noted, OG," I say, earning a glare from the man himself. Alex groans and ushers me inside the car. Omen climbs in the front while Alex slides in beside me. Halo shifts as far away from me as possible which irritates me. "Why are you being a girl?" I hiss when Halo 2 starts driving. OG turns and glares at me.

"Bambi," Alex says in a warning tone.

I throw my hands in the air, utterly frustrated. "So you can just turn up at my hotel rooms, kidnap me whenever the hell you want. Steal my phone, hack my fucking phone and computer but I can't ask questions?" I snap. The car falls silent at my outburst. Alex sighs and scrubs a hand down his face, the fact he's still dressed in his wet clothes gives me some satisfaction though, knowing he's uncomfortable.

"Halo's my twin brother," Halo 2 says, breaking the tension filled silence.

"Wasn't talking to you, clone boy," I grit out while staring at Alex.

"Ask me what you want to know."

I smirk at the Aztec god. "How'd you get the scars on your back?" Everyone plunges into silence again and its starting to work my last frail fucking nerve. I hear Alex's breathing turns choppy, but I refuse to back down. I gave up my brother and told him about Ray, the least he could do is be honest with me.

"I think that conversation is best had alone when we—"

"Shut the hell up, Omen!" I snarl. Alex's eyes darken and I can see I'm pushing him to his limits, but I'm not afraid of the monster he hides inside. "You know everything about me, you've been watching me for months and yet, I know nothing about you. How can you declare me as *yours* if the same can't be said of me?"

That gets a reaction. His upper lip pulls back in a snarl as the car slowly comes to a stop. I refuse to break eye contact and give up on this moment when I know I'm so close to getting the truth from him.

"Desire De Santis is their sister. She is also someone I used to fuck." I fight not to flinch at his cold tone. "I bought our freedom from her family. Those scars you see on my back were the cost." He shoves his door open and climbs out, leaving me sitting here with my mouth wide open. I watch as he stalks toward a plane and climbs the steps without looking backward. Vatican and Pope shoot me a curious glance through the open doorway before following Alex.

"Word of advice, don't push him when it comes to his past," Halo 2 says.

"Your advice means nothing to me. This morning you were the enemy and that still hasn't changed," I grit out, then follow after Alex. Before I can get more than five steps,

Omen grips my arm and spins me around to face him. "What."

His gaze bores into mine. "I know you're mad. I know he fucked up with you tonight, but you need to know the full story before you write him off."

"And what is the full fucking story, Omen? I'm getting really tired of you all turning my life upside down and expecting me to control the monster sitting on that plane, the very fucking monster that your own sister created!" I suck in a deep breath and wait for him to respond.

"She may have created the monster, but we all know you're stronger than her, Tate."

"How?"

He smiles devilishly. "She may have created the beast but you're the one who can control it. We saw that tonight when you brought him back from the brink of blacking out and going on a killing spree. None of us could have stopped him from doing that, but you did." My jaw unhinges. "If he doesn't tell you his story, I will, but it's better you hear it from him because he was the one who lived it."

"Desire will try and kill you because it will hurt him." I turn to see Halo standing beside Omen.

"Why would me dying hurt him?" I mutter.

Halo 2 comes to stand on Omen's other side. "Because he never loved her or looked at her the way she saw him look at you today. You may know nothing about him, but that doesn't mean you feel nothing for The Butcher. You did what our sister couldn't," he says in a tone that brokers on the edge of pride.

"What did I do?" I ask, my curiosity piqued.

"You made him feel." I frown at Halo 2. "He hasn't felt a

single ounce of happiness or any emotion really aside from bloodlust since he buried his little sister. Stew on that while you sit on your high horse and judge him for seeking vengeance against the innocent little girl your brother drugged, raped and strangled to death."

CHAPTER NINETEEN

Alexander

I haven't spoken a word to Tatum the whole flight. She pushed me too far and I had to escape before I said or did something I wouldn't be able to take back. When we landed, I chose to ride alone with Carnage while Vat drove her, Omen, Pope and Halo back to our house.

I can't even find it within myself to be grateful that Carnage got my men released from jail and put on the next flight out of Chicago. The guys tried to get me to talk on the plane but I just ignored them and got lost in my own head.

Admitting to Tatum how I got the scars opened old wounds.

She has no idea the history I share with these guys or Desire. In her head she probably thinks I'm still hung up on my ex, when in truth, she was never my girlfriend. Carnage thought I was in love with her, so did Pope and Vat, but I never was. Desire isn't someone you fall for, she is just someone to pass the time with. Sort of like me. I'm not someone who can love or express emotions. I show how I feel by ripping motherfuckers apart slowly. I'm the guy to get down on one knee and offer you the heart of the person you hate most, not some fucking ring.

"She wants answers, you gonna give them to her?" I just grunt in answer. I have nothing else to say to him or anyone else right now. The second we hit my driveway, some of the tension eases from inside me, knowing we're home and I'll get some peace. I hate the fucking city, it's not a place I even like to visit unless I have to. All the noise and how busy it is screws with my head and puts me on edge. "So this is where you have been hiding, huh?" I don't bother replying. Carnage knew my family had a home out here, and why he never snitched to his sister about it, I have no fucking clue. He parks behind the other car. I spot a few of my guys I left behind as I get out. I nod to them, letting them know to fan out and keep an eye on our borders. I wouldn't put it past that bitch to have someone tailing us. How I missed my tail for months, I have no fucking clue.

Maybe she really was a distraction.

I push that thought away when I see Tatum climb out of the back of the car. She looks directly at me. I see the war of emotions in her eyes and right now, I can't process my own let alone dealing with hers, so I look away and make my way toward my cabin out the back. It's late and I need to sleep. I'll deal with the fall out of everything in the morning.

"Alex?" I pause but don't turn back to face Pope. "Tomorrow morning, we want an explanation." I nod my head, then carry on to my cabin to enjoy one last night of peace before I shatter the rest of our lives with the truth in the morning.

Desire is the only other person that knows why I killed Roberto De Santis.

"Wait, what the fuck?" I hear Carnage shout behind me, but I don't stick around. I head to my house, needing some fucking time to process this shit.

The second I step foot inside my house the tension evaporates. I make my way to the bathroom, needing to shower and to get out of these damp fucking clothes, then sleep. I stand under the spray of the shower and allow it to wash away my stress. I force my mind to go blank and shut down all my thoughts. Me getting lost in my own head never ends well, it's been years since I released all my pent up aggression. The other night interrogating those brothers was just an appetizer.

That reminds me, I need to make contact with that fucker Devon and see what he knows. I know that little shit won't double cross me since I'm the one with the keys to his brother's freedom. He's currently under guard at the local hospital. I paid the doctors to keep him in an induced coma, Devon needs to prove his worth before I allow his brother to wake up. I haven't made contact with him, I need him to get closer to her before he can be of any worth to me.

Stepping out of the shower, I wrap a towel around my waist and use another to dry my hair before I tie it up. I've been debating chopping it all off but I can never bring myself to shave my beard or cut my hair because my sister always loved it. She said it made me look like a fucking lumberjack from one of the books she used to read. I still have all her books in boxes. I just couldn't bring myself to allow my parents to take them when they packed her room up. I know people say there are stages to grief and the final step is letting go, but I can't. To let her go would mean my purpose in life has been fulfilled and that shit makes me feel like I would be acting like she never existed.

I stare at my reflection in the mirror and run my fingers over the tattoo across my heart.

Ellie.

I drop my gaze to the tattoo across my stomach, *De Santis Cosa Nostra.* At the time, I thought I would spend my life serving them and had no issues having that shit inked on me when Desire said it was something I had to do in order to prove myself to her family. How fucking wrong was I? The truth is, the only family I have is the Denver Kings. We aren't a gang or some mafia fucking family, we're just a family who is loyal and will go to fucking war for each other if need be. I turn away from the mirror and exit the bathroom only to come to a halt at the sight of Tatum sitting on the edge of my bed, holding a photo. I can tell from the frame that it's the picture of me and Ellie.

She slowly lifts her gaze to mine and I see the fire twirling in her blue eyes that has my abs constricting and bracing for a fight that I know is about to come.

"She was your world." I work my jaw side to side as I clench my fists at my sides.

"I told you what my breaking point is, don't fucking push me, Miss Lawson," I caution her.

She scoffs. "You've made yourself at home between my legs, Alex, drop the whole *Miss Lawson* bullshit, would ya?" I narrow my eyes but remain silent. "You've based your life on revenge. Why?"

"That's all I have left."

"That's horse shit and you know it," she snaps.

"How the fuck would you know? You think you know me because we fucked a couple of times?" I force a laugh as she flinches at my crass words. "You know nothing. You were never supposed to know who the fuck we are!" I shout as I storm across the room to grab some pants. If we're going to have this argument, then I at least need fucking pants.

"And who's fucking fault is that?" she shrieks as I pull some sweats on, then face her. She stands there glaring at me with her tiny hands clenched at her sides. "I never asked for any of this. I have a job that I love. Friends and people I watch out for and then you come along and ruin it all."

I purse my lips and nod, keeping my face blank of all emotions. "There's the door, Miss Lawson. Use it any time you like, just don't expect me or my brothers to come save your ass when Desire comes for your head."

"Fuck you and your cunt of an ex."

"Watch your vulgar ass mouth, Tatum," I seethe.

She rolls her eyes which has my hand twitching to strangle her perfect little neck. "What are you going to do, Alex? Kill me?" She snorts, then tosses the photo on the bed. I drop my gaze to the image and a pang of guilt hits me right in the chest at the sight of Ellie smiling at me like I hung the fucking moon. "Did she know who you really are?"

I flick my eyes to her and growl. "Watch it."

"Screw you. I've done nothing to you or any of those guys in that house," she screams as she throws her arms in the air. "Much like your Ellie." I take a step forward in warning but she doesn't stop. "I never got a say in who I share blood with. I never asked for the father and brother I wound up with. I'm not them, Alexander."

"But you are!" I yell. "You are a weakness for him. He proved that by coming to you tonight and trying to get you to leave with him."

Her face slackens as she stares at me, her brows drawing in and forming a deep V. "You used me." Hurt laces her tone.

"I warned you, Miss Lawson." My tone is cold and holds a harsh edge. I stalk toward her and don't stop until there is a sliver of space between us, forcing her to crane her neck back to hold my stare. "You don't respond to my methods of interrogation, you can take a fuck load of hurt and still keep your mouth shut." I reach out and cup her cheek, hating myself for what I'm about to do. "I told you I would force your walls down and I did. I'm inside you, Tate, mentally and sometimes physically. You let me in without knowing it and gave me your brother willingly." Her eyes widen, pain blooms in the depths of them as she realizes what's happened.

She smacks my hand away, then shoves me backward. I can see the hysteria rising inside her. "You son of a bitch!" she screams.

"I told you not to call my mother that," I clap back earning another shove from her. Tears glisten in her eyes and I fight my need to comfort her, it's strange to feel this way about someone. I'm the man you call to inflict pain and destroy your enemies, I'm not the guy who tries to take the pain away and comfort you when you're sad.

"I hate you!" she says quietly as she drops her arms back to her sides. Her eyes fill with moisture and I grind my teeth when the first tear falls. "Congratulations, Alexander, you got what you wanted from me. You not only ruined my life, you took the only family I had from me. I guess we finally have something in common huh?"

"What?"

Her eyes harden, then she swipes away her tears with the backs of her hands. "We've both lost a sibling now." My breath hitches. "My brother took yours from you and now you'll take mine from me. When will the cycle fucking end, *Butcher?*" The way she says my name has me tensing, it's filled with so much hatred and disgust. "You wear her name across your heart. I hope you find comfort in that because she is the only woman who will love you for the selfish son of a bitch that you are."

"You think I'm selfish?" I hiss.

"I don't think, I *know* you are. You proved that when you kidnapped the sister of your enemy, lulled her into thinking you might actually care and she stupidly believed you because you are fucking good at what you do. You may destroy the bodies of your enemies but I will be the master-piece of your work."

"How so?" I ask in a deathly calm tone.

"Because you destroyed my mind, my heart and my body. Congratulations, Alex, you won your war and got your man at the cost of breaking me." She turns on her heel and storms out of my house. I wait to hear the door slam but it never comes, instead she leaves the fucking thing wide open so I have no choice but to act as the doorman and close it.

"Fuck!" I roar as I tug on the strands of my hair.

I pull my phone out of my pocket and dial Halo. He answers on the second ring. "Yeah?"

"She took off, get the guys to watch the surrounding fences in case she makes it that far." I bark.

"Alex, it's fucking cold out and she is wearing a dress that is made for a toddler and she's bare foot." The apprehension in his tone grates on my already frail nerves. I take a deep breath and try to tamper my anger.

"Find her."

"What the fuck!" I hear Halo snap, then Omen's voice comes through the phone.

"I'll go after her but this is the only time I'll cover your fuck up with her."

I snort. "Watch it, brother, I'm not in the mood," I snarl.

"Good, you deserve to wallow in it, you fucker. I'm telling her," he says, then ends the call. I throw my phone across the room. When the fucking thing doesn't shatter it pisses me off more.

Was the reward really worth the loss of the woman who saw the real me?

CHAPTER TWENTY

Tatum

I have no idea where I'm going, I honestly don't care either. My feet are aching but the pain is nothing compared to the pain in my chest. I refuse to admit to myself why my chest feels like it's cracking open. I barely know him. I have no right to feel this broken over a guy who used me. I was a fucking idiot. He warned me from the start that he was going to use me, I have no one to blame except for myself. I wish I still had my phone so I could call Vivian and Nova. I know they have both been hurt like this before and if there is anyone in the world that can understand what I'm going through, it's them.

I spot a lone tree up ahead and sigh. I resonate with that lonely ass tree. It's on its own in the middle of an open field, just like me. We are on our own with no one else. I have no doubt Alex will slaughter my brother and claim his vengeance, it's been his mission in life since he figured out who took the person he loves most from him. The sick part about all of this, I get it. I hate that I understand his need to ruin my brother just so he can find peace within himself.

I sit down, lean against the tree and wrap my arms around myself, not really feeling the cold. I know I could have gone to the main house and demanded one of the guys take me to the airport but I'm not stupid. I know women like Desire, even if I told her whatever was happening between me and Alex was over she wouldn't believe it, and would just kill me for the fun of it. I hear a wolf howl in the distance and I can't stop the snort from escaping me.

I may not have blown his straw house down but he certainly destroyed my fragile stick house. Maybe one day I'll find someone who will build a house out of bricks with me. Chances of that happening are slim though, like I've said. I've never had any interest in males and the one fucking time I do, he obliterates me without mercy.

I tilt my head back and stare up at the sky, it's so beautiful.

"The stars are why she loved this place." I snap my head to the side to see Omen walking toward me with a blanket and sweater. He tries to smile but it looks more like a grimace when he hands them to me. I thank him, pull the sweater on and wrap the blanket around my legs. "Uh, I brought you these." I frown as he pulls out a pair of... slippers from his back pocket. I smile my thanks and purse my lips when I realize they are my own fucking slippers—this shit head went through my things.

When Omen sits down beside me I stare at him. "What are you doing?"

He exhales and lulls his head back to stare up at the sky.

"You aren't like every other female, Tatum." I scrunch my face.

"Uh, is that a compliment?"

He nods. "Believe it or not, I don't like women."

I snort. "Gee, I never noticed," I deadpan.

He tilts his head to the side and glares at me. I raise my hands in mock surrender. "You don't do well with pain, do you?"

"What's that supposed to mean?"

"You don't cry and scream, or jump on social media and whine to the world."

I shake my head and decide to be honest with him. "I've never seen the point in crying, it changes absolutely nothing about the situation you're in. Pain is just a reminder of what you've survived and it will pass over time. As for social media? Yeah, that's never been my thing. I don't even have an Instagram, I only scroll TikTok for the cat videos." He laughs and it's strange to hear that sound coming from him.

"You're the first woman I have spoken to in years," he admits.

"Why is that?" I gently push in a soothing tone.

"In order for you to understand I need to explain things to you."

"Okay..." I say skeptically.

"Pope, Vatican, Halo, me, Desire, Wrath, Rage and Carnage are all siblings."

"How does that work exactly? You're all so close in age from what I've gathered."

He nods, his features pull taut before he forces them to relax. "Halo and Carnage are twins, which I'm sure you have already figured out."

I laugh. "Yeah, Halo and Halo 2 look like replicas of each other, but also different."

"They aren't identical, the only identical twins in our family are Wrath and Rage."

"Those two creep me out."

He turns serious eyes to me and I hold my breath. "Never let yourself be alone in the same room as them. Those two are fucking crazy and have no moral compass." I exhale and nod.

"Yeah, I'll do my best to never see them again," I mutter.

"Okay, let me just lay it out for you from youngest to oldest. Vatican is the youngest out of all of us, he's twenty-three. Then it's Pope who is twenty-four. Carnage and Halo are both twenty-five. Wrath and Rage are Twenty-six."

"Where do you and Desire fit into all of this?"

Darkness shrouds him and I tense in anticipation. "Desire is twenty-seven and she is... my twin sister." My eyes widen and nearly bug out of my head.

"You poor thing," I blurt out. His eyes widen, then laughter erupts from him. I can't help but join him.

"It's not a picnic being related to her, but the fact we shared a womb is worse," he admits.

"Why do you have a different last name to her?" I hedge.

He takes a deep breath and nods as if gearing himself up for battle. "Toscano was my mother's maiden name. De Santis was our father's name. Wrath, Rage, Desire and Carnage are De Santis while me, Pope, Vat and Halo changed our names to my mother's."

"Pope told me that..." I try to think of a way to bring it up without upsetting him. "You have different moms?" His jaw tenses and his nostril flare. I reach out and place my hand on his thigh, he flinches but I don't remove it. "If this is too hard you don't have—"

"No. You need to know why he is the way he is." I know who the *he* is he is referring to, but I don't comment. "Pope, Vatican, Wrath and Rage are all full siblings. Halo, Carnage, Desire and me are full siblings. Pope and Vat's mom was my father's mistress. My mother knew about... Rosalina. They knew about each other but never cared because to them Roberto De Santis was a prize and he gave them everything they ever wanted." Pain lances his voice.

"Where is your mom?" I ask quietly.

"She died," he says in a monotone.

"I'm sorry."

"I know Pope told you that I killed his mother." I cringe but don't deny it. "I did kill Rosalina. I have no regrets. She was a vapid bitch and deserved what she got for what she did."

I grab his hand and hold it between mine. He frowns and keeps his gaze focused on the contact. "What she did to you is vile and wrong, you didn't deserve what happened to you, Omen. I may go to hell for saying this, but I'm glad you stopped her." His eyes slowly lift to mine.

"You mean that, don't you?"

I nod. "I do. No one should have to face what you did. You are here. You're stronger than she was. You survived a horrible thing. I was forced to do things... I detested it. I know what it's like to feel caged by the nightmares of your past."

"I didn't. I'm still trapped in that room with her," he whispers and my heart breaks for him. I see the distraught little boy in his eyes and that shit burns.

I reach out with my free hand and cup his cheek, this time he doesn't flinch from my touch. "You're here, with me, sitting under the stars. You'll never be back in that room with her, Omen. If she wasn't already dead, I'd stab the cunt for you." That brings a smirk to his handsome face.

"Your lust for blood may just match his." I scoff and drop my hand from his face.

"I doubt that."

"Look, the point of the story was. We are all related by blood, Alex isn't."

"How did he become a part of your... family?"

"Carnage."

My eyes widen. "Halo 2?" I squeak.

"Carnage and Alex were best friends." That has me sputtering. "Carnage and Alex were tight, Alex had no idea who we were when he met us, he had no idea that my father was the don. When Carnage was cornered one day by the Vatel family, Alex could have run away but he didn't. At sixteen years old he stood firm by my brother's side and fought. Alex killed six of their men. By the time my father arrived Alex had stolen one of their knives and begun cutting them open. When Roberto asked him why he did it, all he said was, "*I just wanted to see how pretty their insides were.*"

"Wow," is all I can say.

"After that, Alex was invited to hang around our house. Carnage was our father's favorite child, he said that Carn would be the one to take over the family because he showed promise. Technically, the role should have fallen to me but I didn't want it, I was too busy keeping his mistress... satisfied." Disgust rolls through me.

"Your father knew?" I bite out.

"Of course he did. He told her to see if I had what it took to be a real man. I clearly failed because the mantel fell to Carnage. Alex only bolstered his reasoning when he and Carnage started doing raids of their own. My father started noticing that Alex loved the blood and gore. When he captured one of our rival family's captain, he brought Alex to the basement and told him that if he could get him the intel he needed, he would be welcomed into the family through marriage."

My jaw unhinges. "Desire," I mutter.

Omen nods. "My sister was in love with Alex. She was obsessed with him and would do anything to get his attention, but he never noticed her. Needless to say, Alex got the intel Roberto needed and from the age of seventeen, Alex became my dad's leading man. Carnage started to get annoyed because Roberto was focusing more on Alex. It only got worse when Alex announced he would take the De Santis last name when he married Desire."

"What happened, Omen? How did it all go bad between your family and him?"

"I don't know but Alex does. Something changed in him after Roberto died. When he turned twenty-two he came to me, Vat, Pope, Halo and Carnage and told us he found our way out. In my family there is no out. You're blooded in and the only way to leave the Cosa Nostra is in a box. When he said we would all get our freedom, we jumped at the chance."

"I get why you would want to leave but why did the others?"

"Roberto forced us to do things we never wanted to do. He beat us. When men would pledge their loyalty to him they needed to be blooded in. It was me and my brothers that would face off against grown men. They had to either knock our asses out or kill us, one guy nearly succeeded in killing Halo until Carnage shot the cunt. He was beaten within an inch of his life for that." Bile rushes up my throat and this time it isn't from the alcohol.

"I'm so sorry."

He waves away my concern. "We didn't know the price of freedom would cost Alex fifty lashes. He was whipped fifty fucking times, ten lashes for each person. His back is shredded because of us. He refused to leave us behind and took that shit just so we could be free of our family." My chest aches at the thought of what he went through. I've seen his back it looks like someone took a grater to it.

"Why didn't Carnage leave with you?"

"He didn't want to live in Alex's shadow anymore is my guess."

"What happened between him and Desire?" I push.

"Honestly, I don't know. She was head over heels in love with Alex but he never cared about her the way she wanted him to. If Alex spoke to another girl Desire would lose it and have her killed. Alex had no idea until Pope told him about what our sister was doing. She lost it when Alex wanted to leave. He has my family's name inked on his skin and refuses to remove it because he says it's a reminder of what we have all survived. I never knew what a real family was like until we all left. Wrath and Rage were never like us and Alex never tried to take them with us."

"I don't blame him," I mutter.

"Not only did he get whipped, he had to swear he would never kill again. *The Butcher* belonged to the De Santis family and upon his release from the family, Desire vowed to wipe his existence from the world so no one could ever hire him or use him against her. He agreed. We can never have our own operations—"

"Hang on, you are the Denver Kings though."

He smiles wickedly and wags his brows. "Are we?" he purrs.

"Oh my God, she has no idea that you are all doing... business behind her back, does she?"

"She does now."

"Why did she leave you alone for years and then come after you now?"

"For two years, the five of us fumbled our way around trying to build something of our own. Alex came up with the Denver Kings. We aren't a gang or anything, we're a family. We sell firearms on the black market and use our moving companies as a front to transport or load across state lines. We've never dabbled in the skin trade or drugs not after..." He claps his mouth closed.

"Ellie," I say for him.

He nods stiffly. "For two years we built our empire from the ground up. Alex has always been our leader but more than that, he's a brother and Ellie, she was our girl. The only woman we would ever let into our sanctuary. Alex's parents wouldn't let him stay in their house. We got our own place and Ellie spent every minute she could with us. Pope and Vatican fell in love with her. I thought Alex would kill them but to my surprise, he just said if she felt the same about them then he wouldn't stand in their way. All he wanted was to see her happy and for a while she was. Pope and Vat made her smile every single day, she was their sunshine from the darkness they were raised in."

"It sounds like you guys really loved her," I whisper, feeling my heart ache for the girl who's life was stolen from her.

"We did. But, Alex loved her more. He told us he wanted to use the arms deals as a temporary solution until we could go legit." That revelation floors me. "He wanted to start investing and build a legal empire that he could leave to his sister one day, and we all agreed because we loved her. His lust for blood vanished when we came back here and Ellie was around. He didn't crave the kill anymore, he was just... Alex. The Butcher was no more until three years ago."

I exhale slowly and drop my gaze to the grass. "That's when she died, isn't it?"

"She didn't die, Tatum, she was murdered!" I flinch at his harsh tone. "That night, when Alex got the call and saw her lying there, he died right beside her. The Butcher was reborn that night. His thirst and hunger for the blood of his victims tripled, he was uncontrollable. We were forced to clean up his mess so Desire wouldn't find out. Anyone that was at that party that night is dead... all except one." I choke on my spit.

"He slaughtered all of them?" I whisper in horror.

"Every single fucking one," he says without remorse.

"The killing only stopped when he was framed for the murders of three women. We all knew he was innocent but we couldn't prove it. We thought we had lost Alex, he wouldn't let any of us visit him while he was inside. He told us to forget about him and live our lives. How the fuck could we have done that when he was the one who gave us our freedom?" I nod, understanding their reasoning. "Our hope was lost until Vivian Tempest showed up and changed everything."

"She got him out."

"Yeah. It goes to show what a fair trial someone can have if the judge isn't being paid off by a scumbag," he sneers.

"I had no idea Thomas did that, Omen. I swear."

He nods. "It's because we believe you that you're still breathing, Tate." I turn rigid. "If for a single second we thought you had anything to do with taking our brother from us, we would have killed you and sent you back to your father in pieces."

"Noted," I rasp out.

"When Alex got out, his vengeance was at an all-time high. We made sure that everyone inside that prison knew exactly who Alexander Denver was, his reputation as the Butcher is what kept him from getting into trouble while he was in there. Not having an outlet for his aggression caused him to come out hungrier than I've ever seen him. He's been fixated on Thomas and Nexus for months, we thought the old Alex was dead to us."

"What do you mean?"

"None of us have seen a hint of the old Alex since Ellie died, but that all changed about four months ago."

"I'm not following."

"You may be their blood but he forgot about that after a couple of months watching you, his focus shifted from them to you. He could have flown to Panama and paid off the guards so he could kill Thomas, but he refused to be away from you." My eyes bug out of my head.

"I didn't even know who he was!"

He shrugs. "Since you came into his life, he's starting to change and he doesn't know how to deal with that."

"Why?"

"For three years he has harbored this hate inside him and the need to destroy anyone who has wronged him. He hates that you're making him feel again, because the last person who made him feel a shred of anything was torn away from him way too soon and he won't survive losing another person he loves."

CHAPTER TWENTY-ONE

Alexander

I barely slept last night. I checked in with Halo at least a dozen fucking times to see if Omen was back from looking for Tate. The last message I received from that dipshit was a picture of her and Omen asleep against a tree in the south pasture. I nearly crushed my phone at the sight of her head resting in his lap. I have no right to feel the way I do. My head needs to be clear and all she is doing is distracting me from what's important and I can't afford that shit right now, not when we are on the brink of an all-out war against Desire and the psycho twins.

I drag my tired ass out of my house and head toward the main one. Just as I'm rounding the bend I spot Tatum and Omen walking toward the house. I remain where I am, out of their sight and listen to their conversation.

"I promise," she says.

Omen nods and shoots her a look that brokers on respect.

"He has some explaining to do this morning, maybe that might fill in the gaps of my story," he mumbles.

She purses her lips then stops walking and grabs his arm, the sight of her hands on another male has fire searing my veins. It's an irrational reaction but nothing about my situation with her is rational.

"If he shuts me out or pulls any of the shit he did last night, you swear to keep your word?"

Omen hesitates for a second then nods. "You have my word, if he fucks up I'll be here." I've heard enough. I round the bend and Tatum instantly spots me, whatever she sees on my face has her dropping Omen's arm and clutching the blanket tighter against her chest. It's only now I notice she is wearing *his* hoodie not mine.

"Well, don't you look cozy, Bambi," I sneer. Omen glares at me.

"Cut your shit, dumbass. It's not what it looks like," he defends.

"Don't explain yourself to that asshole, he can assume what he likes," she snaps.

"Oh, so I kick your vulgar ass out and you have my woman-hating brother falling at your feet for a taste of your pussy?" Tate gasps. Omen launches at me and clocks me across the jaw. I stumble back a step and grip my jaw, then meet his angry stare.

"You want to come at me, then do it... but don't be a bitch about it and use her, you fucking idiot," Omen snarls, then shoves me once more before storming toward the main house. When he slams the door behind himself, I turn to Tatum. She storms toward me and without warning the little shit strikes out and slaps me!

I slowly turn back to face her with murder in my eyes. She doesn't cower or take a step back when I snarl at her. "That was fucking low! After everything he went through, you go and throw that shit in his face? Shame on you, asshole."

My face slackens. "He told you?" My words are laced with surprise.

She scoffs. "Grow the fuck up, Alex. For someone who claims he is a twenty-seven-year-old man who can control himself, you sure have a piss poor way of showing it." For the second time this morning another person turns their back on me and storms off. I grind my teeth and follow after her. When I set foot inside the house, I fight not to roll my eyes at the sight of all the guys waiting for me in the living room. I cut a glance toward the hallway to see Tatum disappearing into Omen's room. I snap my head back to him.

He shakes his head. "Her bags are in there, she's taking a shower," he forces out through clenched teeth. Halo, Carnage, Vat and Pope keep looking between the both of us, trying to work out where the tension is coming from.

"I need a drink," I mutter.

"The fuck you do," Halo snaps.

I wave the idiot off. "I meant coffee, dumbass," I snarl as I stalk into the kitchen. I gave up alcohol when I went to prison, liquor became a crutch for me after Ellie died, I used it to dull the pain and help me get through each day. I swore I would never touch a drop of it again after I got out and these guys have made sure to hold me to my word. I appreciate that shit more than they know because since meeting Tatum, the urge to drink has been ever present. She fucks my head up and I hate being out of control.

"You good?" Carnage asks as he enters the kitchen. I keep my back to him as I pour me a cup.

"You suddenly care?" I throw back as I turn and face him. His eyes darken.

"You gonna be an asshole all day?"

"You gonna keep pissing me off?" I fire back.

"Pull your thong out of your ass and calm the fuck down and I might just fill you in on what Devon sent me this morning."

I work my jaw side to side and inhale a deep breath then answer. "Tell me."

"He says she hasn't called a meeting or anything, she hasn't changed a rotation of guards."

My brows draw in. "She isn't making a move?"

He shakes his head. "My sister is a twisted bitch but I don't need to tell you that. She's up to something but she's being tight lipped about it."

"I'm calling all my men in today for a meeting, I want them all strapped and ready for anything."

"I have some men inside the Cosa Nostra that are loyal to me, I can get them to turn."

I eye him warily for a second. "What happened to you never turning against her?"

His features pull taut and his eyes bore into mine. "That changed when I found out she's working with the cunt who hurt Ellie."

I mull over his words for a minute. "Why do you care so much about my sister?"

Carnage swallows and turns away from me. "I just do."

"Why?" I yell. His eyes close as he slowly turns back to face me, when he opens them again I see it. "It was your drugs," I say barely above a whisper. Guilt burns bright in his blue eyes. I drop my mug and charge him, tackling the son of a cunt to the ground and begin pummeling his face. The guys rush over and try to pull me off him. I fight them off as I keep attacking Carnage, the cunt doesn't even fight back.

"Alex!" I freeze at the sound of her voice. The red haze slowly clears as I lift my head and lock eyes with her. She stands there, staring at me with pity and that sight has me clenching my teeth as I push off Carnage and stand. I stare at his bloody face and feel nothing but disgust and self-loathing for ever considering him as my brother.

"You killed my sister." Carn flinches and pushes into a sitting position. He swipes the blood from his nose with the back of his hand, then pushes to his feet. It gives me great satisfaction when he flinches.

His dead eyes meet mine. "I wasn't the one that sold them to those idiots. That was your ex, you fucking idiot."

"Fuck you!" I roar. I storm toward the back door needing to escape, but Tatum darts in front of me, forcing me to slam to a halt. I shoot her a warning look. "Now isn't the time for your shit—"

She places a hand flat on my chest and stares up at me with sadness. "Stop running, don't let your emotions sabotage this for you. Tell them the truth and it may give you answers to what really happened three years ago."

"None of them were there," I yell.

She nods. "I know. But, you just heard from Halo 2 that his piss flap of a sister is somehow connected to what happened to... Ellie." Hearing my sister's name has the fight draining from me.

"There is only one of me!" I hear Halo growl but no one pays him any mind.

"She's my breaking point."

She smiles sadly and nods. "I know. Just don't let her memory be what destroys you. You owe her that much." I jerk back and suck in a sharp inhale. Tatum grabs my hand and leads me toward the sofas and I let her push me down into one of the seats. It's only then I notice she has showered and changed into a loose off the shoulder navy blue top and black jeans. "You girls joining us or what?" she barks. The guys all snicker but follow her order and claim the spare seats. When she moves to sit next to Omen, he spreads his legs and shoots her a scowl.

"You can sit your ass on his lap, everything happens in threes and so far that's only strike two." She cringes and shoots him a sheepish smile.

"Ah, well, you see, that was actually the third hit of the morning."

Omen scrunches his face. "Who else did he hit?" he says as he looks around the room. I cross my arms over my chest and roll my eyes.

"No one." All eyes turn back to her. "I may have kind of... sort of..." She huffs out a breath then straightens before continuing. "I hit him, okay?" The guys faces slacken.

"You... hit him?" Vat asks, laughter thick in his fucking tone.

She stomps her foot like a spoiled brat. "Yes. He pissed me off when he said something to Omen so I... lashed out." All five of the cock suckers begin laughing. I run my gaze over each of them and make sure they can see the promise of pain in my eyes, but they all ignore it which only serves to piss me off further.

"Sit your ass down on his lap before he comes at us," Pope rasps out through his laughter. Tatum huffs, then stomps back toward me, looking just as displeased about this as I am. She rolls her eyes, then drops into my lap. I hiss and grip her waist in a punishing hold.

"Ouch!" she whines and tries to pry my hands free. I shift her off my dick and shoot her a scowl.

"Next time you drop your ass on me, try not to crush my cock." Her jaw slackens.

"I'll break it next time," she mutters beneath her breath. I pinch her side and she yelps.

"I heard that," I growl.

"You were supposed to," she fires back.

"Enough!" Vat shouts. "I don't want to sit here and watch your brand of foreplay." I grind my teeth and take a deep breath as Tatum swivels on my lap and throws her legs over the arm of the recliner and rests her cheek against my chest. I'm tense as fuck knowing that she is up to something and if I am right, I will throw her ass off me.

"Aww, Vat, don't you want Mommy and Daddy to teach you all about the birds and the bees?" she coos. Vatican's face pales. "You see, the man sticks his penis inside the woman's vagina—" I clamp my hand over her mouth to silence her stupid ass remark. Her eyes are brewing a storm in them.

"Everyone in this fucking room is aware that my *penis* has been inside your *vagina*." Her eyes fill with laughter and I narrow my own in warning. "Now, can you shut your vulgar ass mouth and let us get on with it?"

She pries my hand off her mouth. "They've also seen you

finger my pussy." I inhale and try to latch onto my patience. "But, we won't talk about that," she says in a mock whisper, then crosses her arms over her chest and stares at me expectantly. "Please, continue."

I'm gonna kill her!

I'm going to wrap my hands around her perfect little neck and watch the air leave her lungs.

"Alex, you aren't going to hurt her," Omen hisses. I flick my gaze to him and frown.

"You just told us all how you plan to kill me," Tatum whispers. I close my eyes and take a calming breath, choosing to ignore her and the itch to harm her. Killing her would be bad but the silence, fuck the silence would be bliss.

"What do you all want to know?" I ask after I get myself under control.

"For starters, why did you kill Roberto?" Pope asks.

The air rushes out of me. I knew one day they would figure it out and ask questions about their father's death but I didn't expect it to happen this soon.

"Six years ago I came back to the house with Carnage after a meeting we had in New Jersey with Carlito Vatel. When I went upstairs to my bedroom, I found her." I may hate the vile bitch but even I can show empathy for what she went through.

"Who?" Halo pushes.

"Desire. She was in my room. At first I ignored her and told her I wasn't in the mood for her bullshit. I locked myself in the bathroom, thinking she would be gone by the time I finished my shower. When I came out the lights were off, I thought she was playing one of her games. She wasn't. I went to turn the lights on but she told me to leave them off, then asked me if I stood by the vow I made to her father."

"What the fuck does she have to do with any of this?" Vat asks.

"Shut the fuck up and let him finish!" Carnage snaps.

"I told her to piss off and go find another one of your father's men to screw." They all scrunch their faces in disgust.

"Wait, she was cheating on you?" Tatum does nothing to hide the hatred in her tone.

I ignore Tate's question and carry on. "Desire told me she loved me and asked me if I loved her." I feel Tate stiffen in my hold. I skate my fingers through hers trying to get her to relax, the more worked up she gets I know I will mirror it so I try and calm her. "I couldn't lie any longer. In my head I didn't need to marry her anymore because Roberto trusted me, so I told her the truth."

"Which was..." Tatum pushes. The guys snicker but I ignore them as I lock eyes with her and answer.

"That I cared about her but I didn't love her, I never did. I thought she would pitch a fit but she didn't. She just asked me to focus on the part that cared about her and to try and believe what she was about to tell me. I agreed. She turned the lights on and everything changed."

"How?" Omen hedges.

"She was beaten, her clothes were torn and... I knew her, I can tell when she is plotting, lying or faking shit and I saw none of that in her eyes. For the first time since meeting that cold bitch, all I saw was terror."

"Some cunt hurt my sister?" Carnage rages as he stands and stares at me expectantly. I nod stiffly.

"Everyone thought Omen was the only one to be used by that sick bitch but it turns out, your father was doing the same to your sister." The five of them all start shouting and cursing. Tatum has fallen silent at my declaration. They may all hate her, but each one of them can't stand the thought of what happened to her at the hands of their father.

"So that's why you killed him?" Halo asks.

I nod. "Yes. Now take a fucking seat because I'm not done." The anger in my tone has them all listening. "She asked me to help her get free of her father. I agreed, thinking she meant smuggling her out of the city or something but no, she wanted him dead."

"Something isn't adding up. You didn't kill him because she asked, you had a different reason, what was it?" I bite my cheek to keep from smiling, Tatum is smarter then I gave her credit for.

"I'm getting to that," I answer. "I told her I needed time. She agreed to give me a week before she tried to do it herself. I hated Roberto for what he did to all of you, I made no secret of that. You want the real reason I killed your father? That's it. I wanted the punishments to stop so I agreed to help your sister." All their faces are pictures of shock. "We agreed to make it look like a hit from the Vatel family. I was the one who shot him out front of the restaurant he was meeting the Pakhan of the Volkov Bratva at."

"Jesus, Alex!" Carnage snaps.

I ignore him as I push on. "When it was all done, the De Santis family needed a leader. At the meeting with the other families—"

"What meeting?" Carnage snarls.

"Desire made sure none of you knew about the meeting.

I agreed because you were a loose cannon, Car, you hated living in my shadow. Omen wanted nothing to do with the family and I thought I was making the right call, putting my bid in for Desire to be the leader. The other families agreed, thinking they would be able to fuck her over because she's a woman. Jokes on them isn't it, because she destroyed them all and now they work for her."

"You're not telling the full story," Tatum says quietly.

"I stayed with her for twelve months, guiding her and trying to help her lead the family in the right direction. Carnage became her second, he loved the idea of being higher ranked than me." The man himself glances away from me. "When Desire refused to close down the skin trade we fought. I argued it was wrong to sell women and children. She refused because it made the family the most money. It wasn't until just over a year later I heard her talking to Wrath and Rage." My breathing turns choppy and my anger soars. "Roberto never touched her."

"What?" Omen shouts.

"She lied. I heard her telling the twins that she needed to come up with another plan to keep me in line. I had no idea that she was winning wars against the families with the threat of letting me loose on their loved ones. The twins were the ones who beat her that night. She was fucking your father's men, hoping her pussy would keep them loyal to her."

Tate snorts. "Must be good pussy then," she snarks.

I purse my lips and refuse to take the bait. "Roberto never laid a hand on Desire. She knew how I felt about what happened to Omen and thought spinning me the same story about her would win me over. I confronted her. She tried to deny it until I told her I would tell you all the truth. She asked me what I wanted in exchange for silence... that's when we struck the deal and I got us out. Well, except for her pussy loving brother," I add just to be a prick.

Carnage snarls at me. "I have never fucked my sister. You cunts need to stop saying that shit."

"Why the fuck else would you stay with that crazy bitch? She's my twin and I hate her. She used to stand there and watch us get beaten and smile. She loved when Dad would hurt us, she got off on seeing us bleed," Omen screams.

"Because I was tired of living in Alex's shadow. Our own father preferred him to us because of how unhinged he was. I was angry and I thought with Desire in charge I would finally get my shot."

"Did you?" Tate asks.

Carnage frowns. "Did I what?"

She sighs dramatically. "Did you get the shot you wanted?"

"Yes," he grits out.

"Was it worth the cost of this family you turned your back on, just for her to turn out to be a lying bitch who used your own jealousy against you?" My brows raise at her question. I swing my gaze back to Carnage who deflates and shakes his head.

"Guess, not," he mutters.

"Look, that wasn't the only reason I wanted our freedom," I admit. "Ellie asked me to come home because she missed me. I knew I could never be near her and be The Butcher, so I did what I had to." Tate reaches up and cups my cheek pulling my focus back to her.

Her eyes are bright with understanding. "You did all of

that for her?" I nod and her eyes turn sad. "What is the connection between her and my brother, Alex? None of this makes sense. You got out from under her thumb and then two years later your sister was murdered. I don't believe in coincidences."

"She's right," Vat agrees. I keep staring at Tate trying to work through everything in my head. She holds my gaze. When it hits me, my eyes widen and she smiles. I snap my head up to look at Halo.

"We've been looking at this all wrong, we've been trying to find the connection between Desire and Nexus but it's much simpler than that."

"How so?" Pope queries.

I smirk. "Thomas and Roberto." Pope reels back. "Think about it. There is no connection between her and Nexus but there could be one between Thomas and Roberto."

"Thomas was a real estate tycoon. Could your father have needed to funnel money through buying properties?" Tate asks the guys. Halo stares at her for a minute before nodding.

"I'll look into it," he says, then stands.

But before they can all disappear I ask, "Are we good?" I don't look at Carnage. I keep Vat, Omen, Pope and Halo in my sight, waiting to see their reactions.

"Yeah, brother, we're good," Vat answers. The other three nod. I know it's going to take some time for them to wrap their heads around what I did, and I'll weather whatever punishment they throw my way because they're my family.

CHAPTER TWENTY-TWO

I've made myself scarce all day since Halo gave me all my things and a new phone. He let me know they did track my phone and it was a smart move I made. I appreciate his praise but I didn't do anything really. I still feel guilt churning in my gut over handing my brother over.

I retreated to Alex's cabin when his men arrived to be briefed on what was going on. Omen said I could stay but I declined. I didn't need to listen in on their plans—how they plan to capture my brother and kill him. Knowing it's going to happen is one thing, but hearing the gory details is another. I've buried myself in work for most of the day. I checked in with Andre—my co-manager of Lividica in Hollow Hills—to see how things are going. He assures me he has everything under control. Thanks to Alex and his impromptu kidnapping escapades I'm behind on work.

When I see a WhatsApp message ping across my screen I sigh at the sight of the name.

> V__Temp – You're alive 😃

> TLaw – Yeah, no thanks to you! 😠

> V_Temp – I'm sorry 😔 He just looked so happy to see you.

> TLaw – Yeah sure, got to go. 😳

Before I can close out of the app, a request for a video call with her pops up. I debate hanging up on her but then decide against it. When I hit answer, I fight not to smile at the sight of her and Nova crowding around the screen of her phone.

"Tate!" Nova squeals.

I roll my eyes and fight back a smile. "Hi."

"Oh, don't sound so bitter, we miss you," Vivian says.

I balk at her. "You wouldn't be missing me if you didn't snitch me out to The Butcher!" I scold.

She waves me off. "Girl, lie to yourself if you want but I saw the way you were looking at him." She fans herself with her hand. "I got hot just watching you both." Nova laughs and nods her agreement.

"Thanks to you, I'm now behind on work," I say, trying to bring the subject back to something I can actually deal with instead of my feelings about Alexander–fucking–Denver.

"Don't worry about it, we hired someone to help oversee the finalization of the builds." My breath lodges and I begin to panic.

"A-am I fired?" I stutter.

Both Vivian and Nova's faces fall. "Did the guys fire you?" Vivian shrieks.

"What? No," I rush to say.

"Then why do you think you're fired?" Nova says in a confused tone.

"You just said you hired someone else... so I thought that..." I clamp my mouth closed to stop rambling.

"Oh my God, Tate!" Vivian exclaims. "You are not fired, don't scare me like that again!" she scolds.

"So, I still have a job?" I ask with a cheesy smile.

"Yes!" they both say in unison. I release the breath I didn't know I was holding and smile.

"Thank you," I mutter.

"So, I guess you will be wherever you are right now for a while?" Vivian says with a gleeful look on her face.

I roll my eyes which just causes her to laugh. "I... Yeah, I guess I'll have to work remotely for a while."

"Are you okay?" Nova asks in a tone filled with concern.

"Define okay?" I joke. They share a look before looking at me and I can see the worry lines on both their faces. "I'm fine, I promise," I say, trying to ease their worries.

"How did he know where you were?" Nova asks.

I snort. "I swear he has a tracker on me, that son of a bitch—"

"Stop calling my mom a bitch!" I snap my head toward the door so fast I cringe in pain. I think I pulled a muscle from moving too fast. My eyes widen at the sight of him shirtless and wearing only his jeans, covered in sweat. His hair is out and he looks like a fucking wet dream standing there looking like an Aztec god with no effort at all. He strolls toward me and I fight not to swallow my tongue the closer he gets. He stops at the edge of the bed, putting my face in line with his crotch. I fight the groan of sexual frustration from breaking free.

"Well, shit." I jolt and Alex frowns at the sound of Vivian's voice, I forgot all about the girls being on video call. I turn back to the screen to see them both staring at Alex with dumbfounded looks on their faces. "Hi, Alex," Vi singsongs. I glare at her.

"Hey!" I snap, bringing both their eyes to me. Nova at least smiles sheepishly while Vivian just grins like an idiot. "You have three dicks to choose from, stop looking at mine!" I blurt out without thinking. My eyes widen a second before I scrunch them shut and wish for the floor to open and swallow me whole.

"Your dick, huh?" Alex's tone is filled with smug satisfaction. Vivian and Nova both lose it and start laughing at my expense.

"On that note, I'll talk to you both later," I grit out.

"No, wait—" I slam the lid closed, cutting Vivian off. I bite down on my lip, refusing to even look at him. I'm so embarrassed and right now I would give anything for him to disappear so I can wallow in my own self-pity in private. He's standing so close I can feel the heat radiating off him and it's doing nothing to calm my raging hormones. How the fuck could I have gone eighteen years without caring about sex or even thinking about it, to it now becoming a constant thought?

"By all means, Bambi, come play with the monster's dick anytime you like." I groan and bury my face in my hands. The bastard laughs. "I'm gonna take a shower, sparring with the guys wasn't the cardio I was hoping to do tonight." I gasp, his innuendo was not fucking subtle. While he showers I decide to clean up all my things and put them away, then climb into bed. Maybe if I try really hard, I'll fall asleep fast for once in my life.

Wishful thinking!

The door opens and I scrunch my eyes closed, not wanting to look at him. The second I do I know I'll salivate at the sight of him, and then my thoughts will go haywire as I picture my pussy clenching around him while he's slamming inside me. When the bed dips from his weight, I bite back the groan from breaking free and remain still, praying he will think I'm asleep.

"I lied." I remain still and unmoving. "I had planned to break down your walls but not in the way you think. I was going to fuck with your head not your body or your... heart. Breaking you was never an option." My breathing turns choppy but I still refuse to open my eyes or let him know I'm awake. "You're right, I had six months of getting to know you. I hated you on sight at the beginning. I thought you would be exactly like your brother and father, but turns out I misjudged you. The longer I watched, the more I learned. You were kind because you could be. You helped because it was the right thing to do. You never used Vivian, you worked your ass off. You protected those girls at the clubs. You never did anything for yourself. In the six months I have been watching you I've never seen you buy a single thing for yourself."

I'm trying to latch onto my anger toward him, but the more he talks the harder it's becoming. I know men like Alex aren't the type to explain themselves or even express their feelings, he's showing me the real him. I slowly open my eyes to find his gaze fixed on me. He smiles but it doesn't reach his eyes. He knew I was faking sleep. I release a sigh and push myself up so my back is resting against the headboard.

"Did you mean it?" I ask quietly, as I tilt my head to the side so I can look at him.

"Mean what?" The soft glow of the bedside lamp makes him look like a glowing star. Alexander Denver is certainly not a star, he's more of a meteorite, something that you only see once in a lifetime.

"That you hate me because of who my brother and father are?"

He flinches and shakes his head. "No, Tatum. I said some fucked up things I never should have. I was angry—"

"That's not an excuse to be a dick, Alex," I chastise him.

He rolls his lips over his teeth to keep from smiling. "This isn't easy for me."

"You think it is for me?" I wail. "I've had my life turned upside down, look at it from my point of view. You've been watching me without me knowing. For months I have lived in fear and a gilded cage because I was waiting for you to finally kill me and now look at me!"

"I am looking at you, Tatum." His tone is serious and I swallow trying not to focus on the intensity in his eyes. "When I told you that you were never supposed to know who we were, I meant it."

"I don't understand."

"The night I called you, I told you to stop looking into us. I knew you wouldn't listen so I convinced the guys we needed to go to you and scare you. They had no idea I had planned to bring you back here."

"Why did you bring me here?"

"Because I wanted you." My eyes round in surprise at his honesty. "I still do and I won't apologize for that. I thought if I just got to spend a day or so with you that you would drop the nice girl act but you didn't. Everything I saw on the videos was real and I don't know how to feel about that."

"What do you feel?" I push.

He exhales and slumps back against the headboard. My heart is racing so fast I'm scared it's about to jump out of my chest.

"I've only ever felt love a few times in my life. I love my parents. I love my brothers and even fucking Carnage, but the person who truly made me feel what love meant was... Ellie. My sister was the one person who could see through my bullshit and force me to feel things I didn't know I could. My sister was the only person I loved with all my heart and ever since she was taken from me..." Tears prick the back of my eyes, I can hear the raw pain in his tone and it's taking everything inside me not to try and comfort him. I need to hear this and he needs to say it. "I've been numb. I haven't felt anything. I used to feel the heat of the sun on my skin but that all stopped when her heart did. I relished in the numbness, it made me focus. I saw my end goal clear as day but then, I met a vulgar mouth blonde who started thawing the ice that filled my veins."

Warmth flows through me. "Just to clarify, I'm the vulgar mouth blonde, right? You don't have another kidnapped chick around here somewhere?" He narrows his eyes clearly, not finding me amusing.

"One of you is enough."

I tilt my head side to side. "I love me but even I have to agree I wouldn't be able to put up with a clone of myself." I shift and move until I'm straddling him. His hands instantly grip my hips through one of his shirts I stole from his drawers. I reach out and skate my fingers through his beard, loving the feeling of its texture.

"What are you doing to me, Tatum?" he whispers.

My brows draw in, I cup his face between my hands and stare into his eyes. "I don't know but I think you're doing it to me as well." My declaration has his eyes filling with carnal pleasure. He knows exactly what he is doing to me and he loves it. His mind may be confused because of the feelings I'm inspiring inside him, but him knowing that he is affecting me as well, has the monster inside him flexing.

CHAPTER TWENTY-THREE

Alexander

I press forward leaving a sliver of space between us, my lips ghost over hers as I speak, sending a shiver through her body. "You're taking up space inside me, Bambi."

Her pupils are blown and her breathing is labored. "I want to own a place inside you, Alex." Her honesty not only shocks her but it stuns me. I push her shirt up and grip the tops of her thighs, loving the way her breath hitches. My cock is twitching and aching to be inside her.

"To be owned by me is worse than death, Bambi."

"How so?" she asks, searching my gaze.

"Because I'll demand everything from you. I'll force you past your breaking point, throw you out of your comfort zone, just so I can be your comfort. I'll take all your favorite things and tarnish them just so I can be the center of your orbit. If I give you all of me I expect the same in return. I've never given anyone this type of power, and believe me when

I tell you that you will hold all the power, because you will be the only person in this world that can destroy me. If you say yes to this, death will be the only way you will ever be free of me. That's what it means to be owned by The Butcher. Can you handle that?"

Her mouth parts and she gasps silently, then bites down on her bottom lip, mulling over my words. I don't push her because I need her to make the choice to come to me. She needs to be the one to make this decision. I never thought I would ever be in a position like the one I am now. I know it's crazy. She's only known me a short time but the feelings I already have for her will only grow over time. She will become my kryptonite, she'll be the only thing in this world that can break me and I need to know she is in this with me.

I need her to need me.

"If I give you all of me, I need the same in return. I'm not the type of girl that you leave on read and never call back. I'm not someone who wants to be kept. I love my job and what I do. I won't give that up. I need to trust you, Alex. I've never had... a boyfriend or been with *anyone.*"

"I'll be the only person you are ever with," I growl.

"What if I say no?"

I grind my teeth and tighten my hold on her thighs. She whimpers and thrusts her hips, then gasps when she feels how hard I am for her. "You can say no but I hope you enjoy living like a nun because I'll kill any cunt you make fuck me eyes toward. I'm a possessive motherfucker it seems when it comes to you. Don't taunt me, Tatum, because I don't play games. If you and I have a disagreement and you take off and think flirting with a guy is a good idea, don't. I'll tie your ass to a chair and make you watch as I slice the fucker open, then make you lick the seal on the envelope containing his heart that I'll mail to his mother."

She throws her head back and laughs, earning a scowl from me, then finally meets my gaze again. "One, I was just fucking with you. Two, I have never found a male attractive until you walked your fine ass into Lividica and changed that. Three, I'm 99.9% sure you already own all of me, if I'm being honest with you and myself."

Words are overrated so I use actions instead. I cup the back of her head, yank her to me and kiss her. I can feel her yearning in the way she melts into me and fights for control of the kiss. This kiss isn't like all the others we have shared, there are secrets between us. We've thrown caution out the fucking window and now, we're both jumping into this thing headfirst. It's reckless and dangerous admitting my feelings for her, but I'll be damned if I let her go and risk her finding some motherfucker that is actually deserving of her. I may be a killer and have a bloodlust that rivals Hannibal, but I want her and I'm keeping her right here with me.

Where she belongs.

When I grip the hem of her shirt and attempt to lift it, she breaks the kiss and grabs my wrists, halting my movement. I stare up at her and see apprehension in her eyes. "What happened in the car, with all of them watching—"

I cut her off. "I'll push every single one of your boundaries except that, I'll never put you in that position again. I swear."

She nods. "Good. Because if you do, I'll rip your fucking balls off and I'll lick the envelope myself that I use to send them back to the guys." A smile scratches across my face, this girl is fucking incredible.

"Deal," I rasp out, then yank the shirt over her head. I toss it to the side, then marvel at the sight of her glorious fucking tits. Reaching out to cup them in my hands, I swipe my thumbs over her nipples, relishing in the shiver that rolls through her. I lean forward and wrap my lips around her hardened peak. She jolts against me and I groan at the feeling of her bare pussy rubbing against my cock. She threads her fingers through my hair and holds me in place as she arches her back, pushing her tit further into my mouth. I bite down and love the way she cries out and tugs on the strands of my hair. I release it with a wet pop and try to switch sides, but the filthy minx yanks my head back and slams her lips on mine, pouring everything she feels into this kiss. Her hips continue to gyrate against me. Don't get me wrong, dry humping as a teenager was fine but I'm not some pubescent kid anymore. I wrap an arm around her waist and lift her slightly without breaking the kiss.

Once I free my cock, I line it up with her entrance. She rests her hands on the tops of my shoulders and takes control. She bats my arm away and grasps my dick, sending a shiver rolling through me. The victorious smile on her face only serves to inflate my ego. When the head of my cock breaches her entrance and I feel how wet she is, I throw my head back and groan.

"Fuck, Bambi," I grit out as she slowly lowers onto me, her eyes locked onto mine. I see nothing but heat in the depth of those baby blues. My hands latch onto her waist and guide her down. The second her tight little cunt engulfs my dick she cries out.

"Holy shit, Alex." She pants, I grip her throat and love the way her eyes widen in surprise. Before I can utter a single word she strikes out and grips my throat. "I'm in control, Butcher." My brows hit my hairline. I slowly disentangle my fingers and raise my hands as if surrendering.

"I can't say I've been choked while being fucked," I admit, uncertainty clouds her features for a moment. When she tries to let go, I grip her arm and hold her hand in place. "I never said I didn't like it," I growl, her eyes widen slightly before smugness overclouds her features. When she lifts up and drops back onto my dick, we both moan. The more she does this the tighter her hold on my throat gets and I start to get the fixation of why women love it when guys choke them while they get fucked. It's euphoric, you're literally trusting the other person with your life. At any moment they could get consumed in their pleasure and not realize their grip has tightened too far and end it all. The thrill of this notion has me saying, "Tighter."

Her eyes blaze and her movements grow hurried, I can feel her growing wetter by the second as she tightens her hand around my throat and slams up and down my cock. I grasp her tits in my hands and pinch her nipples. Fuck, trying everything with her when it concerns sex is going to be a wild as fuck ride and I'm so here for it.

"Alex, I need you—" Before she can even finish, I've flipped us and slammed back inside her. She screams out and the monster inside me preens. She digs her nails into my back and drags them down the scars. I hiss but she doesn't stop. My thrusts turn punishing, matching the tempo of her screams. I'm fucking her so hard the bed is scraping along the wooden floor. Right now nothing matters, we could be under attack and I wouldn't be able to pull out of her. I need her to come on my cock more than I need to breathe. I grip one of her legs and throw it over my shoulder, her eyes roll backward when I slam inside her from this angle. "Fuck yes, just like that," she pleads.

I keep my rhythm and don't change my pace, knowing that she needs me to stay as I am. When her nails dig into the flesh of my ruined back, I know she is about to come.

"Give it to me, Bambi. I want to feel you milk my cock," I growl. Her eyes scrunch shut as her back arches off the bed as she comes with my name tearing from her lips. The monster inside me growls and my thrusts grow hurried as I chase my release. I'm on the verge of climax when she shouts out.

"Come on me, I want to feel it." I pull out of her and grip my cock in my hand. She pushes up on her elbows and watches me with rapt focus.

"Bambi," I grit out through clench teeth as I explode, ropes of my cum landing all over her stomach and tits. I'm panting and trying to wring out every last drop as she runs a finger through my cum, then looks up at me as she runs that finger through her pussy and then pushes it inside herself, moaning. My jaw slackens at the sight. Fuck, she looks so sexy covered in my cum and pushing it inside her.

"All your cum belongs to me. Not that rancid bitch in Chicago, am I clear?" I can't form any words as I watch her pull that finger from her pussy and bring it to her mouth. She wraps those sinful lips around the digit and sucks it clean, whimpering at the taste. She flicks her gaze to me and smirks. "Next time, you're going to let me suck your cock so I can get over my fear of my past experiences, okay?"

"*Okay*," I croak out like a fucking idiot. This damn girl has me tongue tied and wanting to bust a nut again without her even touching me. I can tell my life will never be boring with Tatum Lawson in it, and that notion has me smiling. I press forward, forcing her flat on her back and placing my hands either side of her head. The sultry look on her face has my cock twitching and begging to have those sinful lips wrapped around it. "Baby, that bitch has nothing on you."

I stand at the door and just stare at her sleeping, the sight alone has my heart beating faster inside my chest. Last night I couldn't take my fucking hands off her. After fucking her again she passed out, only to be woken an hour later with my face between her legs, eating that beautiful little cunt. The sounds she makes when she comes or when I slide inside her are addictive, and I find myself wanting them every minute of the day.

Tatum did try to blow me last night. The second her lips wrapped around my cock, she tensed. I pulled back and refused to allow her to try again, the shit she went through isn't going to go away overnight and I told her that. I won't let her try that shit again until I'm sure she's ready for it. She argued she wanted to do it for me and I love that she wanted to try, but she can't do it for me, she needs to want to do it for her.

I've never wanted something for myself. The Denver Kings was started so we could have something of our own. The DK's had nothing to do with me being The Butcher, it was just a family selling firearms. My name and reputation as The Butcher helped us, but no one actually knows who I am. A few of the assholes we have done business with have demanded to meet The Butcher specifically, but I'd say no. They were just too stupid to know that they were speaking to him. When my phone begins to vibrate in my hand again for the third time, I sigh and slip out of my house. I hit answer when I step off the small porch.

"What?" I snap.

"We're all waiting on you," Carnage growls.

"I don't answer to you, nor do my men," I snarl, then end the call. If he plans to stick around, then he needs to learn he doesn't call the shots. When I'm out or occupied that role falls to Omen and Halo, they are my go to. Vat and Pope have no desire to lead and are all too happy to leave the decision making to their brothers. As I round the corner, I spot Carnage pacing the backyard, he has his phone pressed to his ear. I slink against the house and listen, he and I may have been close once but that was a long time ago. I don't trust him, he needs to prove to me his loyalty is with us and not with that fucking snake sister of his.

"Don't fucking lie to me, Dez." I tense and clench my fists at my sides. "If you had nothing to do with his sister's murder then why the fuck is Nexus at *our* house?" he whisper shouts, clearly he's taking this call outside so the others don't overhear. I hold my breath and fucking hope that he isn't trying to double cross us because he is one person I won't enjoy killing. "That's bullshit!" he snaps. A moment passes as he listens to her reply. "No, I have stood by you, Desire, and helped you take down every single rival family so no one would oppose your rule, but you couldn't even trust me enough to tell me the fucking truth!" This time he doesn't try to disguise his voice, he's shouting. "Rage and Wrath were in on dad's murder, you tricked Alex! Everything he said about you is true." I should feel happy that he's finally seeing the real side of his sister, but I'm not. "You want me to come back then prove to me you didn't have anything to do with a sixteen year old fucking kid being murdered and I swear to God I will go to war against our brothers and risk Alex tearing me apart." I wait with bated breath, I need to hear how this plays out. "That's what I thought," he snaps and ends the call.

I scrub a hand down my face and sigh. "You make a habit of hiding behind corners?" I bite back my smirk and round the side of the house to face Carnage.

"You knew I was there?" He exhales and nods. "Did you get the answers you wanted?"

He shakes his head. "Believe it or not, Butch, I don't like the rivalry between me and my siblings, never have."

"You got a funny way of showing it."

His eyes narrow. "Do you know how hard it is for me to see my own twin view you as a brother but he hates me. Halo wouldn't piss on me if I was on fire." Bitterness laces his words.

"And you only have yourself to blame for that. I never turned any of them against you. You did that when you chose to side with her and do nothing when your stepmother was raping your fucking brother!" I roar. He flinches but remains silent. "Roberto made them fight for their lives, the only time you ever did anything to help them was when Halo nearly died. You blamed him for the beating you received—"

"He told me if I helped them again he would kill them all!" he screams just as the back door opens to reveal Halo and Pope standing there. Carnage hasn't seen them yet so he keeps going. "Every time they were made to fight I tried to help. I would slip those cocksuckers a pill or something just to give them a fighting chance. When I killed that fucker for trying to break Halo's neck, Roberto told me if I ever did anything to help Halo again, he would have ten of his best men go at him while I watched my twin brother be beaten to death. So, yes, Alex, I left my brothers alone and acted like I didn't care so they would fucking live. My absence seemed to work in your favor though, didn't it?"

My face blanks and shows no emotion. "And how is that?" I say in a deathly calm tone.

"You got my father to turn against me and you even took my brothers away."

Before I can answer, Halo does. "He didn't need to sway us." Carnage whirls around to see Halo and Pope standing there, Vat and Omen standing behind them. "He proved to us years ago that he was there to help, you were just more concerned about pussy and making daddy happy."

"The fuck I was!" Carnage explodes. Halo rushes forward until there is a foot of space between them. I press forward ready to intervene if I need to.

"You checked out on us long before he died!" I flinch at the hurt in Halo's tone. I've always known Carnage's choice to stay with Desire has hurt him, but he would never admit it until now. "You chose that bitch over us. She never loved Alex like you thought. She just wanted him because she knew Dad liked him more than all of us, he was her meal ticket. Roberto was going to hand the De Santis family over to him once he married her." I stumble back a step. I look at the others and they all seem just as shocked as I am.

"What?" Car rasps out.

Halo smiles but its filled with malice. "Yeah, how's that for a bombshell? Alex had no idea he was being used by that bitch. I overheard her talking to Roberto one night. She was furious that he was handing the family business to her future husband and not her." Halo swivels to face me and I can see the regret in his eyes for keeping this from me. "I believe you. I know you killed him for us, but she used that against you. She wanted him dead because she knew you would become the new don of our family and Desire couldn't allow that."

CHAPTER TWENTY-FOUR

Tatum

One week...

This past week has been filled with tension, everyone around here is on edge and waiting for the Cosa Nostra to attack. Alex is gone nearly every day, meeting with people and securing deals. I have no idea what that means but that's what Omen tells me. Every night he comes home, waking me by sliding inside me and making me see stars.

Fuck, he's an addiction I don't want to kick.

I'm catching up on work. It's hard working remotely. I tried to talk to Alex about me leaving to check on Lividica and the builds in New York and Miami but he flat out said no, then walked off. I've been trying to calm myself down for the past hour but it's not working. Who the fuck does he think he is to tell me I can't leave? I can't even yell at him because he left right after he denied me. I called Omen and tried to get him on my side, but the bastard just laughed and said helping me wasn't worth the beating. Apparently *Alex is too pussy whipped* according to Omen, so he wouldn't take it well if they dropped me at the airport for the second time.

To my utter dismay Vat, Omen, Pope and Halo have gone with Alex today, leaving me alone with Carnage. I could go back to Alex's house and wallow in my misery there but I'm too intrigued by Carnage and his pacing. I sit here and watch him for a while, wondering what has him so worked up that he can't even sit still for a second. I know out of all of the guys, he's been the one who is taking this whole thing harder. I can see the tension between him and the others, it's clear he is the outcast and he's struggling with that,

"Stop staring at me!" I jerk in fright. I shake my head to clear my thoughts and face Carnage. His eyes are narrowed and his upper lip is lifted in a sneer.

"Stop pacing then I'll stop watching," I fire back.

"Fuck off back to Alex's house," he snaps.

"Make me, asshole," I clap back. When he takes a step toward me I slink further into the sofa, ready to kick him if he even tries to touch me.

"You have a bad mouth, anyone ever tell you that?"

I roll my eyes. "Have you missed the hundred million times Alex has told me to watch my *vulgar mouth?*" I say in a mocking tone. To my surprise Carnage cracks a smile, the sight of it on his face is strange to see.

"You know what, keep cussing, I love seeing the defeated look on his face every time you say *fuck.*" Without consent, laughter breaks free of me. I've never cussed as much before in my life, but the fact I know it pisses Alex off, I try to do it as often as I can. Like yesterday, I just walked around the house saying *fucking ass* for the fun of it. I watched him grow tense every time the word left my mouth, until he finally snapped and oh sweet baby Jesus he fucked me into submission and had me promising to never say fuck again... but clearly I lied, because I called him a fucking prick just before he left.

"You like fucking with him, don't you?" I ask.

A sly smile works its way onto his face. "Yeah. It used to be one of my favorite things to do." I hear the nostalgia in his tone.

"Why didn't you go with them?" I find myself asking.

He sighs then rubs the back of his neck. "Apparently you can't be trusted to be on your own, so someone has to babysit you." My jaw slackens.

"That son of a bitch," I hiss.

Carnage smirks. "He cares about you, he just wants to make sure you're safe."

"And you volunteered for the job today?"

He purses his lips. "Not exactly."

I narrow my eyes skeptically. "Why didn't you really go?"

"Because they are meeting with the Vatel family and let's just say Carlito doesn't exactly like me." I cock my head to the side and raise my brows, he rolls his eyes then adds, "I slept with his daughter, then I fucked his family over. There, happy now?" I just pinch my lips closed and nod.

"Yeah. That was exactly what I was expecting," I admit.

"What the hell's that supposed to mean?" he growls.

I shrug. "Every male is always getting in trouble over a female."

"You're a female," he points out.

"Duh, but this war isn't over me."

"It's still over a female," he counters.

"She isn't just some female he fucked, that girl was his everything," I hiss with an edge to my tone.

"You didn't even know her."

"I don't need to know her. I know him and that's enough for me."

"Your life is on the line because of him, his need for revenge for the death of his sister has put a target on your back, Tatum. My sister is a jealous bitch and won't let you walk away with Alex. She may have wanted to use him so she could rule the family, but I think some sick twisted part of her really does love him." My brows pinch as I mull over his words.

"She can come after me... she can do her worst and kill me, but she still won't win him. Alex isn't a prize, he isn't a man who wants to be won or tamed. To love him is to love both sides of him."

"How so?" he counters.

I shrug. "Alexander Denver is two people. One side of him is sweet and attentive, slightly overbearing and a possessive asshole... but the other side, that's the side of him that the world gets to see. The Butcher. The monster he has lurking just beneath the surface. The one that thirsts for vengeance for the sister who was stolen from him. To truly control the beast he needs to be fed and it cuts me up inside to say this aloud, but the only way to truly satisfy that beast inside him is to... kill my brother. Only then will the demons of his past set him free."

"I can't say I have ever heard anyone refer to that dick as sweet before." I shoot him a look.

"That's just because you don't know that side of him like I do."

His eyes turn serious and I tense. "I don't think anyone *alive* has ever seen that side of him, Tatum." His words hang heavy between us for a brief moment before he continues on. "He's a good man, he's one of the best I have ever known. I wasn't jealous of Alex because he had my father's attention." His admission shocks me. "I was jealous because I envied him, I wanted to be just like him. Leading comes easy to him, he can garner the respect of every man within a few minutes. After my father was killed, all his men turned to Alex for guidance. If he took control, the men would have followed him without question. I'm torn much like you because I know my sister won't survive The Butcher. Our men will never rise against their true don."

"You mean Alex?" I whisper.

He nods. "He's the one who should have led the family, it was always his destiny to be the head of the De Santis family." I hear no bitterness or jealousy in his tone, just respect and understanding.

"You want me to *butcher* you? Is that it?" I scream as I hurl the fork in my hand at him. He ducks just in time and it sails over him. He stands to his full height and glares at me. I scowl right back because fuck this Aztec god looking motherfucker. I spy Pope, Halo, Vat, Omen and Carnage all peaking their heads around the corner to watch the show.

"What the fuck have I told you about throwing shit at me, Tatum?" Alex roars.

I snort and flip him off. "Suck a dick, asshole!" I scream as I reach for the cup, but before I throw it at his asshole-ish head, he rushes me and grips my wrist. He applies enough pressure to my joint, forcing me to drop it back to the counter. I try to shove him off but he's too damn big. He grips my waist and lifts me, placing my ass on the edge of the counter. He forces his way between my legs. "I'll bite your damn nose off if you try to kiss me," I seethe, the bastard just smirks which fuels my anger more.

The cocky fuck wraps an arm around my waist and uses his other hand to cup my cheek. To anyone else this move would look loving but the firmness of his hold betrays him. "Throw something at me again and you won't like the punishment," he forces out.

"Tell me some mafia fuck wants you to marry their daughter again and I'll burn your damn house down with you in it," I clap back.

He rolls his eyes. "I already told you, I refused his offer!" he snaps. I shove against his chest, forcing him to drop his hold on my face but he doesn't step back.

"I don't care!" I cross my arms over my chest and can't stop the pout from working its way to my face.

"How is it that you can piss me the hell off and instead of wanting to kill you, all I want to do is fuck you." I tilt my head and bat my lashes.

"Probably because I'm not some mafia princess like you're used to fucking?" My tone is thick with sarcasm. Alex groans and cranes his neck back to stare up at the ceiling. His hands cover the tops of my thighs. He leans forward until his forehead touches mine, I can see the anger slowly dissipating from his eyes but I can't say the same for my own.

"I fucked *one* mafia heiress—"

"Only one?" I mock.

His grip on my thighs tighten until I wince, "I am not going to stand here and argue with you—"

"Good, fuck off then, because I'm not staying with you tonight," I fire back.

"Oh fuck no, she is not staying here," Pope shouts. Alex snaps his head toward the five of them and frowns. All of their eyes widen, those pussies just got caught eavesdropping.

"Would you fucking idiots piss off and start arranging the shit we need done?" Alex hisses.

Halo groans. "But it was just getting good and you haven't even told her about—"

"Shut the fuck up," Alex snaps, cutting him off. Omen grabs the scruff of Halo's shirt and drags him away while the others follow close behind. When Alex turns back to me, I eye him skeptically.

"What aren't you telling me?" I push, his eyes darken and I know without a doubt me finding out he was offered the Vatel's little bitches hand in marriage isn't the only bomb he is going to drop on me.

"Devon has found us a way in." My brows raise.

"That's a good thing, right?"

He nods. "Yes, but you won't like how it has to happen."

I uncross my arms and skate my fingers through his beard. He smiles sexually and I allow him to relax slightly, then I yank on the strands pulling him to me. He growls and tries to break free but it is futile, I just tighten my hold.

"Tatum, I'll fucking—"

"You won't do shit because you enjoy fucking me too much. You and I both know you like me way too much to get rid of me, so shut the hell up." He grinds his teeth so hard I can hear it. "Start telling me the whole story or I'm going to start acting like a real fucking brat."

"Watch your vulgar mouth!" he warns. "You always act like a brat unless my cock is inside you, then you suddenly become compliant."

I release him and shoot him a bitchy look. "Not my fault the dick is good," I mutter which just has him smiling. This time when he presses forward and rests his hands on either side of me, I sigh and wrap my arms around his neck and hug him. Just the contact from him has my anxiety and some of my worry over him leaving me for some rich princess easing. "Don't choose her over me," I whisper. His arms band tighter around me.

"Bambi, I feel like I can't breathe when you're not around. My whole fucking focus these days is you. You take the air out of my lungs every time you walk in the room. There is no chance of me choosing anyone over you." He pushes me back and cups my face between his hands, then bends so we are eye level. "I'm going to need you to trust me, baby. Can you do that?"

I don't even hesitate, "I can do that," I whisper. He smiles then places a chaste kiss on my lips.

"Good. I need you to hear me out before you start shouting and cursing me out, okay?" I blow out a breath and nod. "I have to go to Chicago and you can't come." I roll my lips over my teeth and keep my anger in check.

"And why do I have to stay back?" I ask in a strained tone, fighting to keep my composer.

Alex exhales and his eyes take on a pleading look that has me turning rigid. The look in his eyes is putting me on edge and I don't like it. It's surreal how in such a short span of time I can read him and the worst of it, he has a power over me that I never gave him. He took it without me even knowing and it's scary as hell. He told me I had the power to destroy him but what he doesn't realize is he now holds the same power over me.

"I'm meeting with Desire alone."

He's starting to huff and puff, he's about to blow my house down, I can feel it.

CHAPTER TWENTY-FIVE

Alexander

The tension in the room is so thick you could cut it with a butcher knife.

My muscles are coiled as I wait for her to explode. I keep darting my gaze from her to the cup sitting on the counter beside her, waiting for the second she reaches for it and launches it at my head. When she exhales and slides off the counter to stand before me, I don't move. I stand here rigidly waiting. I feel like I'm waiting for one of my enemies to make a move against me when in reality, I think I'm more scared of the five-foot-five blonde standing before me who has no trouble bringing me to my knees whenever she so pleases.

She reaches out and places a hand on my chest. I flinch on instinct expecting pain. When she flicks her gaze up and I see the torment in her eyes my breath hitches.

"Okay." The weight and anguish in that one word nearly

flays me open on the spot. I attempt to reach for her but she sidesteps my touch. I frown but she shakes her head. "You need to close the door on your past before you can fully open the door to the future you could have with me." When she takes a step away from me, I grab her arm, forcing her to stop but she won't face me.

"What the fuck does that mean?" I hiss.

"It means you need to work out what really matters to you. You told me to never go out and flirt with a guy to make you jealous or you would kill him. Imagine how I feel right now, hearing that you're about to meet with your ex—hang on, no sorry your *ex-fiancée*."

I release my hold on her as if she burned me. "Tatum, this meeting with her is just a distraction—" She whirls around and faces me, her eyes burn with unfiltered anger.

"I don't care what it is," she yells. "Not only are you meeting with your ex, you're about to kill my brother so forgive me for not being overjoyed by your plan, Alex." She runs a hand through her hair in frustration. "A sibling for a sibling, right?" she says quietly before stalking out. I don't attempt to stop her because no matter what I say, I won't be able to take her pain. I grip the edge of the counter and hang my head, never before have I ever been so conflicted when it came to executing a plan.

"Omen went after her." I turn my head to the side to see Vat and Halo standing there. I nod, unable to formulate words. "She's eighteen, Alex. This is a lot for anyone to handle. She's still young and saying things she doesn't mean." I appreciate Vatican trying to help but his words mean nothing.

"Her age means nothing," I grit out.

"You've had years of time to live and experience shit, she's still young and falling in love with anyone is hard, but falling in love with *The Butcher* is a fucking tough pill to swallow. The child in her still yearns for the family she was denied. The man she is in love with is about to kill the only person that matters most to her."

I glare at Halo. "He killed my sister," I growl in a tone that has him raising his hands in surrender.

"All I'm saying is, do you think she will be able to look at you when you come home with her brother's blood on your hands?" Halo doesn't wait around for a reply. Vat meets my stare with an intense look in his eyes.

"Take it from someone who fell in love with a girl that I never got a chance to tell how I really felt. Don't allow your thirst for vengeance to outweigh what could be your future. She's good for you, Alex, and I would give anything to have a shot with Ellie again, but you're pissing away your chance with an amazing girl. Don't blow it, because living with regret is worse than death."

I find myself standing here, watching her sleep again. The peaceful look on her face calms the beast inside me. I would give anything to slide under those sheets and devour her pussy like it's my last meal, but getting lost in her won't solve the problems we both face. She needs to know that I can't allow him to live even if he is her brother. I care about her deeply but my feelings toward her won't change the outcome.

I take one last lingering look at her and hope that she will be able to forgive me for what I am about to do. Last night we used each other as an escape, we may be angry and hurting but that just fueled the need to fuck and made sex crazy, hot and fucking messy. She wanted to take control last night but I refused, she needed to be reminded what it was like to be owned and dominated by me. I felt every ounce of her anger last night, the way she took it out on my dick was fucking incredible. She had me busting a nut like a teenage boy.

The second I step outside, I close off all my emotions, my head needs to be clear and in the game. Carlito Vatel has given his word to back the Denver Kings and not to come to the De Santis's aide if they call. The Torrence, Vanchino and Merkule families have also agreed to stay out of it. Their conditions were all the same, they wanted to know the true face of The Butcher. When I announced who I was, they were outraged that all these years they had met me but had no idea I was the one picking off their top guys and forcing them to bend the knee to Desire before I left. With the four of them out of the game, this will be a fight that will come down to who wants it more and win.

Devon's intel has proven good. At this time the De Santis family outnumbers us three to one. The odds aren't great but unlike Desire, all my men have been trained like real soldiers. They know how to blend, hunt, shoot, fight and if needed, they know how to end themselves so they aren't used to extract information. That is a last resort only. I may be private and quiet when it comes to my life, but not when it concerns knowing everything about each person who joins our ranks. When leaders grow too cocky and stop vetting every person who joins them, that's how you get rats.

If you treat your men well and listen to what they have to say, as well as compensating them accordingly, they will remain loyal. Never give anyone a reason to turn against you. I've had that happen before in the De Santis family when Desire took over, killing my own men isn't something I relish.

When I reach the main house, I don't bother going inside. I head around the front to see my brothers waiting for me. Adrian, Marko and Damon are waiting as well. They will be the heads of the three teams we have put together. Each one of them is kitted out with firearms, knives and Kevlar vests. I run my gaze over each of them. Pope and Omen look ready to fight. Halo and Vatican both have blank looks on their faces which tells me they are in the zone and keeping out of their heads. Adrian, Marko and Damon all nod, letting me know they are ready to go. Carnage is the last to draw my attention, unlike the others he stands there looking at me with uncertainty.

"If you aren't ready to commit to this a hundred percent, then you need to back out now, I won't have you being a liability for the rest of us," I say in an even tone.

He releases a breath and shakes his head. "Alex, she gave you two weeks." I quirk a brow urging him to continue. "You know she is a liar, she would have attacked you by now and taken you off guard."

"She doesn't know where we are," Omen states.

Car keeps his gaze on me as he answers. "Something isn't right, brother. I can feel it in my gut. I know her and—"

"You want to be a pussy, then fuck off back inside and stay here with Tate," Halo snaps.

Carnage shoots him a scathing look. "I'm no fucking pussy. Out of all of us, I'm the one who knows that cunning bitch the best and I am telling you something is off." I mull over his words for a minute and debate changing the plan.

"Alex, we have the men in place waiting for us in Chicago. She has no idea we are coming, now is the time to strike," Pope hedges.

I nod in agreement but now that Carnage has voiced his worries, I can't stop thinking he may be right. "Let's go." I find myself saying. Car sighs and shakes his head but climbs into one of the cars. I move to follow the guys, but Halo places a hand on my chest and flicks his head to something behind me. I slowly turn and follow his gaze to see Tatum standing in the shadows by the house looking... nervous.

"Say goodbye. I'll send the others ahead and wait for you in the car," Halo says. I nod, then head toward her slowly. She really does look like a deer caught in the headlights right now. I hate seeing the war of emotions in her eyes.

Pain.

Worry.

Anger.

... Love.

Before I can get too close she darts her arm and places her hand on my chest, forcing me to a stop. She cranes her neck back and stares up at me with glassy eyes. She's fighting back her tears and I itch to reach out, cup her face between my hands and kiss her, wanting to ease her worries but I can't. I won't pity her.

"Don't go," she whispers.

My shoulders hunch. "Bambi—"

"Just listen," she says, cutting me off. I nod and watch as she inhales a deep breath and squares her shoulders. "I know what this means for you. I swear I do understand and if I was in your shoes I probably would be wanting the same thing. But I'm not in your shoes and you have a chance to change the outcome. I know what he did is unforgivable and despicable but he is still my brother." I push her hand away and cup her face. A whimper escapes her when I bend down and claim her lips. Pain ricochets inside me when I pull back and rest my forehead against hers. She grabs my wrists in a vice-like hold and meets my gaze with a pleading edge.

"We're at war, baby," I say quietly. "I've always known I wouldn't live to an age where I would get gray hair and I've made my peace with that." Her brows draw in and her eyes brim with anguish. "Loving me is like loving time, you'll never know how long you have. Today my hour glass might just run out but not before I set out to finish what I started three years ago." Her eyes widen as my words slowly sink in. "I'm sorry, Tatum. My heart may now beat for you and you alone, but it beat for her first." She tries to pull back but I don't let go. "I love you, Tatum Lawson, but my heart isn't in charge today, my head is, which means your brother will die by my hands." I take a risk and place a chaste kiss to her lips, then release her. I turn my back and stalk toward the car, ignoring the sound of her crying.

I climb in the passenger seat and nod to Halo. He plants his foot on the gas and because I'm a masochist I look at the side mirror and watch as she drops to her knees and buries her face in her hands.

"You good?" Halo asks quietly.

"I think I just lost the only woman I have ever loved," I admit.

He sucks in a sharp inhale. "Shit. I didn't see that coming," he mutters.

I shrug. "Yeah, neither did I."

"If she feels the same, she'll—"

I cut him off before he could finish. "Don't do that."

"Do what?"

"Make excuses. You and I both know that if we were in her shoes we would never forgive us either." My anger and pain begins to blend inside me and it's clouding my thoughts.

"Don't fucking lash out at me, but Tate is here, in the flesh and breathing. Ellie isn't. She would want you to be happy and we can all see Tate does that for you, brother. I've never seen you like this before. You stopped smiling when Ellie died, but that girl back there, she is bringing you back from the darkness you've been living in."

I scrub a hand down my face and growl. "Enough. My decision is made. I promised my sister I would avenge her and that is what I'm going to do. I may be a piece of shit but even I don't break my word. Nexus Valerian will die and that is final."

He sighs beside me. "And Desire?"

Bloodlust blooms inside me and my mouth begins to water as the images of what I plan to do to her and Nexus run through my mind like a movie. "Her and Nexus will keep each other company while I work on them slowly."

He exhales loudly and nods. "And the twins?"

I shrug. "That's up to you guys." He nods but I can see there is more he wants to say. "Spit it out, Halo."

"Okay. I know what you have planned for Desire. I may hate Carnage but I could never kill him."

I pick up what he's putting down. "I'm not asking any of you to take part in what I have planned for her." He visibly relaxes. "Will the four of you still be by my side when I finish this or will you all take the same stance as Tatum?"

Halo turns and looks at me with an angry scowl on his face. "You're our brother. We'll be by your fucking side until we're all in wooden boxes or a glass jar burnt to a crisp. We're with you always, brother."

CHAPTER TWENTY-SIX

Tatum

I gather my strength and force myself to stand, my eyes are red and puffy from the tears but I don't care. My heart is breaking inside my chest. Not only am I terrified for what may happen to my brother, but I'm scared Alex won't come back. My mind and heart are warring—one is telling me being with Alex is wrong, he's a serial killer and plans to murder my brother. But the other part, that part is telling me that he is a good man and is just driven by his pain.

Loving me is like loving time, you'll never know how long you have.

His words play on repeat in my head. Is this what it will be like being with him? Him sneaking out before the sun has even risen so he can go off and kill people while I sleep soundly in his bed?

Tatum, my heart may now beat for you and you alone, but it beat for her first.

I don't think I can compete with a ghost. I hold no ill feelings toward Elenor or anything like that, but just knowing that he is starting a war for her, makes me second guess everything. I know Nexus admitted to hurting her but what if it was all just words to hurt me because I wouldn't leave with him?

I love you, Tatum Lawson, but my heart isn't in charge today, my head is, which means your brother will die by my hands.

Bile rushes up my throat and I turn to the side to empty the contents of my stomach. Once I'm finished, I stumble inside the main house and grab a glass of water to rinse the acidic taste out of my mouth. I splash some water on my face and try to gain control of my thoughts and formulate a plan.

4221 means forever together to love one another.

I jerk in surprise as Nova's voice rings out in my head. I remember asking her about what the numbers meant that Vox had tattooed and then showed me hers, and told me that it was something her and her best friend had always said to each other. At that time, I had no care for anything or anyone so the numbers and their meaning meant nothing to me... until now. My chest constricts and I gasp for air. I reach up and clutch at my heart.

Holy fuck, am I in love with Alexander Denver?

I stand up straight and take a deep breath, trying to center myself.

"I mean, I do have feelings for him but love?" I say aloud to no one. Is that why him leaving and me being scared I'll never see him again hurts so much? He just told me he loved me and I said nothing! But, love doesn't change the outcome of what's going to happen, does it?

I pull my phone out of my pocket and start texting him as I make my way over to the sofa and drop down unceremoniously.

Me - Did you mean it? 👀

I nibble on my lip as I wait for him to reply. When the three dots don't appear after nearly an hour, I start typing out another message but my phone rings, cutting me off. I frown at the sight of the random number. It's only like five in the morning but I answer it because it could be a work emergency.

"Hello?"

"Does it bother you that he left you alone and unguarded?" I lurch to my feet at the sound of her voice and look around the room as if expecting someone to be in here with me. "He thought he was smart, but you and I both know women are smarter than men."

I scoff. "You have no fucking idea what I am capable of," I seethe.

She tsks and it grates on my nerves, but I refuse to allow my emotions to get the better of me. "Oh, but you see, Tatum, I know everything he does because he wasn't the only one watching you." My veins fill with ice. "From the very moment Nexus came to me and told me Alex knew everything, we started tracking you and watching," she purrs in a smug tone.

"Why?" I breathe out, feeling more defeated than ever hearing from the cunts mouth that my brother really isn't innocent. I can no longer pull the wool over my own eyes and try to deny that my own flesh and blood is a monster.

"Because he was powerless when it came to you. I'm sure you know by now that you look similar to her, different colored eyes but everything else is the same." A silent gasp escapes me. "Nexus wanted to bring you with him but the second he showed me a photo of you, I knew he wouldn't be able to resist."

I take a deep breath and force myself to ignore her taunts and play her game. "Hmm, does it bother you he didn't kill me?" I say in a cocky tone.

"Not at all, I had hoped he would, but him leaving you breathing meant he finally had a weakness."

"You see, I don't believe you." It brings a smile to my face when I hear her growl. "It must fuck with you every single day knowing he's sliding his cock inside me every chance he gets." I moan just to drive my point home. "I bet you enjoyed it just as much as I do when he flips you over on your hands and knees and eats your pussy from behind while sliding his thumb over your ass driving you insane, wondering if tonight is the night he finally—"

"I'm going to slit your throat while he watches." Laughter comes from me.

"Aww, don't be like that, Desire. I thought we were friends?" I mock.

"You think you're so smart, don't you?"

"I know I am."

"Hmmm, did you wonder how I knew you were home alone?" My eyes widen and my breath hitches but I refuse to crumble now, I won't let this bitch beat me.

"Not really, I'm too occupied thinking about where I'm going to fuck Alex tonight."

"Oh, well that may be a bit hard considering the man

himself is cuffed to the seat beside me." I falter for one fucking second and that's all she needs to know she has won. "Oh come on, we were just getting to know each other! Don't go silent on me now, Tate."

I drop all pretenses and force iron into my tone. "If what you're saying is true, I'll come after you," I vow.

Her mocking laughter only serves to grate on my nerves. I hear the sound of a car and rush toward the other side of the house to peak out the window to see one of the cars from this morning skidding to a stop. Omen, Vatican and Carnage both jump out then rush to the trunk of the car. I frown as I watch Pope and Halo both climb out covered in blood, carrying Alex's guy Damon. I look at the driveway waiting for the other two cars to appear.

"I think you're starting to believe me now, aren't you?" The guys all bust through the door and go straight to the living room. Carnage and Omen both stop at the sight of me and frown. I mouth *Desire*. Both their faces morph into unfiltered fury and anger radiates off them. "Oh, did my brothers just get home?"

My own emotions begin to feed off theirs and I latch onto it. "They aren't your brothers, they are Alex's."

"I think—"

"I don't give a fuck what you think," I say, cutting her off. "What I know is that you are going to die, very fucking slowly if you don't give him back to me."

"You listen to me, you little cunt. You are nothing but a hole for him to sink his cock into. You are nothing. He will be punished for breaking the rules of our agreement and then I'll come for you."

I smirk, forcing Omen and Carnage to frown at me.

"Hey, Desire? Do me a favor and tell my boyfriend I love him too and that I'll be seeing him real, *real* soon."

"You stupid—" I end the call before she can finish. I take a minute to center myself and get my thoughts together before meeting Omen's gaze.

"What happened?" My tone is firm and filled with strength which surprises me given how rattled I am.

"It was a setup, they knew we were flying out this morning. Adrian and Marko didn't make it. Damon is hanging on by a thread. She only got Alex because Desire threatened to kill the five of us if he didn't go with her. Plus, all our men are trapped in Chicago ."

"Why are they trapped?" I ask.

Omen sighs and runs a hand through his hair clearly agitated. "We don't know who is leaking the intel, we can't risk moving them or going after Desire until we figure that out." I gnaw on my bottom lip as I mull over her words. Omen and Carnage stand there watching me as I try and work it all out, the shouting from the other's in the living room becomes white noise.

"I'm just going to point out that you just went and became my sister's sole focus," Carnage says.

"Why?" I push.

"You just declared Alex as your boyfriend and I quote, you told her to tell him that *you love him too*. Alex has never said those words to anyone before."

I narrow my eyes at the bastard. "Well he said them to me this morning."

He nods. "I don't doubt it. I could tell from the second I saw him with you that he had fallen." His declaration has warmth filling me but I tamper that shit down and latch back onto my anger. I need to focus and all thinking about Alex will do is cloud my mind with worry, and I can't have that shit happening.

"She knew I was here alone," I mutter and start to think of all the possibilities.

"Yeah, she saw all of us—"

I cut Omen off before he can finish. "No. She knew that all the guards were gone. How would she know that? No one in Chicago would know that either, would they?" Both of them mull over my words for a moment before they both shake their heads. I keep wracking my brain for a minute until it hits me. "It's not a someone!" I shout as I barge past them and head for the living room.

"What the hell are you talking about?" Carnage snaps. I ignore him as I move around the guys who are... yeah, that is so gross! Halo is stitching Damon's chest closed. I grab my laptop then head back to the kitchen. I hold it out to Omen who just looks from it to me with a frown.

"No one snitched, she knows everything because of me," I admit bitterly.

Omen's eyes darken. "What the hell does that mean?" he growls.

"I sent an email to Vivian last night after Alex told me he was leaving me here alone." Omen just stares at me confused. When Carnage growls I turn to him.

"Her laptop is bugged!" he snaps.

Omen shakes his head. "No, Halo checked it and—"

"You idiot, it's a fucking iMac, you can download apps on that thing. Did he check every fucking one?" At Carnage's outburst, Omen reels back and stares at the laptop like it might leap out of my hands and bite him. I roll my eyes and throw it as hard as I can to the ground. It cracks and bounces but I'm not done. I stomp on it a couple of times before Carnage shoves me backward, picks up the broken thing and then dumps it in the sink and runs water over it. I pull my work phone out of my pocket and toss it to him. He dumps it in the sink as well.

"That phone was linked to the laptop, the only one I have left is the burner Alex gave me to call him," I tell them.

"Damon is patched. He's gonna be down for a few days but he'll survive," Halo says as he comes to stand beside Omen. "And to answer your question, no I didn't check the apps. Alex didn't want me to go through her things."

My heart constricts hearing that. "How did she put a bug or whatever in my laptop?" I ask him.

He smacks his lips together and tilts his head side to side. "She would have had to have had the laptop with her to download the app. The firewall I put in place can't be hacked so it would have had to have happened—"

"Months ago," I utter. Halo purses his lips. "Desire wasn't the one who bugged my laptop," I confess.

"You know who did it, don't you?" Carnage hedges.

I nod. "The only person who had access to my laptop months ago was my brother. I think Nexus was the one who bugged it. I think that's how he knew which club I would be at because my phone and laptop are linked." Now that I've said it aloud, it makes sense and I fucking hate that it does, because it means from the start of all of this he used me!

"Everyone, give me your phones. I'm going to run a deep clean on all of them to make sure." Halo turns to focus on me directly. "Do you have any more of those burner phones?"

I shake my head. "I tossed them all when I got back here

and made my decision to trust Alex." He smiles sadly and nods.

"I hate to say it but you chose right. He would never use you, Tate. You can trust him." I hear the truth in his words but I already knew that. Alex has proven to be overbearing and controlling but he's always had valid reasons. Like kidnapping me. He just wanted to be closer to me. In the start I thought he was crazy and out of his ever loving mind, but now that I know him, I know he only did it because he cared about me. If he didn't take me, I would have still been living my life blissfully unaware that my brother was a lying, scheming piece of shit!

"Fix the phones, sort Damon out, then we need to formulate a plan and get our asses to Chicago pronto." All five of them swing their gazes at me in shock. "What?"

Omen smiles proudly and nods. "Leadership looks good on you." I feel heat creeping into my cheeks.

"You can't come with us." I glare at Carnage.

"Why the hell not?"

"Do you even know how to fight?" he fires back.

I smirk. "I was raised in the system, of course I know how to fight, and I plan to use all the skills I have learned throughout my life to murder your cunt of a sister, who Omen should have absorbed in the womb."

CHAPTER TWENTY-SEVEN

Alexander

There's beauty in torture.

To do what I do you have to have a certain artistry to yourself, carving the flesh from a body is a skill you master over time. If I ever had to give up doing what I do, I would become a mortician. Death fascinates me. It's not something that can be avoided. Death is inevitable, that's why life is so precious and revered because you only live once.

This stupid bitch thinks chaining me up in the very room I used to extract information from many men will have me crumbling and begging for mercy. I'll never beg. Pleading for my life is something I'll never do. Pain is but a fleeting moment and I've survived hell. Whatever she or those fucking idiot twins have planned won't break me. Even if they do succeed in killing me, their brothers will come after them and finish the job I failed to complete.

I know the game she's playing. She tried to get into my

head when she held a gun to Omen's head and said I either come with her willingly or she'll kill them. I agreed without complaint, because one life as opposed to five is not worth it. My life doesn't mean more than theirs. On the plane she had me chained and fucking cuffed to the seat with a gag in my mouth. The dirty fucking rat called Tatum beside me and had it on speaker. Just the sound of her voice calmed the wild rage festering inside me. The way Tate fought back without breaking down and threatening Desire made me hard, but when she said she loved me too, that shit solidified something inside me. It was like something inside me revived and for the first time in years, I could breathe without pain.

Desire saw it in my eyes. She knew I would never come back to her or even work for her again. Yes, I fucked her but I never felt anything romantic toward the twisted bitch. Desire is the type of woman to jump from bed to bed if it meant gaining more power. As soon as I found out she was fucking her way through her father's men, I stopped sticking my dick in her washed up cum dumpster. The second we landed in Chicago, she had her men bring me straight here. From the hunger pains and how thirsty I am I would say I've been chained in here for at least two or three days. I can't feel my arms, they went dead hours after they were chained above my head. My ankles are cuffed, my shirt and pants were cut off, leaving me in my boxers.

They cranked up the AC in here and have blasted some heavy metal shit nonstop to try and get me to lose my shit and go a little insane, but their methods are pitiful and fucking pointless. To truly break someone, you need to find what they care about most and take that away from them, then break their bodies. Induce as much pain as you can while never giving into their pleas. The tactics they are using are childish and half assed, and honestly, I'm offended. When you have someone like me in your midst, you pull out all the stops and hold nothing back.

When the music finally stops my ears ring and for a good few minutes I'm unable to hear anything except for the ghost of the music that has been playing nonstop. I don't show any signs of relief or even change my breathing because I know they are watching, they're trying to figure out what my breaking point is. They'll never find it because she's already dead. They have no leverage on me. The AC is the next thing to go. I fight not to smirk because this shit is hilarious. Desire tried to get me to train a few of her men in my artistry but I refused. This isn't something that can just be taught, there is a hunger and a need that you have to have before you can even stomach the thought of doing what I do. If this is the best she's got, then I'm gonna die of boredom.

I hear the lock on the door turn but I keep my head down and remain still. When it opens and I hear heels clicking against the concrete floor, I fight back my eye roll. Not wanting to give the bitch the upper hand, I speak before she does.

"I'm not in the mood for your bullshit, Desire. I was in the middle of daydreaming about how you'll die slowly and you ruined the moment by coming in here." My voice is scratchy and my throat is drier than a nun's pussy, but I don't let any of that show.

I grind my teeth when she grabs my chin and digs her nails into my flesh, forcing my head up to meet her gaze. Her blues don't offer the solace that Tatum's do. Desire's shine with nothing except for greed, anger and jealousy. Clearly,

Tate's comment is still bristling inside her and she hates knowing that some blonde haired, blue-eyed woman has come into my life without meaning to and stole the one thing she could never have, my heart.

"You are going to regret ever leaving me and choosing that little slut." Malice is thick in her tone. I fight back the urge to headbutt her for speaking about Tate like that. I have never killed a woman and technically, I don't class Desire as one because she's had enough dicks inside her to be classed as one of the boys.

"There was never a choice, because you were never an option for me," I clap back. Her nails pierce my flesh. The sting of pain just brings a smile to my face, knowing I'm the one that is chained but I'm getting to her.

"I've always been out of your league," she sneers. "You are going to scream for me and beg for mercy but you'll never receive it. I warned you what would happen if you defied me."

"You keep spitting that shit and you may just believe it yourself." Her eyes burn with anger at my reply. "You knew I was running game and turned a blind eye until I brought Tatum in. This is why you were never meant to lead the family, you think with your pussy not your head." She grips my cock with her free hand and squeezes. I grind my teeth so fucking hard I swear I heard them crack. When the scornful cunt twists her wrist, a growl filled with pain escapes me which makes her smile. When the cunt begins to stroke me, that's when I start thrashing against my restraints to escape her unwanted touch. I will my cock to remain flaccid and not give this cum guzzling bitch the satisfaction of getting me hard.

"Ma'am, you have to see this." Desire pouts and winks smugly. My chest is rising and falling in quick pants. I flick my gaze toward the door to see it's Devon, the little fuck just earned his and his brothers freedom for barging in here. He glances at me briefly and I give him a subtle nod in thanks.

"What is it?' she bites out, then releases her hold on me. I sag in my chains, relieved to have her touch vanish from my body.

"A blockage has been formed on the street." Desire frowns.

"Who the fuck is it?" she snaps.

Devon glances at me for a second before looking back at her. "We believe it's the Denver Kings," he says warily.

Desire grinds her teeth and it's easy to see that she's pissed off Devon interrupted us. "Get rid of them." Devon opens his mouth to try to speak, but she waves him off. He looks reluctant to leave but he knows if he questions her, she'll kill him and he'll be no good to me dead. When Devon closes the door behind him, Desire moves across the room and drops down into the metal seat against the wall. She crosses one leg over the other and smiles. But there is a sinister edge to that look that puts me on edge.

"You have the wolves howling at your gates, yet you sit here smiling like you've won the war," I taunt.

She lulls her head side to side, never dropping that smile. "I don't need to deal with those idiot brothers of mine. My men will squash them or capture them and bring them here to join you. Either way, I win."

I scoff. "Do us both a favor and get the fuck on with your pathetic attempt at torture so I can go back to daydreaming about your death."

Laughter erupts from her, the sound reminding me of nails on a chalkboard. "Oh, Alex. You know I could never hurt you," she purrs.

"My back would beg to differ," I snarl. She pouts.

"You know I didn't have a choice. I thought you would understand the errors of your way but you didn't. So, I took solace in knowing every time you looked in the mirror or went shirtless the scars would remind you of me."

"You're fucked in the head," I spit out. Her face pulls taut and all pretense of mirth vanishes from her botoxed face.

"Bring him in!" she shouts. I keep my face blank and show no emotion. When the door opens and I see Rage walk in, I roll my eyes. If he's her trump card, then this is worse than what I thought, I might just end up killing myself to escape their idiocy. Wrath follows close behind and wags his brows at me. Before I can even formulate a thought my mind turns blank when I see the last person enter the room. The chill from earlier vanishes as my blood begins to boil when I lock eyes with him.

"So, I hear you've been looking for me?" he says in a cocky tone. "Newsflash, you won't find me hiding out in my sister's pussy." I bare my teeth at him and growl.

"You'll die for what you did, you little cunt," I seethe.

"That's not nice to say, Butcher," Nexus taunts. The way this cunt is standing there acting cocky like he has the upper hand is burning me inside. The fact Desire knows what this little fucker did and refused to hand him over has sealed her own fate. I won't stop until they are both torn apart and gone from this fucking earth. The bloodlust I have been keeping a lid on inside me is no longer controlled, it flows through my veins like a plague overtaking everything inside me and giving me tunnel vision. I have one goal in life, kill both these sons of bitches!

"Des, please let me have a turn. I won't hurt him too much." I bite my tongue to keep from lashing out at Rage, with those idiot twins it's never personal, they just love to cause havoc and inflict pain. Their moral compass is so fucked up, they wouldn't think twice about making the same offer even if it was one of their brothers chained here instead of me.

"No. I told you and Wrath, he's mine and you two get Halo and Carnage." Wrath and Rage both look pissed. They may love destruction and rebel against rules and authority but for some reason, they both follow Desire without question and obey her every demand.

"Tell him to hurry the fuck up then, because I'm bored," Wrath snaps while shooting Nexus a frosty as fuck look. Nexus scoffs then moves toward the table set up with every type of tool he will need. I bite back my scoff when he goes for a pair of jumper cables. Wrath and Rage both roll their eyes, then turn to leave, clearly Nexus is failing to keep their attention but I never had that trouble. They loved watching me work, the sick little fucks.

Nexus is putting on a brave front but I can tell from how pinched his features are that he doesn't have the stomach for what he needs to do. He kneels before me and attaches the terminals to each of my big toes, the teeth of the cables biting into my flesh. I breath through my nose, forcing myself to focus on something else aside from the pain. See, the key to torture is getting the mind to break, not the body. If someone can compartmentalize the pain, then they are harder to break. We use pain to speed the process of breaking down barriers, so that your mind will break in order to stop the pain even though you know deep down in your bones that you will die regardless, you'll still sing like a bird just to give you a minute of reprieve. The point is, you never give your victim a minute to breathe. You continuously apply pressure so they never have a chance to lie when they spew all the information you need.

Nexus grabs a battery next and places it on the concrete floor—this fucker is going to burn the battery out before inflicting enough pain. The dumbass clearly knows nothing about cars or he would know you can't put a car battery straight onto the ground or you'll fuck it up, but I don't tell him that. I just prepare myself mentally for what is about to come. I wrap my hands around the chains on my wrists in a vice-like hold, take a deep breath and close my eyes. It's better to not watch, no matter how hard you try to not lock yourself you won't be able to stop your body's reaction when you see him place the cable to the battery.

My eyes snap open at the exact time a roar of pain tears out of me when electrical currents pulse through my body setting me on fire from the inside. My body jerks as volts of power jar me. It feels like it's been an hour before he removes the cables from the battery. I slump in my chains and pant. My toes are charred, I can feel it but I don't look down to confirm what I already know.

Torture 101, seeing the damage is worse than feeling it.

I can feel the sheen of sweat coating my entire body. I'd love to say I could handle more of that shit but the reality of the situation is, I can't. I would be lucky if I could do another two or three rounds before my heart gives out. I can already feel it pounding inside my chest like crazy. If he was smart, he would shock me again now so my heart didn't gain an even rhythm.

"Fuck, the sight of you chained and bound is a sight I will cherish. You ruined my fucking life, you arrogant piece of shit," Nexus screams.

I force out a bark of laughter, it sounds weak but it does the trick. I slowly lift my head to see him standing there red faced and shaking with his anger. "Do your worst, pup. I can take it but just a friendly warning, whatever you do to me, I will do ten times worse to you when I get out of here," I vow.

"You aren't leaving here alive, you stupid fuck," he snaps. I purse my lips but don't reply. The little cunt yanks on the cables, ripping them off my toes. I bite my lip to keep from yelling in pain, he's torn the skin from the charred flesh and it stings like a bitch. "Let's up the ante," he says, then goes to the table to retrieve a knife. I sigh because I know this idiot has no idea what he's doing so he's going to cut too deep and tear through muscle which is going to hurt like fuck.

I expect him to cut my chest but the little prick surprises me when he goes to my back. The forced gagging coming from behind me has me grinding my teeth.

"Jesus, she really tore you to shreds, didn't she?" My nostrils flare but I remain silent. "How the fuck could my sister touch you?" He drags the tip of the blade along my raised scars. When he pushes it through the skin, I jerk in my restraints and lock eyes with Desire, who is sitting there stiff as fucking ever without an ounce of emotion displayed on her plastic face. I keep my focus on her as he continues to slice through my flesh. I grit my teeth so hard they begin to ache. I refuse to cry out in pain, losing the battle when the little cock sucker buries the blade to the hilt in my shoulder. "Yes! Fuck, I love the sound of your screams," he shouts over my roar of pain.

My eyes start rolling back when he drags the blade downward tearing through my flesh. I jerk and thrash against my restraints but he doesn't let up. Maybe I was wrong, maybe this mutt does have the stomach to do this shit. He rips the blade out only to plunge it back in on the other side. I grow dizzy from the pain. I refuse to let him win by passing out, I want to feel every ounce of pain.

"You know she screamed for you?" I still and quit jerking in my chains. "Yeah, you know who I'm talking about without me even having to say her name." The fire in my veins begins to cool as ice starts filling my veins in its place. The pain from the knife is replaced by the anguish splitting my chest open. "Right before the GHB kicked in, she was screaming for you. She begged me to let her call you so she could say goodbye."

My throat clogs with emotion, I have to force the word out with every ounce of strength I have left. "Why?"

Nexus isn't the one to answer me, Desire slowly climbs to her feet and walks toward me slowly, with a sinister look in her eye. "I told you there would be hell to pay if you left. You thought you paid the price with your back." She shakes her head. "No, to truly break you was to break the thing you loved most." Pain erupts inside me, my breaths turn ragged as her words sink in. "I told Nexus where to find her that night. I gave him what he needed to end that little bitch."

"She was fucking innocent!" I roar, renewed strength flowing through me as I fight to get free so I can kill this bitch. I want to rip her apart and watch her writher in pain and scream for fucking mercy.

"I warned you!" she screams. "I needed someone outside of my family to do it so you couldn't trace it back to me. I met Nexus a few months after you left and I just knew he would be perfect for the job."

"I'm gonna break you and destroy your whole fucking family," I promise.

"You were nothing until I made you what you are!" she snaps back.

"You're nothing but a cunt trying to act tough. You will never be what I am. You're just angry because your daddy wanted me to head the family," I taunt.

"I orchestrated the death of that little bitch and helped send your ass to prison. I won, Butcher." Before I can reply, the door opens and guards drag in Omen and Carnage. My eyes widen at the sight of them. "Oh, look at that, my brothers came to hear the story of how I single handedly destroyed their best friend and ruined him. Well, Carnage did help, didn't you, Brother?"

CHAPTER TWENTY-EIGHT

Never in a trillion fucking years did I think I would be leading an army or be the one planning the attack to save Alexander Denver. Six months ago I would have laughed in your face and told you to lick my ass but now, I can't stop myself from being in a constant state of worry. Anxiety is a bitch to live with on a good day but these past five days have been agony. It's the not knowing part that is killing me. It feels so strange to be so consumed with worry and fear over someone other than myself, this is new to me and I can honestly say, I fucking hate it.

"The tracker's been activated, we have a location!" I dart across the room to where Halo is sitting at the table with his laptop set up in front of him. Halo has been working tirelessly since Omen and Carnage decided three days ago to go after Alex. We had no way to know where he was being held and Devon has gone dark ever since he texted us a warning that we needed to get him out now.

Omen and Carnage offered to go to Desire and get taken, knowing she wouldn't kill them. Carnage has a tracker on him that we've been waiting for him to activate. This is huge. Halo said we would get one shot since the tracker would be able to be detected if he was checked for transmitters. For both of them to offer themselves up like this shows just how much Alex means to them both.

"Where?" Pope asks as he peers over his other shoulder. Vatican comes to stand at the other end of the table with a tense look on his face, I know this whole situation is hard on them as well.

"Downtown Chicago, they're being held at..." Halo clamps his mouth closed and frowns at the map on the screen.

"Spit it out!" Vatican snaps.

"They're at the courthouse, well, underneath it by the looks of this thing," Halo mutters as he zooms in on the map. I press in closer to get a better look but honestly, I have no idea how to read a fucking map, I rely on Siri calling out directions as I drive. "Why the hell would she take them there?" he wonders aloud.

"Because she has the cops on her payroll," Pope grits out. I look up and meet his angry gaze.

"What does that mean?" I ask.

"It means, we'll have to go through the CPD to get to Alex and my brothers," Vatican answers for him.

"How the fuck are we supposed to do that?" I exclaim.

"By calling in the favors you have garnered. Don't second guess yourself, Tate. What you have accomplished in five days wouldn't be possible for anyone else in fifty years." Halo's acknowledgment of my achievements these past couple of days has me preening, I admit, it wasn't fucking easy but I did it. I have no idea who the inner badass was that I was channeling when I walked in that room three days ago, but I had those men eating out of the palm of my hand and I didn't need to flash them my pussy to hold their attention.

"Can we trust them to keep their word?" I ask the guys as I look at each of them.

"Given what you have promised them?" Pope says then scrubs a hand down his face. "Yeah, I think you can because the demise of my family means the rise of theirs and they won't pass that shit up."

I release a breath and nod. "Okay, let's make a call and then get ready to head to Chicago. I want to get Alex out of there because I don't trust that bitch not to kill him."

"She won't kill him, Tate," Vatican says, trying to ease some of my worries but fails.

"I didn't mean literally. She'll destroy his mind first because she knows he can withstand the torture anyone inflicts on him," I admit bitterly.

"What the hell are you talking about?" Halo pushes.

I take a deep breath and meet his gaze with a firm look. "She'll use Omen and Carnage against him. To truly destroy Alex she'll hurt the ones he loves most." All three of them stare at me like they never considered this option. I did. As soon as Omen and Car told us about their plan to cause a distraction so we could meet with the others, I knew Desire would use them to get to Alex.

"Fuck!" Pope roars and punches the wall, leaving a nice little hole in the wall. I frown at him and shake my head.

"Breaking things won't change what's happening," I scold. I know they may all be older than me but the three of them haven't been thinking clearly since Alex was taken. I know they all harbor guilt over that but it wasn't their fault. My brother is to blame. He set all of this into motion. That shit burns me deep. Nexus is no better than our father. I trusted him blindly because he saved me from being subjected to Thomas's wrath that night at the crematorium with Vivian. I thought he did it because he cared about me. My need for family clouded my judgment, all I wanted was for someone to be there for me. I didn't realize it then, but I already had that with Vivian, Nova and even their guys. Now, my circle has widened as I now have Alex and these guys who I care about... a lot.

"Make the call, Tate. We leave for Chicago as soon as the plane is ready. I want my brother's back," Halo grits out as he climbs to his feet and stalks out of the room. Pope and Vat follow after him with their heads down, I can see the tension wafting off them in waves. I know this has to be hard for them. I get it because much like them, I have to face off against my own sibling and that shit is a hard pill to swallow. I push those thoughts away because they will do nothing but eat me up inside, and I can't afford for that to happen. I need to keep a clear head and focus on what's important.

Alex.

I pull my phone from my pocket and bring up my group

chat with Nova and Vivian and hit call. I wait for them to answer.

Vivian is the first to answer. "Hey, how are you holding up?" she asks.

"I'm okay," I answer as Nova joins the call.

"I'm making this a Facetime," Nova says a second before my phone pings, alerting me to accept the change. I do. Both their faces fill the screen and I hate that they both look worried, I never wanted to involve them in this but I was out of options. "Hey."

"Hey," I breathe out.

"Stop pouting, girl, we're here for you," Nova says in a firm tone, bringing a small smile to my face.

"I'm sorry for dragging you both into this—"

"Tate, stop," Vivian snaps, forcing me to clamp my mouth closed. "We're your friends. This is what friends do for each other. We've got your back and so do the guys."

"Are they sure about this?" I press.

Nova scoffs and rolls her eyes. "Tatum, let me tell you something about Vox Hatchett. There is nothing and no one in this world that can make that man do something he doesn't want to do. He'll be there and he'll do what's needed of him because that's just the type of person he is. I promise you, Vox, my brother and the guys will get the job done. You can count on them." Her words should reassure me but the last person I counted on used me and lied to my fucking face. It still twists me up inside, Nexus's betrayal burns like acid through my veins. Vivian and Nova both tried to warn me about my brother but I ignored them. I just thought they didn't know him like I do but I was fucking wrong.

"Thank you both. I know what you are risking by

helping me and I just want you both to know that I will never forget this and I swear, I won't let anything happen to them," I vow. I spend another few minutes talking to them and letting them know the plan before I end the call and dial the next person. My breathing turns harsh and I force myself to relax and channel my inner bad bitch.

"Tatum, what a pleasure to hear from you." I fight not to scoff at his condescending tone.

"Yeah, I'm sure it is." His laughter just serves to grate on my fucking nerves, I don't trust this fucker as far as I can throw him. "Look, we have a slight issue but the guys assure me that you'll be able to aid us." I try to keep the bite out of my tone but fail.

"What's the situation?" His voice is serious and gone is the humor from a second ago.

"We have a location, they're being held at the courthouse."

He snorts. "Of course she would choose that place, the gutless bitch." His hatred for Desire is clear, I think his hatred for her could even rival my own.

"Why do you say that?" I hedge.

"She's the only one who could get those greedy pigs in her pocket. What she pays them is worth those useless cock-suckers giving their life up to protect her."

"Why was she the only one who could get the cops on her side?" I question.

"Because she's the only one with a pussy and willing to allow the Sergeant to plough her rotten cunt to seal the deal."

I shudder in disgust, women like Desire give the rest of

us a bad name. She is the definition of *fucking her way to the top.*

"Can I count on you and your men to be there and support us?"

"I gave you my word." His tone is strong and unyielding. "Unlike the De Santis, when I give my word, I don't break it. " I nod even though he can't see me. "What exactly is the play here?"

"I want minimal bloodshed. All we need to do is cause a distraction long enough for my guys to extract them then... you can do as you like once we're out of there."

"Are you certain they will follow The Butcher?" His tone is filled with caution and I don't blame him.

"I won't lie to you, I'm not certain at all but I'm hoping their loyalty to the true Don will prevail and they will see reason."

"That right there is the reason I agreed to aid you, Tatum."

I reel back in surprise. "What does that mean?"

"It means, you could have lied to me when we first met and you could have lied again right now but you didn't. You would make a great leader."

I scoff. "I appreciate that but I'm not made for this life."

He laughs. "You may not be, but the man you are risking your life to save would burn any city to the ground and not bat an eye at the loss of lives. A man like him needs a woman like you."

"How so?" I find myself asking.

"You are the Yin to his Yang, the goodness inside you breathes life to the darkness inside him. Alexander is lucky to have someone like you by his side."

"I would agree with you but Alex would probably disagree. He seems to think I have anger issues and I do admit, I tend to throw shit at him when I'm mad." His laughter booms through the phone and I find myself smiling.

"Have your men send through the time and positions and I'll relay the information to my own men. You have my word, Tatum, I will not double cross you."

"As you have mine, Mr. Vatel."

CHAPTER TWENTY-NINE

Alexander

"I'm going to fucking rip you apart!" I roar as I grip the bars of my cell and try to shake the steel to get free. Feeling helpless is something I haven't felt since the night my sister died. I swore I would never feel that way again but I was wrong, so fucking wrong!

Nexus turns and faces me with a wide grin on his face. "Can't take the heat can ya, Butcher?" he taunts as he slowly drags the blade down Omen's chest, causing my brother to scream out in pain and thrash against the chains that bind his hands above his head. Carnage is strung up beside him, looking just as defeated as Omen, and it makes me sick knowing Desire has allowed this to happen to her own flesh and blood. I tear my gaze from the little cunt and face Wrath and Rage who sit in the corner with blank looks on their faces.

"They're your brothers!" I yell. They both turn to me in

sync but the looks on their faces are unreadable. "If you don't help them, I'll kill both of you with my bare fucking hands!" I promise. Wrath turns to Rage and nudges him with his shoulder. My anger is the only thing keeping me standing right now. Nexus tried his best to break me with stab wounds and cuts but the little cocky fucker has no idea that pain means nothing to me, it is but a fleeting moment and all you need to do is ride out the wave until it subsides. When Omen releases another scream, I turn back to face him and grit my teeth at the sight of the blade sticking out of his side.

"Oops," Nexus sarcastically says as he moves away from Omen, who is nothing but dead weight in his chains. Neither of them will sell me out and their loyalty is something that can never be bought and something I can never repay. When they told me why they were here, I nearly lost my fucking mind. Unlike them, I knew what was coming when Desire forced me on that plane. These idiots thought their sister was the one in charge, they had no idea she had handed over control to Nexus who has no familial connection to them, which means he won't go easy. If anything, he's gone harder just to fuck with me. Carnage hasn't uttered a word either since Desire announced that he had a hand in my sister's death. I know she's lying, she has to be.

"You want to play, then come play with me, you little cunt," I taunt. Nexus clicks his tongue and shakes his head as he crosses the room sand runs his fingertips over the tops of the weapons lined on a table. He selects a whip with arrow heads attached to the ends. I inhale sharply as he stalks toward Carnage, who hangs limply in his chains. I close my eyes for a second and push the resentment I'm feeling toward him down. As I open my eyes, I see Nexus shift so he's standing behind Carnage and facing me.

"See, I knew you wouldn't break through torture and I was wondering how the fuck I would get you to break." Nexus swings the whip and Carnage lurches forward in his chains, screaming out in pain. His eyes are filled with torment as he looks at me. "The second these fucking idiots showed up, I knew just how to break you." He whips Carnage two more times, smiling at the cries of pain he releases.

When Nexus's gaze meets mine, I shutdown all emotions inside me and latch onto the need for revenge. It's the only way I will make it out of this and hopefully save my brothers.

"Did your daddy teach you how to be a good bitch or was that your mommy?" I ask as I move to the back of my cell and rest back against the bars, then cross my arms over my chest, forcing myself not to flinch in pain from the wound under my armpit.

Nexus's eyes blaze as he rears his arm back and whips Carnage again, but this time I don't react to his screams of pain, I just keep my gaze focused on Nexus. "You won't get to me, Butcher," he grits out.

I shrug. "Maybe, but I sure as fuck got to your sister, didn't I?" I taunt. His eyes blaze with unfiltered hatred. "Hmmm, seems you do care for her after all, huh?" I press. Nexus marches across the room and slams to a stop in front of my cell. I may have been blindfolded on the way here but I'm not stupid, I know where we're being held—beneath the courthouse in the city.

"I'll kill her before I ever let her near you again." Liquid heat licks at my skin at the mention of him touching my girl. I keep my composure and purse my lips tauntingly.

"You could try, but my brothers will put you down before you could get within five feet of her."

"Your men are now under the rule of the De Santis family, you have no one. Those three fuckwits won't be able to save you, but don't worry, Tate will be here to watch you die."

"Just make sure your sister tells me she loves me again before you kill me, kay? I would hate for her to miss the chance to tell me how much she loves me and loves coming on my cock."

Nexus's eyes burn with outrage as he glares at me. "Get the branding iron and brand those cunts," he snaps at the twins. When neither of them move, I raise my brows and bite back a smile.

"I don't think they take orders from you," I tease.

Nexus growls, then turns to the twins. I use that moment of distraction and rush forward, reach through the bars and wrap my arms around him. He tries to fight, but even in the weakened state I'm in, I can still overpower this pathetic excuse for a human. When the side of his head is crushed against the bars and his ear peaks through the gap, I bite it. He roars in pain and fights harder to get free and even calls for the twins to help, but they don't move. I taste his blood coating my mouth and relish in the metallic taste of him. I start to feel his skin giving way and moan at the feeling. The sounds coming from him are fucking euphoric and feed the beast inside me. He rears to life inside me and I allow him to take full control.

I yank backward and release the little cunt who drops to the floor, then scurries backward on his hands. The sight of his tears staining his cheeks and the blood from his ear cascading down the side of his face has a growl vibrating in my chest. I grip the bars and love the sight of fear I see in his eyes. I spit the torn piece of his ear at him and smile. He drops his gaze to the cartilage, then reaches up and winces when he feels the spot where his ear should be.

"You keep walking around here and acting like you're in control, when you and I both know the only reason you feel that way is because I'm in a cage. You better hope she kills me because if she doesn't, I'll come for you. When you close your fucking eyes, I'll be the star of your nightmares. I'll be in the shadows watching you, taunting you and when you think I'll finally strike, I won't, because I'm going to take my time with you. I'm going to cherish every fucking second of destroying the piece of shit you are, not only for my sister but for my girl as well." His eyes widen at the mention of Tate. "Yeah, you heard that right. She's mine and if you touch a single fucking hair on her head, it won't just be The Butcher coming for you, it will be the entirety of the Denver Kings, you cunt."

"Guards!" Nexus calls out as he pushes to his feet, cupping his ear and staggering across the room where the door is opened for him. The little bitch limps out of here like a pussy. When the door closes behind him, I turn to Omen and Carnage to find them both looking at me and grinning.

"There he is," Omen grinds out.

"Welcome back, Butcher. I thought your girl stole your balls." I look at Carnage. When he sees the question in my eyes, he hangs his head and exhales. "I had nothing to do with Ellie dying, but I was there that night." Tension flows through me. I inhale and exhale on instinct but my lungs feel like they can't get enough oxygen. "I had no idea she was there, Alex. Desire sent me there to do a drop."

"You were at the same party my sister died at with your drugs in her system," I grit out.

"He's telling the truth," Rage says. I slowly turn to face the twins and shoot each of them a look of warning to shut their fucking mouths.

Wrath pushes off the wall and stalks into the middle of the room. Both Omen and Carnage glare at their brother but say nothing. "Desire met Nexus through Roberto. The little cock tease had taken over his father's business and Desire needed him on her side."

"Why?" I push.

Rage moves and joins his twin in the center. "Because she made a deal with the Volkov Bratva to obtain real estate for them to expand their operations in the US if they supplied her with drugs and cut off all other families they were supplying."

My brows raise. "They're working together."

Both the twins nod. "Carnage supplying Nexus that night wasn't the first time Desire hooked him up. She was already working an angle with that piss flap. He had no idea who you were or who Ellie was and he didn't care. She promised he would never be caught and that was all he needed to hear. His father came after you on his own accord because he found out what Nexus had done, and didn't trust Desire to keep her word, so he framed you when he found out who you really were from Nexus." Rage's words are like an ice bath, shocking life back into me and renewing my hunger for that bitch's blood to coat my hands.

"Why the fuck are you two only mentioning this shit now?" Omen snarls.

The twins shrug. "You never asked," Rage says in a casual tone that grates on my fucking nerves.

"I'm gonna break both your fucking necks," I force out through clenched teeth.

"As long as you don't bite my ear off. I'm good with a quick end," Wrath replies with sarcasm thick in his tone.

"Why the hell are you both telling us this shit now? Neither of you two gave a shit about anyone aside from yourselves and staying on that bitch's good side," Carnage grinds out with pain lacing each of his words.

"Did you ever think to ask why we have never risen against her?" Rage growls. "Did any of you self-satisfying pricks ever think there may be a reason why we follow her blindly and never question anything she says?"

"Nah, of course they wouldn't because me and you have always been the outcasts of this fucked up family," Wrath adds.

I roll my eyes. "Why the fuck do you follow her?"

"Because she has something that means everything to us and if we step out of line, she'll take it from us. Which is why we won't help any of you. We can't." Rage's tone surprises me because I can hear a hint of remorse.

"Bullshit."

Both the twins turn to Omen and glare. "None of you cared enough to see deeper into us than what we allowed the world to see. That's your problem not ours. We have no issues with any of you, but we also won't cross that line, even though we hope you are victors of this war." My brows raise as it sinks in. Wrath's ominous words make sense to me but not the others.

"She has someone you love and if you try to help us, she'll kill them to punish you." Both of them nod and I realize at this moment, they aren't that different to us. They have been sucked into the black hole that is Desire De Santis, who doesn't give a fuck about anyone aside from herself. We don't get a chance to say more, the door swings open to reveal a pissed off Desire flanked by six of her men. Cowering behind them, holding a rag to his face, is the cunt who is now missing an ear. Wrath and Rage both step back and reclaim their position from earlier, I shoot them both a scolding look. I get their reasoning but that piece of pussy better be worth it because I'll kill them both for allowing their brothers to go through this shit.

Desire struts into the room like she is God's gift to men. I move to the back of my cell and cross my arms over my chest. She ignores the threats spewing from Omen and Carnage as she comes to stand in front of my cell. The cunning look in her eyes is nothing new to me, she always has an ace up her sleeve and won't play her trump card until the very last minute.

"You look upset, Lex," she purrs in what I'm sure she thinks is a seductive tone, but all it sounds like to me is nails on a chalkboard. I remain silent and keep my face blank, not giving away to the fact her mere presence has my skin crawling. "Did my brothers tell on me?" she says with a pout as she looks to Wrath and Rage. Neither of them meet her stare. She sighs dramatically then waves her six guards forward. I see Devon in the mix and can tell he doesn't want to take part in what's happening but he doesn't have a choice. The guard in the front reaches into his pocket and produces a key. I don't move an inch when he opens the cell door and steps inside. I eye each of them with a cold look and smirk when they begin to shuffle their weight from leg to leg.

"Is she paying you enough to withstand what will happen to you and your families when I get out of here?" My tone is calm and even but the threat is clear.

"Ignore him, cuff him and bring him to me." They all ignore Desire's order as I step forward and hold my wrists out to them. I shoot Devon a discreet look of warning. He subtly nods and starts to look around the room, trying to find a way out of here no doubt.

They place the cuffs on my wrists. The fucker to my right makes sure they are tight enough to cut into my flesh. I just shoot him a look that promises retribution—he instantly steps back. Devon grips the chain of my cuffs and drags me out of my cell. My body is battered and bruised but I refuse to allow any of these cunts to see me as weak, so I hold my head high and meet Desire's gaze as I'm brought to a stop in front of her. She runs her gaze over me. I shudder in disgust when she licks her lips and moans suggestively.

"God, don't you miss how messy we were together?"

I snort. "You and I were never together, you deluded bitch," I snarl. Her blue eyes swirl with anger, I know just how to get under her skin so I keep pushing. "You were nothing to me. You were a means to an end. You were never the girl I wanted or even cared about. You are nothing to me, you wretched cunt. I'll make sure you and that elf eared cunt over there die slowly. I'll take my time ripping you each apart, then send you both to hell, deaf, dumb and blind," I vow. I expect her to throw a fit and scream but she doesn't do that. Instead, she lurches forward and buries her blade in my stomach that I didn't even see her holding.

CHAPTER THIRTY

Tatum

Nerves are riding me harder than Alex did the last time we had sex, but there won't be any orgasm coming anytime soon. I can feel it in the pit of my gut that something is wrong with him, I can't explain it but I can feel it. I finally understand why so many chose not to allow themselves to fall in love with anyone. I unknowingly fell in love with the infamous Butcher and because of that, I'm now sitting in the backseat of a car with his three brothers, driving to the courthouse in Chicago to rescue him.

Am I able to fight like Jackie Chan or Bruce Lee?

No.

Can I kill someone like John Wick?

No.

Can I crush skulls with my bare hands like Thanos?

Also, no.

But that won't stop me from going after him, because

ever since I met Alexander Denver, I have changed. My life has stopped revolving around making enough money to prove to myself that I will never be homeless again or eating from a dumpster. I'm stronger because of him. He has brought a side of me to life. I want more than just money now. I want a life, a home and most of all, I just want *him*.

"You ready, we're a block away?" Vat asks.

I release a breath I didn't know I was holding and nod. "Yeah, let's go get our guys back. The Vatel's promised to free our men so they can join the fight." We learned from Devon that all of Alex's men are pinned down at the two locations they were sent to by Desire's men. Desire splitting her manpower is working in our favor. Her armies are split, so it gives us a shot at taking her out before the rest of her forces can arrive and aid her.

"Don't fucking die, Tate," Halo orders.

I scoff. "I wasn't planning on it but if I do, at least I'll make a pretty corpse." Halo glares at me.

"If you die, he'll burn the fucking world down. He won't survive losing someone else he loves." The serious tone of his voice gives me pause. I don't know what to say so I just nod and get my head back in the game. As we round the corner, Vatican slows the car. Both me and Halo push forward to look between the seats. My eyes widen and my mouth parts on a gasp. I underestimated her, she has the street barricaded by armed officers. At the sight of our car, they all turn and raise their guns.

"Where the fuck are the Vatel's?" Pope snaps.

I shake my head. "They said they would be twenty minutes behind us."

"Tate, this shit changes the plan," Vat growls.

"How did you not see this on the cameras?" I direct my question to Halo.

"She's looped the fucking cameras, that's why." He sounds really angry that his sister duped him, but we can't do anything about that now. The shouts of the officers can be heard. Without any warning, I throw my door open and leap out of the car before the guys can stop me. I just need to buy us enough time before the Vatel's get here and for the Filthy Few to get inside the building, I fucking hope CJ Vatel doesn't fuck me over to get back at Alex for aiding Desire in taking down his father.

"Stop right there!" someone yells.

I freeze and raise my hands in the air. I feel the three guys at my back, the anger wafting off them is tangible. "My name is Tatum Lawson. Before you pricks go ahead and get trigger happy you should know my boyfriend is the one that cunt has locked up inside that building." The four of us remain silent as the idiots speak among themselves. I can guarantee Desire would have given orders for these idiots not to kill me, she would want that honor for herself.

The moment one of them reaches for their radio I know they are radioing into their cum dumpster boss that I'm here. We wait for what seems like hours but it's mere seconds until the cop turns his attention back to us.

"Throw your guns to the side, interlock your fingers behind your heads and get on your knees," he calls out.

"You must be out of your goddamn mind!" I shout.

"Tatum," Pope grits out in warning but I ignore him.

"The only man I will ever get on my fucking knees for is being held against his will by that cock guzzling slut who signs your bonus checks. You want me, come get me, you

Fonzi wannabe looking motherfucker." We're met by the sound of every gun cocking and then suddenly our chests are lit up by red laser beams. How these assholes are able to do this in a city as big as Chicago is a mystery to me, we haven't seen a single person for at least four blocks.

"Unless you want the boss to skin you alive, I suggest you don't shoot them!" I turn my head toward the entrance of the courthouse to see a man walking toward us. The officers don't listen and keep their guns trained on us, but the guy doesn't seem to care as he stalks into the middle of the road strolling toward us like there isn't thirty or so guns aimed in our direction. Pope, Vatican and Halo all press in closer to me as the man draws near. He stops a few feet away from me and nods to the guys, which has a frown pulling at my brows.

"Who are you?" I ask.

The man smiles. "My name's Devon."

"You seem important," I reply.

He snorts. "Nah. I'm so far from important it's laughable. I'm what you call expendable."

I cock my head to the side and study him. "Why the hell are you here then?" I grit out.

"Because I'm the only one who is going to take you to Alex." I open my mouth to reply but he pushes on. "There isn't much time, Tatum. Desire has a four inch blade lodged in his abdomen and currently has four men stringing him so she can whip him while Omen and Carnage watch. Did you want to keep arguing or would you like to get in there so we can try to save him while we wait for your backup to arrive?"

A lump lurches into my throat. "Take me to him," I force out through clenched teeth.

"Tate, if we go in there we'll be outnumbered. We need to wait for the others—"

I whirl around and pin Vatican with a look that promises pain if he keeps talking. "You want to wait out here and be a pussy, then go for it but I'm going." I don't wait for his reply as I nod for Devon to lead the way. The three brothers mutter curses behind me, but follow after us regardless of the risks.

Could we be walking into a trap?

Yes.

Do I care?

No.

I shoot the fuckers the middle finger as we pass them. All of the officers begin yelling at me but I ignore those useless fucks. I know without a doubt Alex will deal with them as soon as I can get him the fuck out of here.

"Be warned, this courthouse doubles as the local police station, so it's busy in there but no one will bat an eye at us. Just act normal and don't draw your weapons." The only response I can muster is a grunt. When we push through the main doors, I scan the area and sure enough they're police in here dealing with civilians. My eyes widen when I spot Vox, Ezekiel, Archer and Hayze off to the side speaking to an officer. Ez notices me first and nods subtly before turning his attention back to the woman.

I pull my phone from my pocket and shoot Vox a text.

ME

He's being held in the cells, he's injured, as soon as back up arrives cut the power and get him out.

I pocket my phone and follow Devon down the stairs to the basement level. When we enter the holding area, I'm surprised to see people in the cells. I thought she would have had them emptied. We ignore the shouts and pleas of the people locked up and follow Devon through the middle of the cells to another door. He pushes it open and leads us down another flight of stairs. The air feels charged. I can smell blood and instantly begin to panic. I fight back the urge to run down the stairs. My heart is pounding inside my chest, knowing I'm getting closer to him. Devon stops in front of a closed door at the bottom of the stairs and turns back to face me. I jolt when I hear Alex scream out. I dart forward to push past Devon, but he grabs me and holds me back. When Vat pushes the barrel of his gun into his head, he releases me and raises his hands.

"Calm the hell down," he hisses, earning a glare from me.

"Open that fucking door now!" I snarl. I press forward and get right in his face, gone is the agonizing worry about him being in pain, it's now replaced by the need to kill.

"She's expecting you, she knows you're here. You go in there guns blazing, she'll kill you and make him watch. Rethink your plan and you may just make it out of here alive," he mutters the last part then pushes the door open. I'm instantly met by the sight of Omen and Carnage strung up by chains on my left. They've been beaten and worked over good, but it's the sight of Alex in the middle of the room with his arms chained above his head, that makes me see red. He's naked except for his boxers. His body is caked in blood and grime. When my eyes lock on that blade in his stomach I bite back a whimper. A man steps forward and shoves his cattle prong into Alex's ribs, making his body jerk and convulse as he screams out in pain. The sound snaps me out of it. I don't think as I rush into the room and shoulder the son of a bitch, catching them all off guard. Before the bastard can recover, I snatch the prong from him and shove it against his cock—he jerks and screams out.

Chaos erupts around me, arms band around me and lift me off the ground forcing me to drop the prong. "Touch him again and I'll rip your fucking head off!" I scream out. Everyone's shouting, I fight against the fucker holding me but his grips doesn't ease. I spy Vat, Omen and Halo against the others, I think they may have the upper hand until a dozen more of Desire's men fill the room and aim their guns at the guys.

"Bambi?" I snap my head to the side, only to lock eyes with Alex. For the first time since meeting him I see an emotion I never thought would ever cross his stunning face.

Fear.

"Alex," I breathe his name like a prayer.

He looks past me to see the three guys and his eyes widen. Omen and Carnage are both screaming for Desire to release their brothers, but the bitch herself just stands there grinning at... me. I force my features to blank and stare back at her with nothing but hatred in my eyes.

"Enough!" she shouts, bathing the room into silence. Halo turns toward me and the look of defeat in his eyes spears me. I shake my head, pleading for him not to give up. I know I only met CJ Vatel once, but I believed him when he said he would come to our aid. Even if I don't make it out of here alive, I know Vox and the others will get Alex and the guys out safely. "Lock them in the cell while I talk to my friend." The three guys are disarmed and thrown into the cell. Desire wags her brows at me and slowly comes toward me with a shit eating grin, stretching further across her face the closer she gets.

"You lay a single finger on her and I swear on my sister, I'll fucking kill you slowly," Alex spits out, his tone laced with pain but his features show you nothing.

Desire tsks and rolls her eyes at him. She veers away from me and moves to stand before him. When she reaches out and runs a finger down his chest, I bite down on the inside of my cheek to keep from lashing out at the slut. When the disgusting cum stain grabs his cock, causing him to jerk in his restraints I lose it.

"You sick, fucking cunt, is that the only way you can get him hard for your washed up pussy?" Desire's blue eyes burn with the intensity of a brewing storm. "All I have to do is walk in the room and he's rock hard ready to fuck me on any available surface," I taunt. Her grip on him turns punishing. Alex grunts in pain but doesn't cry out. Alex's eyes close when she begins to stroke him through his boxers. I feel bile rising in my throat but swallow it down.

"God, he's big isn't he? I remember what it feels like when he slides inside me and stretches my tight little cunt." She moans just to drive her point across. Tears prick the backs of my eyes when I see his face contort. Any man can withstand a shitload of pain, Alex more so than most, but no man can control an erection when their cock is being fondled and forced to get hard.

I ignore her and focus on him. "Alex?" He still won't open his eyes. When she begins to laugh I know he's hard, and I can only imagine what he's feeling right now. "Alex, look at me." I force lead into my tone and it works, his eyes snap open and lock onto mine. "I love you." My words seem to ease some of the stress lines on his face but Desire doesn't like that. She releases him and marches toward me. I don't even get a chance to brace myself before her fist sails through the air and my head is jerking backward from being punched in the mouth. The metallic taste of blood fills my mouth. I spit right in her face and relish in the sound of her shocked scream.

"Chain the cunt up!" she screams.

"No. Don't fucking touch her!" Alex roars and begins to fight vigorously against his restraints, causing more blood to seep out around the knife in his stomach. I don't fight as her men cuff my wrists, then throw a chain over the rafters. When they secure the chain to my wrists and hoist me up high enough my feet can't even touch the ground, my shoulders instantly begin to burn but I refuse to give this washed up cunt the satisfaction of seeing me in pain. "Desire, let her go and I'll come back to you. I'll work for you again—"

"Alex, no!" I shout, drawing his focus to me. I implore him with my eyes to see I have a plan and he just needs to hang on until the cavalry arrives. Desire moves to stand in front of me, she holds her hand out to one of her men. I turn my head to try and peer over my shoulder.

"Bambi?" At the hint of panic in Alex's tone I turn to face him. He tries to hide his emotions from me but I can see the worry in his eyes. "Focus on me, baby," he pleads. I want to listen to him but the instant I feel the sharp point of a blade pressed to my chest, I look down and the gleeful look on her face sends dread pooling inside me. Without warning she drags the blade down my front. I bite down on my tongue refusing to cry out and give her the satisfaction of hearing me scream. My shirt is cut open. I can smell my own blood.

"Come pick on someone with balls big enough to challenge the size of yours," Carnage shouts, trying to divert her attention from me. Desire ignores him, she and I both know that she won't stop hurting me. Not only will destroying me kill Alex, but it would break these guys I now consider my friends. They pride themselves on being able to protect those they care about, but right now they are powerless to do anything but watch.

Desire surprises the fuck out of me when she rams the blade into the side of my thigh. A scream so potent and riddled with pain tears out of me. I hear the guys all yelling and screaming but I can't make their words out over the sound of my own screams. Fire is licking a trail throughout my body, sweat coating my brow.

"You thought you were special," she sneers as she pulls the blade from my thigh, drawing another scream from me.

"I'll rip your fucking head off!" Alex roars. To teach him a lesson, she buries the knife into my other thigh, causing the inferno inside me to rise to new heights. Tears trail down my cheeks freely, the pain indescribable and like nothing else I have ever experienced before in my life.

"Utter another fucking word and the next one goes in her throat," Desire spits out as she glares at Alex, who is panting from exertion. He flicks his gaze to mine and deflates.

"I'm okay," I manage to grit out. His eyes tell me what his mouth can't. He knows I'm full of shit and blames himself for me being in this position.

"Calvin, get me two pills." Alex's eyes snap wide at her words. I shake my head, urging him to remain silent because I know her threat isn't idle. She will kill me to teach him a lesson. The man named Calvin approaches and places two pills in her hand. "Hold her head." I try to shake free when he reaches for me but the bitch herself slices my side, drawing a cry from me. She slams the pills in my mouth and gets Calvin to hold my mouth closed. He even blocks my nose, leaving me no choice but to swallow the drugs. When my brother finally comes into view, I just stare at him with disgust as Calvin releases me.

"Is this what you wanted?" I ask him.

Nexus's face is a mask of victory. He thinks he's won this war and now for the first time, I see what everyone else has always seen. A monster.

"No. I wanted you by my side. I actually liked you, I really did, but then you had to go and ruin it and let that fuck face between your legs and caught feelings. I'll be sad to see you go but I won't miss you." Even after everything he's done, his words still hurt.

"I won't save you this time," I utter, feeling the effects of the drugs already taking place.

"No, sister. I won't save you from what is about to happen. I begged you to come with me that night but you refused, so now you will die exactly how his sister did." A whimper escapes me at his promise, my tongue feeling heavy and swollen.

"I'll take all of their punishment. I'll make a statement to the press telling them I killed them, I'll help you take over the fucking country if you just let her go... please." Defeat is not something I thought I would ever hear in Alexander

Denver's tone. He opens his mouth to continue but the sound of gunfire above us draws everyone's attention. My head flops forward and I go slack in my chains, unable to resist the effects of the drugs flowing through my system.

"Get the fuck up there and see what's going on," Desire barks. "Nexus, get her down and stripped. I want him to watch as Calvin fucks her, then strangles her. I want him to picture his sister while watching her."

CHAPTER THIRTY-ONE

Alexander

Feeling powerless is not something I've ever felt aside from when my sister died. It's a feeling I could go my whole life without feeling, but right now that's all I feel as I watch Nexus lower his own sister to the floor and begin peeling her pants down her legs. Blood coats both her thighs. The sight pains me, my anger has vanished, replaced by utter fear. I'm not in control and there isn't a fucking thing I can do to save the girl I've fallen in love with. Tatum was my second chance. She begged me to let this go and I ignored her plea. I thought avenging my sister would give me the closure I craved but I was wrong, all I have done is put the people I love in danger.

I have a reputation as a cold, heartless killer, yet here I am chained like a dog with no power.

"Bambi?" I whisper as that cock sucker Calvin draws nearer to her and smirks down at my girl. When he pops the button on his pants, I see red. "I'll rip your throat out, then I'll go after every single person in your family, women and children included. I'll make sure my face is the last thing they will ever see before I send them all to hell," I decree. Desire snarls when the sound of gunshots gets closer. She drops to her knees beside Tatum, then looks up at me with an evil grin.

"How does it feel to know you lost both times? First your sister and now this whore. I warned you not to leave me, Lex." When she raises the blade I panic.

"Desire, stop. Don't fucking do this!" I plead. Her brothers all begin screaming and pleading for her to stop, but her focus is on me.

"Too late, I'll see you soon, baby," she says, then rams the blade into Tatum's chest. A pain filled roar rips out of me. I yank as hard as I can against my cuffs, ignoring the searing pain in my abdomen. I feel the cuffs biting into my flesh but the pain barely registers as the need to get to Tatum overshadows everything. Desire, Calvin and the rest of her pathetic excuse of men flee. Wrath turns to Halo and tosses him a key before the twins follow after their sister. Halo makes quick work unlocking the cell door. He rushes to Tate's side while Vatican and Pope come to help me down. Screams and shouts can be heard above us, but none of that matters to me, all I can focus on is getting to my girl. When they finally get me down, I crumble to the floor like a sack of shit. Vatican manages to catch me at the last second before I face plant and lodge the blade in further.

"Get them down," I demand, then crawl toward Tatum where Halo is applying pressure to her wound. When I'm close enough I reach for the knife, but Halo grips my wrist and shoots me a look.

"You know better than anyone if you remove that blade she'll die within seconds." His words penetrate the haze. I ignore my own wounds and gather her in my arms—she's dead weight. Her eyes are open and tears leak from the corners. I know she can feel and hear everything going on around her but she can't move or do a damn thing.

This is how Ellie felt.

I push thoughts of my sister away as I stare down at her. Her skin is pale and her eyes are unfocused as I cup her face in my trembling hand. A lump lodges in my throat and I feel tears forming in my eyes.

"Find something you can hold onto, baby," I whisper. "I can't lose you, Tatum, please... please don't fucking give up. Fight, baby, and stay with me," I beg her, tears flowing quicker down her cheeks.

"Alex, we need to move." I ignore Carnage. "We have no idea who the fuck is up there." When we hear footsteps, we all look up to see four masked men enter the room. My face blanks at the sight of the Filthy Few, all four of them have their gazes focused on the girl in my arms.

"The Vatel family have the upper hand, your men have all the exits blocked. They have Nexus and the bitch but we need to get her out of here now." I have no idea which one of them spoke, but it's the one with two horns on his mask that moves toward me. When he reaches for Tatum, I snake my arm out and grip his throat.

"Touch her and I'll snap your fucking neck," I seethe.

"You can't carry her with that knife hanging out of your gut. Let me help you because if she dies, my girl will kill me."

"Alex, he's right. We need to move because we're wasting time here!" Pope snaps.

"She doesn't have much time," Vat implores. He pushes the masked fucker out of the way and gathers Tate into his arms. I grip his shirt and force him to look at me. "I know what she means to you, brother, she means something to all of us now. Let me help her." I drop my gaze to Tate who is now as pale as a ghost.

"I'll search a thousand worlds for you and live a hundred lifetimes trying to find you," I whisper, then release Vat. He turns and races out of the room, with Pope and Halo right behind him.

"Come on, she asked us to get the three of you out of here and I plan on keeping my word," the one with the right horn says. Carnage and Omen both look like shit. No horns and left horn come to me and help me to my feet, left horn throws my arm over his shoulders and helps me out of the room.

"How the fuck did the Vatel family get involved in this shit?" Omen mutters as we climb the stairs.

"All we know is Tate made a deal, your life for the city or some shit like that," two horns answers. We pause at the top of the stairs where we can still hear shouting.

"We're unarmed," I grit out.

"You don't need it, your men and the Vatel family have the cops and all the De Santis men barricaded in the main courtroom. You won, Butcher," no horns says.

"I didn't win shit," I snarl. I feel my strength waning and know I'm minutes away from passing out from blood loss.

"Let's get you three to the hospital," right horn says.

"You make sure Nexus and Desire are alive—"

Two horns cuts me off before I can finish. "You have my word, they will both be waiting for you when you are released from the hospital and so will their men. A favor asked is a debt owed, Butcher. Our debt to you for saving my sister is now repaid."

Seven days...

That's how long I have been sitting by her bed, holding her hand, praying that she'll wake up and focus those big blue eyes on me. Seven fucking days of being in this room listening to the constant beeping of machines. Car, Pope, Vat, Omen and Halo have been here with me since I got out of surgery. The doctors tried to force me to stay in a separate room, but quickly changed their minds when I strangled the fucker. Vivian managed to smooth things over with them so they didn't kick me out after I threatened to kill them if they didn't take me to my girl.

Viv, Nova and their guys have been here every day as well. I loathe to admit it, but I'm in those masked fuckers debt for saving us. They were right when they said our guys and the Vatel family had cornered Desire's crew. Lives were lost on both sides but in the end, the Vatel family came out the winners.

It doesn't feel like a win. I lost that day.

I'm pulled from my thoughts when a nurse enters the room. The five guys all stand straight and wait for any news, I know there won't be any.

"How you feeling today, sweetie?" the nurse asks Tate.

None of the staff speak to me or the guys, it's clear they think we're nothing but trouble and they're probably right, but I don't give a fuck. As soon as she's better, we'll be out of here. The nurse checks her machines and looks Tate over. I wait for her to leave but to my surprise she stops at the end of the bed and turns back to face me. I meet her judgmental glare with one of my own. "That girl is lucky to be alive. An inch closer and that blade would have nicked her artery and killed her. She deserves better." My face slackens. "If you ask me, the best thing you could do for her is to stay away but what would I know." I say nothing as she stalks out of the room.

Everything she just said is shit I've been mulling over for days. I know she's in this bed fighting for her life because I couldn't stay away. I never thought I would fall in love with the girl I was stalking for months but here I am. I still haven't met with CJ Vatel or even dealt with Desire and Nexus. I know they are being held at one of CJ's warehouses, but I haven't had the heart to leave her bedside. She's in here because of me.

"I warned her," I grit out. "I knew if I claimed her it would kill her."

"Butch, you didn't do this—" I snap my head to the side to glare at Omen.

"Don't give me that shit," I growl. "We all know that this life we have chosen takes everything from us. I was a fucking idiot to think otherwise." My hold on her hand tightens as I stand and lean forward to place a kiss on her forehead. I draw back and rest my head on hers, closing my eyes and breathing her in for the last time. "Loving you gave me the freedom I never thought I would ever get. I love you so much. I never thought I would ever feel this way about anyone, but with you, I never had a choice. Loving you was the easiest thing I have ever done in my life. Thank you for saving me, Bambi," I whisper. I pull back and release her hand, then face my guys. All five of them stare at me with varying looks. I ignore all of them because no matter what they say, I won't change my mind. I know she is better off without me. Loving my sister is what got her killed and me loving Tate, that's what nearly got her killed too.

I won't lose someone else I love.

"Let's go. I have a meeting to attend, her brother to kill and your sister to destroy."

Sitting across the table from Carlito Vatel Jr. three days after leaving Tatum is not something I thought I would be doing in this lifetime. I had nothing to do with his father's death and he knows that. What I am curious about though is why he wanted to meet with me. I had nothing to do with him being involved in this shit with Desire, yet he thinks he can sit there and tell me I have no choice but to meet with him first before he hands over those blood bags I plan to drain, while I relish in their screams as I tear them apart for trying to take my girl from me.

I look around the small coffee shop he chose on the outskirts of town and fight not roll my eyes. He has his men disguised as customers occupying tables, trying to act normal but they're failing miserably. Rather than draw this bullshit meeting out I break the silence.

"How about we cut the bullshit and you either send your men away or tell them to stop their bullshit conversations so we don't have to raise our voices." Laughter erupts from CJ. I don't need to see my brother's faces to know the five of them are rolling their eyes behind me. Falcon–CJ's second whistles and soon after the cafe falls silent, even the staff give up the act and head into the back.

"What gave them away?" CJ asks with genuine curiosity in his tone.

I release an annoyed sigh. "They're stiff, the bulge of their guns. They keep darting their eyes around the place, the combat boots, should I go on or do you get the picture?" CJ stares at me like I've just answered the most complex question.

"You're so much more than the rumors led me to believe, Alex."

I scoff. "We're not friends, let's not sit here and act like we are because we'll never be. Where the fuck are you holding those cunts?" My tone is filled with malice. The guy seated to my left shifts, but doesn't even get to move more than an inch before Omen has his gun drawn and aimed at his head.

"Try it, motherfucker, and I'll blow your fucking brains out," Omen snarls.

Falcon spears the bastard with a look that promises reprimand. "Get the fuck out, you don't make a move unless I say." The guy stands and that's when I realize he can't be much older than Tate. He stalks out of the cafe and slams the door closed behind himself. "I apologize for my son, he's young and too fucking eager." I nod because I have nothing to say, son or not if he tries anything I'll kill him before he can bust a nut.

"I was told that I would be dealing with Miss Lawson."

CJ mentioning Tate has my blood boiling and my fists clenching beneath the table. I take a deep breath and force myself to relax. I've only ever had one trigger and I learned to master control of that, but now it seems Tatum is another and I'll have to learn how to control my urge to murder any motherfucker that mentions her name.

"Well, you're dealing with me, *not* her." CJ smiles and it grates on my fucking nerves because he looks smug as fuck about my answer.

"She said you would say that." I turn rigid.

"The fuck does that mean, Vatel?" Omen snaps. Out of all of my brothers, Omen is the one who is closest to Tate. How she was able to manage to get close to him is a mystery to me. Omen has steered clear of all females since Rosalina abused him.

CJ doesn't falter. "I spoke with her last night."

My face slackens. "She's awake?" I breathe out unintentionally. I told Halo to stop tracking her and for the others not to keep tabs on her. In order for her to be truly safe from my enemies she needs to be nothing to me and the only way I can think of to do that is to act like she never existed. It's the cruelest form of punishment to not only her but to myself as well. Tatum Lawson is venom in my veins. She's a plague that haunts my every waking thought. For someone as small as her, she has taken up every ounce of space inside me, there isn't a crack or crevice she doesn't own within me.

CJ nods. "She is and at the risk of pissing off the infamous Butcher, she's pretty fucking mad at you." I grind my teeth and breathe through my nose, trying to tame the anger unfurling inside me. CJ is young and has much to learn—he's only twenty-two and still thinks like a child. If he has any hopes of taking over Chicago, he better harden the fuck up.

"Pissing me off is the least of your worries. Tatum's anger rivals my own so I'd be very fucking cautious of pissing her off. She tends to throw things when she's mad."

CJ laughs and nods, and I fight against every instinct that tells me to leap across this table and smash his fucking smug face in. "She mentioned that as well."

"Just how fucking friendly are you with Tate?" Omen hisses.

CJ crosses his arms over his chest and all trace of humor vanishes from his face, a hard look enters his eyes. "I respect her," he says in a tone filled with malice. "Tatum Lawson is a good, honest woman and someone I consider a friend."

"Yeah, well, she's family to us," Halo bites out.

"Can we get back to fucking business or are we going to sit here all day measuring how big our cocks are?" I snarl, then slam my hand down on top of the table.

"I made a deal with Tatum and I want to make sure you will honor that deal. I may respect her and consider her a friend of mine, but you and I both know that business and personal life should never mix. I want your word that you will honor the terms I agreed to with Tatum."

"What were her terms?" I grit out, hating that I'm on the back foot. I'm still mad as hell that my brothers let her meet with the fucking don of the Vatel family. Tate has no business getting mixed up in my fucked up world. She's too pure and perfect to be dragged into the darkness that I live in. The shadows are my friends, they have offered me comfort for years since I lost Ellie. Tatum is a bright light and chased those shadows from my life for a brief moment and for that,

I will always be forever grateful to the blonde-haired goddess.

CJ runs his gaze over the five brothers behind me before finally settling his gaze on me. "The deal is that no member of the De Santis family will remain in Chicago. They will never come after my family and we are able to take over all their operations."

I narrow my eyes and lean forward placing my elbows on the table. "Bullshit. Tatum wouldn't have handed you everything and left them with nothing."

CJ smirks. "It was worth a try," he jokes but it falls flat, none of us are in a joking mood and all he is doing is pissing me the fuck off. "The operations you don't want for the Denver Kings will be signed over to me."

"You will—"

He cuts me off before I can finish. "Before you even mention it, Tatum has already told me that the supply and demand for narcotics is one you will never want and I have assured her that any product I distribute will be tested and clean. I don't deal in GHB, never have and never fucking will. You have my word on that, Butcher."

Pride swells inside me. "We want the guns and a twenty percent cut in all the revenues that the hotels turnover—"

Again this motherfucker cuts me off. "I can do fifteen percent. I already agreed to give Tate five percent for her helping me and I won't renegotiate on that." We spend another half hour hashing out the details. CJ will have a contract drafted and sent to Terry—my lawyer—to read over. "They are being held in the basement beneath us." I frown and he shrugs. "I thought it was easier to bring them to you as a show of good faith."

"Where are my brothers?" Pope asks.

CJ shakes his head. "I have no idea, we scooped up the shit stain and the bitch before they could flee out the back, but it was only the two of them. I'm assuming from the angry look on your face that if the twins are spotted you want them?"

"You and your men don't fucking touch them. If you spot them you call us and we'll deal with it," Carnage growls.

"If they're in *my* city we'll find them, you have my word," CJ replies.

"Don't fuck this up or fuck *her* over," I warn.

"You gonna beat me up if I do?" CJ jokes.

"No. I'll come back here and strap your ass to my table and give you a front row seat to how I earned the name Butcher."

CHAPTER THIRTY-TWO

Alexander

I stand in the shadows and relish the sight of Desire strapped to my table while Nexus is chained to a seat near her. A shiver of anticipation rolls through me, I've had them here for nearly five days. Those cunts were thrown in the cargo hold of our plane and brought back to Denver with us, where they were transported straight here so I could claim my revenge. Desire is holding it together better than Nexus. He pissed himself within the first hour of being here.

I love this part of the job. The wait always wears them down first and fucks with their heads. They think because I never came to them straight away that maybe I've been distracted or changed my mind. They sit here every day wondering when I'll finally appear and it starts driving them crazy waiting. There is nothing else to do but get lost in your own head and there is no worse place to be than stuck inside your own mind. It will play tricks on you and make you see things that aren't there and hear noises that don't exist, until you are so paranoid you'll even conjure visions.

Fuck, my cock is getting hard thinking about what I'm going to do to these motherfuckers. My mouth begins to water as I step out of the shadows. Nexus is the first to spot me. His eyes widen to the size of saucers, his face pales and his eyes fill with tears. He can smell his own death clinging to the air, he knows he's about to die by my hands. Desire lulls her head to the side and locks eyes with me. Her face is pulled taut and she tries to hide her fear but I can smell it, it's pungent and potent saturating the air. She can try and put on her brave act as much as she likes but I see through her bullshit.

"I'm going to enjoy breaking you and crushing your mind," I pledge as I walk around the table, skating my fingers along the metal, loving the way she flinches away from me. She may try to put on a bold act but her body knows what's about to happen. I stop and face Nexus who is practically shitting his pants. "You know, I had planned to ship your ass to Panama with your daddy so your sister wouldn't have to lose her brother but then..." I let my sentence trail off and as I slowly stalk toward him, I stop just an inch away, "the truth came out and sealed your fucking fate for you."

"I-I didn't mean—" Before he can finish muttering his bullshit ass excuse, I punch him right in the mouth, loving the sounds of pain that escape him. I know without a doubt that Desire will take a lot more to break than this bitch. He won't be able to withstand my usual tactics so I decide to deal with her first. Seeing her suffer will cause him pain, knowing he'll be next. Omen, Vatican, Halo, Pope and Carnage won't be a part of this, they can't and I respect and understand their reasoning. They may hate her for what she has done, but she's still their sister.

"You took everything from me. You tore my world in half over fucking jealousy!" I boom as I get right in Desire's face. Her eyes widen and she swallows audibly.

"Your sister was—"

"I'm talking about Tatum, you stupid cunt," I snap, cutting her off.

Her eyes shine with mirth. "Killing me won't stop the pain of knowing she died suffering because she cared about you."

I laugh but there's no humor in it. "She's alive, you jaded bitch." My revelation floors her and the look of disbelief on her face fills me with great satisfaction. "You get to die knowing you failed, you tried to take her from me and failed."

"But I took your precious Ellie from you." Weeks ago her saying that would have sent me into a tailspin, I would have lost my cool and destroyed her, but not now.

"But you didn't break me. Losing her was devastating but losing Tatum would have ripped my soul right out of my body and killed me inside. Does hearing that grind your nerves? Does it piss you off to know she never had to spread her legs for me in order for me to fall in love with her? I bet it tears you up inside knowing that I could never love you, but I can love her without any effort."

"Fuck you!" she screams and tries to fight against her restraints, but it's futile. She'll never get out. "She is nothing. She's a weak little whore who will never amount to anything. I'm the don of the De Santis family—"

"You were," I correct. "The De Santis family no longer

exists. Chicago is owned by the Vatel family now. You've lost, Desire. This is the last place you will ever see and my face will be the last thing you look upon before you die."

"She'll never love the monster you are. She'll never embrace the beauty in your darkness and help you hone it. I did that, I made you what you are and it's because of me—"

"You just fed the beast inside me, she tamed it." Her eyes blaze with indignation but slowly bleed way to triumph.

"Yet here you are, with me, nonetheless. You know as well as I do that you could never kill me let alone torture me."

I smile. "Wrong," is all I say before I step away from her and retrieve my cart that holds all my tools and wheel it over to her. She clamps her mouth closed and tries to emanate strength, but the terror in her eyes betrays her. I grip the front of her shirt and tear it open in the same way she did Tatum's, then I reach for my scalpel. Her chest rises and falls in quick succession, a fine sheen of perspiration coating her brow as I glide the tip of the blade across her chest, not deep enough to draw blood but enough to elicit fear. I shiver in excitement, this is everything I have been waiting for. I close my eyes and clear my mind of all the fog and distractions, when I get in the zone I lose track of time, sound, smell and even sight.

I guess Tatum is right, Alexander and The Butcher are two different people. When the Butcher takes over, Alex gets a back seat while he conducts his work. I've never had an issue with that until the night I hurt Tatum. I never meant to betray her trust in the car but the beast inside me needed answers and I knew how to get them at any cost.

When her scream rents the air I revel in the sound. I

open her chest, loving the feeling of her warm fluid coating my fingers. I never use gloves because I enjoy the feeling of their blood on my hands too much. Desire is withering on the table and screaming out as I cut her from chest to navel. I drop my scalpel to the side and reach for my spreader. I hold it above her face and give her the same courtesy I give all my toys by explaining what each instrument does.

"This handy little contraption is going to crack your chest open so I can get inside. Will it hurt? Oh yes, it's going to fucking force you to black out as I peel the skin back. Once that's done I'll decide which one of your ribs I'll take first. Then when that's done, I'm going to start removing your toes, fingers, then we'll move onto your limbs. God, I hope you last, Desire, because I want you to be here for the grand finale when I rip your fucking heart out of your chest with my bare hands."

"You've made your point!" she screams. "You won, I lost, now get me the fuck out of here, Lex." I laugh at the delusional bitch.

"The only way out of here for you is in death. You could have lived a long life but you chose to take from me, not once but twice, and for that you will die painfully, you rotten bitch." I've had enough of talking. I ignore her pleas as I get the spreader in place and begin cranking it open, the sound of her skin tearing and pulling open has my cock standing at attention. I don't even realize she's passed out from the pain until I reach for my skill saw. Oh well, I take two ribs from each side and place them on either side of her head.

My mouth waters and I fight back the instinct to crack her rib cage open and rip her black heart out of her chest. I swallow the urge and move to her feet. I peel her socks off to expose her red painted toes. I reach for my hedge cutters and grip her little toe between the blades.

"You're fucking sick," Nexus snaps.

I shake my head and pull out of my haze, I forgot he was even here for a moment. "And you're next but make no mistake, this is me showing some form of mercy because she's a female. What I'm going to do to you is going to take months. I'll take parts of your body and force you to readjust to life that way before I take something else from you. She won't last the day. She's lucky I care about her brothers or I would have made her punishment last as long as yours." I keep my eyes locked on his as I sever the first toe. Desire comes to with a harrowing scream that could peel paint off the fucking walls. She tries to fight and screams for help but no one will come to her aide.

I retreat into my happy place and block out all the noise as I continue to relieve her of all her toes. I can't help but smile as I think of the game my mom used to play with my toes when I was a child.

This *little piggy went to market, this little piggy stayed home. This little piggy had roast beef, this little piggy had none. And this little piggy went crying wee wee wee all the way home.*

Desire lost consciousness again by the time I finish with her toes. Nexus's screams are getting on my nerves so I grab three of her toes, duct tape them together, then stalk toward him. He tries to fight but we both know I'll always win. This little cunt is going to pay and so is that bitch for stabbing me and Tate. I shove the toes in his mouth then wrap the duct tape around his head so he can't spit them out. I step back and shoot the sniffling little bitch a wink.

"Well, if you didn't have a toe fetish, now you do." I return my focus to Desire. Next to go is all her fingers. There is so much more I want to do to her but because of who her brothers are, I'll end it quickly for them and not rip her apart too badly so they can at least see her body before they bury or burn it. I grab her index finger and turn back to Nexus. He recoils as far back into his chair as he can—laughter bubbles out of me. The pussy is scared I'll add a finger but even I'm not that cruel to mix them together. I look down at her and love the sight of her pale ashen skin. Her breathing is labored and shallow, dammit. I really thought she would last longer.

I cross the room and retrieve the bucket of water. I tip it on her face. She comes to with a gut wrenching shriek. Her eyes are unfocused and hazy from the pain, but all I need is for her to see me one last time. Her eyes latch onto mine and the sight of fear I see in them is everything I ever could have wanted, she knows what's coming.

"You took my innocent little sister from me and tried to take my girl from me and for that, I sentence you to death." Her mouth parts but I don't wait for a response. I shift to stand at her side and grip her rib cage in my bare hands and rip it open. The sound that comes from her is almost orgasm inducing, she has mere seconds before she dies so I don't fuck around. I reach inside her and clasp her heart in my hand, then rip that fucker out. A small gasp escapes her, I keep my eyes on hers and it takes a second before she flat-lines. The artery in my hand is warm and pulses for a moment before that too stills. I turn to Nexus who is staring at me with wide eyes and tears streaking down his cheeks. I toss the heart onto his lap, his scream is muffled as he tries to shake it off his lap by bouncing on his chair.

"When you least expect it is when I'll come for you. You'll learn to live as your sister did for months while I hunted her. I'll make sure your fear becomes your best friend. I won't end your pathetic life until you're so filled with terror that your own shadow will have you pissing yourself as vengeance for what you did to Ellie. Unlike you, I would never have used my sister to lure a monster out but don't worry, this monster will always protect your sister from motherfuckers like you. I may not be able to have her, but I'll always watch over her from a distance and keep her safe."

I stalk out of the room and head upstairs to the main floor. I come to a sudden stop when I spot Omen, Vat, Pope, Carnage and Halo all sitting around upstairs while Damon and the others are packing shipments. I run my gaze over each of my brothers. They're all looking at me and judging from the taut expressions on their faces at the sight of the blood coating me they know what happened in that room. I don't regret what I did but I do feel some type of guilt for their loss. They may have hated her but she was still their sister. I focus on Omen and hate the sight of devastation on his face. She wasn't just his sister, she was his twin and that shit will be tearing him up inside.

"How badly did she suffer?" Carnage asks in a flat tone.

"Not nearly enough," I answer.

"Is she alive?" Halo queries.

I shake my head. "As a favor to you all, I granted her mercy even though she never afforded Ellie or any of us the same courtesy." When they stand to head downstairs, I block the door. "I said I granted her mercy, I never said it wasn't messy. Allow me to get her... taken care of before you all see her. Don't allow my vengeance to be the last memory you have of your sister." They share a look amongst themselves before Omen pushes in front of them to stand before me. I can see the anger in his eyes and I'll weather it, I deserve it. I just took his twin from him and he has every right to hate me for what I did.

"She came into this world with me and regardless of what she did, I won't let her stay down there alone without me. She was a bitch and hated everyone, but her and I are the same. I'll be the one dealing with my twin." I nod and step aside. He pulls the door open but doesn't cross the threshold, I wait for him to say whatever it is he needs to. "I don't hate you, Butch. I could never but right now..."

"I get it," I say, finishing his sentence for him. "I'll stay in town for a while. I have meetings with the arms dealers and investors for the properties. I'll deal with all of that while you all... mourn."

CHAPTER THIRTY-THREE

Tatum

Being stabbed isn't something I thought I would ever have to deal with in my life. Getting my heartbroken was something else I never thought I would have to encounter either, but here I am. Want to know the worst part?

The broken heart hurt more than nearly dying.

When I woke up in the hospital and he wasn't there, I knew. Vivian, Nova and their guys were there but *he* wasn't. I tried to play off how hurt I was and told the girls I was fine and it was just a bit of fun with an expiration date, but they weren't buying it. They were horrified when I told them what happened. They were more shocked that I called CJ Vatel and set up a meeting, according to Nova that is bad bitch energy right there. Having the girls here kept my mind off Alex, which was good, but the first night when the nurse kicked them out and I was left alone, I broke down.

The pain was unbearable, my chest felt like it was caving

in. I've never experienced pain like that before in my life. I couldn't breathe. I was so angry at him for making me love him only for him to get exactly what he wanted, then kick me to the curb like I meant nothing to him.

The girls visited me every day. I dare say I've even become friends with their guys which is something I never saw coming. Those four guys don't speak to any females unless it's Vivian or Nova. They may be scary as fuck and kill people but it's clear, the girls are the ones who you really need to watch out for. Ever since I was discharged from the hospital two weeks ago I've been staying at Vivian's old house in Hollow Hills. The first day here I tried to reach for my laptop only for Ezekiel to throw it across the room. I stood there with my mouth agape.

"Rest. No fucking work. You try to do anything aside from that and I'll fire you myself and deal with my girl's tantrum later," he declared. Vox, Hayze and Archer all stood behind him with their arms crossed, nodding in agreement. I feel bad they are all stuck here because of me. I know they need to be back at CHU and I've tried getting them to leave, but none of them will listen to me.

I find it easier to move around each day. I try to keep busy and play board games with everyone to keep my mind off a certain someone, but it's useless. Alex is under my skin, he's in my blood, my heart, my fucking mind and everything I do reminds me of him. Nights are the worst, when I lay in bed alone I try to fight off the tears but they fall without consent. I don't know how many times I've prayed for him to turn up and whisk me away, but he never comes. Vox told me he and the others were at the hospital with me while I was in a coma, but they don't know why they left.

I do.

In Alex's head he would be blaming himself for what happened to me. No matter what anyone says or does, he'll always blame himself and that's on him. He was a fucking coward and turned his back on me, he gave up on us, not me. I thought we would come out on top and be stronger than ever, but I was a fucking fool. Love doesn't win wars and I lost. That pill is bitter to swallow but I've lived through hell and came out stronger on the other side, and I'll damn sure survive this too. I know I'll never love anyone the way I love him, but I won't put my life on hold and wait for a ghost to return.

"Come on." I look up and frown at the sight of Vox standing at the edge of the sofa.

"Where are we going?" I ask.

"Next door." My face falls, I've done everything I can to avoid looking out the windows on that side of the house so I wouldn't have to see the home my brother grew up in and where my father lived his life like I didn't exist.

I shake my head. "No."

Vox sighs. "Either you come with me willingly or I make Hayze throw your ass over his shoulder and potentially tear your stitches... The choice is yours." I peer over my shoulder and sure enough, Ezekiel, Hayze and Archer all stand there with firm looks on their faces. I roll my eyes and push to my feet. I look around the foyer as I follow Vox, looking for the girls but they're nowhere in sight.

"They went to the store," Archer says, answering my unasked question. I follow Vox across the lawn toward my sperm donor's house. My breathing grows choppy as we come to a stop at the front door. Vox turns to me and holds out a key. I stare at it for a long time, no one making a move or a sound, giving me time to grapple with the emotions warring inside me. I inhale a deep breath and reach for the key. I unlock the door and push it open but don't move, I can't.

"This is just a house," Hayze says softly.

"It was their house, they made a life here without me," I reply bitterly.

"If you had grown up here, you wouldn't be standing here right now with us. They would have molded you into the worst version of yourself. You know *he* has your brother and that he won't survive. You need to see for yourself that he was a monster and let them both go or you will be forever frozen in this moment." Archer's words stir something inside me. I square my shoulders and step inside. The house smells stuffy and dusty. I have no idea how long it has sat here untouched and closed up.

"We were going to take you home to Washington, but Nova and Vivi said you needed to come here to face the ghosts of your past. I seem to think they might have been right," Ez says as I walk around the dining room and take in the sight of the photos that line the walls. Nexus is in most of them. It's hard to see the little boy in the photos who looks innocent but the man he became is a demon.

"Thomas ruined him," I mutter as I reach out and trace a photo of him smiling. He must have been only ten or eleven in this image.

"Thomas ruined a lot of people's lives. He took loved ones from families and never cared about their loss or pain, as long as it served his agenda he didn't care. I fucking hate to admit it but Nexus was the only person Thomas cared about aside from himself." Vox's words settle over and calm some of the anger inside me.

I continued looking through the house, seeing Nova's old room gave me pause. When I went inside to take a look, Vox refused to come in saying that was part of his past and he refused to live it again. I have no idea what that meant but I didn't push him either. Nexus's room was next. It reminds me of a typical boys room, clothes were everywhere, the bed unmade and the curtains were askew as if the last time he was in here he just threw them open and left them as they were.

I stand in the center of my brother's room and spin around in a slow circle, taking it all in. His life growing up was so different to mine. I can clearly see the wealth he grew up with but I feel no envy, just pity for him. Our father bought his love and used him. He was nothing to Thomas but a tool to be used in a war of his own making. Tears prick the back of my eyes. I slam them closed and try to breathe through the pain. Yes, Nexus hurt me deeply but he's still my brother.

"I won't stand here and act like I'm sad knowing he'll die, but I do feel sorry for you." I snap my eyes open and swivel around to face Hayze. His eyes soften as he steps forward and places his hands on my shoulders in a comforting gesture. "He's your brother and no matter how any of us feels, there will always be a part of you that will hate knowing he isn't here with you. Part of you hates him for what he did, but a small part of you still wishes for the big brother you thought you would find when you learned you had a brother. I'm sorry, Tate, but that dream will never come true. We may not be blood but we are your found family. We'll always have your back." A lump forms in my throat and tears cloud my vision.

"T-thank you," I rasp out past the lump.

"We know this is a lot for you to deal with on top of Alex fucking off, which is why we have come to a decision about your job." Panic begins to rise inside me. I pull back from Hayze and implore him with my eyes not to do this, my job is the only thing I have left. "Tate, we want you to come to CHU with us and go to school. Once you finish school you can have your old job back if you want it, but we think CHU will be the best place for you." I stare up at him like he's lost his fucking mind.

I shake my head. "I can't afford that," I admit bitterly.

Vox and Ezekiel share a look before Ez comes to stand beside Hayze. "We aren't going to force you but whenever you're ready, there is a place for you at CHU with us. Think nothing of the cost. It has all been taken care of, so has your dorm and everything. This is a fresh start for you, Tate. After everything we all went through, a fresh start away from all of this shit is what we needed."

I mull over his words and nibble on my lip. "Can I think about it?"

Ez nods. "Of course." His tone is filled with pity and it's going to take a long time for them all to stop looking at me like I'm fragile.

"Do you think you guys could give me a minute alone?" I ask. All of them nod and tell me they'll meet me back at the house. I thank them all and wait for them to leave before moving toward his bed and dropping down onto the edge. I twiddle my thumbs and try to sort through my wayward thoughts.

I actually liked you, I really did, but then you had to go and ruin it and let that fuck face between your legs and caught feelings. I'll be sad to see you go but I won't miss you.

His words play on repeat inside my head. I cared for him deeply. I let Nexus in, only for him to use me to get to Alex. He's just as bad as my brother. He lulled me into a false sense of love, allowing me to think I found a home in him, only for him to toss me aside when he got what he wanted.

I guess I lost to a ghost.

I knew his love for his sister ran deep but I guess I just didn't realize how badly he needed to satisfy his demons. I love him and I would have found a way to deal with him doing what he does. I don't condone what he does, but I loved him enough to find a way to deal with that shit.

A part of me envies Ellie. Her brother went through hell to seek vengeance for her while my own just shit on me, used me as bait to lure out the most notorious killer in the country. Alex searched the world trying to seek justice for his sister, while my brother offered me up to a monster on a silver platter.

I let the monster devour me, own me and consume every part of me, only for him to spit me out when I served my purpose.

CHAPTER THIRTY-FOUR

Tatum

Six months…

"Girl, it's bonfire night. You are coming!" I roll my eyes at Janet, her excitement is catchy and it's annoying as hell.

"I have to study, I have a paper due—"

"Tatum! You are coming with us, don't argue." I groan. Janet beams at Nova, knowing there is no way I'll win an argument against her. Vivian joins us then and I know without a doubt that she has already picked all of our outfits out. Janet and Vivian begin planning how we can do our hair. Nova is much like me, we don't give a shit what we look like. I met Janet on my first day here at CHU. I was a nervous wreck and scared as hell, but she clung to me and helped me adapt to everything. The fact she gets on with Vivian and Nova as well as she does makes everything work with our little foursome.

"You okay?" Nova asks as we follow behind Janet and Vivian.

I release a tired sigh. "Yeah, just haven't been sleeping well," I admit.

"Still having those weird dreams?" she asks quietly.

I nod. "I can't shake the feeling that I'm being watched."

She nods. "I get it. That shit takes a long time to get over. If you need to talk, I'm here." I smile my thanks but don't reply. I've been struggling for a couple of months to get more than a couple of hours of sleep a night. I thought I was past this shit but I guess not. A couple of weeks back I woke up and swore I saw a shadow in the corner of my room, but when I turned the light on, it was gone. A part of me wishes it was Alex but another part doesn't. He's clearly moved on and it's whatever.

I tried to reach out to him but his number is disconnected, so are the others. It hurt knowing that the guys cut me off. The one that stings just as badly as Alex is Omen. I thought he and I were friends, but that's just another thing I was wrong about. For the rest of the afternoon I'm caught up in my head and don't snap out of it until we get to the beach. I look around at all the students smiling and drinking like life is the greatest gift. I envy their happiness.

"Dawson is checking you out," Vivian whispers. I snap my head toward her and frown.

"We're just friends," I defend.

She waggles her brows and backs away toward where Vox and other guys stand. "Does he know you've friend zoned him?" she fires back. I roll my eyes and turn toward Janet who squeals and rushes across the sand toward her boyfriend Kyle. Nova bumps her shoulder into mine, drawing my focus to her.

"There is no time frame on healing. Dawson is great..." When I sigh, she smiles and shakes her head. Vox suddenly appears behind her and wraps his arms around her waist. She melts into him instantly and jealousy rears its ugly head inside me. "What I was going to say is, Dawson is a great guy but he isn't Alex." My mouth parts in a silent gasp. "I get it, truly I do. He doesn't have that aura of darkness that clings to your man effortlessly. But, what I will say is, I really like Dawson and he's a great friend. Don't invest your time in him unless you are truly over Alex because I would hate to see him get hurt."

"Witch, I've had enough of hearing you talk about other guys," Vox growls, then drags Nova away. The sound of her laughter brings a smile to my face. That smile slowly fades when Dawson appears in front of me. I feel guilty because Dawson is freaking handsome and any girl would be lucky to have a guy like him, but he just isn't the guy for me.

"Something on your mind?" he asks.

I nibble on my bottom lip and debate how to answer that question. "Dawson, are we friends?" He frowns and nods cautiously.

"I'd like to think so," he says skeptically.

"I want us to stay that way..." Nerves thrum through me, this is the very reason I didn't want to come tonight, because I knew he would find me and I would have to try to find a way to dodge his request to go for coffee or something. It surprises me when he smiles wide and slings his arm over my shoulders and draws me into his side.

"No offense, Tate. I really like you and everything and

I'm sorry if I came off as wanting to date you, but I was genuinely just trying to be friendly because you always look so freaking sad." My mouth parts and I balk up at him. He rolls his lips over his teeth to keep from laughing. Shame washes over me. I bury my face in my hands as his laughter booms out of him and I wish a tidal wave would come and wash me away.

"I'm so sorry," I mumble into my hands.

"I swear, I'm totally good with being friend zoned." The humor is clear in his tone and I want to facepalm myself but refrain.

"Okay, well, now that we have that sorted, I'm gonna go die of shame in my dorm." I turn to flee, only for Dawson to catch up to me a couple of steps later. "Let me die alone please," I beg.

He just laughs and throws his arm around my shoulders. "Never. I'm gonna walk you back to your dorm."

"No you don't have to," I say as we reach the sidewalk that is shrouded in shadows from the trees. The street lamps afford us enough light to see our way until we reach the main street near campus.

"Yes, I do," he counters.

"No, you don't." I slam to a halt at the sound of the voice. I feel Dawson tense beside me as we both stand here watching as a shadow materializes from behind the trees, my breath hitches at the sight and my knees go weak. Dawson instinctively shifts his hold and wraps his arm around my waist to keep me from falling into a heap. His green eyes shine with rage as he stares at Dawson's arm around me. I guess it doesn't help that I'm standing here in a bikini top and denim cut offs. His gaze takes in the sight of the ink across my collarbone and I scold myself internally for leaving that exposed.

"We don't want any trouble—"

He cuts Dawson off before he can finish. "Then I suggest you turn the fuck around and go back to your party," he snarls in a tone laced with venom.

Dawson's grip on me tightens. I try to get my mouth to work but no words come out. "Yeah, I'm not leaving her here with you, asshole."

When he takes a step toward us I tense. I know what's going to happen if I can't get myself under control. He'll kill Dawson and I can't let that happen. When he's mere feet from us I manage to pull free of Dawson's hold and cut in front of him just in time to place my hand against his chest, stopping him from reaching my friend. His eyes blaze at the feeling of my hand on him and has lava filling my veins, having him this close again.

"Tatum, get out of here," Dawson growls.

"Dawson!" At the sound of Vox's voice I look to the side to see him, Ezekiel, Nova, Vivian, Hayze and Archer rushing toward us. Both the girls look shocked to see Alexander standing before me but not the guys. I narrow my eyes when they come to a stop near us. Archer at least has the decency to look guilty when he meets my accusing stare.

"You guys knew he was here," I whisper, hurt lacing my words and the four guys all nod. I scoff, then tear my gaze from them to meet those green eyes I have been dreaming about for months. I can see so many emotions swirling in the depths of his eyes, but I ignore them. I can't handle that right now. "Six months," I say quietly. He exhales and implores me with his eyes not to push him away. "I searched for you, I tried to find you. I flew to Denver."

"I know," he says brokenly.

"Don't speak," I snap. He clamps his mouth closed instantly, tears blur my vision as all the pain I have repressed for six months rushes to the surface, threatening to break me. "You left me. You turned your fucking back on me and now you decide you want to come back?" I shout, unable to control my rising emotions. "Fuck you, Alexander Denver, I hate you," I snap, then shove against his chest. The asshole doesn't budge. "You son of a bitch!" I scream as my tears fall and I pound my fists against his chest. He allows me to continue to hit him and scream at him without doing a damn thing.

"Touch her and I'll snap your fucking neck," Alex sneers. I snap out of my haze and turn to see Dawson frowning at him. Ez reaches out and grabs his arm, pulling him away from me.

"Don't fucking hurt her," Hayze snaps at Alex.

"Wait, I'm not leaving her," Nova says.

"Me either," Vivian adds. I attempt to move toward my friends but Alex grabs my arm, halting me. Without thought I whirl around and slap him. His eyes blaze. I give him an 'I don't give a fuck' glare.

"Get your fucking hands off me, you son of a bitch," I scream.

"Stop calling my mom a bitch!" he snaps. My nostrils flare and his upper lip pulls back in a snarl.

"Witch, walk away now or I'll throw you over my shoulder. Same goes for you, Vivian. This has nothing to do with either of you," Vox barks.

"Like fuck. She's our friend and he broke her heart!" Vivian fires back. Alex flinches at her words. I try to pull free but he won't release his hold on me.

Alex turns to Vivian. "She'll be back at the end of spring break, you have my word." I balk up at him.

"The fuck do you mean?" I snap. Alex bends at the knees, then throws me over his shoulder before I can do a goddamn thing about it. I start punching his back and digging my nails into the scars that mar his back.

"Alex–"

"Vivian, this has nothing to do with you. She's coming with me whether you like it or not. I'm not asking your permission, I'm telling you. She'll call you when she calms down," Alex says.

"I'm not going anywhere with you!" I yell.

"Yeah you are, Bambi," is all he says before he turns and starts walking away. I lift my head to see the four guys holding the girls and Dawson back.

"Hurt her and I'll kill you, Alexander!" Nova yells after us.

"Noted," Alex mumbles.

"Put me down!" I hiss.

"No. Your defiant ass will just try to run away and I'm too tired to chase you," he claps back.

"I don't want you to chase me."

"Bullshit, Bambi. It gets you wet when I hunt you down." I balk at his rudeness but I can't lie and say that his words don't have my pussy clamping down on air. I haven't had any reaction from that nasty bitch for six months, and now, suddenly, mere seconds after being around this asshole, she seems to flare back to life.

"I hate you," I snicker.

"I fucking love you." His words have my breath hitching. I remain silent and don't fight his hold. When he finally comes to a stop, he makes sure I feel every inch of him when he slides me down his front. Fuck, I can feel he's hard for me and its taking a lot more self-control than I want to admit to keep focused. He reaches out and cups my face between his hands, his eyes bore into mine and it's too much. I reel back and shake free of his hold. I spin away from him, ready to run but I come face to face with Omen. A ghost of a smile crests on his lips, his eyes are filled with remorse. I can't stop myself.

I lurch forward and he catches me with ease. I bury my face in the crook of his neck and hold him tight, my tears fall silently and soak into his skin. His hold on me tightens. Neither of us utter a word for a long time. When my tears finally stop falling, I pull back. He places me on my feet and smiles sadly down at me.

"Hi, Tate," He whispers.

"Hi, Omen," I say quietly.

His smile widens but I see the sadness in his eyes. It's consuming him and I know why that is. I reach out and clasp his hands in mine. "I hear we're spending spring break together?" He cuts a glance above my head to look at Alex for a second before focusing back on me.

"If it helps, I packed your bag?"

I sigh dejectedly and roll my eyes. "No it doesn't, but me complaining about it isn't going to change things, is it?" He shakes his head then leads me to the car that's idling at the curb. The back door opens and Carnage steps out. My eyes widen at the sight of him. "I see you're still around."

Carnage scoffs. "Yeah, nice to see you too, brat," he mutters. I slip inside the car and shake my head.

"Of course he brought the fucking calvary." I snicker when I see Pope, Vatican and Halo. The guys laugh. I move to the back of the car, Carnage claims the seat beside Halo and Alex and Omen climb in the back with me, forcing me to sit in the middle. I press in as close as I can to Omen, not wanting to touch Alex at all if I can help it. Omen sighs and shakes his head but I ignore him. Alex is growling and I can feel him glaring holes into the side of my head but fuck him!

"Airport?" Pope asks from the front seat.

"Yeah," Alex clips out.

"Where are we going?" I ask.

"Home—"

"I wasn't talking to you, asshole!" I snap, cutting Alex off. I ignore the four dicks in the front snickering and look up at Omen who has his gaze trained on Alex.

"You know he has a gun pointed at me, right?" Omen says with humor lacing his words. We all know Alex will never pull that trigger.

"He's just got his panties in a bunch because I'm happy to see you and not his mug." Omen bites down on his lips to keep from laughing, but Vatican and Carnage have no issues with releasing their humor.

"*He* can hear you," Alex snarls.

I roll my eyes, forcing Omen to smile and shake his head. "And your point is?" I snap still keeping my back to him.

"My point is I'm about to lose my shit Tatum, and you won't like what happens—" I spin around and face him, pinning him with a look of malice.

"Don't you fucking threaten me!" I scream. I feel Omen

flinch behind me. "You don't get to come back into my life after six fucking months and think I'll drop to my knees and worship you like some fucking God!"

Alex snaps his hand out and grips the back of my neck. He and I both freeze when we hear guns cocking. I dart my gaze to the side to see both Carnage and Halo have their guns drawn, I know without a doubt Omen has his drawn as well. Alex grinds his teeth as he shoots each of the guys a scathing look.

"Don't keep pushing me, Tate."

I snort. "Oh, I'm fucking trembling, Alex. What are you going to do, chain me up? No, your ex did that. You going to drug me? Nope, your ex did that as well. Wait, are you going to stab me?" He releases me and recoils into his side. "Nope, your ex did that as well. Oh, I know. How about you wait till I'm on my deathbed and then disappear from my fucking life after I risked everything to save you!" I don't realize I'm screaming or even crying until I finish. "She nearly killed me," I whisper. He flinches as if I've caused him physical pain. "She was going to have her men rape me while you watched."

"She's dead," Alex grits out.

"You don't fucking get it," I whisper brokenly as the car comes to a stop. When Halo and Carnage climb out I rush to follow after them. I nearly make it to the plane before Alex grabs my waist and yanks me back until I face him.

"What don't I get?" he roars.

"You leaving me hurt more than anything she did. You once asked me *who hurt me*, the answer to that is *you*."

CHAPTER THIRTY-FIVE

Alexander

I knew she would be angry and hurt but I didn't think she would downright hate me. She refuses to even look in my direction. She seems to have no problem forgiving Omen for leaving her or even the others. The only one she is giving attitude toward is Carnage, but it seems like that is their brand of friendship.

"What's your plan here, brother?" Omen asks as he claims the seat opposite me on the plane.

I scrub a hand down my face and sigh tiredly. For six months I have done nothing but work my ass off to become a man she could be proud of and be safe with, but I'm starting to think that it was all for nothing.

"I don't know," I answer honestly.

"I told you she would be pissed."

I shoot him a glare. "You think you know her better than me?" I grit out.

He shakes his head. "Never said that," he defends.

"She hates me," I utter brokenly.

He scoffs. "If she hated you, she would have fought to not be on this plane right now. That girl loves you, Alex, but you have to see that you hurt her. Every person who has meant something to her has left her behind."

I frown. "I didn't leave her—"

"Thomas didn't want her. Her mother left. Nexus used her. She fell in love with you, and formed a partnership with the Vatel family in order to save you. She even got the Filthy Few to put on their masks, even with the threat of the CIA coming after them if they wore those things again. She risked it all for you and you left."

"You know why I did it," I snarl.

"We all told you it was a bad idea. You wouldn't listen and now the great Alexander Denver is going to have to learn how to grovel and kiss ass, because that girl isn't going to forgive you easily." He stands and rejoins Tatum and the others at the front of the plane, leaving me here to mull over his words. I know what he says is true, but I needed to fix the wrongs of my past before I could embrace my future with her. Make no fucking mistake, Tatum Lawson is a part of my future whether she likes it or not.

I'll make her see this big bad wolf will blow down all her walls until I'm the only thing left standing in her life.

When we arrive at the ranch, Tate laughs but there's no humor to it. "Oh, would you look at that, someone's home this time," she snarks. Omen remains silent and follows her out of the car. I knew she would come looking for us, so for the first three months after we left I asked the guys to stay away from here. I knew if she found one of them she would have latched onto them and never left. I follow them all into the main house. Vatican and Halo both place her bags by the back door. Tatum scoffs, then places her hands on her hips. She turns around and my breath hitches for a second until I realize she's only looking this way because Omen is standing beside me.

"I'm not staying with *him*. Can I sleep in your room?"

Before he can answer, I shift forward and stand in front of her. She cranes her neck back and meets me with a hardened stare, her blues a storm of emotions. "I warned you—"

"Your warnings mean shit to me. You said not to go to a club and shake my ass to make you jealous, this is me showing you I don't give a fuck about what you want, Alex. I'm here because I didn't have a choice. There was no way I was going to let you hurt Dawson."

My jaw locks as I close the sliver of space between us. A shiver works its way through her from my close proximity. "Say his name again and see—"

"Dawson," she purrs the fuckers name and smirks. Without any warning I bend and toss her spiteful ass over my shoulder. She kicks and screams but the guys do nothing. Vatican shoves the back door open for me.

"Bye, Tate."

"Fuck you, Carnage!" she screams and I step outside and stalk toward my house. "You better be ready to cuff my ass to your bed because I'm running the first chance I get."

"I'll chase you and when I catch you, you and I both know what'll happen, Tatum." She clamps her mouth closed and remains silent. When I enter my house I stalk toward the bed and toss her onto it. She squeals and bounces up and down. I can't stop myself from staring at her tits and black triangle swim top. My mouth waters with need to taste her.

"Don't look at me like that," she scolds as she scurries off the bed. She straightens her top and pats down her denim shorts. My gaze snags on the tattoo across her collarbone again. I reach out and trace the tip of my finger over it. She begins to tremble but doesn't push me away.

I read aloud. "4221 A.D." She darts her tongue out to moisten her lips, her eyes begin to fill with tears and I hate the look of pain etched into her beautiful face. "What does it mean?"

She swallows then blows out a breath. "I got it after I was released from the hospital." I close my eyes and force myself to remain calm and meet her stare again. "I... I needed to keep a piece of you with me," she admits as her first tear falls. I reach out and cup her cheek but she pushes my hand away. "I was left with a fucking tattoo because the real thing wasn't there. I was alone and terrified and all I wanted was you. I've never had a person before and I let you be that for me. I fucking let you mean something to me." Agony is etched into her words and it kills me to know I'm the cause of her pain.

"What does it mean, Tatum?" I push.

"4221 means forever together to love one another. It was something Nova taught me. I'm sure you're smart enough to figure out what A.D. stands for," she spits the last part. then shoulders past me. I swivel around and reach for her but she leaps out of reach. "I'm going for a shower and your ass is going to stay right here. I mean it, Alex. I'm not falling back into bed with you. I'll bide my time here until spring break is over and then I'm going back to school... *alone.*"

I don't stop her. The urge to kick the door and ignore her plea is strong, especially when I hear her crying, but I respect her enough to let her deal with all of this on her own time. I set out some clothes for her on the bed. When she steps out of the bathroom, I nearly die from the sudden loss of blood that raced to my dick.

"Bambi," I growl in pain. She just scoffs and saunters toward the bed naked! I bite down on my fist and whimper. When she bends over and flashes me her pussy, I nearly cum in my fucking jeans. If I stand here a second longer, I'll lose control, throw her on the bed and fuck the anger out of her until she forgives me. I storm into the bathroom and slam the door closed. The sound of her laughter has me grinding my teeth to the point of pain and my hand itching to spank her ass for being such a defiant little shit.

My shower is ice fucking cold, that's nothing new to me at this point. Every time I think about her I get hard, it's fucking frustrating. It was so much easier to manage my urges when she wasn't standing naked in the next room. I step out of the bathroom and head straight for my drawers. I pull on a pair of sweats and snatch a shirt, then tug it on. When I turn around and see the place is empty I lose it and race out of the house. I head toward the main house but slam to a halt. I slowly swivel toward the pasture and know where she is. I sprint through the long grass. The closer I get, the more sure I am that she's out here. I spot her sitting beneath the lone tree and all the panic drains from me at the sight of her safe and unscathed.

She doesn't turn to face me or even acknowledge my

presence. My chest is burning from exertion, my breathing is rugged from sexual need and from fucking running fast enough to rival Usain Bolt.

"You once told me this was her favorite place," she says quietly. I sigh and sit down beside her, leaving an inch of space between us. I bend my knee and rest my arm over the top of it, staring out at the nothingness in front of me. The stars are shining so bright tonight. "You also told me she was your breaking point." I nod, feeling her gaze on me but unable to look at her. "I told you I couldn't compete with a ghost, Alex, and I meant it." I close my eyes and breathe through the pain in my chest. "I envy the way you love your sister. If my brother loved me even a fraction of the amount you love Ellie, I wouldn't be here right now." I snap my head toward her and stare into her eyes, hating the grief I see in them.

"I would have found you regardless of how he felt about you, Bambi. There isn't a place in this world you could hide from me."

"I hid out at CHU for months without you knowing."

I smirk which has her frowning. "Did you ever ask Vox who paid for your tuition and *single* dorm?" Her eyes widen and her jaw unhinges.

"What?" she shrieks.

"Baby, I knew where you were this whole time. I made sure you would be somewhere safe while I finished what I started. I left you, Tatum, because I wasn't good enough for you then."

"And what? You think you are now because so much time has passed?"

"I told you loving me would be like loving time, you

would never know how long you had. I didn't want my hour glass to run out before I got to experience life with you."

"What the hell does that mean?"

"Five years ago I bought the freedom of me and my brothers from the De Santis Cosa Nostra. I thought we were invincible. We built the Denver Kings and were making something of ourselves until two years later I lost my light. My world turned dark. I was sent to prison for the murders I didn't commit, thanks to Thomas. I thought my life was over until Vivian helped me get my freedom. I was angry. I thirsted for vengeance and I knew I wouldn't be able to rest until I avenged my sister. She became my breaking point."

Tatum nods sadly. "I know. She's the center of your world."

I shake my head and reach out to cup her cheek. She nestles her face into my hand, needing the comfort I offer. "She was." Her brows furrow. "My world was dark and lonely. I had one mission, get justice for Elenor, but then a blonde haired cyclone came into my life and flipped everything upside down. I didn't know it until it was too late, but Ellie wasn't my only weakness. You are my greatest strength and weakness, Bambi. Seeing you chained up..." I clamp my mouth closed and force myself to breathe through the anger. "I couldn't save you."

"I didn't need to be saved, I just needed you to know I would risk it all for you. I had a plan and I just needed you to trust me to save us both."

"And you did."

She shakes her head. "No, I still lost. You won your war, you got your vengeance but it cost you me."

She pulls back and I stare at her with fear thrumming

through me. "Bambi, please don't turn your back on me. I can't let you go—"

"Why?" she screams and climbs to her feet. I mimic her move and stare down at her. "I can't trust you, Alex. You hurt me."

"I know."

"No, you don't. Do you know what it's like to not be able to breathe daily because your heart wants to give up? You didn't just break my heart, you obliterated it. You fucking destroyed me worse than Ray ever could have."

I recoil. "I'm nothing like your foster father."

"You hurt me, maybe not in the same way he did, but you still hurt me."

"I left you so I could do all of this!" I say and wave my arms around me.

"Do what?"

"I gave up everything. I no longer run the Denver Kings. I handed everything over to the guys. I made a deal of my own with CJ."

Disbelief is clear in her eyes. "What deal?"

"The Denver Kings get the firearms. I bought into the hotels CJ owns. You own five percent, the guys own fifteen, CJ owns fifty percent and I own the rest. I knew I wouldn't be able to make a life with you if I was still The Butcher. I couldn't stomach the thought of you hating the sight of me coming home drenched in someone's blood, so I gave it all up. I did all of this for you!" I roar.

CHAPTER THIRTY-SIX

My mouth is agape as I stare up at him in shock. "You gave it all up?" I mutter.

He nods. "When I told you that I loved you, Bambi, I meant it." His words implore me to believe him and eradicate this distance I've put between us.

"No more killing?"

"I won't lie to you. If someone comes after my brothers or you, I will kill again. I can't control the side of me that will come out when someone I love is threatened. Please don't make me promise—"

"I get it," I say, cutting him off. I nibble my bottom lip, debating how to ask my next question. "Did you kill Desire?"

His face blanks of all emotion. "Don't ask questions you don't want the answers to, baby," he warns.

"I'm asking," I push.

"Yes."

"Did she suffer?"

"Not nearly as much as I wanted," he growls.

"Why?"

"I showed her mercy because of who she was to my brothers. Her death has taken a toll on Omen."

I sigh dejectedly. "I know."

He frowns. "How?"

"I saw it in his eyes," I admit.

"He's... dealing," he grits out.

"What about..." I take a deep breath and force myself to woman the fuck up. "What about Nexus?" Alex's features harden, his nostrils flare in anger and I study him for a while, trying to get a read on his emotions but fail. "Alex, I need–"

"He's alive," he grits out through clenched teeth.

"Why?" I hedge.

He scoffs. "So are you mad he's alive and not dead now?" he snaps.

"Fuck you," I fire back.

"Please do, baby, because my balls are as blue as your eyes right now." I gape at him.

"Alex!" I scold.

"What?"

"That's... no... you can't say that shit."

"Why the fuck not?"

"Because... you just can't."

"Why the fuck not? I'm not gonna hide it. I'm rock fucking hard for you right now, baby, and I want to sink my cock so deep inside your cunt that you can taste me on your tongue."

I'm wet.

I can feel my arousal coating the inside of my thighs and

now more than ever I'm grateful he gave me a pair of black sweats to borrow. My pussy is pulsing with need.

"Don't play coy. You loved throwing that shit in Desire's face about how I fucked you." I feel the blush coating my cheeks.

"I did it to distract her."

"Hmmm, so you gonna stand there and lie and say it didn't give you satisfaction telling her I was your boyfriend and rubbing it in her face about me loving you?" I push my tongue into my cheek fighting not to laugh. Alex presses in closer until his front is plastered against me and sure enough, he's rock fucking hard for me. "Admit it, you want me so stop playing hard to get, Bambi, and let me fuck you, then we can fight later."

"Sex won't solve anything." I hate how breathy I sound.

"It would resolve this sexual tension between us so we could focus on actually arguing instead of picturing ways we could fuck."

"Alex—"

He growls. "Fuck, fine, here are your options. One, I fuck you right here, now, and we can fight later, or two, I tell you what happened to your brother, then we fuck all night and don't fight later. Choose!" I balk up at him. I attempt to take a step back but he snakes an arm around my waist and anchors me to him. "Before you try and spit some bullshit, don't. I know you're wet for me, so stop fucking torturing my pussy and let me give her some relief." I snort out a laugh, unable to stop it.

"You ever turn your back on me again, Butcher, and I swear to fucking Christ I will chop you up into little bits myself and make Omen help me bury them around the world." He fights not to smile and nods. "I mean it, don't you dare fucking hurt me again. You're still not forgiven." His eyes blaze and need courses through me.

"I'll fuck forgiveness into you, baby. Now, which option?" His voice is husky and sends a shiver down my spine.

"Two."

"Your brother is alive." My eyes widen to the size of saucers. "Don't get excited, I had planned to drag out his punishment but the guys convinced me that killing him would make you hate me, so I just removed some parts, then sent him to Panama to join your father." He tries to reach for me but I bat his hands away. He flops his head back and groans up at the sky.

"What do you mean removed some parts?"

He smiles sheepishly down at me. "Well, I refused to allow the Valerian name to continue so I removed that sorry ass excuse of a cock. He has nubs for arms and legs. I removed him of his tongue and ears as well. I left the cocksucker his eyes, which I think was very gracious on my part." I stare up at him speechless. When I say nothing his face falls. "Baby, I let him live for *you*."

"I... I don't know what to say," I admit. Honestly a lot of my anger I harbored toward Alex was because I thought he killed my brother, but now I find out he didn't that changes things.

"Are you mad?" he presses.

I shake my head. "No, just shocked." He reaches out and wraps his arms around me and pulls me against him. I don't fight him. I return his embrace and melt into him, instantly loving the feeling of safety he offers me without having to do anything aside from just holding me. "Thank you," I mumble against his chest.

"For what?"

"For not killing him. I know what he did and I know that would have been really hard for you so, thank you." He pushes me back, then claps my face between his hands and bends down so we are eye level. I reach out and skim my fingers through his beard, relishing in the feeling of it again.

"I love you, Bambi, and I'll earn your forgiveness and trust back even if it's the last thing I do."

"Want to earn my trust right now?"

His brow furrows. "How?"

"Don't move from this spot for five minutes." Before he can grasp my meaning, I turn and flee, his booming laughter following me.

"Run as fast you can ,Bambi. I'll find you." I smile when I reach the woods, this place has memories. I lost my virginity here. I know for a fact it hasn't been five minutes when I feel him at my back. I don't turn around.

"You cheated," I say quietly.

His arm snakes around my waist and pulls me back against him. I gasp when I feel his cock pressing against my back. His other hand grips the front of my throat and tilts my head back to meet his gaze. "There are no rules when it concerns me getting to you. You're mine, Tatum." He smashes his mouth to mine and I'm lost to my primal need. I turn in his hold, never breaking the kiss. I wrap my arms around his neck and deepen the kiss—fuck, I've missed this so much. I've missed him. He grips the backs of my thighs and lifts me. I lock my legs around his waist and grind against his erection, needing some form of friction. I gasp into his mouth and break the kiss when he slams me against a tree. "You have no fucking idea how many times I've dreamed of this moment."

"Well, stop dreaming and make it a reality," I taunt, his eyes darken and I relish in the sight. He drops me to my feet, steps back into the glow of the moon and yanks his shirt off. I mimic his move, then push my sweats down my legs and kick them to the side. A delicious shiver rolls down my spine because of the way he's looking at me. He grips his waistband, pushes his sweats down his legs and frees his glorious cock. Oh my God, that sight alone has my mouth watering. I move toward him, loving the look in his eyes. When I drop to my knees before him, his mouth parts in shock. I reach out, grip his cock and love the sounds coming from him when I stroke him.

I press up onto my knees and swipe my tongue across the head of his cock, moaning at the taste of his pre-cum. He shudders and tangles his fingers in my hair.

"Bambi, don't fucking tease me right now," he grits out, sounding like he's in pain.

"Shut up," I snap, then wrap my lips around him and take him as far as I can into my mouth.

"Fuuuuuccckkk," he roars. He doesn't try to control my movements, knowing I need to be the one in control in this position. He allows me to set my rhythm and pace. "Shit, baby, that feels so fucking good. Keep sucking me like that, Bambi." I do as he says, hollow my cheeks and bob up and down faster. The thought of giving someone a blow job was a hard no for me and a trigger, but with Alex, I feel nothing but safe. He's never pushed me or forced me to do this. He's always allowed me to move at my own pace, and it's because of that I have the confidence to do it now. "Baby, you gotta stop or I'm gonna cum down that pretty throat of yours," he forces out through gritted teeth. I pull back and release him with a *pop*. I look up and love the blissed-out tense look in his eyes, knowing I'm the one that put that look on his face is so fucking empowering.

He grips my arms and hauls me to my feet. His lips are on mine within seconds. This kiss is filled with so much longing and passion that it robs me of air. I'm forced to breathe him in or risk passing out from lack of oxygen. His hands roam my body, his touch so sure and practiced as he has memorized every inch of me. When he cups my tits, I moan into his mouth. My nipples are hard and aching, begging for his touch. I arch forward into his hands, demanding without words that he give me what I want.

He breaks our kiss, then dips his head and wraps his sinful lips around my nipple. I throw my head back and cry out. His arm bands around my waist, holding me in place. His teeth scrape my sensitive nipple, sending a shudder through me. He switches sides and draws another sharp cry from my lips. He swirls his tongue around my hardened nipple, then scrapes his teeth along it, causing me to start panting. I tangle my fingers in his hair and love the feeling of the silky strands falling between my fingers.

He releases my nipple with a wet pop, then reclaims my lips. He pushes his hand between our bodies and skates a single finger through my folds and groans when he feels how wet I am for him.

He breaks our kiss and stares into my eyes as he continues to circle my clit. "You saved this for me for six months, didn't you, Bambi?"

My mouth fires off a response before I can stop it. "What makes you think there wasn't anyone else?"

His eyes blaze with jealousy and his features darken. He shoves a finger inside my wet cunt. I gasp in surprise and reach out to grip his shoulders as I press onto my tip toes. He fingers me at a punishing pace, making it hard for me to breathe let alone think.

"I may have told my brothers to stop watching you, but that doesn't mean I didn't have eyes on you the whole time. For the sake of your mask wearing friends, I hope you're lying, Bambi, because I would hate to break my vow to you already and murder some motherfucker while you watch."

There's something wrong with me. I'm clearly sick in the head. His words shouldn't inspire a need within me, yet they do, much like Alex. I guess I have a monster of my own inside, one that thirsts for him and his attention.

"Tell me now, Bambi. Were you fucking someone or were you just trying to make me jealous?" he asks in a tone laced with equal parts anger and lust. He may be mad that I said what I did, but it also turns him on. I can feel my orgasm cresting and I try to latch onto it, needing the relief it will give me more than I need my next fucking intake of air, but Alex slows his pace and I growl in frustration. "I'm waiting."

"No! I never even looked at anyone else. It's only been you. Happy now?" I snap.

The motherfucker smirks. "Ecstatic," he purrs, then presses the pad of his thumb against my clit and quickens his pace. Moans tumble from my lips and my nails rake down his back as I arch into him, trusting him to hold me as I break apart in his arms. My orgasm is so powerful my knees buckle. Alex's hold on me is the only thing that keeps me from falling to the ground. My vision blurs as pleasure surges through me like a current and a sheen of sweat coats my entire body. His name was screamed loud enough for the guys back at the house to have heard, but judging from the smug look on his face he's okay with that.

Alex gently withdraws his finger and brings it to his lips. I watch with rapt focus as he sucks the digit into his mouth and groans at the taste. My pussy clenches on air.

"Fuck, I missed that taste, baby." He then claims my lips, forcing me to taste myself on his tongue. I love knowing I'm the only woman who will ever get to see him like this.

I'll be the only woman he'll ever love.

Alex gently lowers me to the ground and nestles his way between my legs. Butterflies take flight inside my stomach. My body begins to heat in anticipation at what's to come. He leans forward and rests his hands on either side of my head.

"Put me inside you, baby. I need to feel your pussy now." I eagerly obey him and the second he pushes inside me I scream.

"Fuck, holy shit. I forgot how big you are."

Laughter breaks free from him. "Fuck, baby, you're so good for my ego."

I swat his chest. "Shut up or I'll run away from you like last time." Another bout of laughter escapes him.

"You run, I chase," he says. Before I can utter a response, he slams the rest of the way inside me. My back arches off the forest floor as my scream rents the air. "Fuck, baby, I missed this." He growls as he begins to move, not giving me a chance to adjust. I know he's as wound up as I am and right now, so I don't need him to drag this out. I need him to fuck me like a beast, then he can take his time later. Right now, all

I want is to come on his cock and mark him as mine once again.

My nails dig into the scars on his back as I lock my legs around his waist. He growls his approval and slams inside me harder, the head of his cock hitting my sweet spot and with how fucking turned on I am, I know I'll be screaming his name within seconds at this rate.

"Alex, don't stop," I beg.

"Never," he vows as he pulls almost all the way out, then thrusts back inside me.

"Do it again, I need—" My demand is cut off when he does it again and my climax erupts from inside me like a volcano. His name is screamed until my throat is hoarse.

"Fuck, Bambi," he roars, then thrusts once more and follows me over the cliff of ecstasy. He flops forward and buries his face in the crook of my neck—we're both panting and breathless, covered in sweat and dirt. I wrap my arms around him and run my fingers through his hair, loving the relaxed sigh that escapes him.

"This is what I want forever. There won't be anyone else in this world that will ever compare to you, Alex. Don't hurt me again because next time, I won't survive it." He pulls back and stares down at me with nothing but love in his beautiful green eyes.

"I'll never let you go, Tatum. I told you my heart beats for you and I meant it. It's yours to do with as you please. I swear on my sister, I'll never hurt you intentionally again. Almost losing you put so many things into perspective for me. You are the most important thing in my life and I'm done chasing the ghosts of my past. I found my reason for wanting more from life. I choose to live now for you. I promise I'll never hide in the shadows again."

I cup his cheek and fight back my tears. "I love you, Alexander Denver."

He smiles cockily. "I should hope so since those are my initials tattooed on you."

I snort. "You're a real dick, you know that, right?"

He laughs and places a chaste kiss to my lips, then gently pulls out of me. I watch as he stands and searches for his pants. I frown when he grabs his phone from his pocket and hands it to me. I grab it and stare up at him with a raised brow.

"Turn the torch on," he demands, then turns his back to me. I do as he says and the second I shine the light on his back my mouth falls open. "You weren't the only one who needed something to hold onto." I climb to my feet and reach out to trace my fingers over the tattoo that now covers his scars. It's an hourglass in the middle of a forest with a deer set off to the side. It doesn't take a rocket scientist to know that deer represents me, but it's the words at the top that have me fighting back my tears.

I'd live a hundred lifetimes and search a thousand worlds to find you.

Alex turns to face me and smiles down at me. It's hard to believe this Aztec god is mine. It's going to take a long time for me to get used to that fact. "I love you, Bambi."

I fucking swoon. "I love you too," I whisper, then press up onto my tiptoes and kiss him. I was never a believer in Disney movies or happily ever afters, but if I had to choose one of those movies to represent us, I guess *Beauty and The Beast* would be it. I tamed the monster inside him and brought the man lurking inside the shadows out of the darkness to live again.

I guess if you asked Alex, he would say we'd be *Little Red Riding Hood* because he's the big bad wolf and blew down the walls of my houses, so he could make a home inside me.

THANK YOU

I can't even put into words how much I fucking loved writing each of these characters. They were a dream and fuck me dead, it was so fun to write something different. But, it turns out I can't seem to stay away from mafia! I guess I found my home in mafia, which is why Alex had to be the one to bring them in. Thank you for reading this series. I just knew from book one that Alex would have to have a book and I couldn't think of a better woman for him than Tatum Lawson. She is a spitfire and fits him perfectly, don't ya think?

I cannot thank you enough for reading *Filthiest Of Them All*, it means the world to me that you have taken a chance on reading one of my books!

ACKNOWLEDGMENTS

Marky—motherfucking—Beez, my personal butcher of my lady bits! I love you, babe, and thank you for being my rock through all this crazy author journey. I couldn't have done any of this without you and your unwavering faith in me and my ability to get shit done. For that, you get to play with me tonight!

MJ & Ray-Ray, my everything, my world, my demons. You both are the reason I push to write these books and strive for the success that I do, because I want to show you both that dreams can become a reality, you just have work really fucking hard. I love you both more than anything in this world. You two will always be my inspiration.

Leah, my Wednesday fucking Adams. None of this would be possible without you. I mean it. I may write these books but they sell because of your crazy out the fucking gate covers! I love you dearly, babe, and thank you for always being by my side and pushing me. I will forever be in your debt.

Jaye Pratt, thank you for formatting all of these books and being an annoying pain in my ass, sending me reels and TikToks when you were bored and distracting me because you wouldn't work.

My PA, Sarah–fucking–Wilson, thank you! I can't put

into words how much you mean to me and how grateful I am that you have stuck by my side and gone on this fucking crazy ass ride with me. I love you, babe, so fucking much.

My alpha's, Debbie, Clare and Erin, you ladies make these books what they are and for that I can never thank you enough. I love you three so much and I am so honored to have you on my team.

My beta babes, Taay, Amber, Amanda, Nicole, Samantha, Patti, Morgan & Rizzo, I fucking love you crazy ladies. Truly, you are the best fucking hype team and I love that you never spare my feelings in your edits. It's because of that why these books are what they are.

My ARC army girls, thank you beautiful souls so fucking much for always sticking by me and trusting me to mend those hearts that I break.

Lizz, I couldn't do any of this without you my friend! You are so amazing and always so kind and perfect to me when I am an asshole and just send you manuscripts without booking in. I swear, I will try to remember to ask for a slot for edits before assuming next year... maybe... kind of... no that's a lie, I'll still send them and ask for forgiveness later. Hahaha.

My darling dark delicious readers, thank you again for following me and reading each of these books. I know I break your hearts and leave you mad when I end a book on a cliffy but I love that you trust me enough to heal those hearts and come back for more. I love you.

Sam xxx

<u>Fairytales With A Twist</u>

Condemned Beast

Secret Society/ Bully

Filthy Few

Forever Filthy

Filthiest Of Them All

Masked Men Novella (Pure Smut)

Dirty Priest

Dirty Daddy

Sports Romance

<u>Playing For Keeps</u>

Offside

Touchdown

End Game

Hail Mary

Blindside

RH Sports

Hate Us Like You Mean It

MM

Love Me Like You Mean It

Paranormal Romance

<u>The Veil Of Obsidian</u>

Of Time And Carnage

<u>Curse Of Fate</u>

Dream

Fate

Nightmare

Redemption

Anarchy

<u>Brutal Savages</u>

Savage Lies

Brutal Truth

Savage Beast

Brutal Beauty

ABOUT THE AUTHOR

Samantha Barrett is originally from Auckland, New Zealand but living in Brisbane, Australia.

Sam writes all things dirty, dark and delicious with a side of twisted mind fuck.

She is a lover of all things red flags and an anti-hero is a must.